D1134895

KINDLING

KINDLING

TRACI CHEE

HARPER

An Imprint of HarperCollinsPublishers

Library of Congress Control Number: 2023937094

ISBN 978-0-06-326935-4 — ISBN 978-0-06-338135-3 (int.)

Typography by Kathy H. Lam

24 25 26 27 28 LBC 5 4 3 2 1

First Edition

For the young
who fight for us all

THE NORTHLANDS

MORNING DAUGHTER

CAMAS

GATEWAY

WINDFALL

HALABRIX

Part I

THE RESTLESS

LEUM

THE WAR TOOK YOU MANY PLACES ON THE KINDAR
Peninsula (and in the years since the war ended, you've pretty much
seen the rest), but you've never been to the northlands until now.

Too remote. Nothing up here but rocks and cattle—

Cow pies and dust—

It's a harsh land, without a doubt, but that's why it appeals to you.
The ruggedness of it, the relentlessness of it. The plains rising and
falling like waves while the wind howls across the countryside—

Pine, sage, rabbitbrush, stone—

The sun blazing, the heat rising from the road—

A few days in the high desert, and you're parched and sunburned,
with new holes in the soles of your sandals (though, to be fair, they
were already wearing thin weeks ago when you set off for the north).
But you're almost there now, almost to the mountains—

The mighty Candiveras, where the Kindar Peninsula kisses the
continent—

And the nation of Amerand ends.

Ahead of you, that vast and jagged border looms—sharp, immense,
severe. The fortresses of gods or the gods themselves, at the tail end
of summer and still capped with snow.

The Candiveras are all that stand between you and the kingdom
of Ifrine beyond—

The rest of the world beyond.

You pause. You kneel. Scratch your dog behind the ears and adjust the tiny silver medal you wear around your neck.

If you had to take one last look at your country, you couldn't ask for a better view than this.

The Kindar Peninsula had been tearing itself to pieces long before you entered the war. Amerand and Vedra. North and south. For a hundred years, those titans raged, back and forth on the fields, the beaches, the steep mountain slopes—

The flash of steel, the sound of the drums—

And us—

Kindlings. A force of elite, magic-wielding warriors, pink flames rippling from our balar weapons as we carved great swaths through the ranks of our enemies. We fought for Amerand. We fought for Vedra. For a hundred years, we were swept up in two violent, inexorable tides, ebbing and expanding, swallowing cities, villages, outposts—

You can still remember how it felt, fighting on the vanguard, there in the thick of it with a squad of your kin—

The weight of your armor. The give of the earth. The magic sparking wildly inside of you and rushing out through your blade—

But it's been two years since you conjured fire from your fingers, two years since Amerand won the war—

The Vedran royalty slipping quietly into exile—

All the old maps redrawn—

As a testament to the Great and Harmonious Reunification, the Queen Commander (Long May She Reign) outlawed magic on the entire Kindar Peninsula, deemed it too cruel, too inhumane, unthinkable in peacetime. No more child soldiers. No more kids burning out by eighteen.

And the ones who remained?

The ones who survived?

We were given a choice.

Surrender our balar weapons for land and a stipend, or be turned loose, to live and fight and be put down if we ever dared to disturb the new and uneasy peace.

Now you wear your sword across your back, for you no longer need it at your side. A less sentimental person would've sold it already, but you were always a sap, weren't you? Splitting your rations with the replacements, filching a few apples or an extra blanket for the orphans who dogged our convoys, begging for scraps. We gave you a hard time about it, but let's be honest, we all had a soft spot for orphans—

For kids made homeless by war.

If you were smart, you'd sell it. Crossing the Candiveras will lead you deep into the wilderness, or so you've heard, and that means provisions, pack animals, a guide. Since the war ended, you've already sold off most of your armor—

First the sabatons—

Then the shin guards—

The metal skirt that at one time protected you from the blades of your enemies—

The cuirass—

The shoulder plates—

Your helmet, dinged from use—

All you've got left are your sword, your gauntlets, and a handful of copper kidam that won't even buy a meal for you and your dog, much less the supplies for the journey, no stops between the northlands and the outer settlements of Ifrine—

To be fair, you didn't want a dog in the first place, and certainly not a speckled mutt with one half-chewed ear, but we don't always get to choose our companions, do we? Sometimes we just find them, or they find us, clinging to us like sap on our shoe soles—

Sticky and warm—

You told yourself you didn't want a dog, didn't want attachments, not now, especially not now, not after your brother Zan (not your brother by blood, but your brother in all the other ways that matter) shoved you into the street and told you to leave him.

It's none of your business, Leum.

Get out of here, Leum.

There's nothing for you here.

He cried a little, then, and that shook you. You'd never seen him cry before, not in all your months together—

Eleven months together—

Eleven months on the vanguard together, until the official Vedran surrender. You or he or both of you should've been killed or at least wounded seriously enough to be taken off the line, but you weren't. Inexplicably, incredibly, you weren't. Had so much time together. So many furious days in the mud and the dust, your whole squad spattered in blood and stinking of sweat—

Sometimes, when it was quiet, you'd lie around your campfire, saying nothing, staring up at the stars—

Eleven months together.

For us, a miracle of time.

He told you to leave, so you left him, and as you skulked out of the compound, the dog followed. Some stray the smugglers fed from the back door of their kitchens, hungry and flea-bitten—

(A little like you, come to think of it. Both skinny, scruffy, and liable to bite.)

You tried to ignore her as you made camp for the night. Her bright eyes and snuffling breaths just outside the ring of the firelight.

You yelled at her.

You told her to run.

You tried to drive her away, but it didn't matter how much you shouted or how many stones you threw (not to hit her, just to scare her), and eventually you let her lick the dinner off your fingers—

Her tongue warm, her fur oily under your palm—

You fed her the last scraps from your bowl and lay down for the night, angry and heartsick, and when you awoke in the morning, she was still there.

A few days later, after you'd accepted that Zan was right, that there was nothing left for you in Amerand, you grew tired of chasing her off. You decided to call her Burk (which isn't a name we would have chosen, but hey, we're dead, and the dead don't get to have opinions), and you allowed her to stay.

Shortly before noon, you and Burk come to a town at the base of the mountains. Windfall, according to the only trader you saw on the road this morning. It's an auspicious name for an inauspicious-looking place: a collection of rickety wooden buildings topped with thatched roofs and smoking stovepipes, everything looking likely to collapse in the next good rainstorm—

If they get rainstorms up here.

(Of course they get rainstorms up here.)

Until then, the land's cracked with drought, the creek running through the square going dry in the heat. Angrily, you glower up at the searing alpine sun, which, undeterred, glowers back.

Apparently unaffected by the heat, Burk trots ahead of you, sniffing at empty rain barrels and saloon stoops, where itinerants lounge under the awnings, waiting for dark.

In the center of the square, she finds a few merchants from Ifrine, conspicuous with their pale faces and high-bridged noses. You've seen Ifriners before, but you can't help but stare. Near the end of the war, you watched a convoy of them escort a delivery of handcannons to the regiment your squad was attached to at the time. A couple weeks of training—

A few hands and feet blown off—

And every wet-eared grunt became as lethal as one of us.

Cheaper too. An ordinary soldier with a handcannon didn't need seven years of training, didn't need one of those rare and expensive balar crystals. Just pop a weapon into their hands and point them at the enemy—

Boom.

These Ifriners aren't military, though. They're just civilians, bloody and beaten, their carts robbed of whatever it was they were carrying. Whoever attacked them must have been ruthless. Among the Ifriners' injuries you spy a shattered ankle, a gaping eye socket, more lacerations and bruises than you can count . . . In the shade of an empty cart, one of the men is weeping openly beside a dead body, covered by a dirty sheet.

You glance toward the Candiveras. You'd heard there were bandits in the mountains, but you didn't know they'd be as brutal as this.

(And this is supposed to be peacetime?)

Burk bounds over to the traders, docked tail wagging, but before she can reach them, one of the Ifriners lets out a cry, shooing her away with his large white hands. "We have nothing!" he shouts in his accented Kindarian. "It is all been taken! There is nothing here for you!"

"Hey!" You stalk up to him. (Hardly a menacing sight. You barely come up to his armpits.) "Leave my dog alone."

He eyes you dubiously through his bruises. Let's face it, you're not much to look at. (Never have been.) You're small. You're grubby. Your robe, frayed; your belt, tied in the feminine style, stained. Your topknot, which should've signaled that you're a warrior, is currently a mess, overgrown locks falling around your windburned cheeks.

"We have nothing," he repeats.

"Raiders?"

He nods.

You know you shouldn't ask (it's none of your business, really), but you can't help yourself. Compassion, duty, valor, honor—

Protect the weak—

Defend the defenseless—

You used to have a code . . . once.

"When?" you ask.

He shakes his head. "This morning."

"Did they have handcannons?"

At your line of questioning, his gaze darts to the sword on your back. During the war, every kindling was given a weapon set with a balar crystal, that rare gem found only on the Kindar Peninsula, through which to channel their magic—

Some of us got daggers—

Gauntlets—

Spears—

Shields—

You got your sword. Since the war ended, you've taken to wrapping the hilt in linen, so no one can see the balar crystal there—

So no one will try to mug you for it—

So no one will know what you are.

(Were.)

(Used to be.)

The Ifriner may not have met any of us before, but in a hundred years we've become legends far beyond our borders. Kindarian fire soldiers. Young, ferocious, unrelenting. Given your age (only sixteen), your sword, your messy topknot, he must suspect. "Why does it matter?" he asks. "Who are you to know?"

And you hesitate.

You want to tell him you're a warrior.

You're a *kindling*. You could do something about this. You could

dispatch a pack of bandits quicker than the Ifriners could bury their
fallen comrade.

You're—

"Nobody," you say, and you turn away.

You find the antiquary in a particularly ramshackle shop in a particularly ramshackle part of town, squashed between the remains of
what must have been a school and a one-room hostel renting straw
sleeping mats for ten kidam a night.

Outside, a girl about your age is approaching anyone with a
weapon (no matter the quality or how well they carry it) with some
kind of job offer. Mercenary work, maybe, though you doubt she
can afford it. In her frayed sandals and faded clothes, she looks almost
as poor as you are.

Most passersby avoid her, shrugging her off and stalking away,
others pausing only to laugh at her proposal and shake their heads.

As you try to slip past her, she catches your eye. Her gaze sharp,
her jaw set. She straightens her shoulders. She takes a breath.

But you're not interested in hearing her sad story or her offer
of work. You're not going to take it. You're not going to be here
more than a couple days. Before she can reach you, you duck behind
some other fool with a staff slung across their shoulders, putting them
between you and the girl as you bound up the steps to the antiquary.

Leaving Burk outside, you enter the shop, where you're greeted
by a laughing wooden statue of the Rice Keeper, Lesser God of Merchants and Commerce, whose belly you rub (out of habit more than
belief) as you close the door behind you.

But it doesn't look like the Rice Keeper has been around lately.
Inside, narrow shutters cast bands of light over the bare shelves: a
rusty hand axe, a few bolts of cloth, an old plow propped in a corner.
Briefly, you wonder if the supply shortage has anything to do with
the Ifriners getting robbed, but you tell yourself not to care.

What catches your eye are the ceremonial knots displayed on a high, dusty ledge. One is a general's emblem. One is a kindling commendation. Several more are shaped like spider lilies, presented to soldiers who were wounded in battle—

And they're up there next to the chamber pots.

You want to be angry, but let's be honest, in those early days, when we were hungry and the demand for war paraphernalia was high, we all pawned our medals first. Better our medals than our armor—

Or our balar weapons.

Behind the counter, the antiquary's an old woman, broad-faced, with shrewd eyes and beaded bracelets of fine artistry you didn't expect to see this far north.

"You're wearing *Vedran* trinkets?" you snap. Can't keep the accusation out of your voice.

Enemy trinkets.

She glances up from the shoulder guard she's repairing, quickly taking stock of your grungy appearance. "They're Amerandine trinkets now." (Her eyes unkind, her smile thin.) Then she returns to the damaged armor, threading pink cord through each plate with expert fingers.

You're used to people dismissing you, but you've never learned to keep your temper, so you reach into your pack and slam one of your gauntlets onto the counter—

The clank and clatter—

Calmly, the antiquary sets down her needle, examining the tattered knots and flaking lacquer. After a moment, she squints at you. "You got the pair of them?"

"How much for just the one?" you ask.

"One fifty."

A hundred fifty han is less than you'd like, but not much less than the armor's actually worth, so you begrudgingly place your other gauntlet beside the first.

The antiquary barely bats an eyelid. "Two fifty."

"Four hundred," you counter.

"Not in this condition." She prods a line of missing scales you lost during a fight with a Vedran kindling three years ago—

A boy—

One of us—

Maybe thirteen—

Behind his face guard, he had freckles like distant starlings, caught flying across his cheeks.

The memory of heat flashes along your forearm. Without thinking, you smooth your sleeve over the blazing red scar.

"How much do I need to cross the mountains?" you say.

The antiquary strings another length of cord through her needle. "Two fifty will fetch you a nice horse and something to feed it, but the journey over the Candiveras is long and dangerous. It'll cost you at least six times as much, and that's without protection."

"From who? Raiders?" You tell her about the Ifrine traders, their empty carts.

"The Ifriners got hit?" She curses. "I was counting on them for resupply."

"This been happening a lot?" you ask.

"Every summer since the war ended. But Adren's gotten greedy this year"—the antiquary gestures at the barren shelves—"as you can see."

"Who's Adren?"

"A pain in my ass." The old woman clicks her tongue. "She and her raiders would think nothing of robbing a little thing like you."

Grumbling, you shove your first gauntlet back into your pack. "I can handle raiders."

The antiquary's gaze flicks to the sword on your back, then the small silver medal you wear around your neck. It's no bigger than a thumbnail, stamped with the image of a dayfly, but she smiles knowingly. "Is that a Wind Runner medallion you've got?"

You scowl. Hardly anyone recognizes the Lesser God of Kindlings. Hardly anyone's heard of the little boy with the wind in his limbs. But maybe it's part of her trade. Maybe she heard of him from whoever sold her one of our commendations, sitting high on the shelf—

Outside, Burk begins to bark.

You glance over your shoulder. There's some kind of commotion out there. Whooping, cheering—

"Balar weapons are illegal in Ifrine, you know," the antiquary continues, jabbing a crooked finger at your sword. "If that's what I think it is, you might as well turn a profit off it now while it'll still do you some good. I promise you, selling *that* will get you over the Candiveras with more than enough left to get you settled wherever you want."

But you're no longer listening. Can't concentrate on leaving when Burk keeps barking like that, and now over her racket you can hear the noise of a scuffle: shouting, wheezing, the soft sounds of flesh on flesh—

You know those sounds—

Someone's being beaten out there—

But you tell yourself it's none of your business, like the Ifriners were none of your business—

Like Zan was none of your business.

You may wear the sign of the Wind Runner, but you're not a kindling anymore. Technically, there *are* no kindlings anymore. We're outdated, outlawed—

Relics, like the ceremonial knots up there on the shelf—

You've almost convinced yourself you shouldn't interfere when someone comes crashing through the door. She stumbles, knocking over the statue of the Rice Keeper, and they both tumble to the floor.

It's the girl from the street. Her lip split, one eye swelling. She's clutching her ribs—

Kicked, most likely—

Multiple times. You can see the scuff marks on her robes.

As she lies there, groaning, a boy in rusty greaves leaps in after her, grabbing her by the chin. "You learned your lesson yet, peasant?" He sneers. Contemptuous, cruel. "Your kind has no business talking to our kind."

You should intervene—

You can't intervene. Fighting isn't your job anymore—

But you've still got your sword, Leum—

Use it.

You don't move.

"Get out!" the antiquary snaps from behind the counter. "Keep your business on the street where it belongs!"

The boy laughs. Starts hauling the girl off by the collar. Outside, Burk continues barking, hopping from foot to foot in her rage.

You should warn the boy. You should give him a chance. If he lets the girl go, you might not have to fight him—

But your pack is already dropping from your shoulder. Your sword, though still in its scabbard, is already in your hands—

You vault after him, through the doorway and into the road, where he and two other boys are wrestling with the girl, who's recovered enough now that she's bucking and shouting, nearly throwing them off her with a desperate, panicked strength.

Across the street, a crowd has gathered, eager for violence. Like they forgot they lived with it for generations. Like two years was more than enough to erase all those lifetimes of war.

One of the boys sees you coming. He runs at you with an antique-looking spear, but you duck easily. You're under the arc of his weapon and appearing again inside his reach, striking him in the stomach, the arm, the chin. He staggers, dropping his spear, and you kick it away before he can grab it again.

Whirling, you turn on the other two—the one in the greaves and another in pauldrons—who shove the girl at you. Before you can extricate yourself, there's a cry, a quick tangle of limbs, giving the boys time to draw their swords—

Cheap things. The kind given to draftees—

And these boys are too young to be draftees. Must have bought their armaments, or stolen them, thinking it'd be funny to play warrior, to walk a path of violence—

But they have no idea.

The boys rush toward you. They try to cut you, but you're too fast for them, hitting them above the greaves, between the shoulder blades—*thwack! thwack!*—your sheathed weapon finding them again and again and again unchecked.

The boy with the spear runs at you, but he's still unsteady from that blow to the chin—

You catch him by the arm and send him sailing over your shoulder, into the front of the antiquary, where he smashes through the shutters, splintering them from their frames, while Burk barks at him from the stoop.

"Not helping, Burk!" you shout.

Maybe the boy in the pauldrons thinks this is enough to distract you, because he lunges. You block him easily, twisting his sword out of his grasp, and take his hand in yours like you're dancers, or lovers (not that you ever had the inclination for such a thing)—

You snap his wrist.

Shrieking, he staggers away from you, and now you're turning for the last boy, the one in the greaves, but he doesn't charge you again. No, he's got the girl on the ground—

His foot on her back and his blade at her neck—

He points at your sword, its hilt still covered. "Is that a balar weapon?" he says, panting. "Are you one of them?"

You don't answer. You're considering, now, the best way to kill him—

Your blade through his gut, or maybe his ribs—

Or just the old standby, removing his head—

"Throw it over here," he continues, oblivious to the danger he's in, "or I'll—"

But we never get to know what he'd do, because a hooded figure, a girl (tall, slender, swathed in fine, airy garments), strikes him like lightning out of the clouds. One second, the sword is in his hands; the next, it's gone—

It's in hers—

She's got it leveled at his throat.

You blink. You're fast, but you're not *that* fast.

The boy's got this look on his face like he can't believe what just happened, can't believe the fact of his own empty hands. He stands there, bewildered, while the girl in the hood lifts the sword, tapping him in the chin with the flat of his own blade.

"Run," she whispers.

And he does. They all do. Stumbling, they scoop up their cheap weapons and scamper off down the road. For a moment, you consider going after them. You might be able to sell off those swords, that spear, that rusty armor. Would they fetch you enough to cross the mountains?

Not likely.

Gradually, the crowd disperses, muttering with disappointment, while the girl in the hood goes to fetch her horse: a beautiful, enormous bay with striking white socks, more fitting for the battlefield than the backwoods.

Settling your own sword across your back again, you walk up to the girl on the ground. Extend your hand. "You okay?"

For a second, she doesn't look at you. Shakes her head, wipes her eyes. (You wonder if she's ever been in a fight or if this is her first time.) Finally, she takes your hand, hauls herself to her feet. "No," she says. This close, you notice another wound at her collarbone—

Deeper than the rest but scabbed over—

Maybe a week old at this point—

"What happened?" you ask.

She leans over, gagging, blood dribbling from her lips. "I asked them for help, but they said it was beneath them. I guess roughing me up was just for fun."

"Bastards." You grunt. "You should be more careful who you ask."

She looks at you like you're joking.

(You're not. You don't have enough of a sense of humor for that.)

"I don't have that luxury. It's hard enough getting anyone to listen." Straightening, she wipes her mouth with the back of her hand. "You didn't."

You don't know what to say to that, so you glare at her. Then, reaching into your pocket, you offer her a handkerchief.

She takes it, her expression softening. (Weariness, grief.) "Thank you, though, for stepping in when you did."

You nod.

"I'm Tana," she says.

"Leum."

The other girl slides by you, leading her horse. "And I'm going." With a flick of her fingers, she twitches her hood into place, although up close you can see it's not a hood at all but a scarf (a nice one, nicer than any you've ever seen, much less worn or even felt between your chapped fingertips), dyed a brilliant gold you can't find anywhere in Kindar—

Of Yansenite origin, maybe—

From the empire across the sea—

But she's not Yansenite. In the shadow of her scarf, you glimpse angular Kindarian eyes, straight Kindarian hair that flows from under her head covering and down her back like an ink stroke.

Your breath hitches in your chest.

You *know* her. You've only seen her once before, high on a mountaintop with the clouds amassing behind her and a balar crystal blazing at her forehead. You'd assumed she would've burned out by now. She was, what, sixteen, when you saw her on that ridge, calling bolts of fire from the heavens?

But it's *her.* After that night, you'd know her anywhere.

"The Twin Valley Reaper," you whisper.

AMITY

YOU HAVEN'T HEARD THAT NAME IN MONTHS. TRUTH be told, you never thought you'd hear it again, anonymous as you are in the northlands, without any of the pageantry that used to accompany your rank and renown.

(Which was, of course, why you came to the northlands in the first place.)

You turn around, leaving your old charger, Comet, stamping impatiently in the street. His temperament's mellowed since the war ended, but whether that's out of old age or boredom, you can't say.

The girl with the messy topknot (Leum, she said) hasn't stopped staring at you. She's got the quiet intensity of a dog, head lowered, neck taut—

But you've never been partial to dogs.

Inhaling deeply, you adjust your scarf. It was presented to you by the lord of some castle you helped liberate from Vedran occupation. Imported, beautiful, made from lotus silk and dyed a luxurious saffron. You harbor no sentimental feelings toward the lord, whose name you can't even remember, but that battle earned you your title. That battle made you a legend long before you or anyone else had ever heard of Twin Valley. You may have abandoned most of your belongings when you left the capital five months ago, but you couldn't bear to part with this scarf.

"It's just Amity now," you say firmly.

Leum nods, and you wonder how she knows you. Not just your nickname (practically everyone in Amerand knows that) but your face. Maybe she's another kindling, Senary or perhaps Quinary Class—

A vanguardian, most likely, with a heavy two-handed sword like that—

Maybe you were stationed together once, attached to the same battalion before being called off to other slaughters—

Or maybe she's Vedran. The south knew you by a number of monikers too, both flattering and not.

"Amity?" The other girl, Tana, looks startled, the way most people look when they realize who you are. What you've done. The destruction you've caused and the lives you've taken. "*You're* the Rea—"

"Quiet." You glance across the street, where a few bystanders, alerted by Tana's tone, turn toward you curiously.

"My brother used to tell me stories about you," she continues, softer now. "He—"

You cut her off with a smile. "It's a little hot out here today, don't you think?" She looks confused, but you don't have time for her confusion. All you wanted when you left your cabin this morning was to run your errands and slip away unnoticed, same as you've been doing for months, but you can't do that if you get caught in a crowd. You need to get out of here, lie low until the furor dies down. More importantly, you need to make sure Leum and Tana, who know who you are now, don't cause you any more inconvenience than they already have. You motion them down the street, toward the taverns at the town entrance. "How about I buy you both a drink?"

"No one's going anywhere!" The antiquary, who's been survey-ing the damage to her storefront, smacks you on the shoulder, which, in other circumstances, would amuse you. (During the war, no one would have dared.) "Look at this mess! Look what you've done to my shop! Who's going to pay for this?"

Your gaze darts to the crowd again, some of whom have started in your direction now, eager for more action.

Swiftly, you press a handful of han into one of the antiquary's wrinkled palms. "For the repairs," you tell her, "with extra for your silence on today's events."

She eyes you thoughtfully, bouncing the money in her hand. "Feels light. This won't cover—"

"Don't haggle with me," you interrupt. "I know what those shutters are worth."

At the edge in your voice, she retreats a step. Can't help herself. You could be her granddaughter, but in your limited years you've cowed older, more formidable forces than she.

The crowd's almost reached you now, moving with a purpose that reminds you of certain court toadies and minor lords, so you turn back to Tana (who's dabbing at her bloody lip) and Leum (who's looking impatient). "Now, how about that drink?"

The others have scarcely agreed when you lead Comet off at a brisk pace, forcing Leum and Tana, who are both shorter than you, to jog to keep up. True, you ought to slow down. Behind you, you can hear Tana's uneven gait, her labored breathing—

A broken rib, most likely—

Terribly painful, but there's nothing anyone can do except wait for it to heal—

And it's not like you're responsible for her well-being. You just need to get her out of there, buy her silence. That's the extent of your obligation to her.

Nothing more.

"Hey," Leum says, trotting up to you. "Hey, Amity."

Neither you nor Comet slow down. "What?"

"How are you here?"

You purse your lips. Decline to answer.

"I mean, how old are you now? You've got to be at least nine-teen . . ."

"Twenty next month," you say.

"And you haven't burned out?" she asks, blunter than you're used to, although, let's be honest, you've barely spoken a word to anyone in months.

You shrug, tightening your scarf around your throat.

That was always the problem with kindlings, wasn't it? The reason the Queen Commander was so eager for the power of powder and shot—

We die too quick.

Our magic's always been fueled by our life force, each sickle of fire, each dart of flame taking days, months, years from us—

Shortening our time here—

Shortening our lives.

Supposedly, in the early years of the war, when Vedra had only just begun annexing all its little southern neighbors, kindlings didn't start training until they were grown. By the time they hit the battle-field, they had only a few months before the magic began to devour them from the inside, hollowing them out until they were nothing but charred shells.

But conflicts, in those days, were shorter. Vedra gobbling up Chenyara, Gamaran, Parvanaya in a matter of months before moving on to consume other islands, other nations, other peoples.

As the conquest dragged on, however, the northerners in Amer-and grew uneasy. They began looking for ways to maximize their assets—

And that included kids like us.

By the time Amerand rose up to stop the Vedran expansion, they'd discovered that if they started training us at age five, we'd be battle-ready by twelve, after which point they could get a good six years out of us before we burned out.

Of course, we'd still be dead by eighteen (nineteen at most), but for a kindling, there was no higher purpose, no greater calling than that.

"I got lucky," you say, although you're not sure if you mean it. "I suppose we both did."

When you're certain the bystanders have lost interest and drifted away, you slacken your pace, allowing Tana to catch up. She's clutching her side (definitely a broken rib, then), but she hasn't complained or asked you to slow down, and you find that intriguing—

You didn't expect such fortitude from a civilian who spent most of that skirmish under someone else's heel—

As you make your way through town, you pass a trading post, an abandoned gemologist's, an old weigh station, now overgrown with sedge, which the dog stops to sniff before padding quickly back to Leum's side.

It wasn't always like this. According to your research, some prospector discovered a vein of balar in the Candiveran foothills a hundred years ago, prompting the Amerand military to dispatch their miners and crystallographers to collect the gleaming pink gems from the earth. Windfall blossomed. Hotels, card rooms, merchant shops; buildings popping up one after another like weeds; everyone hoping for the next big lode.

They never found it. Over the years, the mines dried up. The town shrank. Gradually, a few peasant families moved into the hills above Windfall, establishing farming villages in the lush alpine meadows. In wartime, their primary contributions to the Queen Commander's army were rations and draftees—

But let's be honest, given the choice, we would've preferred more to eat.

Now, Windfall's pretty much abandoned, and with the Great and Harmonious Reunification still underway in the south, the northlanders have been left to their own devices. Little law enforcement. No real government to speak of. Maybe they get the occasional incursion of thieves and highwaymen, but that kind of thing isn't any bother to you. No, for you, it's quiet—

Peaceful—

Dead.

That's why you chose it, after all.

The only drawback to a deserted town is there's no decent place to drink. Out here, the best you can get is at the Grand Hotel, an eight-room establishment that by no means lives up to its name. Sagging beams, warped shutters. But its lobby restaurant has a selection that's halfway palatable (which is more than you can say for most places around here), so it's the only place in town you'll drink.

Tying Comet outside, you usher Leum and Tana into the lobby, followed (much to your dismay) by the dog.

You're not the only one taken aback either, because as soon as the proprietor, a thickset man with an even thicker mustache, sees her, he starts forward, jabbing a finger at the door. "No! No dogs!"

Sliding out of her sandals, Leum flips him a ten-kidam piece and shoulders past him, she and the dog trotting swiftly across the worn straw mats.

Too stunned to protest, the proprietor pockets the coin in silence.

Tana looks thoughtful as she slips off her shoes, her mind apparently occupied by other, less canine, concerns.

You frown. You don't consider yourself a snob (though you are), but a dog has never been your idea of a good drinking companion—

Not that you have much choice now.

Crossing the restaurant, you weave between a handful of sunken firepits and low tables, only two of which are occupied—

Locals, from the looks of them, which troubles you. You've only been in the northlands five months, but that's long enough to have learned that at this time of year Windfall should be crawling with merchants, stocking the shelves for winter. The restaurant should be packed with them.

Last time you were in town, you heard that raiders were striking the trade routes, but you didn't think the situation had gotten this out of hand. If they can't bring in enough supplies during the warm season, it's going to be a hard few months in the northlands—

Not that it matters much to you.

Leum's chosen a corner table (her back to the wall, a good view of the dining room), and as you settle in beside her, she says, "So, you're going to buy us lunch, huh?"

"I said a drink," you reply delicately, "but a meal is fine too, provided you keep my identity to yourselves."

Leum nods, pleased with herself. "Done."

But Tana shakes her head. "I don't want anything except for you to hear me out."

Leum turns away, trying to flag down the serving girl. "No thanks."

Tana frowns briefly at the covered sword Leum's laid across her lap, then she inhales deeply (if painfully, due to that broken rib), and when she looks up again, it's with more bravado than you suspect she's used to. Chin tilted, shoulders back. "You will," she says, "unless you want everyone to know you've got a balar weapon on you."

Leum scowls. "And when they come after it? That's a lot of lives you're willing to put at risk."

A little of Tana's bluster fades, and behind it you can see how desperate she is, how serious, how resolute. "I know," she says. "That's how much it's worth to me."

Ultimately, you buy them both a meal. After all, they look like they could use it, and it's not like you can't afford it, so you don't hold back. A bottle of plum wine, three brimming dishes of rice and bur-dock root, a stew of mountain potatoes, some kind of beef. As soon as the bowls hit the table, Leum ladles a few scoops into her hand for the dog, who gobbles it down in several wet bites.

You grimace.

Meanwhile, despite her insistence that she didn't need lunch, she wasn't that hungry, Tana is wolfing down her meal nearly as fast as the dog.

While the girl fills her stomach, Leum gestures at you with a spoon. "What are you doing up here anyway?" she says. "Thought you'd be in some big city manor or something."

You turn your cup between your hands, watching the surface shimmer in the light. "I was," you say. "But I gave it up."

"Why?"

"I guess I just wanted a little peace."

Which isn't a lie, exactly. When you left the capital, you sold most of your possessions (your house, your furniture, your finery) and bought a cabin outside Windfall. Nothing special, you say, but it's peaceful. You keep to yourself, mostly—

You tend the garden. You chop the firewood—

You ride Comet over the foothills—

You like it here. You're *happy* here. It's nice, you tell her. Peaceful—

"You already said that," Leum interrupts.

"Well . . ." You take a sip of your drink. "I suppose that makes it true."

"Not for everybody," Tana says, picking the remaining grains of rice from her bowl. "That's what I want to talk to you about."

Leum ignores her, prodding the last of her lunch with her spoon.

"My village is in trouble," Tana continues. She tells you she's from Camas, a little farming community two days out of Windfall, up in the hills. "We were hit by raiders a week ago."

You glance at the empty seats in the dining room, thinking of the absent merchants, the deserted roads. There have always been law-breakers, of course, but after the war, there seemed to be more. Most soldiers went home (kindlings being the exception, since we had no homes to return to, all record of us destroyed when the kindling collectors took us and all longing for us erased by healthy stipends for our former families), but not all of them stayed.

To be fair, not all of them became thieves and cutthroats either, but after years of violence, it was like some of them no longer cared about the difference between pillaging and burglary, between battle and murder, like the rules of peacetime didn't make any more sense than the rules of war, and there were more than enough of those to form roving bands of outlaws, or, in the cities, criminal enterprises buzzing with misdeeds—

Some of us were guilty of that too—

Abandoned our code to become enforcers, assassins—

It was what we were good at, wasn't it? It was what we knew.

"For the past two years, raiders have come every season to take more of our stores, our livestock, our horses," Tana continues.

You lift an eyebrow. "And you've given it to them?"

"We didn't think we had a choice."

"But you think you have a choice now?"

"My brother did. He—" Her mouth twists. "It was his idea to find kindlings to defend us," she says finally.

Leum crosses her arms. "So why isn't he here?"

You shoot her a look, not that she notices. (But she doesn't seem to notice much, does she?)

Tana stares at her empty bowl, trying to blink back tears. "He tried to stand up to them, so they killed him. When I tried to help him, they . . . they made me watch while he bled out on the ground." Gingerly, she touches a wound at her collarbone, just visible beneath the folds of her robes.

You've seen injuries before. (Too many of them, if we're being honest.) But the sight of her wound unsettles you somehow, over-turns you. You picture her at the point of a sword, caught between further injury and the urge to help her kin, the tip of the blade digging deeper and deeper into her skin.

You frown. You may have been ruthless, in your time—

But you were never cruel.

Tana clears her throat, passes a hand over her face. "They'll be back in little over a month, when we bring the cows down from the high country," she continues. "Just like last year. Only this time, we won't have enough left to survive the winter. My brother wanted to come here, to hire kindlings who'd fight for us. He believed you could drive off the raiders, so they'd leave us alone for good."

Leum's expression doesn't change. "How much are you paying?"

For the first time, Tana looks ashamed. "Food and lodging," she mutters.

"Then find someone else to fight for you."

"I've *tried*. I've been in Windfall three days, begging for help. And you know what that's gotten me? A black eye and some broken ribs."

"And lunch," Leum adds.

Tana eyes her coldly. "Lunch won't save my village."

Leum may not have control over her mouth, but at least she's got the decency to look appropriately chagrined. Her face reddening. Her gaze darting away.

If you knew what was good for you, you'd leave now. Pay the bill, run your errands, return to your cabin, your garden, your rides through the hills. You wanted that life, remember? That slow, unchanging crawl of days.

No, you *earned* that life. You bought it with your own years, paying for it, little by little, every time you donned that crown, every time your balar crystal burned with magic.

And yet—

You lean forward. "It's always the same raiders?"

"Yes." Tana frowns, like she didn't expect you to be interested, expected you to reject her like all the others before you. But you're not like all the others, are you? (Never have been.) "They're led by a girl named Adren," she says.

"Adren?" Leum straightens.

You cock an eyebrow. "You've heard of her?"

"She hit some Ifriners this morning. Saw them when I first arrived." She pauses. "It didn't look good."

"Did you see any balar burns?" you ask.

"Balar burns?" Tana echoes.

"From kindling magic." Leum pulls up her sleeve, revealing a forearm spiderwebbed with brilliant pink scars.

Tana inhales sharply, but you don't react.

You've got them too. (We all do.) The scars vary in color from red to fuchsia to rose, the color of the burn always matching the color of the magic that got you, the color of the balar crystal burning in your enemy's weapon.

If you were good—

(If you were lucky—)

You got up. You kept fighting. You made the light in that crystal go out.

Leum tugs her sleeve back into place. "Just looked like regular old bloodshed to me."

But you have to be sure. You turn back to Tana. "These raiders. Are any of them kindlings?"

"I don't know." Her hands flutter uselessly over the tabletop. "Some of them have kindling armor, but we haven't seen any of them use magic."

"Armor?" Leum perks up at that. "How much?"

You flick your fingers dismissively. "They could've bought their armor. What about balar weapons? Handcannons?"

"Not that I know of."

"Hmm." You sit back, running your fingers through the tail end of your scarf.

Get up, Amity. Go home.

That peace you said you wanted? The peace you came up here for? Left everything behind for? Your whole life behind for?

You can still have it.

But you don't want it, do you? Maybe you never wanted it. Tried to convince yourself you did but failed, every day, every long and agonizing day in the garden, the hills, the quiet—

All these months of failure, and only now do you realize how much it bored you, irritated you, sanded you down until there was nothing left of the person you used to be but dust—

So you stepped in when you saw your chance to fight again, to be a warrior again, to be victorious again, however briefly—

And now you don't get up.

"How many raiders does she have?" you ask.

"Sixty. Maybe more."

"I see." The fabric slides between your fingertips, back and forth, back and forth as you think—

Sixty—

Sixty raiders against a little farming village.

Maybe the Camassians have a veteran or two, if they're lucky. A couple of cheap swords. The rest of them unarmed, untrained—

Against sixty raiders.

Inwardly, you're already counting the fighters you'd need for a battle like that, can't help it, can't stop the dreadful calculus from running through your head—

"Are your people willing to fight?" you ask.

"Of course," Tana agrees. Then, more quietly, "Of course."

Leum scowls at you. "You're really thinking of doing this?"

You give her a little smile (sad, reckless). "Aren't you?"

She grunts, and that's all the answer you need. You lean forward again, feeling yourself drawn in again, reeled in again, like a fish that's caught and released and caught again, for one more battle, one last battle—

It's what you're good at, isn't it? It's what you were trained for—

Made for.

Not peace but war.

You jab a finger at Tana, leveling it between her eyes. "No magic," you warn her. "No one burns out on this job."

(Not that you'll need magic for this mission, not for chasing bandits off a mountain.)

She nods solemnly.

Beside you, Leum has gone quiet and thoughtful, scratching her dog between the ears. "Who keeps the weapons?" she asks. "The armor? The good stuff, I mean."

"You can have it," Tana says quickly. "We won't need it, not after this."

"And we'll be done before the passes close?"

"Long before."

Slowly, Leum nods. She lifts her gaze to meet yours. "How many are you thinking?"

You feel your smile go wide and vicious, and deep inside you, the old fire flickers to life once again. That old desire for combat, for bloodshed, for victory and glory—

One last time.

"Seven," you say. "Seven kindlings."

She snorts. "You think you can find seven of us all the way out here?"

"I found you, didn't I?" You flatten your scarf against your chest, feel your bones beneath your fingertips. "Only five to go."

LEUM

YOU SELL YOUR GAUNTLETS SO YOU CAN SPEND A couple nights at the Grand Hotel while Amity recruits more of you to the cause. Maybe you could've saved your coins by renting a mat at the hostel or finding a spot outdoors on the edge of town, but after weeks of camping by the roadside, sleeping in barns and woodsheds, you're willing to shell out a few extra han for a bath and a private room.

Besides, you won't want for funds once you strip Adren and her raiders of their armor. Kindling armor, Tana said. Just a handful of halfway decent pieces and you'll have more than enough to get you over the Candiveras, into the snowfields of Ifrine.

So you get a room. Second story, nothing fancy. Two han a night, plus a little extra for Burk, the proprietor sweeping the coins from the counter and grumbling, "Keep that mutt off the furniture."

Now she's nosed under the covers, snoring soundly, and you're climbing through the window, digging your hands into the thatch and hauling yourself onto the dormer, where you lie back against the roof to breathe in the night sky. The air feels clearer up here—

The stars, closer—

The wind, fiercer and smelling of snow. In the distance, the white peaks look hand-carved in the moonlight. It's pretty, but if you've learned anything since you went looking for the rest of your squad, it's that a lot of places are pretty—

The sea-scoured sentinels of the west, where you found your brother, Aran, buried on a cliff—

The blue lagoons of the south, where your sister, Kida, was last seen paddling toward the ocean—

The giant cedars that grow along the misty eastern coast, where you walked for days, searching for your sibling, Vo, wanted on three counts of crimes against Amerand and now on the run—

Nearly a year you spent looking for them, and the only one you found was Zan—

Zan, who didn't want you—

Zan, who told you to leave—

But you shouldn't have left, Leum, or at least you shouldn't have left him alone.

He could've come with you. He could've been here now, could've been one of you. Together, you could've spent a month shooing bandits away from Camas—

You and him and a squad of your kin, fighting together for the first time in years—

The seven of you, all seven of you, together—

You never should've left him alone.

You sit there with the roof at your back and the wind in your hair, watching the constellations turn. The Sisters, the Dread Empress, Kemera the Weaver, whose needle points north—

You used to pray to her, the Greater God of Fate—

You used to follow her needle—

Age seven and bivouacking across the plains, learning to navigate in the dark.

Age ten and in maneuvers, preparing yourself for war.

Age twelve and on the battlefield, where, again and again, you watched us, your kindred, burn out.

Now you've followed them to the Candiveras, and when the month is over and the job is done, you'll follow them north again, to some foreign city. You and Burk and thousands of barley-haired Ifriners who never knew the war or the people who fought in it and therefore can't betray their memory—

There, the constellations will be different. No Sisters. No Empress. No Kemera to sever our lifelines when we've been spent. There will be new names, new histories, new wounds, and you'll be a stranger to all of them.

But you'll no longer be a stranger in your own land.

You don't sleep. You spin your medallion on its cord. You watch the light change on the mountains, the highest peak looking almost like a kneeling girl in the moonlight. Down below, the drunkards in the bars and cardrooms are closing out their tabs and drifting slowly into the night, sloppy and content—

Their stumbling footsteps, their drowsy farewells—

Until it's just you and the stars and the wind howling across the foothills—

But you can't sleep. You still can't sleep—

Don't like to sleep.

There's this lullaby we used to sing after lights-out. The little ones (only five years old when the kindling collectors came for them) always cried when they arrived at the Academy, and this was what we did to comfort them, for this was what had been done for us.

Oh-oh-ohhh . . .

No words, just a melody. You don't know who came up with it—

The nations of Kindar had been at war so long, and kindlings died so fast, it could've been ten years old or fifty or as ancient and constant as the sea. You sang it for the little ones (wet-eyed and whimpering like new mice), so they could sing it for the little ones who came after them, and the ones who came after that, and sometimes, even though you weren't little anymore, when you were reeling from the beatings, the weariness, the loss—

Then you sang it for yourself.

Ohhh-oh-ohhh . . .

You're humming it now, don't even realize you're doing it until another voice joins yours (higher, clearer), finding harmonies you're not clever enough to know were there—

Oh-oh-ohhh . . .

You stop.

On the peak of the next dormer, perched in the thatch and peering out at the mountains, is a girl your own age. She's got a square face and a hard jaw that looks like it could take a punch (and probably has, if she knows that song). Maybe she had a topknot, once, but now she lets her hair fall freely to one side (impractical for battle, but maybe that doesn't matter anymore).

When she notices you glaring at her, she gives you a quick grin. "I haven't heard that song in years."

You sit up, frowning. You don't like being snuck up on, and it doesn't happen very often, so that makes you dislike it even more. "How long have you been there?"

"I dunno. A few minutes, I guess."

You squint at her. You don't recognize her from the Academy, but you were only familiar with House Kemera—

The other three houses (Callula, Vastari, Omayo) were spread out across Amerand in case one of you was overrun.

"I wake you up?" you ask.

She avoids your gaze, drums her fingers along the thatch. "What do you think?"

You let it go at that.

"I'm Ket," she says.

"Leum," you tell her. "You been in Windfall long?"

"I'm never anywhere for long."

"If you're planning on moving on, I might have a job for you. In Camas."

"Never heard of it."

"It's out there." You gesture toward the highest mountain.

Her gaze darts to the peaks, too quick to be casual, though her voice is light when she says, "Oh yeah?"

It seems like you've got her attention, so you tell her about the farmers, the bandits, the spoils you hope to collect.

She whistles, which makes you jealous. (You've never been able to manage more than a half-tuneful whisper yourself.) "Sixty raiders?" she says. "Against how many?"

"Just me and Amity so far."

Ket laughs. "Amity?"

"Yep."

"Amity, Kindling Primary Class, *Deathbringer* of Her Queen Commander's Army? *That* Amity? Is all the way out here, fighting bandits for food and lodging?"

"Yep."

Ket whistles again.

To be fair, the rank sounds grand, all spelled out like that, but Amity *was* grand, wasn't she? "Deathbringer" was a title applied only to the most lethal of us, the ones who could slay a dozen enemies in a matter of seconds. By the time she was commissioned, there hadn't been another Deathbringer in a decade—

The last one having burned out at fifteen—

Each massacre taking a greater toll on him than the last.

"Did you get to see her crown?" Ket asks.

She means Amity's balar weapon, custom-forged for her by the smiths of House Vastari: a golden crown set with a crystal of deepest garnet. You saw it that night at Twin Valley, when she stood on that peak with two Vedran battalions storming both sides of the ridge, thousands of them roaring, surging over the rocky terrain—

But you haven't seen it since. You don't even know if she's still got it or if she gave it up for that little cabin she talked about, so you shake your head.

Ket clicks her tongue. "Too bad."

"Join us, and maybe you'll see it for yourself."

She laughs again. "A month in some northlands backwater? With nothing better to do than clean up after the cows? I'll pass, thanks."

"You got someplace better to be?"

"I dunno. There's a lot of world to see." She looks to the mountains again, tapping thoughtfully at her breastbone. "But I might have another lead for you. A duelist who's performing in Gateway, not far from here."

"A kindling?"

"I dunno. Have you heard of the Sparrowhawk?"

You nod. You recognize the name. A girl, a knife-thrower. People say she's so quick with a blade, she can strike songbirds out of the sky, which you doubt, but you've never paid much attention to these traveling entertainers, these little sideshows that popped up after the war.

"Have you seen her throw?" you ask.

"Nah, but I've been meaning to." She grins at you. "Tell you what, I'll help you find her, if you introduce me to the Reaper."

"Tomorrow morning," you tell her. "Breakfast in the lobby."

"Great." Swinging one leg over the dormer, she clambers nimbly down the thatch and pauses at her window. You can't be sure, with the light so dim, but you think she's smiling—

Sadder this time.

"Hope you can sleep, Leum," she says.

"Same to you."

But you remain on the roof when she lowers herself inside, and you don't move for a very long time.

KET

YOU CLIMB THROUGH THE WINDOW, CAREFUL NOT to wake the girl in your bed. (Her slow and steady breathing, her hair spilling across the pillow.) For a moment, you watch her curiously. You can't remember the last time you slept like that—

Uninterrupted, serene—

If you were thinking about it, you'd realize it's been years since you made it through the night, made it to morning without dreaming, waking, scaling the roofs or roaming the streets—

But you're not thinking about it.

You tiptoe across the floor, picking up discarded clothes. A robe, undergarments, socks, each one peeled off and flung aside in your urgency—

Fingers fumbling, knots coming undone—

"Ket?" The girl stirs, her voice slurred and lovely with sleep. "What are you still doing up? Come back to bed."

You don't need to be told twice. Dumping the clothes into a pile, you remove your robe and trousers and crawl under the covers, where you pull the girl into your arms—

Her body soft and willing, her skin warm—

Rema, that's her name. The hotelkeeper's daughter. Sneaks out of her room at night to come tumbling into your bed and leaves again before her father's any the wiser—

Barefoot across the corridor at dawn.

She was the first one to welcome you to Windfall when you showed up four nights ago, looking for a clean room and a hot meal.

Well, you've come to the right place, she said. *Which do you want first?*

You chose the meal. Polished it off in minutes and spent the next hour lingering over a cup of barley wine so you could watch her weave between the tables, brisk as a summer breeze—

A smile, a flourish of her sleeve—

So what're you doing in Windfall, soldier?

You asked her if it was that obvious. She nodded to your balar sword, bound in some of your old dress robes, and for a second, you thought she'd ask about the war. That's what most people do when they find out you were in the military. They want to know what you did—

If you saw anyone die—

How many people you killed.

But she didn't say any of those things, and that's when you knew you liked her.

You fixing to stick around? Or are you just passing through?

I dunno. You drummed your fingers against your sternum. (Your gaze sweeping over her, your grin going wide.) *Is there anything worth sticking around for?*

She blushed, then. *There's plenty.*

Oh yeah?

By this point, the restaurant was mostly empty (not that it had been very busy to begin with), just you and a couple haggard-looking merchants arguing over the bill, so Rema unfastened her apron and plopped down across from you, elbows on the table, dimples in her grin.

Yeah. I've lived here my whole life, you know.

So you know the mountains pretty well, huh? What's that big one called? The one I saw on my way in?

She tilted her head. A curl of hair brushing her neck. *The one to the northwest? Morning Daughter.*

Funny name for a mountain.

I think it's kind of romantic. She's the first thing the light touches every day. Although . . . Rema leaned across the table, whispering conspiratorially. *Some people say it's really supposed to be* Mourning *Daughter. Because she looks like a girl at prayer.*

Oh yeah? You didn't let on that you already knew this, knew the story of the mountain. You just needed to confirm which mountain it was. *What's she mourning?*

Depends on who you ask.

And if I'm asking you?

I think she's mourning her mother. Her smile dimmed and faltered, like a star at dawn.

How come?

And she told you. How she lost her own mother. (Fever.) How her father raised their family alone. (A struggle.) She told you story after story—

The abandoned mine shafts she explored with her brothers—

The deer skull she found when she was eight—

The lakes she liked to swim in, naked and up to her neck in snowmelt—

Naked? You grinned, imagining her bare limbs, her exposed back pimpling in the cold—

Sure. It's the middle of nowhere. No one around to see.

You would've liked to hear more about that (her being naked, that is), but instead she wanted to know about you. Where you were from. What your plans were in Windfall.

But you didn't want to talk about that, so you just shrugged and slid your coins onto the table and told her you'd better go.

She looked up at you, confused. *I thought you wanted a room?*

I do. You smiled. *But there's a lot of world to see.*

You left the restaurant then, tapping your fingers along the siding, but it didn't take her long to follow. (Her footsteps on the wooden sidewalk, her breathing quick and eager.) She caught up to you in the shadow of her father's hotel, and she didn't try to make conversation this time, didn't ask you any questions, didn't want anything from you but to push you against the wall and kiss you in the darkness, her lips urgent and begging you to stay.

Simple.

Easy.

But the beginning's always easy, isn't it? The look, the gentle conversation, the kiss—

You took her to bed that night, have taken her to bed every night since. Under the sheets, Rema sighs and pulls you closer. (Her lips at your collarbone, her fingers at your chest.) Careful not to disturb her, you reach over the side of the mattress and remove a slip of paper from a hidden pocket of your discarded robe.

There's not much light to see by, but that doesn't bother you. In your fingers, the paper is soft and the pleats are deep, and you know its contents so well already, read and reread them so many times on your travels, that you could read them now with your eyes closed—

It's a list, still incomplete—

Things to do. Places to see. Locations scattered all across Amer- and, from the God's Cradle at the heart of the peninsula to the black beaches of the Parvanayan archipelago, and wherever you crossed one off there was another girl, another conversation, a kiss—

A shared bed, a damp embrace—

But never for long.

Quietly, you fold the list along its old and tender creases, tuck it back into the inner pocket of your robe. Your fingers smoothing out the fabric like you're sealing it inside—

A secret—
A wish—
You still can't sleep, so you look to the window.
There's a lot of world to see.

AMITY

THE NEXT MORNING, LEUM AND HER DOG COME
down to breakfast with a girl you don't recognize. She's taller than
Leum, and neater too, her travel-worn clothes clean and pressed—

More clean and pressed than she's used to, you suspect. The pleats
too tight, the folds too crisp. As she weaves through the restaurant,
she keeps tugging at her robes, fiddling with her belt to make her
covered saber sit properly at her waist.

Another kindling for the mission?

You glance at Leum, who shakes her head.

Pursing your lips, you tap your fingers on the rim of your teacup. Either the new girl isn't a kindling, which you doubt, because
you can smell the Academy training on her from here, or she *is* a
kindling, but she isn't joining you.

And you need her to join you. After you left Leum and Tana yesterday, you spent a few fruitless hours digging around Windfall for
fighters, beggars, itinerants—

These days, we're all disguised, but if you look closely, you can
still spot us—

Straight backs, weapons wrapped—

But you didn't find anyone. The day was waning by then, your
head swimming with fatigue, but you steeled yourself against your
exhaustion and hauled yourself onto Comet's back. Together, you

took the road to Halabrix, the nearest town to the east, and in the cool of the evening you stalked the saloons and gambling parlors, one by one, searching for more of us.

Leum looks to your right, where another girl is seated beside you, her attention entirely consumed by a large bowl of rice porridge. She's younger than you (eighteen or so) and nearly as tall, but broader and browner, with gray in her eyes and dark hair she leaves long and wavy, like a thundercloud down her back.

You nod.

Leum grunts in acknowledgment and drops down on one of the floor cushions, pulling her sword across her lap. "This is Ket," she says. "She knows where to find another kindling."

"So do I." You survey the girl critically. "What class were you, Ket? Senary?"

She laughs, but she doesn't deny it. "You don't waste any time, do you?"

The girl to your right snorts into her porridge.

You permit yourself a restrained smile. "Some of us don't have time to waste." You gesture for Ket to sit.

She does, settling herself comfortably between you and the dog, whose nose you can see over the edge of the table, black and wet. "These farmers really got you invested, huh?"

"Just one." Lifting your hand, you wave down the serving girl, who's been bustling back and forth from the kitchen with chipped trays and hot kettles. "You should hear her out."

Ket chuckles. "Hey, I'm just here for the food . . ."

Her voice trails off when the serving girl arrives with two more bowls and a fresh pot of tea. Leaning over Ket's shoulder, she unloads her tray with practiced ease and departs again, trailing her fingers across the back of Ket's arm.

"But I guess the company's not bad either," Ket adds, grinning after her.

"Ah," you say, pouring her a cup of tea. "How long have you two been together?"

"Together?" She laughs and helps herself to the porridge.

"You mean you aren't . . . ?"

"Nah, I don't really do commitments. No promises, no attachments—"

"No hard feelings?" you add.

She stirs her breakfast and gives you a grin. "That's the idea."

"Hmm." You let your gaze drift over her shoulder, toward the kitchen. "I suppose that's worked out well for you so far?"

She glances behind her. From the edge of the dining room, the serving girl gives her a quick wave.

Ket's smile falters, if only for a second. "Yeah," she says. "It's worked out fine."

You incline your head, as if that's the end of it, although you're far too stubborn to simply let her go. "Well, we're happy to have you while you're here." Setting down your teacup, you gesture to the girl on your right. "Ket, Leum . . . this is Emara."

Emara drains her cup, waggling her eyebrows by way of greeting, and promptly returns to her second helping of breakfast.

You sigh. You tell the others you met her last night in one of Halabrix's cardrooms, losing hand after hand to a pair of leathery gray-haired women called Hope and Haru, twins (or so you gathered) with identical wolfish smiles, the only difference between them the silver rings on Hope's fingers and Haru's rich Vedran wrap. By the time you arrived, Emara was already deep in the hole, nothing left to her name but desperation and two cloth-wrapped daggers, reluctantly unbuckled from her waist.

You stopped her before she could place them on the table. Offered to pay off her balance, to get her out of the game. In exchange, all she had to do was join you. One month in the mountains, that was all you were asking.

Better than losing her balar weapons, right?

Emara shovels another scoop of porridge into her mouth. "Eh, that was going to be a winning hand."

"So why didn't you play it?" Ket asks.

"Why bother?" Emara waves at you with her spoon. "I had Queenie."

"Queenie?" Your lip curls with distaste.

"You know, because of your crown."

Ket pours herself another cup of tea. "You saw her crown?"

Emara laughs. "Not yet."

"I retired my crown," you say firmly. "And don't call me Queenie."

"Sorry, would you prefer Reaper?"

"No."

"Thunderhead?"

"No."

"Red Death?"

"No."

"*No.*"

Your enemies called you a lot of things during the war. Red Death, Doomsday, Fist of Amerand. You didn't mind. You wanted them to fear you, to fear your name, as if repeating it would summon you like a bolt of judgment (which was, incidentally, another of your monikers).

"Red Death?" Leum frowns. "Haven't heard that one before."

Ket chuckles. "That's what the Vedrans used to call her."

Leum turns on Emara. (Her jaw tight, her voice low and dangerous.) "You're Vedran?"

You glance at Emara to see how she'll react. You'd hoped this wouldn't be an issue. She assured you it wouldn't be an issue, her working for you, her old enemy—

But you hadn't reckoned with Leum.

Emara squints at her for a long moment, chewing slowly, before giving her a wink and a mock salute. "Chenyaran, actually."

Now that's a surprise. Chenyara was one of the first nations to be annexed by Vedra over a hundred years ago, near the beginning of the war. Much of the historical record has been destroyed since then, but from what you understand, it was a bloody time—

Most of the Chenyaran resistance massacred, the remaining population forcibly assimilated into Vedran society—

Their archives burned, their festivals outlawed, their art stolen and sold off to the Vedran elite—

You'd assumed their lineages would have been lost by now, but the truth is, our lives are so short, we rarely concern ourselves with the past. What's ancestry to a kindling who's been stripped from their family? What's a century to a child who'll die before they hit twenty? No, we measure our time here in months—

Weeks—

Days—

Beneath the table, Leum's hand tightens on her sword. "Chenyaran, Vedran. Same enemy, different name."

Emara hasn't gone for her daggers yet, but you recognize the tension in her shoulders, the way her knuckles have gone pale.

On your other side, Ket's leaning back from the table, looking for the exits.

But you can't have her leave—

You can't have any of them leave—

You need seven kindlings for this mission, and you'll take what you can get. Tertiary Class or Senary, Amerandine or Vedran or Chenyaran. You can't be choosy out here.

"Stand down, Leum." Your voice is cold; your gaze, severe. "There are no enemies anymore."

She whirls on you. "You can't be serious. During the war, her kind slaughtered—"

"The war's over," you snap. "And we all got the same ultimatum when it ended, no matter our name, our country, our rank—"

You pause. You didn't mean to say that last part, didn't mean to let it slip, and now you feel the words floating between you like a secret—

Embarrassing and intimate—

Disturbed, you pull your scarf closer to your throat.

Leum glares at you. But after a moment she begrudgingly returns to her breakfast.

Unabashed, Emara helps herself to another serving of porridge, apparently more interested in filling her stomach than in feeding these old animosities. But you shouldn't be surprised. Vedrans always valued their creature comforts above anything else—

(Including winning the war.)

You pour them all some tea. You've smoothed their hackles, for now, but that doesn't mean they'll work together. You can still feel Leum's hostility rising from her like miasma from a swamp.

You need to bring them together somehow, or your mission is over before it's even begun.

"So, Ket, you know where to find another kindling," you say.

She nods. "A knife-thrower. I've actually been meaning to go see her—"

"Oho!" Emara brandishes her spoon, flicking grains of rice into the air. "You want to challenge her, eh?" Across the table, Leum glowers at her, but either Emara doesn't notice or she doesn't care.

"Nah." Ket leans back with a shrug. "I've got nothing to prove."

"Yeah, but it'd be funny."

"So why don't you do it? I'd pay to see that."

"Nah."

Ket chuckles. "Had enough of losing, huh?"

"Tch." Emara wags a finger at her. "Don't talk to me about losing when your kind spent the last months of the war hiding behind your cannoneers."

You bristle at that, and you know Leum and Ket do too. None of us *asked* for Ifrine's handcannons—

They made us obsolete.

But you're determined not to let the conversation devolve into another altercation, so you turn to Ket. "What else do you know about this knife-thrower?"

"Just that she's called the Sparrowhawk."

You steeple your fingers. The name is familiar. When you lived in the capital, you recall hearing rumors about a kindling-turned-street performer. You didn't expect her to be this far north, but then again, no one would've expected to find you out here either. "Do you mean Ben?"

"I dunno. You think you know her?"

"There was a knife-thrower at House Vastari by that name, two years below me." Through your mind flits the image of a child, mantis-thin and just as quick, flinging blades in an Academy court-yard, but you can't remember her face. Can't remember any of their faces. With your unique talents, you were schooled separately from the other trainees. Separate housing, separate meals, separate everything. It meant you were skilled, superior, feared—

It also meant you were alone.

"Where is she performing?" you ask.

"Gateway. It's your last stop if you're heading over the mountains, a half day's ride from here."

You sip thoughtfully at your tea. Half a day to ride to Gateway, half a day to ride back. You might have to miss recruiting Ben yourself, but you need to generate a little momentum, to show Ket that it's easier to fall back in with the rest of you than to stick out her current commitments, such as they are.

You'd feel bad for the serving girl, but sympathy is a luxury you've never been allowed.

"Do you know how to get there?" you ask Ket.

"It's not hard."

"Good. Then you can lead the way."

"Uh . . . what?"

"You said you wanted to see the Sparrowhawk, didn't you? Don't tell me you have other plans?"

"Nah. I don't plan, remember?"

"I do." You smile. "Do you have a horse?"

"You're volunteering my horse now too?"

"Tana will need a ride. Leum, you and Emara can take Comet."

Leum balks at that. "I'm not riding with—"

"I get to be in front!" Emara declares.

Leum growls, although that could have been her stomach. (Or the dog beneath the table.)

You sigh. You hope sharing a horse softens them on each other, although you doubt it. Leum will need more than time to get over her old resentments.

But Leum's a good soldier, and Emara's indebted to you. They'll fall in line, even if they aren't happy about it.

"Who's Tana?" Ket asks.

"The one who hired us," Emara says. "I heard she took a real good beating yesterday before Grumpy and Queenie here stepped in."

Leum bristles at her new nickname, but she doesn't pick a fight about it. (Yet.) "You're not coming?" she asks you.

There's a twinge in your chest. The truth is, if you're going to miss out on today's expedition, you've got other matters to settle before returning to the battlefield. "When I came to town yesterday, I didn't plan on running off to fight raiders for the rest of the season," you say. "I need to find someone to see to my property while I'm gone."

"Property!" Emara laughs and pounds the table, although you

wish she wouldn't. Vedrans aren't known for their manners, but since she's Amerandine now, eating with Amerandine kindlings, you'd think she'd make more of an effort. "Well, aren't you fancy? Did you trade your crown in for that, Queenie?"

You dig into your purse, lay your coins on the table. "How do you know I traded it in?" you say archly.

"What?" She bolts upright with a cry. The other patrons stare. "You said you retired it!"

"For a scrap of land in the hills? Please." You stand, brushing imaginary dust from your robes, and make your way to the exit as the others scramble after you—

The last of the tea drained, a few more spoonfuls of rice shoveled into their mouths—

The hustle of footsteps, familiar in its urgency—

It seems you haven't lost your touch after all. In the old days, you were something of a celebrity among the powerful and the wealthy, and when you weren't on the battlefield or planning your attacks, you were often tasked with garnering support for the war effort: promises of weapons, rations, coin, draftees. You used to do it with panache, but after two years, you didn't know if you still had it in you, if you could still attract a following, could still mold and direct them as you wish—

Ket catches up to you in the foyer. "I heard you could get a mansion for that crown."

"She had a mansion," Leum adds, slipping into her sandals. "She told me."

"Well, Queenie?" Emara slides open the door for you. "Do you still have your crown or not?"

You flash her a grin. "Wouldn't you like to know?"

Before any of them can question you further, you step into the road, forcing them to clamber after you like children begging for sweets. Not all of them like each other. Not all of them have agreed to join you. But you've united them in their curiosity, all their hesitations and old animosities forgotten, at least for the moment. You've given them purpose, trivial as it is.

But you can work with that.

KET

.

YOU DON'T ENTIRELY KNOW HOW YOU'VE BEEN roped into riding half a day to Gateway to convince some knife-thrower to join a cause that you yourself have no interest in, but you've never been one to swim against a current, so here you are, standing in the street with your little buckskin mare, Callie—

Her breathing gentle—

Her nose soft under your palm—

To the north, you study the Morning Daughter in the sunlight. Her bowed head, her somber features, her hair glinting with ice. Briefly, you wonder what the view will be like whenever you finally reach her. Something new? Something dazzling and bright?

Or will you see what you always see from all the tops of all those mountains you've already climbed?

(More of the same?)

You don't have time to wonder long, because Emara is drawing up with Amity's old warhorse, and Leum and her dog are appearing around the corner, and soon you're being introduced to a girl named Tana, the girl who brought them together—

You don't know what you were expecting out of a farmer (let's face it, you weren't really expecting anything, seeing as you weren't planning on joining her anyway), but what you get is a girl your age, bruised and beaten, with dark eyes like chips of obsidian.

"I can't believe Amity found two more of you already," she says, looking from you to Emara. "My brother would've been—"

"Wait, sorry." You lift your hands. "I'm actually just here for the day."

She frowns. "You're not a kindling?"

"I didn't say that." You try to smile, but she seems less than pleased with your evasiveness, and your expression fades.

"So you're helping someone else already?" she asks.

Her persistence makes you uncomfortable, so you rub the back of your neck and avoid her gaze. "Just you," you say. "Just today."

"I don't under—"

"Ket doesn't do commitments," Leum adds unhelpfully.

You shoot her a glare, though you don't think she notices.

"You what?" Tana stares at you, a furrow appearing between her brows, and it's almost like she recognizes you, though you've never met her—

Would've remembered meeting her, would've remembered those sharp eyes, that thoughtful frown—

"But I thought that was part of your code," she says. "We all heard the stories, after the war. They said you weren't soldiers anymore, but you were still helping people, protecting them when no one else would."

Emara snorts, but Leum glares at her, and she backs away with an exaggerated bow.

"They said a lot of things about us," you say. "Not all of them true." Your voice is sadder than you expect. More honest, more revealing. You don't know why, but something about her sets you off your guard.

"Oh." Tana blinks a few times, and for a moment it's like you can see all her thoughts swimming behind her eyes, surfacing and submerging like dark fish in a dark pond—

You wonder how often she's like this, with a whole world churning inside her—

(It must be exhausting. You're tired just watching her.)

"Okay." She shakes her head and takes a breath. "It's fine. It's going to be fine. There are going to be others, right?"

She's pretending, and you know it, but you've always been comfortable with pretend. "Sure," you say with your usual grin. "Why not?"

She smiles, like she's trying to believe you. "Okay."

A few paces off now, Emara claps her hands. "Well. Sounds like you all have it handled, eh? You don't need me for this."

"Good." Leum climbs onto Comet's back. "Time to go."

But Tana doesn't move. Her frown reappears as she turns to Emara. "Why aren't you coming with us?"

"How many kindlings d'you think it takes to watch a duel?"

"Three," Tana replies flatly.

You chuckle.

Emara winks at her. "I guess you've got a lot to learn about kindlings then." She stuffs her hands into her pockets and pulls them out again. "Say, none of you happen to have a few extra han to spare, do you?"

Ignoring her, Leum urges Comet into a trot, leaving the rest of you standing in the middle of the street.

Emara looks at you expectantly.

You shrug and toss her a couple coins. "So where are you off to while we do all the work?"

"I thought you Amerandines liked work!" With a wave, she pivots away. "I've got some unfinished business to take care of. Drinks on me tonight, eh?"

Tana stares after her, looking perplexed. "Are all of you like this?" she asks.

"Like what?" You climb into the saddle, offer her a hand up.

She takes it. Wincing only a little at her injuries, she settles herself behind you, smelling of something sweet and wild, like some kind of flower you never bothered to learn the name of—

"I don't know," she murmurs into your shoulder. "You're hard to pin down, I guess."

You don't answer. (You don't want to think about the answer, don't like the answer or the memories it dredges up.) Clicking your tongue, you urge Callie into a trot, then a gallop, Tana gasping, her hands tightening about your waist, and you ride for a while like that—

Hard and fast out of Windfall—

Into the hills, breathless and quick—

You move, and when you're moving like this, you don't have to talk, and you don't have to think.

But you can't ride like that forever, with the wind in your ears and your heart in your throat. Eventually, you have to slow down. Eventually, things go quiet and still.

Sun, sweat, Tana's gaze on the back of your neck—

You don't like awkward silences, so you try to fill them. *You know the Candiveras pretty well, huh? What's it like, growing up in the northlands?*

She tells you about the sunsets in the mountains. She tells you about the lambs in the spring. She tells you about Camas, describing the old creaking houses, the mid-autumn feasts, the children plucking raspberries from the brambles and wearing them on their fingers like plump red thimbles—

And it all sounds nice, but nice exists everywhere, doesn't it? You've already seen it. You know it doesn't last.

Then silence again—

She tries asking about you, and you don't want to talk, not about anything serious, not what you're doing here or where you've been, but something about her opens you up—

Not her fingers in your clothes or the pressure of her body on yours, but the way she seems to see you, for all she met you this morning, seems to know you like you've known each other for years. You tell her you've been traveling. You tell her you wanted to see the mountains, which isn't particularly specific, but it's more than you've said to anyone else, and that unsettles you—

So you ride again.

You're relieved when you finally reach Gateway, because it means you have more to focus on than each other—

Her voice in your ear, her breath on your neck—

The town's smaller than Windfall but better kept. Fresh horses for sale in the livery. Armed wagoners dotted among the trading posts. Gateway's the last stop between Amerand and Ifrine, so it's where most travelers hire their guides and stock up on supplies for the dangerous Candiveran passes ahead.

It's busy enough that it doesn't take you long to learn that the Sparrowhawk's dueling in a corral on the north edge of town, where you find a crowd already assembled and placing their bets.

You dismount and turn to help Tana from the back of your horse. (Her hands on your shoulders, your hands at her hips.) She alights in the brush with a sigh.

"You okay?" You remember to let go of her.

"I had the whole morning," she says, "but I didn't convince you, did I?"

You choose to play dumb. (You're good at that, at least.) "Were you trying to?"

She frowns, curiously this time.

"What?" you say.

"Hey!" Leum calls from up ahead. "Are you coming?"

You wave her off. You turn back to Tana, whose mouth twitches sadly. "Nothing," she says. "You just remind me of someone." She shakes her head as she steps past you, leaving the scent of wildflowers (lilacs, you think, and something woodsy) floating in her wake.

Trailing after her, you pick your way through the bunchgrass to find two people placing wooden cups on opposite ends of the corral. You've seen duels like this before, competitions to see who can knock their opponent's cup off the fence post first. Today's challenger is broad and bearded, with a masculine knot as his belt and a one-handed sword at his side.

His opponent, in contrast, is short and slim, dressed in a white robe and loose trousers, with a wide straw hat shading most of her face. She doesn't wear a sword, but you count fourteen knives of varying lengths tucked into her belt and a dozen more in leather holsters strapped across her narrow chest.

Leum eyes her from the fence. "Is that Ben?"

"I guess so." You slide into place beside her, hooking your arms over the rail.

Trailing her fingers across each of her knives, Ben selects one from her belt and flips it over her knuckles. Simple blade, plain wooden grip. It's nothing special, but she handles it with such careless grace, you can see why people pay to see her perform.

You let out a low whistle.

Leum grunts.

You knew you'd get along with Leum as soon as you heard her singing on the roof last night, but since this morning you've gained a greater appreciation for her prickly, taciturn ways. With Leum, silence is just silence. No weight, no expectations. She's exactly who she is, and she takes you exactly as you are.

"So Ben's a kindling?" Tana asks. "That's not her balar weapon, is it?"

Leum sniffs. "No crystal."

You gesture at the clean linen strips Ben wears around her hands.

"Knife-throwers' gauntlets were set with balar crystals, so they could throw magic if they ever ran out of blades," you explain, though you don't have to. But you can't seem to stop yourself around her, can you?

That familiar furrow appears between Tana's brows as she absorbs this new information. You can almost see her tuck it away in a corner of that cluttered mind of hers—

You imagine she even gives it a little pat, like a neatly folded towel.

In the corral, Ben removes her sun hat, revealing a narrow face and a tidy topknot (neater by far than Leum's). As she tosses the hat aside, the sunlight catches on a thin spiderweb of balar burns, brilliantly vermilion against her forehead.

You wince.

Whatever happened to her, it must have hurt.

With a nod, she salutes her opponent, who salutes back. They let their hands fall to their sides.

As the crowd quiets down, a balding official lifts his handkerchief.

On Leum's other side, you see Tana's hands tighten on the rail.

The handkerchief comes down. Across the corral, there are twin flashes of steel, and the cups fall from their posts with a clatter.

A surprised murmur rises from the crowd, followed quickly by a speckling of nervous laughter, a rumble of displeasure.

"Who won?" Tana asks.

"Ben," you say. It happened so quick, you barely caught it. You're not surprised some of the civilians didn't.

"How can you tell?"

You're about to answer when Leum interrupts. "Experience," she says.

Before Tana can press the matter further, the official clears his throat. "And the winner is . . ." He jabs a finger at Ben. *"The Sparrowhawk!"*

On the north side of the corral, a scrawny kid with big eyes and baby fat on her cheeks lets out a whoop. She's a slip of a thing (maybe fourteen years old), perched precariously on the fence with a shrouded weapon at her side—

The mark of a kindling, trying to blend in—

But the greatsword's much too big for her. Maybe she bought it. Maybe she stole it. But you know just by looking, it wasn't made for her the way a balar weapon should be.

Around you, the rumbling of the crowd has grown louder. Some spectators are even refusing to pay the official, claiming he called it wrong, declared the wrong winner. Has he got something in his eyes? Or is he a cheat and a thief?

As if emboldened by their discontent, the first duelist pulls another knife from his belt. "Again," he snarls.

The official waves him off. "Walk away now, Kiban."

"Again," Kiban repeats, leveling the blade at Ben. "For real this time."

She ignores him. Silently, she retrieves her sun hat and places it back on her head before padding across the corral to collect her knife from the dust.

As she passes Kiban, he grabs her by the arm. "What's the matter? Are you scared?"

She stares at him for a moment, sizing him up. You can see it in her eyes, in the faint purse of her lips. She doesn't have to fight him. She already knows she'll win.

Jerking out of his grasp, she retrieves her blade and sheathes it. "You can pay me my winnings later," she says to the official. "I'll be in town."

"No!" Kiban starts after her. He lifts his knife.

Across the corral, the little kid on the fence shouts, "Ben!"

This time, it happens so fast, you *don't* see it—

Ben turning on her heel—

The knife glinting in the air—

Then Kiban is staggering back, gasping, with Ben's blade buried hilt-deep in his shoulder.

You blink.

She didn't kill him. (She could've killed him.) She was fast enough to kill him, faster than anyone you've ever seen, in the war or since.

"Did she miss?" Tana asks.

"No." You point. "She went for his throwing arm, see? He didn't even get a chance to lift his blade."

In the corral, Ben stares at Kiban, the tips of her fingers twitching.

With a gasp, he wrenches her weapon from his shoulder. For a second, you think he's going to charge her with it—

Ben must think so too, because she adjusts her stance, ever so slightly, and wearily lifts her chin.

But he must be less of a fool than you think, because he just tosses the blade into the dust and storms through the crowd as they shove past him, dropping their coins duly into the official's open handkerchief.

While he doles out Ben's share of the winnings, Leum climbs through the fence. "Stay here."

"Shouldn't I go with you?" Tana asks.

"Why? You think you know how to convince her?"

Tana looks hurt, but she tries to hide it, scowling down at her fingernails while Leum stalks away.

"Don't mind Leum." You shrug. "She's just being a jackass."

"She's not wrong, though." Tana picks at the fence, peeling bits of lichen from the weathered wood. "I couldn't convince you, could I?"

"Yeah, but that was a battle you were never going to win."

Tana frowns, watching Leum and Ben talking in the corral. "Ben was so fast," she murmurs. "Are all of you that fast?"

You lean back. You drum your palms on the rail. "No one's that fast."

"Adren was fast."

You recognized the name when Leum told you about the attack on Camas, had heard it floating around Windfall, a rumor of violence in the hills—

Villages terrorized for crops and cattle—

Merchant caravans attacked and looted—

Bodies left to rot in the road—

"I don't think he even knew she'd cut him until he was on the ground," Tana says quietly.

"Who?"

She's silent for so long, at first you think she's ignoring you. Then a couple teardrops spatter her forearms. (Small and gleaming.)

"My brother," she says. "Vian."

Oh.

You remember now. She mentioned her brother. It's the first thing she said to you, when she thought you were joining her.

My brother would've been—

But you cut her off.

(Which kind of makes you a jackass too.)

She shakes her head, like she's seeing it all over again. "He looked so confused. But he was *never* confused. About anything. All our lives, he was always so infuriatingly sure of himself." She sniffs, wipes her eyes with the back of her hand. "You remind me of him, you know."

"Because I infuriate you?"

She smiles faintly. "Because I could never convince him to do anything he didn't want to do either. Even when he was wrong."

You chuckle. You can't help it. (Even though you're not wrong.)

"This was his idea, you know? Our mother always wanted him to

take her place as village leader, and this was the first time he actually wanted to do it. He would've been here now, if he hadn't . . ."
Tana's voice trails off for a moment, comes back again diminished.
"He could've gotten you to join us. He might've even let you think
it was your idea."

You doubt it, but you don't need to tell her that, so you just say,
"Sometimes we lose the best parts of us."

Tana glances up at you, surprised, like she didn't expect that kind
of sincerity from you. (Honestly, you're a little surprised yourself.)

But she doesn't press you for details, and after a moment you
settle against the fence again, the silence between you comforting,
though sad.

Neither of you moves away.

BEN

WHILE THE CROWD THINS, YOU COUNT YOUR WIN-
nings. Kidam by kidam, han by han. Each coin clinking gently in
your palm. After this, you'll have all you need to fund your journey
across the Candiveras, into Ifrine.

By the fence, a skinny child is watching you intently. She's
attended every one of your duels in Gateway, studying you with the
ferocity of an acolyte, though you've got no interest in followers—

You've got no interest in anyone, really—

You're better off alone.

You return to your winnings. When you first started dueling, it
took you a while to get used to having an audience, to playing a part,
to putting on a show.

Now, you think you'll almost miss it. For the next few weeks,
there'll be no one to duel but your guide, no one to watch but the
wildlife.

Since the war ended, you've performed up and down the peninsula, fought opponents in the capital, the farmlands, the ruined
southern cities. You've earned your epithets, throw by throw by
throw. Sparrowhawk, they call you. Quickest Blade in Kindar. And
you are. You've made sure of it. You've tested yourself against officers, grunts, civilians, kindlings, Vedrans and Amerandines.

None of them have bested you.

So it's time to move on.

As you drop your winnings into your purse, you hear footsteps approaching in the brush. Short strides, an even gait. Someone small and self-assured.

You don't bother to look up. "I'm not taking on any more challengers today."

The response is gruff and impatient. "Not here to challenge you."

Lifting your finger, you tip back the brim of your hat. Before you stands a girl, scowling and straight-backed. With a posture like that, you wouldn't be surprised if she's a former soldier. She may have even been a kindling, once.

But she's gotten sloppy. Her clothes, rumpled; the sides of her head, in need of a shave. Her sword, which should be hanging properly at her side, is slung uselessly across her back, like baggage.

Still, she looks strong and light on her feet. She might've made an interesting opponent, actually, if she'd wanted to duel with swords instead of knives, but she's already said she's not here for that.

"Leum," she says by way of introduction. "Senary Class."

"Hey, Leum. I'm Ben." Then, out of respect for the old ways, you add, "Quinary Class."

She snorts. "You're kidding."

"I'm not." Brushing past her, you cross the corral to collect your bloody knife from the dirt.

She follows. "Come on. You had to be Quaternary Class, at least."

"I wasn't." You wipe the blade with a handkerchief and slide it into its sheath. If Kiban had known what was good for him, he would've relented after your first throw. You'd already won, that was clear enough. After that, spilling blood was superfluous, although in the past two years you've been forced to spill plenty. You try to live by the code (tranquility, honor, compassion), but there's always someone who won't accept defeat—

Always someone who won't let up until they're bleeding—

You understand having something to prove.

But it's not you they have to prove it to.

"They should've promoted you," Leum says, still disbelieving.

"They didn't."

A long time ago, you believed you'd make Primary Class before you burned out. Had the ambition for it, the arrogance, the foolishness. You thought you'd be a specialist, a Mistwalker, an assassin as deadly as you were swift—

Quick, untouchable, perfect.

(But you weren't, were you? Not when it counted.)

For an instant, vermilion light flashes across your vision, bright as a flame.

You blink.

Back in the corral, Leum's still speaking. She wants to offer you some kind of job, it seems.

"Not interested," you say.

"You haven't heard the offer."

"I don't have to. Whatever it pays, I don't need it."

"It pays food and lodging, but we get to keep the spoils."

"Then I definitely don't need it."

She barrels on as if she didn't hear you. "We're defending a village. Up in the mountains. Sixty raiders against seven kindlings, if we can find enough of us out here."

Now *that* surprises you. "How many do you have already?"

"Four, including you."

You glance over her shoulder, where a couple girls are speaking softly by the fence. The one with the saber could be a kindling, but you doubt the other's seen a day of battle in her life.

"No thanks." You cross your arms. "I'm no gambler, and those odds are slim."

"Amity doesn't think so."

You pause. "This is Amity's job?"

You never had the chance to see the Twin Valley Reaper in combat, but like everyone on the peninsula, you knew the stories. She became a Deathbringer nine months after leaving the Academy, made Primary Class by the time she was fourteen. In a handful of years, she'd become more myth than girl. Magnificent, accomplished, precise—

(She was exactly what you wanted to be.)

But sixty to seven?

Sixty to four?

It's not that you're scared. You've faced death before. You were bound to it for years. (We all were.) You never ran from a fight, never backed down from a challenge. You ran gladly toward death, again and again, in pursuit of excellence, perfection, magnificence—

You believed in the cause. You believed in the code. You would've killed for it—

(You did kill for it.)

You would've died for it—

(You almost did—)

But not for this. *This* won't prove anything.

You can't be perfect if you're dead.

"She's back in Windfall at the Grand Hotel," Leum tells you. "She sent me to recruit you."

"What's the Twin Valley Reaper doing all the way out here?"

"Fighting bandits."

You smirk, although you don't think she means to be funny.

Leum stares at you. "So . . . are you in?"

You're almost tempted. During the war, you would've given a year of your life to train with the Reaper, to study from her, to learn from her—

But this isn't the war—

And you don't have to fight in it.

"Not this time, Leum." Waving her off, you head for the fence.

She refuses to give up, trailing after you like a dog on a scent. "Why not?"

"Because I've got fifteen hundred han in my pocket and the best guide in Gateway waiting for me in town."

She halts, surprised. "You're getting out?"

"Aren't you?"

"I'm staying the month," she says stubbornly. "You can too."

"No offense, but you look like you need the money."

She scowls at you, which tells you you're right. "We can't do it alone," she says, lowering her voice. "We need you."

You know.

You *know.*

But you're done with bloodshed. You've been done with it for years. You're not a warrior anymore; you're a performer. You duel only for the chance to hone your skills. You may be the Quickest Blade in Kindar, but you don't throw to kill.

"Sorry," you say. "I'm done with violence."

She glares at you, fists clenched. "You're a kindling. Violence is part of you, whether you like it or not."

You shake your head. You climb through the fence. Your guide is waiting for you. The Candiveras are waiting for you, looming close and oppressive over the northlands. Maybe in a few weeks, you'll find an Ifriner worth challenging, some fair-haired warrior from that cold and mountainous kingdom—

And if not, there are always the lands beyond Ifrine—

Riven—

Kun-kala—

Or Yansen, across the sea—

You don't need Leum. You don't need Amity. You have your knives, your skill, your speed. You'll keep testing yourself. You'll keep improving. True, you won't be a Mistwalker—

(You'll never be a Mistwalker.)

But as long as you're diligent, cautious, persistent, precise—

As long as you're alive, you've still got a chance. You can still be who you were always supposed to be.

Quick.

Untouchable.

Perfect.

EMARA

YOU DIDN'T THINK YOU'D BE ON YOUR OWN TODAY, but you're more than happy to spend Ket's coins on a rented horse from the livery. You're more than happy to see the back of Leum's scruffy head. Maybe you would've joined them, if they'd been interested. Maybe you could've helped.

But they weren't interested, and they didn't want help, not from you—

Just as well, you think. They gave you the chance to slip away, so you took it.

Your mother used to say that luck favors those who look for it, so you're always looking for it. Openings, opportunities. Gifts from the Shell Collector, Lesser God of Games and Chance, can come from anywhere, she said (or you think she said, you can't quite remember), so you'd better be ready to receive them.

Hence, the horse.

And the return to Halabrix.

Your mother would be proud, or at least you hope she'd be. To be honest, you can't really be sure. You remember her (you remember more than most of us), but you don't remember much.

Her face—

Her name—

Emara. When you were born, she gave you her name, which is the main reason you remember it. The name of your mother, the name of your town. You remember nettle farms on the hills and the acrid smell of the dyes in their vats, bundles of fibers hang-drying in the doorways and the clacking of looms drifting out of so many windows—

Your memories like wind-tattered flags—

Or garments left hanging on a line before an evacuation—

You didn't have much to go on, but you had enough to find your way back there when the war ended, to find your way back home when the war ended, but when you arrived, you discovered that home—

The home you remembered—

The home you clung to all those years—

It no longer existed. Gone were the farms, the vats, the looms—

The entire town emptied while you were away, made a battleground while you were away. The population fleeing the Amerandines the same way they fled the Vedrans nearly a century ago and only now beginning to trickle back.

You wandered the streets, asking after your family. *My mother,* you said. *Her name was Emara.*

Did you know her?

Do you know where she went?

You followed her name to a city. A camp for refugees. A village in the country.

My mother. Her name was Emara.

You didn't find her.

Couldn't find her. Couldn't find any of them. No trace of them left but a single scrap of cloth, ragged at the edge, encoded in a dying Chenyaran language of color, weave, and thread—

Here is the story of Emara, daughter of Rava, Weaver of Livia—

The ride to Halabrix takes nearly four hours, which should have been ample time to come up with a plan, although let's be honest, you're not a planner (never have been). In fact, the most planning you've ever done brought you here, to the northlands, where, promptly upon arrival, you nearly lost your balar weapons to a couple of old card sharps with yellow teeth.

Dismounting, you let your horse slake its thirst in the fountain while you creep up to the windows of Harana's Cardroom, where Amity found you last night. The place looks different during the day—

Smaller, dingier—

Holes in the seat cushions, cobwebs in the rafters. When you were little, your mother would tell you to leave a single spiderweb whenever you were cleaning—

For luck, she said—

You and a dustcloth, kneeling in the corners, while she dipped bundles of bast fiber into murky buckets of dye—

Livia, your town, was known for its textiles. Robes, coats, wraps—

Beautiful, light wraps in double ikat, with embellishments embroidered in expensive cotton threads. You remember your little fingers tracing each nub of yarn. Dots and dashes, crosses and braids. A code, your mother called it. A Chenyaran code, passed down in secret by generations of textile artists, who recorded the stories of your people in complex patterns, stitched across each colorful wrap.

Here is the story of Emara, daughter of Rava, Weaver of Livia—

You found the cloth fragment at the last place anyone saw your mother, half price at an open-air market, being hawked by some loudmouthed vendor—

Shame it's not a full wrap, but not bad for true Chenyaran weave, eh? Look at those stitches!

No, I don't know who made it.

I got it off some traveling merchant. Don't know where he got it. Didn't ask.

Why does it matter?

Are you going to buy it or what?

You bought it. Didn't know how to find your family after that, all the clues leading nowhere, all the trails going cold, but Chenyaran wraps were considered precious, rare, works of art from a vanishing culture, fit for collection by wealthy merchants and members of the nobility.

Maybe you couldn't find your family, but you could find their stories—

Chenyaran stories, though Chenyara no longer existed—

(And neither did your family—)

You could track their artifacts down in galleries, museums, mansions, across the former Vedran territories and into Amerandine lands, and maybe, if you were lucky, someone, somewhere, could tell you what happened to your mother.

You found a second wrap in the hold of a ship bound for Yansen. Not your family's work but another's. Not a personal history but a cultural one.

Here is the story of Vana, Third Queen of Chenyara, as recorded by Saya, Weaver of Nemera—

You arrived just in time to abscond with the wrap—

The anchors lifting—

The sails unfurling—

Your wild leap from the deck to the dock, where you landed by accident among several officers of the port authority, who tried to hold you for questioning, but the Shell Collector gave you an escape and you took it.

Luck favors those who look for it.

So you kept looking. Cities, collectors, black markets. Eventually, you heard rumor of another wrap in the northlands—

A *Livian* wrap this time, in the possession of a professional gambler named Haru, who won it in a card game.

So you went north. Tracked Haru and her sister from town to

town until you reached Halabrix, where last night you discovered in Harana's Cardroom an old woman wearing a Chenyaran heirloom around her skinny northern shoulders like it was some common hempen cloak.

You should have studied her.

You should have made a plan.

Instead, you threw down your coin purse and entered the game. Wanted to win the wrap from her but nearly let her take your daggers too. Then the Shell Collector sent you none other than the Twin Valley Reaper, who was at one time your deadliest enemy, but you were Vedran then, and there is no Vedra now.

You're hardly enthusiastic about having to fight bandits for a bunch of farmers, but it's better than being indebted to Hope and Haru. (Probably.) In any case, you'll only be here a month—

A month in the company of some Amerandine snobs who think you're sloppy and self-indulgent and all those other preconceptions they have about Vedrans up here—

They think you lost the war because you lacked *discipline* and *force of will*—

Not because they had handcannons by the end.

It's not like you care what they think of you anyway. You're not one of them. (You're not one of anything anymore.) So they don't matter.

No, the only thing that matters now is that Haru is seated beside her sister at one of Harana's scratched tables, her gnarled fingers expertly flipping cards from her deck, and she's no longer wearing the wrap.

You grin. You send a prayer of thanks to the Shell Collector.

You may have lost most of what you had on you last night, but you didn't lose your wits. As your meager pile of coins slowly dwindled down to nothing, you learned that one of Hope's rings holds a dram of poison, you learned Haru's adept with a knife. You learned how many weapons they carry and how many enforcers they employ, and, most importantly, you learned where they're staying.

If the wrap isn't on Haru now, it'll be there, in her room. At the Last Stop Inn.

In the lobby of the Last Stop, you stumble into a couple perfumed Amerandine travelers (hoity-toity and impeccably dressed). "Whoops!" Your arms pinwheeling, your long legs tangling in their luggage.

It tumbles to the floor.

"Excuse me!" Blunderingly, you fumble a package. As you loosen its ties, its contents spill—

Scarves, undergarments—

You scoop them up only to let them fall through your fingers again like water. "Oh my, I'm so sorry! Please, let me help you—"

Irritably, they wave you aside as the innkeeper comes dashing out from behind the desk. You lift your hands. You back away. You sneak a peek at the ledger, find Haru's name.

One upward glance tells you her room's on the second story, at the back of the building, so you slip out of the lobby and make your way to the alley behind the hotel.

A jump, a climb, a scramble, and you're at Haru's window. You're unlatching the shutters. You're climbing inside.

The room is a mess. The bed unmade, the floor littered with clothes, bottles, overflowing ash trays. You rummage through Haru's belongings, searching for the wrap. Rip the sheets from the mattress, toss the pillows against the walls. You dig through the drawers, pawing through socks and jewelry, loose coins (which you pocket) and winter coats.

You finally find the wrap stuffed into a chest beside the saddlebags and spare sandals. Extricating it gently from the tangle, you lift the fabric to your face and inhale—

The faint scent of dye—

Grass—

The sour smell of someone's sweat—

You lower the wrap, running your fingers over the cloth. *Here is the story of Callula, Greater God of War, when she came to defend the coast from the Tide King, as recorded by Maryam, Weaver of Livia*—

You swallow.

You don't remember a Maryam.

You barely remember this story. Something about the Tide King, in his anger, threatening to consume the ports, and Callula riding into battle on her warhorse with his many hooves of flint—

But who angered the Tide King?

And why was Callula moved to intervene?

The details are beneath your fingers, in the warp, the weft, the pattern, the embroidery—

But you can't read them. Can't read all of them anyway. Have forgotten so many of the words, lost them somewhere during your thirteen years away.

And you call yourself Chenyaran?

What does that even mean, if Chenyara doesn't exist anymore? It was wiped from the map by Vedra, before Vedra was wiped from the map by Amerand. All these nations obliterated. All these identities erased.

Does that make you Amerandine now?

Not according to Leum. To Leum, and maybe to the rest of them, your hair's too wavy. Your eyes are too gray. You're too loud. You don't have their nice Amerandine manners, their vaunted martial discipline. You have your wine and your weeklong festivals, and a couple years ago they would've killed you on sight.

(Not that you wouldn't have done the same to them.)

You turn the wrap in your hands.

No, if you're anything now, you're alone.

Then, in the hallway, footsteps—

Haru's voice, scratchy with smoke, filtering through the door—

You leap to your feet as a key turns in the lock. Throwing the wrap around your shoulders, you dash for the window, where you clamber out of the room as the door slides open.

Haru sees you immediately—

(Not that you're hiding or anything—)

And her eyes narrow with recognition. "You!" she snarls.

Pausing on the windowsill, you wink at her. "Me."

A knife strikes the wall beside you, quivering in the wood, and you're going to run out of luck if you linger any longer, so you fling yourself from the second story, rolling in the dust and coming up running.

Above you, Haru appears in the window. Her teeth bared, her canines dog-sharp. *"Emara!"*

Cheerily, you flick her a salute.

And what's not to be cheery about? You got what you came for. You got the wrap, your third wrap, and soon there will be others. You'll spend a month in the northlands, a month of free meals (though you could've asked for better company), and after that you can head south again. You can continue your search again. You'll find more Chenyaran artifacts, more scraps of your culture.

If you find enough of them, maybe you'll also find your way home.

LEUM

AFTER LEAVING BEN IN THE CORRAL, YOU AND THE others ride back to Windfall, your disappointment clinging to you like sweat.

She could've joined you. She could've been one of you, fighting side by side against a band of raiders—

Fierce—

Ferocious—

Resplendent. It wouldn't have been like it was in the war, but it would've been something, wouldn't it? To fight together again? To be together again?

You've almost reached the livery when you pass an alley reeking of vomit, the slop of a binge gone wrong. Ordinarily, the stink wouldn't stop you. (You've smelled worse, after all.) But there's another smell in that alley too, a familiar one—

Blood.

You swing down from Comet's saddle.

Beside you, Burk sniffs at the air.

In the shadows, there's a person leaning against one of the alley walls, face-first against the wooden siding like a crooked fence post. Their clothes are stained and half-heartedly patched, their belt looped in a loose nonbinary knot that looks like it'll slip from their hips at any second.

A snore rattles in their throat.

"Something wrong?" Tana says.

Ket dismounts, leaving the farmer on the back of the little buckskin mare. "Leum?"

You ignore them both. The figure in the alley has cropped hair, messy but soft, like even after this, they could run their hands through it and still come out looking good.

If it weren't for the bruises—

And the blood—

And the puke.

But you recognize that hair, don't you? That way of sleeping, like a half-felled tree. You remember teasing them about it, years ago at House Kemera—

The two of you shorter and ganglier back then, dumber and livelier and quicker to laugh—

They always dozed off when they were supposed to be on watch, allowing your fellow trainees to sneak up on you during the night—

You step into the alley. "Kanver?"

They mumble something, and now you're sure it's them. You know that rough voice, like an ember crackling in their throat. You used to drift off to that voice, curled up in the lower bunk while they rambled on about the food in the mess hall, the other trainees, a cloud they saw that day—

You used to think they wanted someone to listen to them.

Now you think they knew you couldn't fall asleep in the silence.

Tana dismounts behind you. "You know them?"

"We were at the Academy together."

As you lever Kanver's sleeping form away from the wall, Ket steps forward to steady their body.

"I can do it," you tell her.

She doesn't let go. "I know."

Between you, Kanver throws up on themself, bile dribbling down their chin.

"Hey," you say.

Their amber eyes are bleary. "Leum?"

You wipe their mouth with the cuff of your robe. "Yeah."

"Oh, damn. Am I dead?"

"Not yet."

They laugh, vomiting a little more in the process. Then, seeing Ket, they blink. "Who're you?"

Ket grins. "I'm Ket."

"Hi, Ket."

"Hi."

"They need water." Tana appears behind you, holding a gourd. You tense, thinking she's going to reach for Kanver too, but she seems to understand, even without you telling her, that she's different from the rest of you. An intruder, an outsider, peering in on something private.

She passes the gourd to Ket. "Vian liked to drink too." Then, more quietly, she adds, "I always cleaned him up so our mother wouldn't catch him."

Ket eyes her thoughtfully. "You were a pretty good sister, huh?"

Digging into her pockets for a handkerchief, Tana looks away. "Not good enough to save him."

Ket says nothing. Offers Kanver a sip of water. Carefully, you steer them onto a nearby crate, where you check them for injuries—

A black eye—

A broken nose—

Some bruised ribs—

They're better off than Tana was yesterday, but only just.

"What happened to you?" you ask.

They shrug in an exaggerated way, like they're trying to shimmy out of their own skin. "Got drunk."

"No kidding."

"Somebody wanted to fight me, and I said, 'Okay, I'll fight you.'"

Ket plucks a sliver of wood from Kanver's hairline. Knuckle-length and bloodstained. "Was that someone a door?" she asks.

Kanver squints at her. "Who're you?"

"I'm Ket." She picks another splinter from their forehead, which causes them to flinch.

"Hi, Ket."

Taking back the water gourd, Tana wets a handkerchief and passes it to Ket, who dabs at Kanver's wounds. Glancing around, you check the alley for Kanver's polearm—

The long, beautiful weapon the smiths of House Kemera presented to them when they were promoted from trainee to Octonary Class—

But you don't see it.

"Did someone take your glaive?" you ask.

Kanver gives you a sloppy grin. "I hid it." They giggle. "I buried—hey, you have a dog."

Standing behind you, Burk wags her stump of a tail.

"Her name's Burk."

"That's a stupid name for a dog."

Ket laughs.

"What do you know?" you grumble. "You're drunk."

Kanver belches. "Yes, I am."

"Come on." Gingerly, you and Ket help Kanver to their feet. "I've got a room."

They snort, swaying between the two of you like a sapling in a breeze. "Show-off."

"Shut up."

As you lead them back to the street, they drag their fingertips along the siding. "I'm going to miss my wall."

"There are walls in my room," you tell them. "Four of them. You can take your pick."

Beyond the alley, the sunlight is harsh, illuminating all the nicks and scratches on Kanver's hands and arms and neck, the dried specks of blood and vomit on their collar. Blinking, they look at you, watery-eyed, like they're only just seeing you now.

"Leum?"

"Yeah?" You gesture for Tana to take the horses, and with a sad glance at Kanver, she leads the animals toward the livery.

"I'm a mess, huh?" Kanver says.

You keep walking, steering them past the saloon, where you see a cracked doorframe, a ripped curtain.

These broken things.

Ket shrugs. "No more than the rest of us."

Kanver burps. "Who're you?"

"I'm Ket."

Kanver chuckles. "Hi, Ket. What're you doing hanging around with this old grump?"

"Shut up," you grumble.

They shake their head, which causes them to retch. You and Ket pause, waiting for Kanver to finish.

At last they straighten, wiping their mouth. "I'm glad you lived, Leum," they say softly.

You nuzzle the side of their head, and despite the sick and the blood, their hair is just like you remember it—

Soft—

Feathery—

Comforting against your cheek.

"Same to you," you whisper.

KANVER

SOMETIME IN THE LATE AFTERNOON, YOU COME TO—

Bleary and dry-mouthed—

On someone else's bed. You don't know exactly where you are or how you got here, but there's clean sheets and a little speckled dog, and maybe you should be worried because you don't really understand what's happening, but let's be honest, you haven't had it this good in months, so you just close your eyes again and hope things are clearer when you wake.

They are. After another short but blissfully dreamless sleep, you find out you're in Leum's room at the Grand Hotel. Apparently, she plucked you out of some alley in Windfall—

She's in Windfall too, imagine that—

Before she found you, you remember stumbling into someone, fists swinging, your face hitting something hard and splintery, a breath of air, the morning sky—

Then nothing.

Leum's changed since the Academy, you think. She's still short (and short-tempered), but there used to be a brightness about her that's all gone dull now. Her voice, her stare. Blunted, blunted. She reminds you now of a cloudy sky—

Of rain on the horizon—

Gray water and a windswept cliff.

She doesn't say anything as she wets a cloth for you, averts her eyes as you swipe your face, your neck, your pits. You stink, and now you remember throwing up on yourself. The tang and bitter surging up your throat, sloppy and warm.

"Sorry," you mumble.

She shrugs.

The dog (who's called Burk, which is a stupid name for a dog) is lying on the floor, staring up at you with limpid brown eyes. Shame-faced, you turn your back on her as you shuck off your soiled clothes and reach for the new ones Leum's laid on the bed for you.

They're not hers, you notice. Too big for her. Maybe she got them from that girl, Ket, who you can only recall as an easy grin and a gentle arm, and if that's the case, Ket's got good taste, because the clothes are nicer by far than yours—

Diamond patterns in the robe, stiff pleats in the trousers—

You'd like to appreciate that for a minute, but to be honest, all you can think of is how they'll be a mess again in the morning, or if you're careful, the morning after that, or maybe the afternoon, the evening, the night, the next—

It's only a matter of time.

Leum says she needs your help, something about fighting, something about the code, and you don't know if you believe in all that anymore, but it means she didn't drag you out of that alley solely out of the goodness of her heart, and that's a relief because it means despite everything you can still be useful—

Or at least she believes you can still be useful, which is almost as good—

You're sitting in the hotel lobby in a restaurant you didn't even know was here, but how could you have known? You can't afford a hotel. You've been sleeping on the ground (and in alleyways, you guess) since you were chased out of that barn last winter.

The food's not bad, and the wine's drinkable, or at least that's what Amity tells you as she fills your cup. You're tempted to tell her you've found that practically anything can be drinkable if you're desperate enough, but she's the Twin Valley Reaper, and you may be a fool, but you're not foolish enough to argue with the Twin Valley Reaper, so you keep your mouth shut and try not to embarrass yourself.

You're not sure if you're succeeding. More than half the table already saw you in that alley, sloshed and reeling, which is a first impression you don't think you can shed, no matter how clean your clothes are, your borrowed clothes, or how politely you can make conversation.

They're nice enough about it, you suppose. Leum and Burk. Ket, seated thigh to thigh beside a girl named Tana, who you don't remember at all from this afternoon but who regards you with some consternation (thin-lipped and frowning) when Leum tells her you're joining them.

You manage a smile. A two-fingered wave.

Her frown deepens, but she doesn't tell you to leave, so that's something.

"We're glad to have you," Amity says, and you don't know if she's lying—

(Lying seems beneath the likes of the Twin Valley Reaper—)

But you're happy to believe it, or at least you're happy to try. The truth is, you don't know what to make of her. Her graceful movements, her gracious manner. You don't understand why she's in the northlands, why she's wearing that scarf over her hair. If it's a disguise, it's pretty thin, although none of the other diners seem to be aware they're in the presence of battlefield royalty, so maybe it's working.

What you really don't get is why she's here. With you. You and

Leum are kindlings, and maybe that means something if you're not one of us, but among our own kind you're nothing special.

Infantry—

Expendable—

During the war, a specialist like Amity wouldn't have given you the time of day.

Now she's serving you wine?

Stranger still, she's roped a Vedran into helping her. (Not that these things are supposed to matter anymore, although try telling that to Leum.) Emara's splayed out between you and Amity, who keeps pulling away like she doesn't want to be touched, or maybe she just doesn't want to be touched by a Vedran—

Old habits, maybe. Older enemy.

Not that you mind. You like Emara already. You like her long arms, her gap-toothed smile, her generosity—

"Hey, drink up!" she says, signaling the serving girl for another bottle of wine. "It's my treat, eh?"

Amity, who's still nursing her drink, declines politely. Ket laughs and beckons for more. Leum scowls down at the table. (She hasn't had anything to drink at all.) Smiling, you tap the top of your cup with your palm, the suction making a little *plop, plop* that only you can hear.

The serving girl arrives, wedging herself between Ket and Tana to set the bottle down. You wonder if she has something going on with Ket, because ever since you arrived in the restaurant, she's found excuses to touch her (a hip, an arm, a shoulder), like she's trying to weave a net around her with nothing but her touch.

Maybe she's concerned because Ket's sitting so easily with the rest of you, drinking and laughing so easily with the rest of you—

Like she's already one of you, even though she said she isn't.

The serving girl withdraws.

"How did you get the money for this again?" Tana asks, frowning.

Emara winks at her. "Trade secret."

"What trade? Gambling?"

"Theft, probably," Leum grumbles.

You always knew when she was going to blow up, could tell from her pinched mouth, her lowered brow, so you lean into her, just a little, just enough to stop her from exploding. Your shoulder to her shoulder, your arm to her arm, like you used to do at the Academy.

She lets out a breath.

Her fists unclench.

You're not good for much of anything anymore, but it's nice to know you can still do this.

"However you got it"—Ket reaches for the bottle, refilling Tana's cup and then her own—"I'm happy to take advantage of it."

Emara grins and tosses her a couple han. "I couldn't have done it without you, eh?"

Everyone except Leum lifts their cups. You drain yours in a single gulp, and you don't know what Amity's talking about, because the wine's more than drinkable, it's *good*—

Better than anything you'd have bought for yourself, although that isn't saying much—

More importantly, it's plentiful. Emara splashes more wine into your cup. "I think I'm gonna like you, Kanver."

You smile. You drink. Maybe you should head south after this. You've never drunk with a Vedran before, but if Emara's any indication, you can see where they get their reputation. Vedrans are notorious for their revelries, their festivals and feasts and weeklong debaucheries. You'd always been told they were wastrels and sybarites, which was why Amerand crushed them in the end, but maybe being a sybarite suits you.

The softness of it—

The haziness of it—

You shake your head. You drain your cup. You drain your cup

again. Maybe there's a meal (you can't say for sure), but before you know it, the restaurant is emptying, and nobody but Emara is ordering drinks because all the real drinkers are headed for the taverns, where there's music and entertainment, which, to be fair, you wouldn't say no to—

You like the sound, the noise, the cacophony, so loud you don't have to think—

But you're so far gone already, you're not thinking, not remembering, not anything. You're nothing, and you like that, and here the drinks are free.

Soon it's just the six of you and the dog and the serving girl, still lingering by the kitchens, even though the cook has left for the night and all the other tables have been wiped down and Emara's finally run out of money, so you're down to the last bottle of wine.

"When did Adren say she'd be back?" Ket asks.

Adren. The name sounds familiar, but all these names sound familiar to you. *Adren, Amity, Amerand—*

"End of the season," says Tana.

Ket drums her fingers on the edge of the table. "And how far is your village from here?"

"Two and a half days by foot."

You nod, trying to look sage, although you're worried you only look drunk (which you are, but you hope no one notices). The truth is, you've had enough wine that you no longer know what anyone is talking about, although, strictly speaking, it no longer matters to you either. You sip your drink and squint your eyes and everyone is a pleasant blur: Leum and Emara and Amity, Ket and Tana and the serving girl in the corner.

"We should leave in the morning," Tana says.

Amity shakes her head. "We need more kindlings."

The farmer frowns, an expression she wears as easily as Leum wears her scowl. "We already have four of you."

"Four against sixty," Leum mutters. "Won't be enough."

"What?" Emara stands, which must be hard for her, because she's almost as drunk as you are, and levels an accusatory finger at Amity. "You told me it was *eighty*, Queenie."

Amity smothers a smile.

"And you still came?" Ket grins at her. "When you thought the odds were that bad?"

Emara huffs and sits down again, toppling into you with her big cloud of hair. It's smells nice, which you like, but it's also in your mouth, which you don't like at all. "Don't you know?" she says with a laugh. "Chenyarans are suckers for bad odds."

"But we *can't* wait," Tana says. "We already searched Windfall, and Halabrix, and Gateway. If there were more kindlings out there, we would've found them by now. The village isn't ready. We need time to prepare."

You blink, and things swim into focus—

Sharper, harsher—

Leum with her arms crossed. Amity at the head of the table, looking grim. Ket squirming like a worm on a hook.

You may have missed something.

"She's got a point," Emara says, as if to ease the tension, which you appreciate, even if you don't know what the tension is about.

You consider trying to duck under the table if the fists start flying, but you can't figure out how to make your bottom half go wobbly enough to slide out of the way.

"How well can you prepare?" Ket asks. "When you only have four kindlings?"

Emara shrugs. "She's got a point too."

Tana frowns, not at Emara but at Ket. "Well," she says sharply, "we could've had five."

Ket averts her eyes. A muscle twitching in her cheek, fingers drumming restlessly at the collar of her robe.

"Ket's right," Amity says. "The numbers don't lie. We won't succeed without more of us."

"But we can't stay here, doing nothing, while we wait for more kindlings to wander into town," Tana counters. "Even if someone showed up tomorrow, there's no guarantee they'd help us."

Beside the table, Burk woofs. (A low, affirmative sound.)

Leum glares at her. "No one asked you, traitor."

If dogs could shrug, you think Burk would do it now, but she just lays her head on her paws, and you're the only one paying enough attention to hear her woof again, as if in protest.

"What about my people?" Tana leans forward. "You said you'd train us."

Amity eyes her coolly. "We will."

"So? Won't that be enough?"

"You're not kindlings."

"We're better than nothing."

Amity gives her a restrained smile. "An unskilled soldier is a greater liability than no soldier at all."

Tana's eyes flash. "It's our *home*. We'd die to defend it."

"And it's my job to make sure you don't have to."

Tana stands, and you decide you like her courage, which you have to admit is abundant. Arguing with a Deathbringer? You don't know anybody else who'd dare.

You raise your cup to her, but you're disappointed to discover that you've already drunk what was in it, and before you can ask for a refill, a girl bursts into the lobby, dragging a greatsword behind her.

She's small, with large, round eyes in a large, round head that looks funny on her scrawny frame—

She can't be more than fourteen, you think, more of a kid than any of you—

She takes one look around the table, chin jutted forward like she's daring you to throw her out, although you don't know why you'd do that, you've never seen her before in your life. (At least, you don't think you have.)

"I'll join you," she says. "I'm a kindling."

SIDDIE

THEY STARE AT YOU—

Steady, skeptical—

Taking in every spot and speck and detail—

And you can't see yourself, but you can feel your neck and cheeks turning red with embarrassment, which isn't the kind of first impression you wanted to make, but you've already stepped in it, Siddie—

Too late to take it back now.

You've been stalking the Sparrowhawk for a week, trying to work up the courage to talk to her. *Hi, Ben, remember me? Siddie? From House Vastari?*

Although you don't think she'd recognize you, because why would she? You weren't an exceptional student, worthy of notice—

Not like her—

Or Amity before her—

Besides, she kept to herself at the Academy. Always training. Always alone.

Then Leum, the crabby one with the messy topknot, approached Ben at the corral. Leum, Senary Class. You heard her recite her rank that afternoon in Gateway. A kindling with a greatsword, like yours—

A kindling who could train you, like the Swordmaster was supposed to.

So you followed her and the others to Windfall. (Took you a while, without a horse of your own, but you made it.) You listened to them talking from outside the hotel. It wasn't easy to hear what they were saying, but you heard enough to know they're up to *something*.

And you want to be a part of it.

"Sorry, private party," one of them says. She's big and beautiful, with dark hair crackling around her face and her eyes with a bit of gray in them, like fog at night.

"My name is Siddie," you say, trying and failing to keep your voice from trembling, which makes your next words come out in a squeak. "I'm one of you."

Leum snorts. She crosses her arms, and you can see her two-handed sword laid across her lap.

You bite your lip. You'd hoped to impress her. "I am!" you say, although you immediately regret it, because it makes you sound like a child, which you're not. Then, because you're getting desperate now, you pull the wrapping from your sword, hoping it will come off in a nice dramatic flourish.

It doesn't.

Instead, it gets caught on the scabbard, so you have to wrestle it free, struggling a little with the weight of the weapon, which you hope the others don't notice, although the sinking feeling in your stomach tells you they probably do. You bite back a cry—

The frustrated kind, not the teary kind—

(Well, maybe a little.)

A balar crystal glows blush-colored in the dim restaurant. Its light is faint, the way it always is when it's not *your* balar crystal—

When you're training on a generic Academy weapon—

Or wielding a borrowed sword—

But the light's there. You *are* one of them.

You lift your chin, as if to say, *See?*

Leum growls. "Where'd you get that?"

"It was forged for me," you lie.

"You steal it?"

You try not to take a step back. "No."

Which *isn't* a lie, because you and the Swordmaster were friends, weren't you? Traveling together. Cooking over the same fire. You carrying her pack. You mixing her tinctures. Her teaching you what it took to be a kindling.

And if you weren't friends, then you were at least master and apprentice, which might not have been how she'd have phrased it, but she still gave you her greatsword—

Left it lying in the dirt for you, wrapped in one of her old cloaks—

Right before she burned out, her veins a bright and scathing red beneath her fevered skin—

Maybe it's not technically *your sword* the way Leum's is hers, but so what? It's yours *now*.

At the head of the table, Amity studies you through her ink-flick lashes. She almost looks the same as you remember from House Vastari—

Six years older than you, distant and cold—

But she seems thinner now. Paler. More determined.

"You didn't make it out of the Academy, did you?" she asks. Her voice is gentler than you expect—

You could have taken it if she'd been harsh with you, like the Swordmaster was, but instead her soft words strike you square in the chest. Your face warms again, this time with shame.

"How close were you to graduating?" she asks.

You rub your arm across your eyes. "A few weeks."

A few weeks, and you would've gotten your very own balar sword. A few weeks, and you would've been Octonary Class instead of a trainee. A few weeks, and you would've been like any of the rest of them.

But the war ended, and you didn't even get the chance to trade in your weapon like a real kindling, because you didn't have a weapon.

(And you weren't a real kindling.)

"She could be an asset," Amity murmurs, more to herself than anyone else.

Leum grunts. "Not if she's dead as soon as she hits the battlefield."

You don't like that they're talking about you like you're not even here, but it seems like they're considering your offer, so you keep your mouth shut.

"She's a trainee," Amity replies, "not some civilian."

Leum shakes her head. "She's a child."

"I am not!" You start toward her, trying not to let the tip of your weapon touch the floor. "I'm only a few years younger than the rest of you!"

"Yeah?" Leum looks you up and down quickly, dismissively, in a way that makes you feel two feet tall, even though she's only got a few inches on you at most. "You think you can join us?"

You nod.

She gestures to the empty place beside her. "Then join us."

You can't believe it. A seat at *that* table? With Amity? You feel a relieved laugh bubbling up inside you as you take a step forward, but before you can sit, something smacks you in the shin. You stumble backward.

Across the table, the one with the gray eyes clicks her tongue. "Watch your feet, Piggy," she says.

You grimace. You don't know why she's calling you that (you're not particularly piglike), but you can tell from her tone it's not good.

"Shut it, Vedran," Leum snaps. "This is none of your business."

You blink, surprised. You've never met a Vedran kindling before. What's she doing with northerners like Amity and Ben?

"Hey." Beside Leum, a kindling with feathery hair nudges her with their elbow. (You assume they're a kindling, anyway, even though they don't seem to have a weapon on them.) In a low, crackling voice, they say, "Leum. C'mon."

Leum glares at the Vedran for a full second before turning back to you. "What's the matter? Thought you wanted to join us."

You shouldn't be this confused, but you are, so you start forward again, and this time you see it when she lashes out at you, quick and hard, forcing you away from the table.

Someone smothers a laugh.

You glare at the others, but you can't figure out who did it.

Leum gestures you forward again, and you're determined to make it this time. When she kicks at you, you dodge, neatly sidestepping her, but you don't see her hand coming up to shove you aside. Her palm catches you in the arm, thrusting you back again.

And she isn't even on her feet yet.

The girl at the end of the table (one of the ones you saw at the corral) is watching you uncomfortably, like she's not sure if she should say something, although you wish she would. *She's* not a kindling, you're pretty sure. If you had to guess, you'd say she's just the civilian who hired them. Even if you can't fight Leum, you're a better fighter than a *civilian*, aren't you? You don't know why that doesn't make you good enough to join them, but you know it's not fair.

Grunting, you charge the table, wielding your sword in its worn wooden sheath.

Again, Leum strikes you in the shin, the knee, grabbing your wrist as you tumble forward. You swing your weapon around, hoping to catch her in the side of the head, but she leans back, letting the scabbard whisk harmlessly past her ear.

She shoves you away.

Her mistake. You swipe at her with your fist, and as she ducks, you lunge for your place at the table.

Then something hits you in the stomach, and all the air goes out of you. You fall, tripping over your scabbard, and land hard on your backside.

Slowly, Leum returns her covered sword to her lap.

Stupid, Siddie. You forgot about her balar weapon.

She stares at Amity for a long moment, something unspoken passing between them, and when she turns back to you, her voice is hard. "You're a child," she repeats. "Get out of here."

No one laughs this time. Their grim expressions, their pitying eyes.

You look to Amity, but she shakes her head.

You start crying—

(Not a lot, but enough to notice when your vision blurs—)

And you don't want to let the kindlings see you cry (especially not Leum), so you grab your sword and you scramble to your feet and you run.

Thankfully, you make it out of the hotel without embarrassing yourself any more than you already have, and on the street you pause to dash the tears from your cheeks.

Inside, they're arguing again. Raised voices. Sharp words.

You tighten your grip on your sword. You couldn't even sit down with them, could you? You couldn't even do that.

But that doesn't make you less than them.

That doesn't make you worth any less.

You were at the Academy. You have a *balar* weapon. You have as much right to call yourself a kindling as any of them, and one day, soon, you're going to prove it.

BEN

AFTER YOU LEAVE LEUM IN THE CORRAL, YOU TRY TO forget about her. Her heavy brows, her stubborn jaw, the way she glared at you like you were a coward and a traitor—

But you can't have betrayed her, can you? You never pledged yourself to her cause in the first place. You don't owe her anything—

Your skills, your loyalty—

(Your life—)

So you return to Gateway. You pay your guide. You spend the afternoon helping him load supplies onto the cart, listening to him tick off items as they're stacked and secured—

Tents, soap, pots and hand tools—

You keep your mind on the minutiae.

Bags of rice, grain for the horses—

It helps not to think about Leum. Her offer. Her disappointment. Her chances for survival.

Bottles of vinegar and boxes of tea—

You saddle up your horse, Penumbra. You count her steps as you climb into the Candiveras. You make it past a thousand before you forget not to look back.

Sundown on the foothills, dusky and red. In the distance, you can just make out the winking lights of Windfall. The hotels, the rattling saloons.

You try not to imagine Leum out there, Leum and whoever else she found, if she found anyone else to help her—

But you rejected her offer, didn't you? You're not supposed to care what happens to her now.

You click your tongue. You knee Penumbra forward. As you draw up beside the cart, your guide, Kereb, leans over with a crooked smile. "Nice night for traveling," he says. "Clear skies. Good weather ahead of us."

You nod, but you're having a hard time thinking about what's ahead of you. The steep cliffsides, the winding mountain trails. You feel like the world has tilted beneath you, all the soil sliding away, all the weeds uprooted, all the rocks tumbling southward, end over end—

Wreckage—

Rubble—

Dust and blood—

But you don't have to worry about that anymore, because you're getting out of Amerand. You got what you wanted, didn't you? You're the Quickest Blade in Kindar. You don't have anything else to prove.

Not to Leum. Not to anyone.

So you try not to think about her as you listen to Kereb ramble on about some early winter festival the Ifriners have, these little black cakes they serve on street corners. "You ever tried one?" he asks.

You shake your head.

"I thought as much," he says. "You've got to get the ones with the seeds on top."

To be honest, you're not particularly interested in cakes, or festivals for that matter—

(Although you would be, if you knew how much you'd miss them when they're gone—)

But you don't tell him that. You don't have to. He'll fall silent soon enough. You just have to wait, and you're good at waiting. You're good at silence.

You're good at being alone.

At the Academy, you always preferred your own company to the company of your kin, who you found to be loud, lax, undisciplined. The cacophony of the training courtyard, the chaos of the barracks. Instead, you took to the rooftops, the gardens, anywhere you could find a little silence, a little calm.

That's why you wanted to be a Mistwalker. So you could work alone.

Except you didn't, did you? Work alone? You weren't good enough yet, weren't fast enough yet. You may not have been infantry, like Leum, but you were still assigned to a squad like anyone else—

The four of you tasked with kidnappings, interrogations, assassinations—

At least for a time.

You flinch. You can't help it—

The pain in your forehead searing, bright—

You got what you wanted, in the end. You were alone after that. In recovery after that. Bandaged and bedridden until the Vedran surrender.

At the top of the first ridge, Kereb halts before a roadside shrine. Rotten beams, shingles strewn with lichen, a chipped idol of the Crane Brother, Lesser God of Travelers, huddled inside. Rummaging in his satchel, Kereb pulls out a small late-season peach and places it at the idol's feet.

You scan the stacked stones arrayed beside the shrine. "Graves?" you ask.

Kereb straightens, scratching his chin. "For the ones who didn't make it across."

Some of the cairns have been adorned with flowers, dry as insect husks on their fragile stems, but others are so old they've collapsed in the weather, the winter, the snow—

Their names (if they ever had names) eroded, their deeds erased. The anonymous dead, vanishing into the topography as if they'd never lived at all—

You try not to, but you can't help wondering how many more fighters Leum found after she left you. Another two? Three, if she was lucky?

Three kindlings—

You close your eyes.

Three bodies—

The corpses of your squad, stiff and cold, and you, the only survivor, staggering from the rubble—

You don't have to do it again, Ben.

You don't have anything to prove, remember?

"Ben?"

You open your eyes to find Kereb squinting at you in the low light. "What?"

"I asked if you were ready to go."

You look toward the mountains, black and jagged against the stars. You look toward your future. Ifrine. Riven. Kun-kala. So many contests untested, so many challengers unchallenged. You could continue improving, picking up speed, learning new techniques from foreigners you meet. You could be the best in the world, Ben.

But the world will have to wait.

You turn back to Kereb.

"What do you mean you're not going?" he asks.

You tell him you have unfinished business in the northlands. "It'll only be a month," you say. "You can take me across then."

He gestures at the laden cart. "Some of these supplies won't last a month."

"So sell them." Lifting the reins, you turn Penumbra back down the road. "We'll buy them again when I get back."

"Get back from where?" Kereb asks.

But you don't answer. You're already riding southward, faster and faster, surer and surer with every step. Down the mountain. Across the darkened hills.

Because you have to know.

You tell yourself you have to know. You have to know you're good enough to save them this time. You're fast enough to keep them alive. They're not going to die, nameless in the mountains. You're too good for that now—

Too perfect.

So you ride, and you ride. The dusty road, the dry wind, the skies yawning overhead. In Windfall, you make your way to the Grand Hotel, where you come across a child stumbling into the street, the same child who was at your duel this morning. (Large eyes, larger sword.) Odd that she's here, but you don't stop her as she shuffles past you, sniffling and swiping at her eyes.

Entering the hotel, you find Leum and a few others hunched around a table in an otherwise empty lobby. The kitchen closed, the lamps burning low. They look up at you as you enter: Leum and the girls from the corral; Amity, who you recognize from House Vastari; and two others you don't know.

"Ben." Amity's voice is unruffled, as if she's been expecting you (which maybe she was). "Nice to see you again."

You're surprised she remembers you. At the Academy, she studied alone. Trained alone. Lived alone.

(Like you tried to.)

Leum lowers her chin, scowling at you from the opposite end of the table. "What are you doing here?"

You touch the handle of one of your knives. "You said you needed me."

"We need a kindling, not an entertainer."

You chew the inside of your lip. You'll have to fight. That's un-avoidable. You'll have to come to grips with the violence, with the blood you'll have to spill. But if you're quick enough—

(If you're perfect enough—)

Maybe this time you won't have to kill.

You shrug. "What if I told you I need this too?"

The corner of her mouth twitches.

You're bound to them now, Ben, bound to the mission, bound to these kindlings and their cause—

Now *your* cause—

In the silence, one of the girls from the corral (the civilian, you think) turns to Amity. "That's five," she says. "Five kindlings. Will that be enough?"

"Hardly." Amity sniffs. "But it'll have to do." Standing, she adjusts her scarf. She's taller than you remember (and leaner too). "Get some rest, all of you. We leave at dawn."

As the others file past you, you look each of them in the eye. You force yourself to look each of them in the eye. Leum, Amity, the others whose names you don't know. You force yourself to see them, and you make each of them a simple, silent promise.

You're going to live.

You're going to live, and everyone else will too, and when the mission is over, when the job is done, you're going to leave this country, this unforgiving, indifferent country—

No regrets, no lingering questions—

After this, you'll have nothing left to prove.

KET

WHEN YOU FINALLY RETURN TO YOUR ROOM, REMA IS waiting for you. Drowsy and beautiful. "Hey."

"Hey." Removing your sword, you climb onto the bed, where you trace the shape of her foot, her ankle, her calf beneath the sheets. Sometimes you try to be content with these things. These things could be a world, you think. A girl in your bed, the stars in your window. This narrow slice of things and nothing else mattering beyond—

(As long as you don't think about it too hard.)

Rema yawns. "You've been busy today."

"Yeah." You circle her knee with your thumb.

"Who were those people? More soldiers, like you?"

You shake your head. Soldiers? No, you're more than that. You're kindlings, which means you're kin, not by blood or by history but by training, by trauma, by your tragic (and now defunct) fate. Today, when you were with them, it was simple. Easy. You just had to fall in line again, taking orders, supporting the mission, and that was nice, because it meant you didn't have time to think about anything except what was in front of you. Not the past, not the future, not your list—

"They offered me a job," you say.

"In Windfall?"

"Have you heard of Camas?"

"Yeah." A catch in Rema's voice sends a prickling sensation along your arms. Tiny fishhooks, attaching to you one after another after another. "Are you going to take it?"

You hesitate.

There's an awkward silence, laden with expectation. And you realize she wants you to stay.

But you can't stay. *No commitments, no hard feelings.* That's what you told yourself. That's how nobody gets hurt.

Maybe you're wrong. (You hope you're wrong.) Maybe that's not want in her voice but weariness. So you try to make a joke of it when you look back at her and grin. "What, are you tired of me already?"

You want her to grin back. You want her to curl her fingers into your collar and kiss you. You want things light and hardly touching you. You want it to be easy.

But her smile is faint, and you know she isn't joking. "I could never get tired of you, Ket. Not even if we had years together."

Years?

You frown.

Years.

You can't imagine it, can't allow yourself to imagine it. You measure your life by nights, by girls you've kissed and sheets you've rumpled and left cold by dawn. Maybe you've managed to string together a couple weeks, here or there, but since the war ended, you haven't seen the moon rise twice on the same town.

You try to laugh. "You've only known me five days. What if I snore?"

"You don't snore."

"What if I start snoring?"

She regards you seriously. "Then I'd listen to you snore."

You swallow. You avoid her gaze. You know she means more than she's saying. She's not talking about snoring anymore but about something else, something steady and permanent—

It's not that you don't like her. You could maybe even love her, given time, given enough time, but that's time you don't have to give her. (Have never had to give her.) You were always going to move on, that echo driving you forward like a tern on the wind—

There's a lot of world out there, Ket.

There's a lot of world to see.

You need to be untethered. You need to be free.

"Ket—" she says, and you can already hear the ache in her voice, the pain, though you didn't want to hurt her, didn't want to hurt anyone, though you have, again and again, couldn't seem to help it, all these towns, all these girls, all of them temporary—

They just didn't know it.

But you don't want to think about that yet, don't want to hurt her yet, so you do the only thing you can do right now.

You kiss her. You throw yourself at her, pulling at the bedsheets until she's naked beside you. Your lips and hands traveling her body, roving the hills and dales of her, the dark and tender places. You make her gasp, softly, and arch, deeply, until she's shuddering and inarticulate, all her words dissolving like vapor into the close, hot air.

When she falls asleep again, you lay the covers across her body. You tuck her hair behind her ear. You kiss her temple, and you whisper, "I'm sorry."

You gather your things: your discarded clothes, your pack, your sword. You can't stay here, can't give her what she's asking. You should've stolen away while things were easy, because you like easy, but you know it doesn't last. Turns serious too quickly.

Things get painful when people get attached.

But your kindred are only asking for a month. A month and some fighting. Simple, easy. No more than you can do, no more than you're willing to give. And that's better, isn't it? They get what they want, and so do you, because once you're in Camas you'll be one step closer to the Morning Daughter, to the next item on your list—

You remove the slip of paper from the hidden pocket of your robe. No promises, no long-term commitments except for this.

In the doorway, you take one last look at Rema and hope when she wakes, she doesn't miss you. Curses you, maybe. Hates you, even.

But you hope she doesn't hurt.

AMITY

YOU'RE PERCHED ON A ROCK JUST OUTSIDE OF town, where you told the others to meet. Ben and her horse were already here when you arrived, which didn't surprise you, but you didn't think Emara would be next to wander down the road. After the drinking she and Kanver did last night, you were fully prepared to head back to Windfall and haul her out of bed.

Now, the three of you are waiting and watchful, breathing silently as the northlands come alive around you—

The stillness—

The gray air—

The birds fluttering in the thickets—

You like the hush of it. The solitude of it. You're all here together, but each of you is here alone: Emara with her back to the rock, Ben in the sagebrush with the wind in her clothes, you with your thoughts on the battles ahead.

Leum, Kanver, and the dog show up next. Kanver looks half-asleep, yawning and dragging their feet behind Leum, who's even sloppier and more sour-faced than she was yesterday, with dirt on her trousers and a polearm slung over her back beside her two-handed sword.

You lift an eyebrow. If Kanver trusts her with their balar weapon, they must be closer than you thought. (In the eight years since you graduated from the Academy, you've never let anyone *near* your crown.)

Leum grunts at you as she draws up, and Kanver gives all of you a tired wave. (The dog goes off to sniff at a cow chip or something equally distasteful.)

Tana appears when the sun does, the light turning the mountain-tops a perfect balar pink.

You stand, looping your pack over your shoulder. "Are you ready?" you ask.

Inhaling deeply, she takes a look at the five of you—

Five kindlings—

Five warriors—

The best she could scrape together with only her desperation and determination—

"I wish Vian were here," she says finally. "He'd know what to say. He'd know how to thank you."

Emara hops up, dusting herself off. "Thank us when it's done, eh?"

Morning's racing down the ridges now, recklessly bright, the whole world transforming before your very eyes, and you know your time is growing short.

Then, as if at some hidden signal, all of you turn south, toward the rest of the peninsula—

Toward Amerand—

The vast scrublands are turning color now: silver and gold and green, the rills flashing white in the low places and the insects buzzing in the rushes. Disturbed by the presence of some unseen predator, a flock of waxwings rises from the brush, scattering across the sky.

"I didn't think you were coming," Kanver says suddenly.

You turn, surprised, and standing behind you is Ket, leading a spry buckskin mare. At the sight of her, Tana gives a little start, but when Ket doesn't meet her gaze, she frowns and begins leading the way through the grass, toward the mountains—

The jagged slopes—

The pines gilded in sunlight.

Wordlessly, the others follow.

Ket glances at you like she expects you to ask why she's here, but you don't say anything. You don't have to. You can guess what happened. (You could have told her it was coming.)

It's that restlessness. You've all got it. You were never meant to stay here, never meant to linger like everyone else. You're meant to be quick, to be a flash of light in the darkness, to be glorious and fleeting.

And you are—

Even though the war is over—

Even though you're supposed to be free—

You keep leaving.

She left a girl. You left your cabin, your garden, the peace you kept telling yourself you wanted. The truth is, you would have left them all sooner or later—

Come victory or come death.

The others are trailing northward now, a broken line feeding into the wilderness, and as you watch them climb into the hills, your hand goes to your throat, splaying your scarf across your skin.

It's better this way, you think.

You and a battle—

You and a mission—

You and your kin.

Interlude

THE WRATHFUL

ADREN

ONE WEEK AGO

YOU WAKE, AS YOU ALWAYS DO, WITH A KNIFE IN your hand and sweat upon your brow. You were dreaming, but you never remember your dreams, try not to remember your dreams—

The way they unseat you, like a rider thrown from a horse—

You stagger to your feet. Laying the blade beside your water basin, you splash your face. A soft gasp. The cold trickling down your jaw.

Drip, drip, drip—

You're here, or at least that's what you tell yourself.

Your chipped basin, your sagging cot, your rumpled blankets, your wooden trunk—

You number these things. You let them ground you.

You're here.

You're awake.

Outside, night relinquishes its hold, and the shadows upon the walls of your tent fade to a gentle lavender. A warm bath of a color—

Serene, perfect—

Fleeting. As the sun rises, the sounds of the company cooks rattle through camp: iron-on-embers, water-and-kettle, the scrape of food sacks being lowered from their bear-proof perches in the pines.

You dress in quick, methodical movements and grab your sword, sliding it through the wide belt at your waist. It's not the weapon you would have liked—

Nothing about this life is what you would have liked—

But for assaulting a little mountain village, it'll do.

You're not bad in hand-to-hand combat (the feints, the fencing, the well-timed strike), but your favorite part of battle has always been the advance—

The gap between the spring and the clash—

The thunder of hooves surrounds you. The air is filled with the smell of sweat and dust and horses. From your position at the front of the charge, you feel like you're at the prow of a mighty wooden ship, slicing effortlessly through the sea.

The village nears—

Sloped roofs. Fenced gardens. Ducks and children darting along the roads.

You allow yourself a smile.

There's a split second between the roaring in the blood and the spilling of it, before the swords come down, before the choices are made, when everything is possible: victory, defeat, valor, disgrace, the naked blade, an arrow in the shoulder, a killing blow, the whisper of steel, the last gasp, the downfall of your company, the slaughter of the innocent, broken fences, smoke, split knuckles, bare teeth, eyes, lungs, the smell of scorched stone and singed hair, a burst of flame, battered bodies, death—

And after, the looting.

Your raiders abscond with sacks of barley, bushels of onions, sides of cured pork, chickens (newly strangled and tied together at their nubby ankles), woven blankets, tanned hides, coils of rope, bowls, baskets, rice—

You never allow them to take everything. You don't want the farmers to starve, but you need them hungry enough to keep producing, weak enough that they won't fight back.

Onna, the village leader, informs you the cattle won't be down from the high country for another month at least, and with a smile you tell her you'll be back for that, but for now you take a few of their goats, a couple of horses, their saddles and tack—

In the village square, you study the farmers as they stand helpless beneath their thatched eaves. (Fear, silence, anguish.) You wonder at their motionlessness, like rabbits trapped in a burrow, can almost hear their little heartbeats quivering inside their chests.

But paralysis doesn't stop the fox from coming—

The snapping jaw, the pointed teeth—

One of your lieutenants fetches a horse from the stables: a young black stallion, huge and beautiful. Strong teeth, sleek mane. You first saw it galloping across the meadow last spring—

Quick as lightning, powerful as flame—

It was still being broken then, but it's ready now for a rider. You take the reins, run your hand across its withers. Smooth coat, hard shoulder.

The horse of a commander—

The reason you're here—

(Though you're not saying no to the other spoils either, since you came all this way.)

As you stroke the stallion's soft nose, you hear a voice from behind you: "Whoa, whoa. Not that horse. Not him."

You're surprised by the tone. Affable, agreeable. Not like you're conqueror and conquered but peers—

You turn around. One of the villagers, a boy about your age, steps out from his doorway. Broad-shouldered, wide-mouthed. Handsome. You've seen him before, lurking behind his mother, Onna, as she yielded to your demands again and again and again, but until now he's done nothing worth paying attention to.

He advances on you, hands raised.

Such recklessness. You almost admire him. An unarmed civilian speaking against the marauders who've got his village under their heel? You wonder what it's like to be made of such foolishness, such innocence, such nerve.

The girl beside him (a younger sister, maybe, with the same tanned face, the same intelligent eyes) grasps after him like he's a kite caught by the wind. "Vian! Don't!"

Vian ignores her. He saunters to the edge of the square, where he lowers his hands and says in the same easygoing voice, "You can't take him."

You lay your hand on the horse's neck. "Actually, I can."

To your surprise, he laughs. (A nice laugh, you have to admit. Full and warm.) "Okay, okay, but what I mean is, you don't want him. He's too stubborn. Hates to listen."

"You're one to talk," you say dryly.

"Huh?"

"You were given explicit instructions to stay in your homes."

"Heh, okay." For a second, he looks chagrined. Rubbing the back of his neck, he glances at his mother, as if for permission, but she shakes her head sharply. He turns back to you with a shrug. "Look, if you need a horse, I can get one for you. A better one. I'm training up a filly by the same sire. Different dam, but she's more even-tempered. You'll like her, I promise."

You smile. (You can't believe you're smiling, but even you can't resist charisma like that.) In another life, you might've liked him. His looks, his charm and chatter, the glint in his eyes. You might've even been friends—

Partners—

Lovers—

But you don't relent. "I like this one fine." Taking the reins, you start to turn the stallion away, but the horse jerks back, hard, when you try to lead it.

"See?" Vian follows, out of the garden and into the square. "Stubborn, right?"

Turning on him, you draw your blade. The villagers murmur. In the doorway, Onna's grip tightens on the sister's arm.

"Whoa, whoa." Startled, Vian lifts his hands again, though he doesn't retreat. "Look, I'm working with some of the other villages around here. We're starting a breeding program. In a few years, we'll have the best horses in the northlands. The best-trained ones too. You can be part of that, if you want."

You cock your head at him, letting your sword dangle limply from your hand. "A lot of people have tried to bargain with me."

"This isn't a bargain. It's an opportunity."

"A lot of people have said that too."

"Hey, do I look like 'a lot of people'?" He grins, then, because he knows he doesn't. "You're mobile. We're not. We supply the horses. You sell them down south. We can be partners. Just leave the horse. Leave us enough to get through the fall and winter. None of this works if we're starving, right?"

You consider his offer (if it's an offer, if it's not a lie to let him keep his horse, to buy the village a little more time). You almost envy him. His vision. His confidence. His naive smile. His weaponless hands.

Mostly, though, you despise him. His brazenness, his stupidity. (You haven't been allowed to be stupid since you were five years old.) What's he thinking, trying to negotiate with you? It's like he doesn't know how dangerous you are, even after two years, like he doesn't know you'd murder his family in front of his eyes at the faintest hint of deceit.

You take a step forward. He still doesn't retreat.

Again, that feeling—

Admiration. Envy. Hatred.

"How old are you?" you ask.

He frowns, a line like a knife cut appearing between his brows before he grins at you again. "Nineteen," he says. "Almost twenty."

Something flashes inside you. Something small and painful and hot as a flame.

"Wrong." You lash out, splitting his throat with the tip of your blade. Blood spills down his collar as he reaches for his neck with those stupid, empty hands.

The sister runs for him, but you level your sword at her collarbone, pinning her in place.

"No," you say.

She almost tries to help him anyway, almost moves toward him, the point digging into her collarbone while Vian writhes at her feet—

Wide eyes, wet gasps—

Behind him, Onna is screaming. They're all screaming. All the little villagers.

Mercy.

Mercy.

Let her go to him.

Let her save him.

Mercy, Adren.

You watch the boy choke. You watch him bleed.

"You're nineteen," you whisper. "You'll always be nineteen."

Part II

THE HAUNTED

LEUM

YOU MAKE YOUR WAY INTO THE MOUNTAINS. RIDGE after ridge, rise after rise. You don't know what you expected out of the Candiveras (something stark and overbearing, perhaps, an environment fit for the giants who roamed the peninsula in the days when the world was young), but you discover that the highlands are startlingly minute in their beauty: white stretches of scree pebbled with sedum, meadows of aster and balsamroot and barbed mountain rose.

It's a hard land. Hard sun, hard stone. As the others climb ahead, you pause in the shade of a juniper tree, twisting antler-like out of the granite, and look back the way you came. From this height, the mighty nation of Amerand looks so small—

A dusty footprint—

A fading shadow—

Something to leave behind.

But some things won't be left behind, will they? Below, you spy a skinny figure scrambling up the gravel.

Siddie.

She's little more than a speck at this distance, but if you squint you can pick out her gangly limbs, the shape of her sword, now strapped to her back like yours.

"Stupid kid," you mutter.

At your feet, Burk grumbles peevishly in the dust.

You sniff. "No one asked you."

"Asked me what?" Amity draws up beside you. (Her face flushed, her breathing shallow.) Gently, she leads Comet into the shade, where she unhooks her water gourd from his saddle.

You jerk your head in Siddie's direction. "You see this?"

"Hmm." Amity lifts the gourd to her lips. "She's stubborn."

"She's going to get herself killed."

"I doubt that." Amity offers you a drink, which you accept, the water cool and slick on your dry throat. "I still think we could use her. I always said I wanted seven of us for this mission."

You scowl. "She's *not* one of us."

"Not yet." Amity smiles faintly, although you don't know why. There's nothing funny about a kid risking her neck, pretending to be a soldier.

"Not ever." Wiping your mouth with your sleeve, you shove the gourd back into Amity's hands. "Not if I can help it."

Sometime after noon, you stop beside a lake. The horses drinking, soft-lipped in the shallows; your fellow kindlings finding cool spots beneath the pines. Nearby, a few dragonflies flit among the grasses, pearlescent wings humming, while on the far shore, there's the faint splash of a fish surfacing for a meal.

"Hey." Kanver's shadow falls over you. "Where'd you get my glaive?"

Looks like they've finally sobered up enough to notice you carrying their polearm up the mountain for them.

You hand it over. "You told me where to find it, remember?"

"I did?" They heft it once or twice, as if to make sure it's really theirs.

"Why'd you bury it anyway?"

They shrug. "Last time I drank this much, I almost let someone take it from me." Sitting down behind you, they lay the weapon in the gravel. "So this time I buried it *before* I started drinking."

You lean back, the way you used to at the Academy, the two of you sneaking a break during kitchen duty, marches, drills, and you feel them resting against you, spine to spine.

"You ever consider not drinking?" you say.

You feel them shrug. Up, down. The movement of their shoulders comforting, familiar. Then a sigh. "Nope."

Packs are opened. Provisions are passed around. You tuck into a meal of millet cakes and pickled plums, supplemented by some currants Tana scavenged, chalky and sweet. By the water, Ket and Emara slide out of their sandals to cool their feet in the lake, while Amity fans the sweat from her face.

You feed Burk a few bites of millet and stare down the trail, where Siddie sits on her haunches, watching you hungrily. You wonder how much food she's got on her, if she grabbed some berries when Tana did—

Not that starvation is what'll kill her out here. More likely she'd slip and break her ankle, die of thirst or heatstroke, collapsed on the trail—

"Give it a rest, Piggy!" Emara calls, shattering the peace. "Get outta here, eh?"

You hunch your shoulders. Amity said Emara's part of the mission, so she's part of the mission, but you don't have to like it.

Don't have to like *her*.

Sucking the last of the flesh from a plum, Emara pitches at Siddie. Not hard. Just enough to scare her off, the way you tried to do to Burk when she first started following you.

The pit sails through the air and falls short, bouncing down the slope. Siddie watches it roll to a stop in front of her, but she doesn't move.

Emara casts about for something to else to throw (a rock, a stick, a fallen pine cone), but Ben glances up from where she's flinging knives at a wind-scoured log. "Leave her be."

"It's fine, Knifey. I won't hurt her."

Ben doesn't reply.

"Whatever." Emara stuffs the last of her millet cake into her mouth. "Dumb piggy."

You remain silent. Privately, you agree with Emara, but you'd never admit to agreeing with Emara about anything, so you have to settle for glowering at Siddie from the shade—

Willing her to give up—

Willing her to go home, if she's got a home to return to, if she has anywhere else at all to go—

Before it's too late.

Near dusk, Tana calls for you to make camp. You and Ket see to the horses. Kanver gathers the firewood. While Amity prepares a fire and a spit, Ben slinks off into the woods, returning half an hour later with several squirrels and a rabbit dangling from her shoulder. Gray tails, limp paws. They're butchered and roasted over the embers, their entrails offered to the fire with a prayer of thanks to Vastari, Greater God of Death.

Later, when the coals are banked and the bedrolls are unfurled, you volunteer for the first watch. You want to stare into the darkness, want to make sure Siddie's not there.

On a rise above camp, you sit with Burk at your feet, watching for movement.

The stars come out.

The conversations dwindle to whispers, until only Ket and Tana remain awake, their voices drifting up to you on the breeze.

"I've been meaning to thank you," Tana says. "For deciding to help us."

"Don't worry about it."

There's a pause, and for a moment you allow yourself to hope they've fallen asleep. Then you hear the soft scrape of gravel, the sound of someone turning onto their side. Tana, you think, inching closer in the darkness. "What made you change your mind?" she whispers.

"Would you believe me if I said it was your pretty face?"

"No," she scoffs.

"Oh, then it must've been that even temper of yours." Despite the distance, you can hear the smile in Ket's voice.

"Ugh, fine. Don't tell me."

"Sorry, I mean, it was your endless patience."

"Ket."

You roll your eyes. You wait for them to shut up.

Down the ridge, a fire sparks.

Siddie.

She's still here.

You scan the peaks, searching for movement. If Adren and her raiders are in the vicinity, they wouldn't think twice about robbing a kid of her balar weapon, slitting her throat or leaving her trussed up in the wilderness until the animals come.

But you're alone out here.

From your vantage point, the fire looks small, a little thing flickering in the night like a candle, the emptiness of the Candiveras threatening to swallow it whole.

For some reason, you're reminded of the war orphans. Dead family. No one to take care of them. Dirty, barefoot, starving. Maybe you'd get one a pair of sandals. Maybe you'd sneak them a handkerchief of rice.

They'd still end up dead. Sick, hungry, cold. Sometimes they'd get caught in an ambush, end up trampled on the battlefield.

But you don't want that for Siddie. She didn't fight in the war, didn't have to see any of it, suffer any of it, *do* any of it. She gets to be free of it—

She gets to be young—

She gets to be a kid, the way none of the rest of you did. You can keep her away from this, all of this, the violence, the danger, the mission. You can make sure she grows up better than you.

But you have to keep her alive first.

SIDDIE

YOU WAKE TO THE SOUNDS OF SOMEONE STOMPING out your fire. Sandals and embers, smoke and sparks. You sit up, coughing. "Hey!"

Over the dying flames, Leum glares at you—

You can't believe it. Leum's *here*—

"What's the matter with you?" she snarls. "You trying to kill us all?"

"What?" You rub the sleep from your eyes. "I mean, no—"

She kicks dirt over the coals. "One spark, that's all it takes. The whole mountain goes up, and us with it."

You leap to your feet, trying to help her, but all you manage to do is get ash on your robes. "I'm sorry!" You didn't know. How could you have known? You were trained at House Vastari, near the ocean. Everything moist and moldering, the rocks slick with mist. You're not used to the high desert, these tinderbox forests. You made a mistake. You didn't know—

Leum snaps her fingers at you, jolting you out of your stupor. "Water."

Reaching for your water gourd, you upend it onto the ashes. (The hiss, the sizzle.) The center of your firepit turns to mud.

Leum stirs it with a stick, smothering the embers, while her dog watches you judgmentally from the edge of camp.

"I'm sorry," you repeat. Hugging your elbows, you sink to your knees. "I was cold."

"Ever heard of a blanket?"

In response, you lift the remnants of the Swordmaster's cloak, weather-worn and tattered with use.

"That's not a blanket."

You twist the fabric in your fingers. "It's all I have."

Somewhere above you, you hear her grumbling, but you don't look up. Don't want to see the anger and disappointment in her eyes. You made a mistake. You were trying to prove you could keep up with them, but the only thing you managed to prove was that you're a liability.

Leum shifts in the pine needles. Her footsteps retreat, and for a second you think she's going to leave you out here.

You squeeze your eyes shut.

You try not to cry.

Then she sighs. "Come with me."

It's the last thing you expect her to say, so you don't really hear it, not at first, don't really understand it as you sit there uselessly with your hands in your lap.

But then she turns around. Her shoulders hunched in the darkness, the starlight on her disheveled hair. "What's wrong with you? Come on."

"Who?" You straighten, resisting the urge to look behind you, because you know no one's there. "Me?"

She doesn't stop this time, stalking into the shadows with the dog at her heels.

You blink rapidly. She wants you to follow her? She wants you to join her? After yesterday night at the hotel, you can hardly believe it's not a joke, but it doesn't matter. You can be the butt of another joke, but you'd never forgive yourself if you missed your chance to fight alongside *real* kindlings.

You gather your things. You check the fire one last time. It's cold, but you kick more dirt over it anyway (just in case) and scramble after her.

You've almost reached the kindlings' camp when something shifts among the boulders. A bear? A big cat? You've never fought a big cat before (or a bear, for that matter), never even seen one, but it's not an animal at all. The shadow unfolds into a slender figure, hooded in the moonlight—

Amity.

You startle, but you manage not to yelp in surprise.

Of course they posted a watch. Why didn't you think of that? You should've been up all night on lookout, or, if you wanted to get some rest, you should've slept in a tree instead of exposed on the ground beside a smoking fire.

"Siddie, isn't it?" Amity's voice drifts toward you from the darkness. "Welcome to the team."

Ahead of you, Leum grunts. "She's not part of the team."

Amity doesn't answer, but you swear she smiles at you as you pass.

Beyond her, you find the others arranged around the firepit (banked for the night). The Vedran, Emara, spread-eagled on her bedroll; Ben curled on her side among the rocks. You tiptoe past them, trying to be quiet, but as you creep after Leum, another of the kindlings (you think she's called Ket) sits up, sweeping hair out of her eyes. "Looks like Leum finally gave in, huh?"

You try to look humble, but you can't stop the smile from spreading across your cheeks. "I'm sorry. I didn't mean to wake you."

She drums her fingers along the edge of her collar. "You didn't."

Near the edge of camp, Leum pulls a blanket from her pack and shoves it at you. "Get some rest," she says.

As she stalks off again, you burrow into the blanket, which is thick and warm and smells like Leum. Dust and sagebrush.

You smile to yourself.

Amity said you were part of the team.

(Amity, the *Twin Valley Reaper*, knows your name.)

And if Amity said you were part of the team, that means you have to be, doesn't it? Part of the team? Even if Leum said you weren't? Because Amity's the leader, so whatever she says goes, right?

There's a rock digging into your back, so you turn. You tuck your arm beneath your head.

By the firepit, someone gets up. They shift around for a while. They lie down again. You wonder if they're as excited as you are, if that's why they can't sleep.

You're one of them. You earned your place. Yawning, you close your eyes. You're floating, now, in that dark in-between space—

You're a *kindling*, and you're going to prove it. You're going to listen. You're going to watch. You're going to keep your head down and do what you're told, and by the end of the month, no one, not even Leum, will be able to deny you're one of them.

It's still night when you wake to the sound of someone screaming.

At first you think you're under attack, so you fumble for your sword, but no one seems to be going for their weapons, no one's leaping into action, no one's even searching the perimeter—

In fact, Amity's sweeping in from her perch among the rocks, muttering, "Ben, take the watch."

With barely a nod, Ben disappears. The others converge near the firepit, the shapes of them blurred in the starlight.

Belatedly, you let your sword slide back into its scabbard. It's not an attack.

It's one of you—

The Vedran—

Emara. She's on her knees among her blankets, crying—

No, not crying—

Moaning—

Sobbing. Tears on her cheeks, saliva dribbling from her lips. She's so changed from the girl who threw a plum stone at you yesterday afternoon, you scarcely recognize her. The leanness of her. Her mouth wide and aching, revealing this big wide emptiness inside of her you didn't know was there—

Couldn't have known was there, concealed as it was by her winks and her laughter and her throwing arm—

But it's there. And now you know it.

Amity starts forward, but before she can reach her, Kanver appears at Emara's side. Near her but not touching her, their voice gentle but firm. "Emara," they murmur. "It's Kanver. Remember me? You bought me a drink in Windfall. You said we were going to get along. We're up in the northlands. We're on our way to Camas, see? You're safe."

"Get back!" Emara scrambles away, wedging herself among the rocks. "Get away from me!"

You creep up behind the others, peering between their still forms like a bystander. "What's wrong with her?" you ask. (Too loudly. You wince at the sound of your own voice.)

Amity's gaze snaps to you so fast you recoil, bumping into Ket behind you.

"Same thing that's wrong with all of us," Ket says, tapping the edge of her robe with her thumb.

"What does that mean?"

The northlander, who you've heard them call Tana, draws up beside you. "My father had dreams like that, after he came back from the war," she murmurs. "At least that's what my brother told me."

You scowl at her. Why does a farmer, of all people, have to explain these things to you? She's not a kindling. She's not even a soldier.

You're about to say as much when Emara stands. Hollow-eyed, ashen-cheeked, still unsteady on her feet. You think she recognizes you now, you see the recognition dawning in her face—

(But you don't think she likes what she sees.)

Kanver backs up a step. "Emara?"

Emara's face contorts, not with fear this time but shame—

That, at least, is familiar—

(You're well acquainted with shame.)

Which means you're not at all surprised when Emara ducks her head and plunges into the darkness, away from the rest of you.

Kanver sighs and rubs their eyes.

In the uncomfortable silence, you look from one of the kindlings to another. Their faces unreadable. Their expressions austere. No one seems like they're going to say anything, so you say (more loudly than you mean to), "What was *that* about?"

Leum growls. "Shut up, Siddie."

You step back, surprised. You didn't expect Leum to snap at you, not about Emara. You've been studying them as you followed them up the trail. Leum *hates* Emara.

Why would she be defending her now?

You want someone to defend *you*, to stick up for *you*, but as you look around at the others, they avert their eyes. They shift away from you. And you feel it again—

Shame—

Ear-burning, stomach-shrinking *shame*—

You don't get it. How do they all know whatever it is they know? About what's going on? You want to shake them until they tell you, until they let you in on their secret, whatever secret this is, whatever this thing is that they and a *Vedran* and a *farmer* know, but you, somehow, don't.

Because you're one of them now, aren't you? You're supposed to be one of them?

You're part of the team, that's what Amity said.

A comrade in arms. A kindling.

But you're standing there watching them crawl back under their covers, watching them turn their backs to you as they curl up in the dark, and you look down at your stupid useless hands, still clutching your sword, and it's clearer than it's ever been.

You're still not one of them.

They may have accepted you (kind of), but they've still got something you don't, and you don't know how to get it.

You don't even know what it is.

AMITY

AFTER THE NIGHTMARE, FEW OF YOU SLEEP. EMARA pacing, wrapped in a blanket. Siddie sitting, vigilant, by the newly kindled fire. The others rotating through the watches while you stare up at the sky, biding your time until dawn.

You count stars. Three of them, flashing across the heavens—

Six—

Eleven—

You consider getting up. You consider breaking camp. You could be in Camas by dawn if you leave now.

But the others deserve to rest (if they can rest), so you lie still. You continue counting.

Twelve—

Fourteen—

Nineteen. A star for each year of your life.

The air is lightening now, the stars enveloped by day now, and you can't wait any longer. You get up, and you stagger to the nearby creek to wash. You feel faint—

Not enough sleep, you think. A heaviness in your limbs, a dull ache in the back of your skull.

Kneeling, you glance around to make sure no one's watching, and you unravel your scarf.

Your hands dipping into the creek. The water trickling down

your neck, frigid with snowmelt and soothing against your throat.

You don't bother to dry yourself before you don your scarf again. You have to keep moving. You don't have much time.

You approach Camas by way of a wide, hard-packed road that winds back and forth up the mountain until it finally flattens out at a vast alpine valley. Towering skies. Mountains on all sides. A river rambling past a cluster of barns and slope-roofed houses, well thatched against rain and snow.

You purse your lips. You can already see the road's too open; the land, too even. You and your kin will be hard-pressed to secure it against the mounted invaders Tana described, but you're already dreaming up ditches, barricades, water defenses—

Passing a number of homes, you and the others follow Tana into the village square, bordered on three sides by farmhouses, each one large enough to fit several families: a sprawl of parents, siblings, aunts, uncles, cousins, the generations piling on top of each other through the decades—

New children born, elders growing old and creaky in the long mountain winters—

You find it unfathomable. You could never imagine having that much time.

"Tana?" A woman rushes from the house on the north side of the square. Seizing Tana by the shoulders, she pulls her into a swift (though none too gentle) embrace. "Are you hurt? Where have you been?"

You eye them curiously. Same shoulders, same eyes, same wide mouth. She must be Tana's mother, Onna.

To your surprise, you feel a pang of jealousy. You haven't been hugged like that (like a child, like someone's baby) since the kindling collectors took you fourteen years ago. You don't even remember what your mother looked like—

If she had your height, your complexion, your hands—

Would she recognize you, as you are now?

(War-hardened? Battle-scarred?)

Would she know you were hers?

Cautiously, the other Camassians begin to emerge from their houses. Tanned faces, rough hands. In the doorway nearest you, a few children poke their heads out from behind an old man, his skin as wrinkled as a dried plum.

"Who's that?" He gestures vaguely in your direction, as if his clouded eyes can't quite see you clearly. "Who are you?"

None of you answer. You're waiting for Tana and her mother to finish whispering to each other. On the west side of the square, Ben studies the slope: a narrow trail that leads to a cabin, a creek tumbling off the mountain, a shrine. Ket, Emara, and Kanver take up easy positions along one of the garden fences, waiting for orders.

Another man, this one with a wide forehead and soft eyes, appears in the doorway. "It's Tana, Old Man," he says.

"Tana? I thought she ran off."

"She came back. She's brought . . ." His voice dwindles into silence.

They never know what to call you, do they? Are you kids? Are you something else? What's the word for a child forged in war?

(For a child who was supposed to kill for you?)

(Die for you, though you'd never met, somewhere across the peninsula, on a battlefield hundreds of miles away?)

"Others," he says finally. "They have weapons."

"Weapons?" The Old Man's expression turns petulant. "So someone's finally going to stick their necks out for us, huh?"

"The Twin Valley Reaper?" Across the square, Onna glances at you with a familiar mixture of fear and distrust. "You brought *kindlings* here?"

Her reaction doesn't surprise you. The stories that circulate among the civilian populace paint us as horrors as much as heroes. For all the legends of valor and good deeds, there are lurid accounts of children who fight like wild creatures, children who murder their enemies while they sleep. You doubt Onna believes you're the monsters the tales describe, but there's no denying you're different, uncanny, strange—

A shiver goes through the villagers, who begin muttering among themselves.

"I thought they'd be younger," someone whispers.

"That one's young."

"That one's not a kindling. She can hardly carry her sword."

Beside you, Siddie squirms uncomfortably. Leum, who's taken up a post beside her like one of the Queen Commander's Shieldbearers, murmurs under her breath, "They didn't know we were coming?"

You frown. "Apparently not."

An unfortunate development. It seems Tana's put you in a tricky position. You can't defend the village without the Camassians' cooperation, but considering their consternation, you doubt they're in a cooperative mood.

"We can't afford kindlings," someone else says. "Adren barely left us enough to feed ourselves. What are they going to do to us when they find out we can't pay them?"

"They don't care about pay. They have a code of honor."

"Yeah, but they can't eat a code of honor, can they?"

"It's about time we got some help around here!" The Old Man's voice rises querulously above the rest. "It's what they were trained for, isn't it? Let them do their job, I say."

You sigh. You've heard enough now to understand your circumstances: Onna's resistance, the villagers' uncertainty, their fear, their curiosity, their willingness to use you for their own ends. (People are entirely too predictable; you get the same reaction everywhere you go.) You step forward.

The villagers fall silent.

As you approach, Onna gestures Tana toward the house at the north end of the square. "Get back inside. Keep an eye on Poppy."

Tana starts to slink away, but after a moment she takes a breath, like she's mustering her courage, and turns back to her mother. "Vian would've—"

Onna's voice sharpens. "Don't you hide behind his name." You can see where Tana gets her intensity. Her cutting gaze, her furrowed brow. You're almost amused by the resemblance—

(Almost envious.)

Defiantly, Tana glares at Onna for another second before she finally heads inside.

"You should be thanking her," you say, watching her slam the door behind her. "It sounds like she was the only one willing to fight for you."

Onna regards you with the usual fear, but now that you're closer, you detect a sadness in her eyes. Pity, perhaps, though you resent it.

You're a Deathbringer. You're not one to be pitied.

"It might be difficult for someone like the Twin Valley Reaper to understand, but not all conflicts can be resolved with violence."

You lift an eyebrow. "What do you know about violence?"

Her hand goes to the faded infantry knot hanging at her neck. Her husband's? You remember Tana mentioning her father last night. Said he came back from the war with nightmares.

(You wonder how many of them were of your kind.)

"You may not think much of us," Onna says quietly, "but the war touched us too."

"Not the way it touched us."

"No." Her mouth twists. There's that pity again, odious and slick. "But I saw what violence did to my husband when he came back from the war."

You frown. You can't help but wonder why she's wearing his

memorabilia, why it matters to her when she has such obvious distaste for what it represents.

"It's taken more of us in the past two years than I care to say," Onna continues. "Now it's taken my son. I won't allow it to consume more of us."

Now it's your turn to pity her. Such softness, such naivete. "Tana's already explained your situation. Starvation may not be violent, but it still results in death."

Onna studies you for a moment, and you wonder what she sees. A girl? A warrior? A veteran? The truth is, you have more in common with the Old Man than her daughter, living every day with your death staring you in the face.

By battle or by burnout, that's what they used to tell us.

"How old are you, Amity?" Onna asks.

You tug at your scarf. "Almost twenty."

She winces and looks away, as if the answer pains her. "You're only children," she murmurs. "How can I ask you to fight for us again? It's supposed to be over. We said we were done."

No more kindlings sacrificed for the war effort—

No more children killing and dying on the front lines, while the rest of the country continued on without them—

"You'll fight for yourselves," you tell her. "It won't work otherwise. You have to show Adren you're more trouble than you're worth."

"And causing that trouble will mean losing lives."

"Yes."

Her brow creases, and you can see her weighing her options. How many Camassians will die if she refuses you? How many will die if she accepts? You've done this yourself already. You know the numbers, the odds, the cost—

It's high.

Whatever happens, the price will be high.

She nods uneasily. "All right, Amity. We'll do it your way." You don't know why, but she looks tired already, holding the fate of her people in her hands. But that's what a leader does, isn't it? You've been carrying that responsibility since you were thirteen—

Entire battalions under your protection—

Cities you were tasked to defend—

You want to tell her to toughen up. She'll need to be stronger than this for the battles to come.

She looks to the other kindlings, her gaze lingering for a long moment on Siddie. "Did you like it?" she asks. "What you did in the war?"

You purse your lips. "I was good at it."

"That's not the same."

You don't answer. The truth is, you don't know if you liked it or if it was simply all you knew. Death, destruction, slaughter. You and your balar crystal. You and your power. The sensation of it searing through you, devouring all the years you might have had, all the lives you might have lived—

You could have been a painter, a merchant, a beggar, a mother, a thief—

A gravedigger, a poet, a drunkard, a nun—

You could have been a daughter—

Someone's daughter—

But you burned up every one of those futures each time you donned your crown. You weren't any of them. (You were never going to be any of them.)

You were fuel.

You were a weapon.

You were exceptional. You were glorious.

"Yeah," you tell her. "I liked it."

KET

AFTER SEVERAL HEATED DISCUSSIONS, THE VILLAGERS finally agree to put you up in the Old Man's two-room cabin on the slope above the square. The Old Man protests his eviction, of course, but the fact is no one else will host you. No one wants you in their homes. No one wants you sharing space with their children.

So the seven of you are crammed into two small rooms, one of which is also a kitchen, and it's lucky none of you brought more than a pack and some saddlebags, because there's barely enough space to lay out your bedrolls as it is.

But we all lived like this during the war, didn't we? (When we lived?) First the barracks, then the field. The crowded bunks, the cluttered floors, the sounds of our comrades breathing in the dark—

You'd find it comforting, but beyond the walls of the cabin it's much too quiet. No muted conversations. No officers playing cards late into the night. No music, strummed by some lonely soldier, aching for home.

In the silence, your thoughts drift to Rema. How she's doing. How you left her. How you keep running away, because whenever you aren't moving, your mind fills up with all the things you did, all the things you have left to do.

You throw off your blanket. You grab your weapon and tiptoe

past the sleeping forms of your kin. It's a little early for your watch, but after last night you don't think Emara, who's currently patrolling the west edge of the village, will mind the extra rest.

Outside, you find Ben asleep in the grass. Maybe it was too crowded for her inside. Maybe she couldn't stand Kanver's snoring. Maybe she wanted to see the sun rise on the river.

You don't linger. Down the steps and through the village. You find Emara on her rounds, tell her to get some sleep. Officially, none of you will be touring the village until morning, but Amity wants you to start learning the terrain, so you make a quick study of the roads, the landscape, the fences.

Across the creek, you skip up a narrow set of steps to a little shrine for the Grain Mother, where a worn wooden idol is seated inside. Bundles of herbs cloaking her shoulders, crude carvings of livestock in her arms. At her feet, you notice a small whittled sheep, tipped on its side in the moss.

You pick it up, rub the grime away with your thumb. The Lesser God of Hearth and Harvest was never a deity you paid much attention to. Kindlings, if we worshipped, worshipped the Wind Runner, the Weaver, the Dread Empress, the Sword and Spear. We wanted the blessings of war and fire, not the bounty of some field we'd likely never reap.

You haven't prayed since the end of the war, and truth be told, you don't know if you ever really believed in such things, but tonight you nestle the sheep in the Grain Mother's hands and deep in your heart, you wish for peace.

From the shrine, you continue north toward a break in the forest, where you stumble upon a little cemetery. The trees cleared, the slope dotted with cairns—

And the Morning Daughter rising over the ridgeline, stark and tall against the night sky.

There's a lot of world out there, Ket.

You have a future now, Ket.

What do you want to do with it?

But you don't want to think about the future now. You've already spent so much time thinking about the future, always looking toward the next thing on your list.

You're about to leave when a shadow shifts down the hillside, and you duck behind one of the cairns, hand on your saber.

But you recognize that figure—

The broad shoulders, the strong arms—

It's Tana. She's standing at one of the graves, tracing a stick of incense through the air. The glowing ember, the scrawl of smoke. A prayer to Vastari, the Dread Empress, who receives the dead—

(Or some of them anyway—)

(The ones who don't linger, who don't hover about the living, telling tales no one can hear—)

As if she senses you watching her, Tana straightens. "Who's out there?"

You wince. You didn't want her to know you were spying on her, but you can't skulk off now, so you step out of the shadows. "It's me."

"Ket?" She drops the incense as you draw up beside her, the embers flaring in the dry grass before she crushes them with her heel. She's been crying, you think. Her eyes swollen, her nose tinged pink.

"You okay?"

"Just visiting my brother." She gestures at the nearest cairn, which looks newer than the rest. Fresh flowers, crumbled earth. "He and Ma used to fight all the time when he was alive, but now that he's gone, I guess that task's fallen to me."

You drum your fingers along the hilt of your sword. You never had parents to fight with. You had drill sergeants, commanding officers, and you didn't argue with them. You obeyed, and you did it without complaint, or you faced the consequences—

You think about digging holes, digging them and filling them up again. You think about marching until your legs collapsed beneath you. You think about stone walls and no windows—

"What are you doing out here?" Tana asks.

Your fingers go still. "Patrolling. Amity will want the rest of you to start taking watches tomorrow."

"Ma won't like that." Tana sighs. "She's having a hard enough time accepting you're here."

"Oh yeah? We couldn't tell."

"Ha."

"Is she going to get on board? We won't be able to do this without her."

"She'll get on board. She's just stubborn."

You crack a smile. "Must run in the family."

"Ugh. You don't know the half of it."

"I bet it didn't help that you didn't tell her we were coming."

"She'd never have agreed. She hates violence. She has for a long time."

"Why?"

"I don't think she ever forgave what it did to my father. And now with Vian dying the way he did . . ." Tana bites her lip, like if she opens her mouth, she'll start crying again, and if she starts crying again, she might never stop.

You stand with her among the stacked stones, the deep shadows. There are generations of Camassians buried here, in the same place as their parents, their grandparents, their great-grandparents—

Their brothers—

"He was trying to stand up for us," Tana says finally.

"Sounds brave."

"You mean stupid."

You chuckle. "Can't you be both?"

She only hesitates a moment before she smiles wearily. "I'm afraid

I've never been much of either."

"Uh, aren't you the one who got us all here?"

"I was just trying to do what he would've done."

"And you don't think that's brave?"

She tilts her head up at you, and all of a sudden she's so close that you can count her freckles in the darkness, feel her breath on your jaw. "Not stupid, though?"

You lick your lips. "I can think of a lot of things to call you, but stupid isn't one of them."

Her eyes flash, as if in challenge. "Oh yeah?"

Then she kisses you.

At first you're so surprised that you let her. (The weight of her in your arms, her fingers tightening in your robe.) But you're not here for this—

A look, a conversation, a kiss—

You back away. "Tana, wait—"

"What?" She frowns. (That line between her brows.) "You don't want to?"

"No, I *do* . . ." You swallow a few times, fighting the urge to kiss her again. "But I don't do commitments, remember? I'm only here for a month, and after that . . ."

Then what? The mountain?

And beyond it?

(More of the same?)

You expect Tana to look hurt (and let's be honest, she doesn't look happy), but at your words she only appears more determined. Almost desperate. "I don't care," she says.

"What?"

"I don't care if you stay."

"You don't?"

"No." At her sides, her fingers curl into fists. "I want this, right now. I want you. I want something to be different."

"From what?"

"From when he was alive."

Oh.

Her brother, Vian.

There are tears in her eyes, but she doesn't move to brush them away. "Something has to be different, doesn't it?" she says. "Now that he's gone? *Something.* It can't be the same as it was before. *I* can't be the same as I was before. I have to be different. Because if nothing is different after he dies, what was it all for?"

You don't know what to tell her.

Sometimes people die. Sometimes nothing changes.

"I don't care what happens later," she says, advancing on you again. "Do you want to be here? Right now? With me?"

You consider her offer.

No past, no future, no commitments?

Just now?

Just this?

You reach out.

Tana gasps. A small, quick sound, almost painful—

Then she's in your arms. (Your lips in the darkness, your eyes falling closed.) She's rushing into you, and you're staggering backward, almost toppling one of the cairns.

She laughs into your neck. "Not here." Taking your hand, she leads you up the hill, out of sight of the village, and kisses you again in the shadows. You're careening across the slope as you cling to each other, stumbling, faltering, until you catch her by the waist and press her against the rough trunk of a tree—

Her face upturned in the moonlight—

Your hand at the nape of her neck—

As you lower your mouth to hers, she starts pulling open her robes. The rustle of fabric, the shiver of skin. She's drawing your hands to her breasts, and you're not thinking about the mountain anymore, absorbed as you are now by Tana's body—

Curve and thumb—

Nipple, teeth, tongue, and throat—

She guides your hand between her legs, and as your fingers slide between the folds of her, your world suddenly, exquisitely, narrows—

To warmth—

To darkness—

The slick of her against you and the way she trembles at your touch—

You're floating away. You're flawlessly here.

No past, no future.

You feel movement at your waist, and when you look down, Tana's fumbling with your trousers. "Is this okay?" she asks.

"Yes—" More of a hiss than an answer as your belt comes loose, as your saber drops to the ground beside you and her hand slips beneath your clothes—

"I've never done anything like this," she whispers.

"You don't have to if you don't want to."

"I want to."

"Okay."

You put your hand over hers.

Her movements are tentative at first, exploratory, but the more you lean into her, the more you buck and groan, the more confident she becomes, and then you're touching her again, and she's clasping you to her, tighter and tighter, and then from her lips comes a cry, sharp and bright—

Your tongue at her throat, your voice in her ear: "You're going to draw attention."

"I can't—" Another cry escapes her, brighter this time, so bright you have to close your eyes—

And in the darkness, you grin. "Shh."

"Make me."

First you laugh. Then you kiss her. You kiss her as she whimpers and moans against your lips, again and again there, among the trees, moving against you so perfectly as you, in turn, move against her, and for a little while, for just a little while, you forget there's anything else out there, anything else at all, anything out there in the world to see—

KANVER

YOUR FLASK IS EMPTY, WHICH IS ODD BECAUSE YOU could've sworn you refilled it before you left Windfall. Sneaked a bottle of plum wine off the tabletop and dribbled it into your flask when you thought no one was looking—

Your hands unsteady—

The liquid sloshing over your fingers—

(Such a waste.)

Maybe you and Emara drank it all last night when she returned from patrol. The two of you giggling in the garden, passing the flask back and forth while you shushed each other and declared with increasing conviction that one of you was going to wake Ben—

Which you did—

You remember the look she gave you in the darkness, annoyed and half-lidded with sleep—

But you don't remember much after that.

Now you're standing by the bridge on the north edge of the village with Amity, Onna, Tana, and Ben, who hasn't spoken a word to you all morning—

But you're used to that, used to being ignored by your betters. Amity and Ben are the experts, the tacticians. They're smarter than you, more skilled than you. A specialist and an assassin, and you?

You're nothing. You're Octonary Class, same as you were when you left the Academy—

Never got promoted, not once in your years of war—

Didn't deserve it either, weren't good enough, disciplined enough for it. If not for your squad, you would've been killed in your first month on the line. Let's be honest, the fact that you made it out of there at all was some sort of cosmic joke.

You slide your flask back into your pocket. You're supposed to be preparing for the defense of the village, but Amity and Ben are doing all the talking, analyzing, planning—

You're only here because you didn't get up early enough to leave with Leum and the others, who are scouting the surrounding area today, learning the terrain. To be fair, you wouldn't have been much use there either—

You're no good with horses—

Or scouting—

Or much of anything, really, except drifting. You like to drift, absentmindedly watching the creek as it tumbles beneath the bridge and pell-mell through the gully, careening toward the river below.

"How many roads into the village?" Amity asks.

Onna frowns at her. At first, you thought Onna disliked her, but now you just think Onna doesn't know what to do with her. Amity may be young enough to be her daughter, but Amity doesn't act like a daughter, like she was ever anyone's daughter. You wouldn't be surprised if Amity sprang out of a mountainside fully formed, like Callula, Greater God of War, who clawed her way out of the rock and emerged fighting all the monsters that tried to drag her back into the darkness.

In the awkward silence, Tana shifts uncomfortably. "Three," she says. "This road leads to the mountains, and there's a loop from the square to the farmyard, but we're the only ones who use those."

Onna glances sidelong at Amity. "Outsiders always approach by the south road."

It's not lost on you that you and Amity and Ben are the outsiders in question, but that's nothing new, is it? You're used to being an outsider, used to being removed—

Distant—

Drifting—

"Hmm." Unperturbed (maybe even pleased, you think) by Onna's prickliness, Amity returns to studying the landscape. "We'll have to dismantle the bridge, at least temporarily, and post archers above the creek."

"Our archers are good," Tana says.

"At shooting game," Onna counters, "not people."

Amity flicks her fingers dismissively. "Game is quicker, and it's more difficult to shoot."

Ben glances at her from under the brim of her hat. "But it doesn't shoot back."

Amity's brows draw together in surprise.

Privately, you agree with Ben and Onna. There's a big difference between killing an animal and killing a person, between the weight of them on your conscience, between the shift in your soul. But you don't think anyone wants to hear your opinion, so you let your gaze float past them to the farmyard by the river—

A few horses in the paddock. Some scrawny hogs in the pens. Villagers moving in and out of the barns in mesmerizing patterns like little ants—

You're drifting higher and higher, and everything is so far away, pleasantly far away, where you can't touch it, can't mess it up—

You can't be sure, but you think there's some discussion about the bridge, the archers, the guard posts along the creek, and then you're following the others toward the farmyard, along the rim of the gully and past the terraced gardens that lie below the square. Down here, among the corrals and stables and storage sheds, you can hear the river—

Lovely, lovely—

The sound of the water over the stones, smoothing the edges off knobs of quartz and granite and chert—

Amity tells Onna they'll have to flood the farmyard. It's too exposed down here, too vulnerable to attack. They've got to move the animals to higher ground and post lookouts in the abandoned barns, or Adren will slip right into the village, quick as a knife.

Onna doesn't like that, but to be fair, who would? All around you, the villagers are pausing in their chores to mutter and stare. They're wondering where the remaining livestock will go, what they'll do about the inevitable water damage, the subsequent repairs. And for what? Because a bunch of flatlanders say so? How do they know you're even really kindlings?

One of them nods at you, says you look drunk.

(You're not drunk.)

They say you're just a kid.

(Kids can be drunk.)

They don't know how you're going to save them when you can't even keep your shirt clean.

You look down, notice a bloodstain on your collar. Yours or someone else's? You don't know. You don't remember.

You wish you weren't here. You wish you were across the river and into the meadow, where the wind is moving across the wild rye like a giant invisible hand sweeping gently, gently through the grass—

You like the idea of being a giant, of being very big, looking down on things from a great height—

Behind you, someone giggles. Such a strange sound, you think, among the protests and malcontent—

Darting and carefree—

You turn to find several children clustered behind a nearby willow shrub. They're whispering and pointing at you, and you don't know why, but it doesn't really matter. You're used to being whispered about, pointed at—

(That's what you get when you pass out on a street corner in a puddle of your own sick—)

You cross your eyes. You thumb your nose at them.

They laugh, covering their mouths with their small, grimy hands.

One of them, a girl of eight or nine, wrestles a dead branch from the willow. It catches in her braided hair, pulling a few strands loose, but she tugs it free with a determined frown and swipes it experimentally through the air.

You smile. Unslinging your polearm from its place on your back, you spin it a few times—

The whir of the blade—

The blur of the shaft—

The other kids gasp and duck behind the willow again, but the girl holds her ground. (Fierce eyes, a furrow between her brows.) She even attempts a few twirls herself, though she only succeeds in waving the stick back and forth a little.

You salute her.

She beams.

Apparently finished with their survey of the farmyard, Amity and Ben lead the way up the slope to the south road. They move quickly, arguing over defensive strategies with Onna and Tana, and they're all so preoccupied with one another that you're the only one who notices when the girl with the stick starts to trail you through the field.

The other children follow, diving into patches of greasewood and giggling into their hands when you catch them sneaking behind you.

You don't mind.

You think it's funny.

You even pretend not to see them so they have the chance to catch up.

As you reach the road, you find Amity pacing the width of it, kicking here and there at the hard-packed earth. "So this is the main route into the village," she says. Then, with a knowing glance at Onna, she adds, "The one for outsiders."

Tana looks embarrassed, but you almost think you see a smile tugging at Onna's lips.

(Maybe.)

(Fleetingly.)

"It's too open," Amity continues. "If we don't fortify it, Adren and her raiders will make it to Camas in a matter of seconds."

"You want to barricade the road?" Onna asks.

"I want to barricade the entire field." With her finger, Amity draws a line across the landscape, from the rocky west edge of the village, across the meadow, and down to the river. "It's likely they'll still attack from the south, but at least the area will be defensible."

Onna looks unconvinced. "So you want us to take out the bridge, build some guard posts, flood the farmyard, and erect a barricade—"

"Not in that order," Amity interrupts with a wry grin.

"And you expect all of it to get done in the month before Adren arrives? Have you considered the farm? The harvest? The animals? We can't just drop everything and—"

"Ma," Tana says softly.

Onna glances at her, quick and sharp as a slap.

Tana draws back, the space opening between them like a wound, though you wish they wouldn't fight. They've got enough fighting ahead of them. They don't need to start now.

So you try to focus on something else. The field, the river, the children in the bushes. You squint at them, give them a wink.

There's a high little laugh—

A shiver in the branches—

"Fine." Onna turns back to Amity. "We can cut the lodgepole pines behind the cemetery to use for the barricade."

"We'll need a stand of oak as well," Amity adds.

"Of course you do."

"Your people will need spears."

"And that means they'll need training on top of everything else, I'm sure."

Amity purses her lips, no longer amused. "You agreed to this, remember?"

"I know I did." Sighing, Onna rubs her temples. "That doesn't mean I can't regret it."

But you're no longer paying attention. You're turned around, making faces at the children. Eyes rolling. Teeth bared.

"Kanver," Amity snaps.

You freeze. (Your fingers in your mouth and your tongue sticking out.)

Onna looks cross, though not with you. "Poppy! What are you doing here?"

The girl with the stick freezes, but the others scatter, scampering off through the field like jackrabbits—

"Where's Hemmen? He was supposed to be watching you." Taking the girl by the arm, Onna starts walking her back to the village, and now that you see them together, you can also see the resemblance. (Those fierce eyes, that furrowed brow.)

You turn to Tana. "She's your sister?"

Tana nods. "She was born just after our father . . . well, after he was gone."

A sister—

You shake your head.

A little sister—

You take a step back. Ahead of you, Onna is still scolding Poppy, who's prodding at the grass with her stick. "Hemmen said we were done for the day," she insists, "and we wanted to help the kindlings . . ."

She looks back at you then, but you can't do anything to help her. You can't help anyone, not even a little kid—

A tiny one—

Nine years old and no more—

"Kanver," Amity says.

You blink. You're on the south road again. Ahead of you, Onna and Poppy have reached the edge of the village, and Ben and Tana aren't far behind. You don't know how they made it so far so fast, but Amity is staring at you like she wants to peel you open to see what's inside, and that doesn't sound pleasant to you, so you hurry after the others.

She follows. "I'm counting on you to train them, you know. The Camassians."

You grimace. "What about Ben?"

"Ben isn't an expert in polearms."

"Neither am I."

"Kanver," she says.

You don't stop. "Yeah?"

She draws up beside you. (She's breathing harder than you are, the air rasping a little in the back of her throat.) "Can you do this?" she asks.

"Do I have a choice?"

"No."

You should be used to that. You should be used to taking orders. You're not a person. (You haven't been a person in years.) You're a soldier. You eat when you're told, sleep when you're told, fight when you're told, die when you're told—

At the edge of the square, Amity joins Ben and Onna, who are reviewing the western slope: the Old Man's cabin, the creek, the shrine. The hillside is too sheer for an assault, Ben says, but a couple of skilled scouts could make it down the rocks in the night.

Amity agrees. Watches will need to be posted.

You shake your head, though she's not paying attention to you anymore and therefore doesn't see. You can't do this. You don't have it in you. You can't be responsible for all these people, for training all these people. You can't be trusted to keep anyone alive—

Not the villagers—

Not the kids—

There's movement on the hillside above you. The Old Man, wrestling a keg of wine from his cabin—

His thin arms, his muffled curses—

And you drift away again. You meander up the steps while no one's watching, because why would anyone be watching you? You're no one of importance, you're barely there already. You ask the Old Man if you can do anything, and he eyes you suspiciously, but he lets you help him remove two other kegs from the crawl space under the house.

"Can't let you kindlings take my home and my wine too," he says. Then he offers you a drink, which you take—

"Say, aren't you a little young for this?" he says.

You shrug. "We're a little young for a lot of things, I guess."

Cackling, he offers you another drink, and another, and another, and you don't decline those either.

Things are more distant after that. You're more drifting after that. No one watching you anymore, no one needing you, depending on you. No duties, no responsibilities. Just you and your flask, which is full again. Just you and the fields of grass and the light rippling on the river. You don't remember where everyone's gone, but at some point they all come back. You come back, and it's night, and everyone is sweaty and tired, and you're drifting among them, not touching them, not really here at all, and then they're crawling under the blankets and you are too except then you're not, you're supposed to be standing somewhere, watching, even though you're tired, and as your eyes close you think you see something in the darkness—

Gray fur, or gray hair—

A flash of silver—

There and gone, although to be honest, you're not sure if it was ever there at all. You see a lot of things these days, not all of them real, and sometimes you can't tell the difference. A ghost in the trees, a figment of your imagination, a stranger. Whatever it was (if it was anything), it was new, and you find that comforting, because you'd rather see this new thing than the things you usually see.

EMARA

YOU'RE DREAMING AGAIN, BUT UNLIKE THE OTHERS, this dream is slow. A swamp of a dream, sluggish and hazy. Something noxious on the air (if there's air in a dream, if you can breathe, if you can scream). Sickly. You're trapped and gasping, and someone, somewhere, is calling your name. Someone is shaking you, someone is shouting, and you know you're dreaming now, know you're asleep, but you can't wake up, can't move your limbs, can't open your eyes. You have to breathe, but you don't remember how, something wrong with you, with your lungs. You wonder if you're dying.

(You're not dying.)

But you have to get up, Emara, quickly—

The others need you—

You have to wake up—

You open your eyes, but you still can't breathe. The air thick with smoke, cloyingly sweet—

Poppy powder. You recognize it instantly. An instrument of your enemies. During the war, Amerandine assassins were known for dispatching guards and stealing over your defenses, where they'd dust the braziers with poppy powder to slow your reactions and sow confusion among your ranks. An entire field camp dazed and coughing, and only later would you find the corpses—

A high-level target, some commanding officer or visiting general—

An unfortunate watchman or two—

You're under attack. Not by assassins this time but someone else—

Adren? No, you'd be dead already.

But who else knows you're out here?

You cover your mouth, but your senses are already clouded. Wasn't someone supposed to be on watch? Kanver, maybe? You remember waking them for their patrol. You remember them stumbling out into the darkness.

Why didn't they raise the alarm?

You roll over. Your eyes are unfocused; your body, sluggish. The front room of the cabin is empty, but it looks like someone tried to stomp out the kitchen fire, left a few charred powder packets smoldering on the earthen floor—

(You suppose it's the least they could do before leaving you here alone.)

Distantly, you hear the sounds of violence. The other kindlings, fighting, shouting. You could've been out there. You could've been helping them. But maybe they didn't want you, didn't need you, didn't think you were worth the trouble of waking—

You go for your daggers, but you drop one of them with a clatter, the hilt slipping cleanly through your drugged fingers—

Clumsy, Emara. Don't prove them right about you.

Blinking a few times, you're leaning over to retrieve your weapon when someone curses behind you.

Leum.

She's in the back room with Amity, trying to loop an arm around her waist, but Amity keeps coughing and shoving her away.

Leum curses again. "Come *on*, Amity."

Amity shakes her off, gesturing at you through the doorway. "Get . . . Emara . . . out of here . . ."

You pick up your dagger, give Leum a messy wink.

She grabs her greatsword. For an instant, you think she's going to attack you—

(And who can blame you? Your battle-honed instincts? Your kind fought each other for years—)

But she lunges past you and disappears through the open door as if you weren't even there. Outside, you hear the clash of weaponry.

"C'mon," you say to Amity. "Let's get you on your feet, eh?" You stagger toward her as she crawls from the back room, her hair trailing limply over her narrow shoulders, but before you can get close to her, she jabs her finger at the door.

"I'm fine," she croaks. "Help Leum."

You try to obey, but your body is in no mood to cooperate. The room spins around you as you stumble backward, and through the haze you catch a glimpse of Leum fighting someone in the garden—

Swinging, slashing, sword flashing—

But the poppy powder must be affecting her too, because she's slower than she should be. She gets cut across the arm, then the thigh—

Her opponent quick and clearheaded, lithe and leathery—

You squint, trying to get your eyes to focus. You recognize that shorn gray hair, that wolfish grin, the same grin she wore when she and her sister tried to take your daggers in Halabrix—

It's Hope. She and Haru must have tracked you all the way to Windfall, then to Camas—

For the wrap? The Chenyaran wrap, bundled neatly away with the others?

"Hello, Emara." Hope points the tip of her polearm at you, although it's not *her* polearm, is it? It's Kanver's. Without them, the balar crystal in its socket is cold and clear, pulsing only faintly pink with you and Leum so near.

Leum glances back at you. "You know her?"

"Oh yes." Hope bares her teeth at you. "She stole something from us, and we don't take that lightly—"

You snort. "Eh, I think you mean *reappropriated*—"

"So we gathered up some friends," she continues smoothly, "and we're happy to take your weapons as recompense. It seems only fair."

Your stomach twists.

You should've seen this coming. Hope and Haru wanted your daggers at the cardroom, didn't they? Maybe they'd have let you leave with them if you hadn't come back for the wrap, but you did. You made yourself a target. You made everyone a target. Sloppy, Emara. That's exactly the kind of thing the others would expect of a Vedran—

"What'd you do to Kanver?" Leum growls.

Hope shrugs. "Who?"

Leum charges her.

You're only seconds behind, but Leum's swings are too big, too wild. You can't fight like this. You can't get close enough. She nearly slices through your nightshirt before you stumble out of the way.

She doesn't stop to see if she cut you. Lunging forward, she slashes at Hope, forcing her down the path.

Hope hisses, but she doesn't counter with Kanver's glaive, doesn't try to maintain the distance between them. With a feral grin, she beckons Leum closer, the starlight flashing on her ringed left hand.

But why would she let Leum within the reach of her weapon? It doesn't make sense. You blunder after them, trying to remember. You know there's something about those rings—

One of those rings—

Something about it—

Something secret and dangerous—

Part of it opening up, you think, revealing a sliver of a blade—

Poison.

You remember her bragging about it over a winning hand of cards. *Killed three men with this beauty,* she said. *Two of them ex-husbands.*

Hope's luring Leum in, close enough to nick her with the tip of that concealed blade, the poisoned edge of it plunging swiftly toward Leum's exposed arm—

"Look out!" You barrel into Leum, tackling her out of the way before the ring pierces her skin, the two of you tumbling to the ground as Hope lunges after you with the glaive.

You roll aside, pulling Leum with you before she's sliced across the back, but she claws at you and shoves you away.

"Get off me!"

You try to tell her the ring's poisoned, but she's already on her feet again, already rushing Hope again, so you leap up and run after her, the two of you racing toward Hope with your blades in your hands—

But Leum must not see you—

(She can't have seen you, right?)

She's not thinking clearly, she's drugged and dizzy, she can't see you there to her right, just there to her right, because you're still within the arc of her weapon when she slashes at Hope again, the greatsword slicing across your shoulder—

Keen and bright—

You're knocked aside as Leum charges forward without you, around the side of the cabin. You clamp your hand over the wound, trying to convince yourself she didn't see you. She can't have seen you, right?

(Wrong.)

(You know she saw you.)

(She just didn't care.)

The two of them are in the garden now, exchanging blows in the grass, and you could leave them to it. Leum doesn't need you. Doesn't want you.

You, a Vedran.

You, her enemy.

You're about to leave them to it when Leum's balance falters. A loose stone, a wet patch of grass, an opportunity—

Luck favors those who look for it—

And Hope, a gambler, is always looking for it. She knocks Leum to the ground—

The glaive gleaming in the starlight—

The glaive coming down—

Belatedly, you launch yourself at them, but you know you're never going to make it. You're too far. You waited too long. You were too slow, too sloppy. You hesitated, and now it's going to cost you Leum.

But before the blade reaches her, there's a flash of pale, blush-colored light. It carves through the air, severing Hope's arm above the elbow.

She howls.

Flesh smoking.

You duck out of instinct. You'd know that light anywhere.

Kindling magic.

"Leum!" Siddie dashes across the grass, skidding to a stop between Hope and Leum with that ridiculous sword of hers trembling in her hands. "Are—are you okay?"

SIDDIE

LEUM LEAPS TO HER FEET, SHOVING YOU BACK. "WHAT do you think you're doing?"

You blink, but you're not looking at her. You're looking at the severed arm in the grass. (How strange it looks without a body attached to it.) You can't stop staring at it, actually, can't stop thinking about it—

The sensation of your magic sparking inside you, the ripple of it through your arms, your hands, your blade—

It made such a clean arc, didn't it? Carving through the air? The Swordmaster would've been proud, you think—

(Or, if not proud, then at least more interested in you than usual—)

Such a perfect cut—

The perfect sizzle of flesh and bone—

You feel light-headed, although the effects of the poppy powder should have worn off by now. No, wait, that's nausea. That's bile coming up your throat. You swallow a few times, try to stop yourself from retching.

"Lay off her, Grumpy." Emara staggers up to you, winding a strip of her robe around her wounded shoulder. "She saved your life."

"Yeah? And where were you?"

"At the pointy end of your sword, apparently!" Emara knots the bandage, tying it tight with her teeth. "Whatever. It doesn't matter.

We've got other fires to put out, eh?"

You finally notice the smell of smoke on the air. Thick, black, noxious. Maybe *that's* what made you so sick—

(Not the sight of the severed arm in the grass—)

Down below, someone has set fire to one of the thatch-roofed houses, Parker's, you think. (You remember him helping you move into the Old Man's cabin. His high forehead, his kind and drooping eyes.) The little woodshed on the north side of his house is ablaze, all that fuel igniting quickly in the dry night air, the flames clawing greedily at the walls.

Leum stares at it for only a second before she snatches up Kanver's polearm, advancing quickly on the woman in the grass. "Where'd you get this?"

The woman doesn't answer.

Or she answers, but in a painful, gibbering moan.

"Grumpy, come on!" Emara says. "They need our help down there!"

Leum ignores her. She smacks the woman across the face with the butt of the glaive. "Where's Kanver? What'd you do to them?"

Blood and spit. Teeth dribbling from the woman's lips like cherry pits.

You sway on your feet.

"Leave her to me." Amity stumbles from the cabin, although you don't know why she's still so unsteady. She was in the back room when Ben discovered the drugs in the fire, so she shouldn't be feeling this faint. "Leum, go find Kanver. You two, see to that fire."

Leum glares at her, but she's too used to taking orders to argue, so she nods, briefly, and races off into the trees.

"Let's go, Piggy." Emara nudges you with her good arm, jostling you out of your stupor. "Hey, Pig. C'mon."

You make a face. "Don't call me—"

She doesn't wait for you to finish. Pulling you after her, she bounds down the slope to the village below. You're at the intersection of the south road and the village loop—

Flames leaping skyward—

Sparks flying toward the stars—

You've never seen a fire like this before. You're still in the road, and you can already feel the heat on your cheeks, the smoke in your throat—

You don't know how anyone can stand it, but Ket and the villagers are already lashing at the fire with rakes and shovels, spreading out the embers and smothering them in the dirt, while Onna organizes a water brigade, passing buckets all the way from the creek to the house, where they're emptied onto the flames and sent back up the hill with kids your own age—

Which, to your dismay, is where Emara puts you—

"Why?" You try to keep the whine out of your voice. "I want to be wherever you and Ket are!"

"You'll be safer running buckets, so don't get any ideas, eh?" Emara ruffles your hair. "Or Leum will have my head."

You don't know what she means, because you're pretty sure Leum couldn't care less about you, but you're determined to prove you can be useful, so you retrieve an empty bucket from the water brigade and sprint back to the creek. You try to focus on your job, the job Emara gave you, but you can still hear screaming—

The woman screaming in the grass—

You didn't expect her to scream like that, didn't know a person could make a sound like that, high and panicked like an animal—

The stump of her arm—

The smell of singed fat—

Then the scream—

"What are you doing?" One of the villagers, a girl named Fern, is yelling at you. "Don't just stand there!"

Surprised, you look down at the bucket swinging limp and empty in your hand. You're still ten paces from the water, still haven't passed the pail to the rest of the brigade. You didn't know. You didn't realize. You rush to hand off the bucket and hurtle downhill again to retrieve another, but as you vault over the fence and into Parker's garden, you hear a sharp, distorted cry—

At first, you think it's your imagination. The woman again. Her arm falling so suddenly from the rest of her body.

But it's not her.

"Jin!" Parker is shouting for his partner. Crop-haired, crow-eyed. Nonbinary, like Kanver. Parker's running through the garden. Singed hair, charred clothes. He's checking the fire team. *"Jin!"*

Onna takes him by the shoulders. "Did you see them leave? Do you know if they got out?"

As if in answer, there's another cry, this one from inside the house.

On the fire line, Tana hesitates only a second before she drops her shovel. Without a backward glance, she pulls her robe over her mouth and rushes into the flames.

Onna lunges after her. "Tana, no!"

But Ket catches Onna before she can reach the blaze. "I've got her. Don't worry."

Then Ket disappears into the fire too.

Seconds later, part of the roof collapses. A rain of sparks. A deafening roar. The north corner of the house has fallen. Through the smoke, you see blackened beams, scorched walls. No bodies yet, but that doesn't mean they're alive—

Onna lets out a strangled cry.

"Damn it." Whirling on you, Emara grabs you by the arm. "Listen to me, Piggy. I'm going in there to get them. Whatever happens, *don't* come after me. You stay out here. You stay safe. We're going to need you, okay? We're going to need your help when we get out. I'm counting on you, Pig. Do this for me, eh?"

You nod, though in your confusion you don't really know what you're agreeing to. You just know she's counting on you. She needs you.

"Good Piggy." Patting you on the cheek, she races into the house.

You don't know what to do, but you feel like you have to do *something*. You're darting through the garden, trying to get a better view through the snapping flames, the billowing smoke—

You can't see them. You can't see anything. You don't even know if they're still alive. But they've got to be alive, right? All of them? They can't just be gone, just like that—

You've almost reached the south side of the house when you hear footsteps behind you.

Someone on the road?

Glancing back, you catch a glimpse of gray hair, a narrow face, and at first you think it's the woman again, the woman from the garden, the woman you maimed—

But no, her hair is longer, she isn't wearing those silver rings—

(She still has all her limbs—)

A sister, maybe, a twin—

She runs past you with three people you've never seen before. Mercenaries? Enforcers? Dressed in black and armed to the teeth—

But they're fleeing, not fighting, now, and as they sprint down the south road, a knife flies out of the darkness and strikes the gray-haired woman in the neck.

She collapses. (How strange a body looks when it's no longer alive.) One second she's moving, she's escaping, she's panting, she's afraid—

Then she's none of those things, and Ben is racing by you, stopping only to pull her knife from the body, and it moves, a little, but strangely—

Not like a body at all, even though it still looks like a body—

(Not like an arm at all, even though it still looked like an arm—)

You throw up, the liquid slick and sour in your throat, on your lips. It hits your sandals, splatters the dirt, and behind your closed eyes you can't stop seeing that woman's face—

Her scared eyes—

Her mouth opening and closing like a stranded fish—

"Ben!" someone shouts.

It's Ket, bursting through the back door on the south side of the house. She's got Tana with her. They're both coughing, but they seem unharmed. Faces black with soot.

"Ben, come back!" Ket calls again. "Emara's still inside!"

But Ben doesn't hear or doesn't want to, because she draws another knife and disappears down the road.

You wipe your mouth. You stagger toward Ket. "Where's Emara?" you gasp.

Coughing, wordless, Ket waves at the house.

You take another unsteady step. You should follow orders. Emara told you to stay out here. But Emara needs help, doesn't she? You should run in after her. You should go after her like she did for Ket—

But you're scared—

Scared of the fire, scared of dying, scared of what's happening to Emara in there—

You don't know what to do, so you hesitate.

Then Emara emerges from the house with Jin, who's limping, their leg badly burned. But they're alive, and so is Emara. They collapse in the garden as the fire team beats out the last of the flames.

You shake your head. You can't believe it. They're putting out the fire. They've put out the fire. The house is damaged, but it's still here.

You're all, miraculously, still here.

Ket and Tana—

Emara and Jin—

Behind you, Leum and Kanver appear at the edge of the square, Kanver looking disoriented but otherwise unhurt.

Ben returns from the south road. She keeps wiping her hands on her trousers, but there's too much blood. Her sticky fingers, her slick palms. If you didn't know better, you'd think she was as sickened as you are.

Amity descends from the stairs by the creek, and the Camassians are cheering for her, cheering for all of you, thanking you for defending their village, for fighting the fire. They cluster around you, all of them trying to touch you, to put their hands on you, on each of you, as if to welcome you the way they didn't welcome you when you arrived—

But if they're congratulating you, you can't hear them. You're watching the other kindlings. Their grim expressions, their dead eyes.

It shouldn't have been this easy for the attackers to enter the village, but you were lax, undisciplined, unprepared. You were disorganized. You squabbled and fought. You forgot your orders or purposely ignored them. You almost lost two villagers, who you swore to protect. You almost lost Emara and Ket.

This wasn't a victory.

This was a disaster.

And if you perform like this when Adren comes, you're going to get yourselves and everyone else killed.

LEUM

AFTER THE ATTACK, AFTER THE FIRE IS EXTINGUISHED
and the prisoner is secured, after the bodies are retrieved and
cocooned in burial white, you'd think you'd be able to sleep; but
though your eyes are dry and your bones are weary, your heart won't
let you rest.

You get up. You strap on your sword. With Burk yawning at your
heels, you sneak past Siddie, who whimpers and turns over in her
sheets—

(You try not to think of the flash of pink light, the quiver in her
blade—)

You should've seen her coming. You should've stopped her. You
would've, if Emara hadn't gotten in your way—

You descend the steps. You wander into the meadow. (Starlight, schist, the river murmuring below.) You relieve Vander, one
of the villagers, who's watching the south road. Your sleepless gaze
searching the fields, the trees—

Against the lightening sky, the long black pines remind you of
spires rising out of the sea. The towers of rock, eaten by waves. That's
where you found your brother Aran's grave.

But you were too late.

You were days too late. If you'd been a little faster, if you'd
searched a little harder, if you'd wanted it a little more, you could've

saved him. You could've stopped him from starting the drunken brawl that claimed his life.

Then you found Kanver in that Windfall alley, and you knew it was a second chance. You'd lost your family once; you weren't going to lose them again.

Dawn glimmers in the east. Sunrise, bulrush, flycatcher, wren. Beside you, Burk perks up at movement in the farmyard: the villagers drifting from their houses to begin their morning chores.

Onna herself comes to replace you, but you don't think she's slept either. Ash in her hair, eyes swollen and red.

"Where's Vander?" she asks, a rasp in her throat.

"He needed the rest."

She straightens the infantry knot she wears around her neck. "My husband had trouble sleeping too. He'd never tell me why."

"Maybe he was trying to protect you."

She regards you thoughtfully, and you wonder if that's true, if he was trying to protect her or trying to protect himself, or the memory she had of him, of the man she knew before the war. Or maybe he wasn't thinking of her at all, or of his children, and he was just trying to survive, just trying to get by. You don't know. You can't know. You can't see inside his mind.

"Or maybe it was none of your business," you add sourly. As you shoulder past her, she almost lifts her hand, almost tries to touch you, to touch your arm, the same spot where that Vedran boy got you three years ago, though she can't know that.

You duck out of her way. You motion to Burk and quicken your pace. Along your forearm, the webbing of scars burns.

As you round the bend below the Old Man's cabin, you hear voices above you. "I suspected," Amity says with a cough, "when Leum brought you to the hotel, but I was so intent on the mission that I ignored my misgivings. I'm sorry I let things get this far."

A murmured response, velvety and low.

Kanver.

You dash up the stairs, taking them two at a time.

Last night, after you left Siddie and Emara in the garden, you found Kanver passed out among the trees, uninjured and smelling of drink.

You cradled them in your arms. You whispered their name.

Kannie.

A name you haven't used since you were six.

Kannie, wake up.

Huh? Their muddy gaze. The slick of saliva at their lips.

Your relief. Your dismay. Your pity. Your fear.

Kannie, what have you done?

At the top of the steps, you find Kanver and Amity beside the creek. Kanver's downcast eyes, their hair falling limply across their forehead. Amity twitches the end of her scarf, and you can see her doing that invisible calculus of hers. Surveying, measuring, assessing, weighing—

You'd never admit it, but you know even before she speaks that Kanver's going to come up short.

Amity glances at you (almost pityingly) as you draw up beside them. Then she turns back to Kanver, clearing her throat. "If I can't use you, I can't have you here."

You plant yourself beside Kanver, fists clenched. "You can't do that."

"Actually, I can."

Burk growls at her.

Kanver only shrugs, like they knew it was coming. (This rupture, this ending, this inevitable disappointment.) Like it was only a matter of time.

"They're family," you say.

Amity coughs. "They're a liability."

"You can't—" You try to continue, but you know she's right.

How can you trust Kanver after what happened last night?

But you can't let them go. Not now. Not after you found them again.

You're not losing any more kin.

"Who are you willing to risk next?" Amity asks you. "One of the villagers? Ket? Siddie?"

You don't answer. You can't answer. You already failed Siddie once. You can't fail her again.

Kanver taps you on the shoulder. They rub a hand along their cheek. "It's okay, Leum. I'll go."

"You can't," you say. "We're supposed to do this together."

They tilt their head thoughtfully. "What do you mean 'supposed to'?"

You don't know how to answer that, so you scowl at them for confusing you. "If you go, I go."

Amity lifts an eyebrow, and you know you've stumbled onto the only leverage you have against her. "I'd hate to lose you, Leum," she says.

"Then don't."

Her face is expressionless, but you know she's considering your usefulness now too. You're only Senary Class, only a vanguardian, only a grunt. How much are you worth to her, really?

Fortunately for you, you never have to find out, because Emara emerges from the cabin, tucking her injured arm into a sling. Her shoulder is neatly bandaged now, but you try not to look at it—

You didn't mean to cut her, but she was too slow—

She should've gotten out of your way—

There's a twinge of guilt in your belly, but you choose to ignore it, choose anger instead. (You've always been better with anger than guilt.) After all, she was the one who led Hope and Haru to Camas, wasn't she? If not for her, Siddie wouldn't have had to fight. If not for her, Amity wouldn't be trying to send Kanver away.

The edge of your anger is blunted, however, when Emara looks at you (gray-eyed and solemn) and says, "I'm with Grumpy."

At first, you think she's joking. You almost took her arm off last night (almost got her killed last night, if we're being honest), but she doesn't waver.

"You keep all of us," she says to Amity, "or the village falls, and your mission fails."

You glare at her. "What are you doing?"

Doesn't she want you gone? Doesn't she hate you for everything you and your kind did to her in the war? The way you slaughtered them? The way you demolished them like swallows feeding at dusk? The bloody fields, the mountainsides strewn with corpses, survivors limping back to their outposts. How could she survive all that and still want to be one of you?

"I'm saving the mission." Emara slings her good arm around Kanver's shoulders, and they give her a watery grin. "We need all seven of us, eh?"

Amity frowns, but you know she can't afford to lose all three of you. She can't afford to cut her fighting force by half.

She needs you.

She needs Emara.

She needs Kanver, though she doesn't know it yet.

"Fine," she says at last. "Kanver can stay. But as long as they're here, they have to remain sober. No drinking, do you understand me? Not a drop. You clean up your act, or you're gone, and *you*"— she looks from you to Emara—"both of you stay until the job is done."

Late that afternoon, you find Kanver curled up in the cabin. Sweating, shaking, feverish, pained. Something's wrong, you think, something's seriously wrong. The altitude, maybe, or the mountain chill. You've got to get help, so you bolt for the door, but Kanver croaks at you from the floor: "No, wait. I'm fine—"

"You're *not* fine."

They look up at you from beneath their blanket. "This always happens when I can't find a drink."

The tremors, the headaches, the nausea—

Sometimes they have nightmares—

But it'll pass, they think.

They sit up, shivering. "It's almost dinner?"

"Yeah. The others will be back soon."

They reach for a nearby pail, pulling it to their chest. "Help me into the garden, will you?"

"Why?"

"If I smell anything cooking in here, I'm going to throw up, and I don't want to put *everyone* off their meal."

So you guide them into the garden while the others filter back from their duties. A quarrel over who's supposed to fix dinner tonight. A cook fire started. A pot put on to boil. As the sun sets over the ridge, the two of you sit at the top of the stone terrace with Burk, watching the shadows lengthen along the south road.

Kanver throws up anyway.

You sit with them. You remind them to drink water. Burk lets them knot their fingers in her fur. At some point, Ket offers you dinner, but you wave her away.

Evening falls. A meadow like a dark ocean, star-tipped grasses billowing like waves.

After a while, Kanver says, "You didn't have to stand up for me. With Amity."

You shrug and lean back on your hands. "Why wouldn't I?"

"I don't know. We haven't seen each other in years. How do you know I'm still worth standing up for?"

"You're still Kanver, aren't you?"

They shake their head slowly, their threadbare blanket rustling against their chin. "Sometimes I don't know anymore."

You don't know what to say to that, so you shrug. "Well, you're still family."

They rest their head on your shoulder.

Not to be left out, Burk noses between you. A warm bundle of oily fur.

You almost tell them about Aran and Kida and Vo and Zan. How you just couldn't seem to hold on to them, no matter how tightly you clung. But that was another family, a different family. You already lost them. They're already gone.

Instead, you say, "I'm getting out of here, you know."

"Out of where?"

"Out of Amerand." You tell them about your plan. Why you took this job. The spoils you'll sell in Windfall. The guide you'll hire to take you into Ifrine. "You can come with me."

"Me?"

"Of course, dummy."

After all, there's nothing left for them here. There's nothing left for either of you here.

(Except us.)

(And we don't want you to go, can't follow you out there, out past our borders, past our land—)

(The land that birthed us—)

(And took us away again.)

Shivering, Kanver plucks at their blanket. "I'm afraid I'm no good to you like this."

"You'll get better, won't you?"

"I guess."

"It'll be better once you get out of here. We'll be better out there, the both of us. You'll see."

As you speak, you see three figures on horseback riding up from the loop road: Vander, Hemmen, and the prisoner, Hope, with her balar-burnt arm in a sling and her good hand tied to the saddle horn.

Amity wanted to hold her until the mission was complete. That's what you would've done in the war. Housed her and fed her and kept her locked away until the danger had passed.

But Onna said Camas couldn't afford a prisoner. They're barely feeding their own as it is. What was she going to do? Ask the children to give up their rations for the enemy? No, Hope would've starved in their care.

So they're doing what they do when one of their own commits an unforgivable offense.

They're banishing her.

Near Parker's ruined house, they turn down the south road, the sound of their hoofbeats fading into the field, the distant trees. They're taking her into the mountains, where she'll be stripped of her clothes and set loose in the wilderness, her fate decided not by mortals but by the Stone Shepherd, Lesser God of the Candiveras, and whatever other deities deign to intervene.

"Cowards," you mutter. "They want her dead but they don't have the courage to do it themselves."

"It's hard to find that courage," Kanver says.

"We don't have trouble with it."

"Well, we didn't have much of a choice. We did it so they didn't have to."

You fought on the front lines. You defended their country. You stopped Vedra from seizing the northlands. You stopped the war from reaching their hills.

You were their hope for the future, they said. You were their salvation. You didn't choose to be born into this war, but you could end it. You could fix things. You could make the hard choices, though you were just kids.

"One more mission," you say softly, "and then this is all over."

Kanver plucks at a nearby tuft of grass. "Will it ever be over?"

"What do you mean?"

They don't answer.

Down below, you think you see a shadow stealing southward through the pines. A wild animal, perhaps, a wolf or a cat roaming its lonely range. Burk sniffs the air and grumbles softly, but her hackles don't rise, and after a moment she settles her head upon her paws.

Minutes later, another shadow stalks into the trees.

BEN

AFTER THE ATTACK, YOU TRY TO KEEP TO YOURSELF.
You take your meals in the garden. You volunteer for patrol. In the evening, you slip away while the other kindlings regale Siddie with stories from the war: tales of Windcatchers stealing behind enemy lines or Shieldbearers with their walls of fire. Leum claims the Queen Commander's guards could summon a balar barrier broad enough to protect a full complement of infantry, impenetrable to everything from arrows to cannon shot—

You want to say you'll believe it when you see it. (Though the war's over, so you're never going to see it.) But it's not like you're going to join them around the fire.

You escape into the woods. Clover, fern, bracken, loam.

The silence, your knives.

You're better off alone.

But you can't avoid the others forever. Two days later, while everyone else is digging ditches by the river or taking down pines for the barricade, Amity chooses you to cut spears with her. None of her fortifications will last without defenders, and no defenders will last without weapons to train with, fight with, kill with, so you end up felling saplings in a grove of oaks some miles below the ridge, the air shady and sweet.

Kanver would've been the obvious choice for this job. They're better with polearms than any of you. But Kanver's in no condition to do more than sit on the bank of the river, sweating and shaking, and if we're being honest, Amity's been avoiding them since she tried to dismiss them the other day.

Amity lays down her axe, a sheen of sweat on her brow. She's been moving slower than you today, but to be fair, you've been moving quickly, trying to get ahead of her, trying to put a little distance between you so she won't try to make conversation.

But she has you trapped here with her, most likely by design, and you can't run away when she finally breaks the silence.

"Are you going to tell me why you continued to pursue Haru and the others when they were already retreating?"

You shrug. You grip your hatchet and swing.

The blade bites into the narrow trunk, snapping it free of its stump.

The night of the attack, you were the first one to wake. The familiar scent of poppy powder, oddly sweet. You knew it immediately. The soft *pop* of sachets in the fire, the billowing smoke—

Your old arsenal—

A Mistwalker's arsenal, for stealing into the ranks of your enemies. For slitting their throats in bed.

The others were moaning. Their bodies on the floor, thick-limbed and whimpering in their half-drugged sleep—

Panic gripped you, then, tight around the heart.

(You never wanted to feel that again.)

Removing the sapling's branches, you toss it into the pile with the rest and slip away in search of another tree to fell. Green but not too green. Straight and unmarred by age.

Undeterred, Amity follows you deeper into the grove. "Leum thinks you wanted to add to your kill count."

You dig your axe into another tree. At the Academy, you heard that all Mistwalkers had kill counts. Notches on their weapons, tattoos on their ribs. A record of devastation, and you wanted one too. You still have it, in fact. A brand on the inside of your belt for every life you took, black and permanent.

"I stopped keeping track," you say, which is the truth, though not all of it.

The truth is, until last night you hadn't killed anyone since the war—

(Since you failed to save your squad—)

That's why you became a performer, isn't it? You could still throw your knives. You could still master your skills. You could still be perfect.

But no one had to die for it.

You knew when you came here that you'd have to hurt people again, and you accepted that. It was the cost of protecting your kin.

But you didn't expect this—

Once you smelled the smoke, you were on your feet in an instant, kicking the sachets from the fire. Scorched socks, the smell of stray embers burning on the kitchen's earthen floor. Grabbing your knives, you burst from the cabin, your enemy scattering before you like beetles from a broken log.

You could have seen to your kin. Could have gotten them up. Could have made sure they were safe.

But you couldn't go back in there. (Couldn't bear to watch them writhing and helpless on the floor.)

You were scared.

You were so scared that Hope and Haru had hurt them, would come back to hurt them (again and again and again), that when your enemy was within range and your knives were at hand, you didn't hold back. You tracked your enemy through the village, felling them one by one as they fled.

Dead.

Dead.

Dead.

You chased them all the way to the south road, past the fire, past Ket limping from the flames, calling to you, calling your name—

Ben, come back!

Emara's still inside!

But you didn't go back.

(Couldn't.)

You couldn't watch it. You couldn't stand there, powerless, while the fire took Emara from you. No, you couldn't take that, not again, couldn't wait around while you lost another of your kin.

Not after last time—

It was supposed to be a simple mission. Nothing was supposed to go wrong. Your squad charging toward the darkened tower, supposedly undefended except for one or two sentries, nodding off at their posts—

You've gone over it (again and again and again) in your mind. You thought you heard something in the shadows. The scrape of a sword. The whisper of an attack. You *knew*. You knew it was coming.

But you were too slow to react.

Then an explosion of light—

Then a pain in your forehead—

When you came to, your squad was dead. Crisp corpses. Rubble and dust. Your head was ringing. Your body was broken. You had to fight your way out of there, alone and injured. You barely made it out alive.

But you made it out. You were the only one who did.

And then you had to live with it.

In the grove, Amity watches you take down another sapling. "Tell me what happened on the south road," she says.

You strip the branches. Twigs and leaves like confetti. "I eliminated a threat."

"They weren't a threat by that point."

You could see your quarry in the distance, shadows moving against the silvery grass. Hardly menacing. Their leaders killed or captured. The others dead in the village gardens, lying across the fences and in the roads.

You could have let them go.

But you were too scared. Desperate, panicked. Your instincts took over. You forgot you didn't want to hurt anyone. You forgot you didn't want to kill. All you knew was that you had to stop them, couldn't allow them to retaliate against you, against your kin, couldn't allow them to live.

Your breaths came fast as you threw your knives, flashing one after another in the starlight.

In the meadow, the shadows fell, one after another, until there was no movement left.

You shrug and move to another tree. "I couldn't let them escape."

"You could have taken them prisoner," Amity counters.

Your axe falters, skimming the bark and narrowly missing your shin. Amity doesn't say anything, but you can feel her gaze burning into your back like a branding iron.

With forced nonchalance, you wipe your hands on your trousers. "Like the woman Siddie caught for you?"

Amity says nothing. You know she fought Onna's decision to banish Hope. You know she wanted Hope to live. She's a kindling, and kindlings abide by the code. We treat our prisoners with dignity and respect.

But that isn't what happened, is it?

You try not to think of Hope, naked and wounded in the darkness, with the cold closing in.

Some deaths are worse than others.

(That's what you tell yourself, at least.)

You rub your eyes. You swing your axe. The hard cut. The exposed heartwood, pale as flesh—

"Do you think she'll be back?" you ask. You keep your eyes down. You keep your voice light.

You know Amity's watching you from beneath her hood, but you don't look up, don't want to meet her gaze. "No," she says finally.

You nod, as if that settles it, although of course it settles nothing. "Good."

You don't want to spend any more time with the others than you have to, but you can't escape your duties when after the evening meal Amity gathers all of you in the garden to make spears. Seven faces lit by the firepit, seven sets of hands. Hardly anyone speaks (not even Emara, who keeps staring at you through the smoke), the only sounds the scrape of knives, the clicking of bark chips in the grass, the rasp of the scouring brush.

Amity's the quickest, which is to be expected, peeling each sapling clean in a matter of minutes before reaching for the next. You're almost tempted to stop what you're doing so you can watch her. No wasted movements. Each stroke an act of grace. You could probably learn more from watching Amity craft a wooden spear than sparring with anyone else.

But after your interrogation this morning, you don't want to draw any more of Amity's attention. You don't want her to suspect.

So you keep going. One spear after another.

Siddie makes it halfway through a sapling before she stops to stare at the flames. You don't even think she blinks, her round face drawn and pale in the firelight.

Across the flames, Kanver's damp with sweat, but at least they're no longer shaking. For a while, they're even keeping pace with Amity. But then their hand slips. A narrow miss. Setting down their knife, they breathe deep and study their fingers, opening and closing on their thighs like sea creatures in a tide.

One by one, the others drift off to bed, until it's just you and

Emara on opposite ends of the fire. You reach for a spear. You start to carve. Chip, flake, blade, pith. You whittle the end into a point while Emara watches you with her gray and curious eyes.

"What?" you say finally.

"Eh . . . I just can't figure you out, I guess."

"What does that mean?"

"It means I get Queenie. I get Piggy. I even get Grumpy, if you can believe it. But you? Your whole thing?" When you don't answer, she takes up a stick and prods at the embers. "I followed you last night, you know."

Your knife falters, nicking the tip of your finger. Blood wells from your flesh, but you don't move to stanch it. "Why?"

"Because sneaking off in the middle of the night is *weird*, Knifey." She pokes at the firepit again, sending up sparks. "And because I needed to know."

"Know what?"

"If I could trust you after you left me to burn in that fire."

You don't look at her. If you look at her, you'll have to admit that you couldn't stand to see her scorched and broken and streaked with ash. You'll have to admit that you couldn't stand to look at her or Ket without seeing your old squad, dead in the rubble—

"I thought for a while you were like Grumpy, eh? You left me there because I was Vedran?" Emara rubs her chin thoughtfully. "But after last night, I know that's not it. You're messed up, but you're not messed up like that."

"What did you see?" you ask carefully.

"I saw enough."

She was out there, then. She was out there when you followed Vander and Hemmen out of the village. She was out there when you tracked them through the pines. She was there when you watched them take Hope's sandals, her clothes, everything but the bandage on her arm—

She was there when they left her huddled and miserable on the granite, and you stepped out of the shadows with a blade in your hand.

"What's your deal, Knifey?" Emara asks. "You're not a performer. You're not the Sparrowhawk. You're not even really the strong, silent type the Sparrowhawk's supposed to be. So who are you? What're you doing out here? You just want an excuse to kill people?"

"No." You're on your feet in an instant. "That's not—"

Emara wags a finger at you. "You better tell me the truth, eh? Or everyone's going to hear what happened out there."

You sit back down.

Hope begged you to spare her. She pleaded. She wept. You remember her tears glistening on her cheeks—

Pale as heartwood—

But you told her it was better to die by the knife than by tooth and claw. Better to die quick than shivering in the cold.

Some deaths are better than others, that's what you said, and as you sank your blade through her temple, you tried to believe it.

You want to tell Emara you're a kindling. You were trying to do the right thing.

But kindlings are supposed to have a code. Protect the weak. Defend the defenseless. Adhere to the tenets of honor, duty, loyalty, compassion—

Mercy—

"I lost control," you say softly.

Emara looks skeptical. "You seemed pretty in control to me."

"I forgot the code."

"This is about your code?"

You finally notice you're bleeding. Sticking your finger in your mouth (a bitter, mineral taste), you nod. "Didn't you have one?"

"Of course we had one, eh? Without it, we'd be monsters."

You flinch at her words, and she lets out a weak laugh. "Sorry, I'm kidding."

"Ah."

But she's right. We were trained to believe the code made us different, made us better. Living and killing and dying by it meant we were warriors, not murderers—

Heroes, not monsters—

But you didn't kill by the code this time. You were so scared, so desperate, you didn't even remember you had a code.

"Hey, don't look like that, Knifey." She gets up and sits beside you, pulling you under her arm. "We did worse during the war, eh?"

You stare into the fire. Ash, ember, glimmering coal. During the war, you had your orders. You had your targets. If you didn't kill them, they'd kill you. It was your job to stop them before they had the chance.

Is that what you did last night? Is that what you've always done?

"Were we always monsters then?" you murmur.

Was that what they made us? Was that what they trained us to be?

"Whoa." Emara's arm slides from your shoulders. "Who d'you think you're calling 'monster'?"

You blink at her, confused. "You're the one who said—"

She grins and draws you close again. "Look, I don't see much point in names these days. Kindlings, monsters, Vedrans, northern scum"—she waits for you to meet her gaze before she winks at you and continues—"we are who we are. I'm just glad you're on my side this time, eh?"

And you want to believe her, but you keep thinking about the fear curdling in your stomach, the hollow beat of your footsteps against the earth, the sensation of your blade sinking into Hope's skull—

Emara stands, yawning. "C'mon, we should both get some sleep."

You nod, but you don't follow her into the cabin.

You thought you were a kindling, or if not a kindling anymore, then a veteran, a virtuoso with a knife. But how can you be those things if the code you built them on was a lie? Where's your honor, Ben? Where's your compassion? Who are you without these things you used to believe?

Are you an assassin, an entertainer, a butcher, a beast? Protector or predator, violent and unyielding?

You don't know. You can't reconcile it.

You go over it (again and again and again). You don't sleep.

KET

YOU'D FORGOTTEN HOW MUCH TROUBLE IT IS TO live with someone you're not sleeping with, much less six of them, who have all the usual disputes over whose stuff is in whose space, who didn't do the dishes this morning, who's supposed to cook dinner, who left their laundry hanging from the rafters *again*—

(Emara. It's always Emara.)

And none of them can be solved with a kiss or some time in the sheets (or by leaving, for that matter), so you have to figure out other ways to deal with them. After the fourth squabble over the crusty pots, Amity puts everyone on a rotating list of chores: sweeping, dusting, mopping, cooking . . .

Most nights, you volunteer to do the dishes, because you don't mind it. You like the quiet of it, actually. The smooth circles of the scrubbing brush, the soft slop of the water. Sometimes Kanver joins you, says they need something to do with their hands. Taking up a cloth, they dry the cutting boards, the bowls, the wooden spoons, and place them all neatly back on their shelves.

Kanver's easy to be around. Sweet-tempered, undemanding. Since the end of the war, they've been wandering the peninsula. No plan in mind, no place they're going. Usually they walk, but they're not choosy. They've hitched rides with merchants, wood-cutters, a traveling sideshow, a monk. Once, they even fell asleep on a barge drifting down the Jivana River and didn't wake up until they reached the roaring green falls.

"What'd you think of them?" you ask. "The falls?"

Shrugging, they scratch their cheek. "They were loud."

You laugh. You tell them you've been there. (It's one of the items you crossed off your list.) Soon you find yourself comparing the places you've been. Jivana Falls, the Queen Commander's Citadel, the Temple of the Fire God, and beneath it, House Omayo of the Kindling Academy. Kanver's the first person you've shared these things with, but you don't mind sharing.

(They're restless too.)

Leum's still picking fights with Emara at the slightest provocation, so after a few days of her bristling and snapping, you switch rooms with Emara, (who's taken to calling you "Roamie") to keep her out of Leum's path. Better for you to be in the front room anyway, since you still get up to wander the village at night.

Soon, you notice Leum sneaking off to train before dawn, returning red-faced and drenched in sweat, so you start making sure you have a pot of tea ready for her, cool enough to drink. She doesn't thank you. (Of course she doesn't.) But she quaffs the first cup and holds it out for more, and coming from Leum, that's thanks enough.

While her breathing evens out and the sweat cools upon her brow, the two of you stand in the garden, watching the valley in the morning light. The birds in the wild rye. The flashing of the river. Inside the cabin, there's a muted cry, the sound of someone shifting in their sleep.

You glance over your shoulder, but the windows are dark and still. "Siddie or Emara?" you say to Leum.

"Siddie." She glowers down at her cup. "It's been happening since the attack."

"I heard she saved you."

Leum looks at you sharply. "Did Emara say that?"

"Does it matter?"

She shrugs. "I didn't ask for Siddie's help."

You laugh quietly. "You didn't need to. I'm pretty sure that kid would do anything for you, whether you want her to or not."

"She asked me to train her again."

"Oh yeah?" You're not surprised. As far as you can tell, Siddie's nothing if not persistent. "What'd you tell her?"

"To get lost. Same as always."

"Ha. D'you think she'll listen this time?"

Leum downs the last of her tea in one quick gulp. "If she knows what's good for her."

And that's the end of the conversation, which suits you fine. You stand there without speaking, just the two of you, watching and listening. You've always liked these moments, these gaps between things when the world goes still—

Between the thunder and the breaking of the rain—

Between the withdrawal of the water and the incoming wave—

Between the dreaming world and the waking, when everything is possible, there's this: you, Leum, the cooling tea, the pines, the gray light of morning, the shadows in the thickets, the sun on the mountains, the dust, the quiet, the calm—

Once the spears have been completed, Amity splits you into teams. You, Siddie, and Emara fell trees for the barricade while Leum and Ben dig ditches in the meadow and Kanver, newly sober, trains the villagers—

When the villagers can be spared from their chores, that is—

It's a point of contention between Onna and Amity, who flits between your logging operations behind the cemetery and the flood preparations in the farmyard, but to be fair, you don't think any amount of time would've been enough for Amity.

What this means for you is that sometimes Tana joins you among the lodgepole pines. You expect things to be awkward since you slept together, because let's face it, all your trysts have ended poorly—

You've been slapped and screamed at—

You've had more than one drink upended in your lap—

But Tana, just as she promised, seems totally unruffled after sleeping with you. In fact, it's Tana who gleefully topples the tree where she let you kiss her that first night, laughing as it crashes to the forest floor.

You lay down your axe with a sigh. "I guess you really aren't the sentimental sort, huh?"

"Why?" She gives you a grin. "Was it supposed to be memorable?"

"Wow."

The preparations continue: trees felled, ditches dug, spears jabbed into haystacks like pins. Despite the fuss they made when you got here, the Camassians eagerly take on their new duties. (They're better woodcutters than you, and they like to prove it, although you don't mind because it means the work gets done faster.) Little by little, you learn the rest of their names. Jin, Parker, Poppy (Tana's little sister), who trails after Kanver like a duckling. Hemmen, Vander, Ferra, Fern. They make you compresses to soothe your aching muscles. They show you how to slide your hand along the axe so all the force goes into the blade.

As the forest opens up, so does your view of the Morning Daughter. Her tilted head, her half-closed eyes. You spend a lot of time studying her, learning her from a distance. Her moods, her expressions in the sunlight. You're obvious enough about it that Tana notices, calls you out on it one day.

"So what's with you and the mountain?"

It's almost evening, and you're lashing pines to the logging cart so Jin, whose burned leg is slowly healing, can drive them to the south road for unloading.

You check your knots. You slap the side of the cart to let Jin know they can take off. "The Morning Daughter, you mean?"

Tana steps back, waving dust out of her face as the cart rattles away. "Yeah."

"I've heard the stories." Which is true, although it doesn't answer her question. "Who do you think she's mourning?"

"When I was little, I used to think it was her father. I mean, it's in the name, right? Mourning *Daughter*." Tana leans against a nearby boulder, tracing the green crags of lichen with her thumb. "I don't remember him very well, though. My father. I was only four when he was drafted, and Vian always said he was different when he came back. Not long after that, he was gone."

"What happened to him?"

"We don't know. One night, he just . . . left."

You sit beside her, though not near enough to touch her. You like how things are between you. Don't want to make things weird. "When?" you say.

"About a year after he came home. Poppy wasn't even born yet, so she doesn't remember him at all." Tana squints up at the mountain. "He was obsessed with the Morning Daughter too. Sometimes I think that's where he went, when he walked out into the snow that night."

You drum your fingers along the edge of your collar. You imagine a man disappearing. A shadow, swallowed by white, howling and empty—

You wonder if he was haunted like you. You wonder if he had nightmares like you. You wonder if he was running like you.

"I'm sure he would've stayed, if he could've," you say.

"You didn't know him."

You smile at her sadly. "I know a lot of people came back from the war running from something."

She frowns, and by now you know her expressions well enough that you can tell she's not displeased or disappointed with you but merely curious. "Does that mean you're running too?"

You trace the edge of your robe, where you still keep your list in its hidden chest pocket.

Of course you're running. You've been running for years. Even when you're not moving, you're running.

(Even from what you love most.)

Instead of answering, you nod toward the Morning Daughter. "You think she's mourning something different now?"

"Yeah. Now I look at the mountain, and all I see is my brother." Tana shrugs and crosses her arms. "Sorry to be obvious."

"What's wrong with being obvious?"

She stands, brushing off her trousers more times than she probably needs to. "I'm actually heading out there in a few days. It's my turn to check on the cows."

You try to picture cattle on those precarious cliffs. "There are cows on the Morning Daughter?"

She laughs. (She's got a nice laugh. High and bright. Though you don't hear it often.) "Nearby. There's some good pasture at the base of the ridge."

"You just leave them out there?" you ask.

"Sure."

"Aren't there wolves?"

She looks at you like she can't believe you're asking. "Of course there are wolves."

"And bears?"

"Yeah."

"And mountain lions?"

She laughs again. "Yes, Ket, there are mountain lions."

"And the cows are just allowed to wander around free?"

"If you don't believe me, you can come see for yourself."

"Really?" You try to imagine it. The peaks, the cows, the narrow mountain valleys greened by glacier-fed creeks—

"Sure. Ferra was supposed to come with me, but I can see if she'd rather stay in the village." Tana shrugs. "I should warn you, though, it's hard work."

"Hey!" You're almost offended. You show her your blistered palms. "Do I look like I mind hard work?"

You have to get Amity's permission to take a few days off, but she doesn't push you to stay. Actually, she seems preoccupied, seems to have caught a chill or something since she's been here, hasn't been able to work alongside the rest of you, preferring instead to take over the training of the villagers, shooing Kanver away to dig ditches with Leum and Ben.

(Apparently, Amity's an impeccable instructor. Tana tells you she's almost as good with a polearm as Kanver.)

Amity glances out the cabin window, where, silhouetted against the evening stars, you can see Ben and Emara on the terrace. Emara's sprawling limbs. Ben's tidy, cross-legged sit.

"I'll put Ben in charge of the barricade while you're gone," Amity says. Then after a moment she adds, "Since she and Emara have been getting along."

You grin. "Weird, right?"

Amity chuckles, trying not to cough. "Very."

They spend every evening out there together, while you and Kanver wash the dishes and Leum sharpens her sword. At first, you assumed Ben was throwing knives at the hillside behind the cabin, but she hasn't done that since the attack. In fact, she's been leaving her gauntlets in the cabin (which is to be expected, because she can't work an axe or a spade in her balar weapons), but she's also stopped wearing her knives.

So you're pretty sure she and Emara just talk. Through the windows, you can hear Ben's restrained murmur, Emara's soaring laugh.

"Just don't fall off your horse while you're out there," Amity says.

"I need you in fighting shape when Adren comes."

You chuckle, but you're careful when you head out at dawn the next morning. You and Tana and the horses, the dogs streaking through the grass. As you make your way into the highlands, the land sharpens—

Mountains appearing around you like giants rising out of the granite—

Bristlecone pines twisting out of the cliffs—

It's so vast up here, you can scarcely understand it. The scale of things. The enormity of them. You could die out here (exposure, heat stroke, a fall from the mountain) and no one would notice but the flies—

The vultures—

The impassive face of the Morning Daughter, praying over your bones—

You expect it to be overwhelming, but you almost find it comforting to be so small, to live so quietly, to pass unnoticed, hardly making a mark, at the feet of something so tall.

Below the Morning Daughter, you find cows grazing between clusters of whitethorn. Bells clanking, calves trailing their mothers through the shadows of passing clouds.

"I guess they are all right up here alone," you say, sitting back in your saddle.

With a laugh, Tana shakes her head and turns her horse up the trail. (You try not to notice how she sways in the saddle, the smooth way she moves when she rides.) "Well yeah," she says, "they like it this way."

And, much to your surprise, so do you.

In the mornings you wake to the sounds of lowing. You cook up breakfast in the little stone cabin the villagers have up here, on the edge of a glacier-blue lake. The creak of the floorboards, the crackle of the fire. During the day, you walk the fences. Maybe you retrieve a heifer that's wandered away from the herd. You doctor a couple wounds. You repair what needs repairing.

You like the simplicity of it, the even pace of it—

The freedom of it.

Up here, you're not running. Not away from anything or toward it. No past, no future. No restlessness, no list. Just you and the trails, just you and the cattle, just you and Tana and the little cabin by the lake—

Simple.

Easy.

Dusk is strange up here. First, the sun goes. Things dimming, the forest draining of color. Shadows pooling in the low places. It's only after the land's gone dark that the sky turns to fire—

Coral, vermilion, magenta, red—

Balar colors—

Kindling colors—

The air burning catastrophically above you for a few beautiful minutes before the light disappears again.

You and Tana are watching it now, on your last night, before you return to Camas and another pair of villagers rides up to see to the cows. You're splayed out on a rock near the water, watching the light explode across the firmament, when Tana turns toward you, propping herself up on her elbow. Her fierce dark eyes, her hair brushing the nape of her neck.

"So," she says with a grin. "I've been thinking about your first night in Camas . . ."

You swallow, remembering the darkness, the smell of the pines, the kiss. You try to keep your voice neutral when you say, "Uh-huh?"

"I lied." She licks her lips. "It was memorable."

You sit up. You look down at her. The swoop of her collar

revealing the shape of her clavicle, the soft curves of her chest. "Oh yeah?"

"Do you want to do it again?"

You let out a small, strangled laugh. (Because of course you want to.) But you don't say yes, not yet. "Nothing's changed," you warn her. "I'm still leaving when this is all over."

She straightens. "I haven't forgotten."

"And you're going to be okay with that?"

She pulls at her belt. A tie loosened, a knot undone. "Do I look like I care?"

Your breath hitches in your chest. You've never seen her naked, half-clothed as you were in the darkness before, but the only thing you're thinking of is getting her naked now, seeing with your eyes the limbs and breasts and back you've already explored with your hands.

"I guess not," you say.

"Then kiss me."

You've managed to keep your hands off her for days, but you don't stop yourself now from pulling her toward you. Your arms encircling her, your mouth finding hers. Warm and wet—

Behind her, the last of the light leaves the Morning Daughter, high above the ridge, but you're not watching the mountain. You're gathering Tana to you. You're staggering up the shore. You're entering the cabin, where you lay her down upon your bedroll and peel off her clothes. Lips and hands, traveling, ravenous.

You kiss her with the heat of the cook fire warming your calves. You kiss her, tangled in the blankets. You kiss her. You kiss her. You kiss her.

Over the coals, your dinner burns.

SIDDIE

THERE'S SOMETHING DIFFERENT ABOUT KET SINCE she returned from the high country. Before, even though she got along with almost everybody (even Leum), it was like she was always only halfway here, like she was already halfway packed and out the door, always one step away from walking out of your life and down the dusty road.

And maybe she's a little like that, still, in the same way that all the kindlings are, but ever since she and Tana got back, it's like she's more present, more settled, more grounded in the rustle of weeds in the meadow, the motion of the river and the wind in the trees. She's happier, you think, more relaxed, especially around the villagers, and when she sinks one of those sharpened logs into the soil, it's like she's embedding herself just as deeply, solidly into the earth.

You keep wondering if anyone else notices the difference, but if they do, they don't show it. But they don't show a lot of things, these kindlings. Don't say a lot of things, except when they're yelling at you, which they do often.

Stop that, Siddie! Let go of that, Siddie!

Go away, Siddie!

Where are you, Siddie?

Get back to work, Siddie!

In truth, you resent it, because haven't you proven yourself by now? After the attack? After you saved Leum's life? After a week of building this stupid barricade without even a peep of complaint?

Okay, so maybe you don't always show up on time. And maybe you take longer breaks than everybody else. And maybe you're not as fast or precise as the others.

But you're still here, aren't you? That ought to count for something.

Anyway, you're still determined to prove yourself, and you know you can't do that by whining about your mistreatment, so you keep your mouth shut. (It's what any of the others would do.) You don't talk to them about anything, not even your dreams of the attack—

The furor of it—

The confusion and commotion of it—

The other kindlings scrambling around you, racing through the darkness—

Then a fire inside of you—

A flash of light—

Hope's face twisting in horror and pain—

Then you wake, and it's morning. Gray light in the shutters, songbirds rustling in the thickets. Someone else is already up. Leum, you think. You recognize her heavy tread, Burk's nails clicking on the cabin floor.

You wonder where they're going this early in the morning, what they're doing in the dim light before dawn.

(You're always the last to get up, so you don't know what any of the others do before then. Let's be honest, you'd always kind of assumed they slept in as long as possible, like you.)

You lie still, biting your lip, while they pad across the room. A door opening. A breath of air. As soon as you know they've gone, you get up, pulling on your clothes and sliding groggily into your sandals, and trot after them. You follow them at a distance, through the square and over the wooden bridge to the north road—

The river singing in the meadow—

Clear water over stones—

Across from the wild rye, they duck into the woods, heading over low ferns and fallen logs until they reach a round cap of granite peeking through the pointed canopy. Pawing at the earth, Burk lies down beneath the branches of a pinyon pine while Leum removes the wrap from her sword, her face lit by the blazing amaranth of her balar crystal—

A dark and vibrant color, like raspberries and blood.

As the sky lightens, she swings the sword a few times, as if getting reacquainted with its weight. Then, with the sun cresting the ridgeline, she starts running through her forms. Thrusting, spinning, slicing. Her movements are quick; her stances, firm. She makes it look easy, though even at this distance you can hear her grunting with the force of every strike.

Slashing, parrying. Again and again while the mist rises from the river and dawn crawls across the valley, and soon it's light enough for you to see the way she continues to adjust her breathing, her footwork, little by little, every repetition bringing her closer to perfection.

You want to ask her how she does it. You want to ask her for her help. You want to have a mentor, a real mentor, not like the Swordmaster (who, let's be honest, treated you more like a servant than an apprentice), but a *real* teacher. Someone to show you all the things you missed when the war ended, who can teach you how to fight like a kindling, how to live by the code.

But every time you ask her, Leum tells you no, tells you to get lost, rejects you over and over and over again, and you're tired of being rejected, so you bite your tongue and slink away before she's done.

You follow her the next morning and again the next. You continue to observe her from a distance, and you aren't caught except one time when Ket creeps up behind you while you're putting on your sandals. Her cheek creased from her pillow, her hair mussed with sleep. "What's Leum going to say when she finds out you're spying on her?" she whispers.

You slide open the door. "She's not going to say anything, because no one's going to tell her." Then you glance back at her, unsure. "Right?"

Ket lets out a soft laugh. "Do I look like a snitch? I'm just saying, you've got to be careful, or she's going to find out."

"I'm always careful."

Which isn't exactly true, but it's true enough. You're sneakier now than you used to be; you learned it from watching Ben.

But there's only so much you can learn by observing the others. Ben and her stealth. Leum and her sword. You have to practice if you're going to get better. (And you're determined to get better.) So that afternoon when the Camassian cooks arrive with the midday meal, you shoulder your weapon. You glance toward the river.

From up here, you can see the progress they've made toward flooding the farmyard: the water temporarily diverted through a series of ditches, a few logs (which you helped cut) laid across the riverbed for the base of the dam. That's where Leum is now, piling mud onto the foundations while on the shore Burk sleeps peacefully.

Good. Leum's not watching you. In fact, no one is. No one really cares what you do during your lunch break. Ket and Emara make friends with the farmers, regaling them with travel stories that may or may not be true. Kanver sleeps in one of the haylofts while the village kids race about the farmyard with their tiny blunt-ended spears.

Part of you wishes you could join them. You could show them how to wield their makeshift weapons. You could lead them, leaping and dashing, through the corrals.

But you're not a child, and you're certainly not a farmer's child. Such things are beneath you—

(Even if they look like fun.)

Anyway, you have better things to do. It's too far to the granite cap where Leum trains in the mornings, but you find yourself a rocky promontory on the western slope, hidden enough among the pines that no one can see you from the meadow but close enough that you won't be late when the afternoon shift starts—

Though, as it turns out, you often are—

So absorbed are you in re-creating Leum's movements (jabbing, cutting, skirmishing with countless invisible enemies) that you usually lose track of time, and the only thing that calls you back is Emara shouting from the south road, "Piggyyyyy! Where are you, Piggyyyyy?"

Then you rewrap your weapon and race back down the hill, and when you arrive, you're panting and drenched in sweat, and everyone looks at you like you're just an annoying kid, no more crucial to the preparations than any of the farm children—

But it's working. Day after day, you feel yourself getting stronger, more skilled. You're still nowhere near as good as Leum is, but you feel it in your muscles, your lungs, your limbs.

You're improving.

"What are you doing?" someone snaps from behind you.

Startled, you spin around to find Leum climbing over the lip of your promontory, advancing quickly.

You back away from her, loose pebbles shifting under your feet. "N-nothing!"

"Doesn't look like nothing."

Guiltily, you glance down at your sword. Its blush-colored crystal. Its gleaming length of blade. You almost consider trying to conceal it behind your back, but it's much too big for that. (Besides, you've already been caught. No use trying to hide it now.)

"How'd you know where to find me?" you ask.

"I needed an extra set of hands for the dam this afternoon. Ket said you'd be up here." Leum crosses her arms, scowling at you. "You've been following me."

You gape at her. "You knew? Since when?"

Does that mean she was okay with you watching her? Does that mean she *wanted* you to watch her? She *wanted* you to learn? She *was* teaching you, all this time? In her own way?

"Since now," she says.

"What do you—"

"You think I don't recognize the drills I run every morning?"

"Oh." You try to swallow your disappointment. She wasn't secretly training you after all. You look down at your feet. "I wanted to learn, and I didn't think you'd teach me."

"You were right."

She turns to go, but you don't want her to leave yet. Don't want to give up hope yet. "Why won't you?" you ask, planting yourself in front of her. "It's not like I can't learn."

"Maybe I don't want you to learn."

"Why not?"

She grimaces, and when she speaks, it's with more gentleness than you've ever heard from her: "Maybe I'm trying to protect you."

That makes you madder than if she'd yelled at you. You could've taken her yelling at you. (You've taken it before.) But you don't want her to be gentle with you, like you're fragile, like you're a child. *You* saved her, didn't you? In the attack?

(Though you don't like to think about the attack, because whenever you think about the attack, you think about Hope's arm falling from her body, you think about her wailing in the grass—)

No. You're *not* going to think about that. "Protect me?" you scoff. "From what?"

"From being one of us."

"But that's exactly what I want!"

"Only because you don't know what it's like!"

"Then tell me!" You stick out your chin. "Teach me! Please."

For a moment, she looks pained, almost sorry, but you don't want her to feel sorry for you. "I can't," she says.

You want to protest again. You want to pout. You want to scream and stamp your foot and argue with her, but you can't. Over two weeks with these kindlings, and you still don't understand them. Can't understand them. Can't even imagine, really, the things they've done, the things they're running from. Things that make Emara scream at night. Things that make Kanver drink. And that's the worst part of it, you think. That they still won't share these things with you, won't let you carry them, even though you're pretty sure you could. You could carry them, you could share them, and maybe those things, whatever they are, would weigh a little less.

You can feel your eyes burning, but you don't want Leum to see you cry, don't want her to think any less of you than she already does, so you take your sword and race down the hillside, slipping on loose rocks and skidding in the mulch. At the meadow, Emara tries to hail you, but you don't want her to ask you what happened, don't want her to sling her arm around your shoulders and call you Piggy while the farmers stand around and laugh.

You run back to the village, up the steps and to the cabin, where you plan to curl up and wait for the day to be over, but when you slide open the door you find Amity sitting by the window, her hair uncovered, with a burnished mirror in her lap.

"Amity?" You're surprised to see her. She's supposed to be in the farmyard today, training the villagers to use their wooden spears.

Quickly, she flips her scarf over her head, loops the end around her throat. "Siddie," she says, turning to face you. "Shouldn't you be helping with the barricade?"

"I just needed a break, I guess."

Amity stands, tucking the mirror into her robe with her careful, bony hands. She's thinner than she was when you met her, you notice. More fragile. She keeps blaming it on the elevation, but no one else is showing signs of altitude sickness this long into your stay. "From what?" she asks.

You start wrapping the hilt of your sword again, covering the crystal little by little. "From everyone."

"But Leum in particular, perhaps?"

"How'd you know?"

Amity clears her throat a few times. "She cares about you, you know."

"She has a funny way of showing it."

"It might be the only way she knows how."

You make a face. Like the Swordmaster, Amity has a knack for telling truths you don't want to hear. A lot about Amity reminds you of the Swordmaster, actually. Her rigor, her ruthlessness, her unexpected frailty—

You cock your head at her. "Is everything okay?"

"Everything's fine," she says, but her smile is strained. "Why don't you go back to work now, Siddie?"

She's lying. You don't know how you know it, but you do. She's hiding something from you, just like the others.

Amity sighs, or she tries to, but the air won't come out right. It gets caught in her windpipe, somehow, snarls up there like a knot. She coughs, doubling over, and all of a sudden you remember the Swordmaster—

The storm—

Lightning crashing, trees billowing overhead—

You remember the cave where you took shelter from the rain—

She was panting and shivering as the water dripped down her neck, her veins a bright balar red against her fevered skin—

Amity's cough finally subsides, leaving her gasping as she tries to stand, smoothing her scarf again over her neck—

You stare at her, open-mouthed.

She stares back.

And you know.

You *know*, and you wish you didn't, because you know now why the kindlings don't talk about some things, don't give them air, don't let them breathe—

They don't want them to be real.

These memories, these nightmares, these fears—

These whispers, these rumors of disease, of the thing that takes you, no matter how strong you are, no matter how skilled or capable or fearsome or magnificent—

Without another word, you duck out of the cabin.

Some things are too terrible to say.

EMARA

YOU'RE JUST OVER TWO WEEKS INTO YOUR STAY IN Camas when something goes horribly wrong. Not in the "we're-under-attack-again" sense, but in the sense that you're halfway through your morning shift on the barricade when Ket suddenly steals away without a word to anyone, which leaves you and the rest of your team standing by the south road, staring at the empty length of meadow you need to blockade before nightfall, and you don't know how you're going to do it without someone to lead you.

It can't be Siddie. Siddie's been morose to the point of uselessness all morning, something nagging at her, though she won't tell you what. (Besides, Siddie's never been that useful to begin with.)

And it's not going to be you. You're Emara. You're Vedran. You're a loafer and a glutton and a slovenly southern layabout. You're not supposed to be trusted with something like this. That's why Amity put Ket in charge in the first place.

But you'll eat your own shoe if you have to be the one to tell Amity you've fallen behind on your plans. You're not going to prove them right about you.

You beckon to Siddie, who's halfheartedly stamping the earth around one of the new posts. "Hey, Piggy, did you see where Roamie ran off to?"

"Ket?" She looks around, confused, like she hadn't realized Ket was gone. Then she shrugs. "She's probably with Tana."

"Tana?" You chortle. You haven't had a good romp in the sheets since you came to the northlands. You're glad someone else gets to.

"They've been sneaking off together ever since they came back from the mountains. You want me to find her?"

"Nah. Let her have some fun, eh?" You clap Siddie on the shoulder. "It'll be just you and me today, Piggy."

"Lucky me."

"Lucky everybody! Tell you what, if we get through whatever Roamie and Queenie had planned for us today, we can all take off early. How does that sound, eh?"

Siddie appears unenthused, but the villagers cheer. You get them started on the next set of postholes. Your shovels sinking into the dirt. Upheavals of dead weeds and dry roots. Sharpened logs hefted onto your shoulders and lowered carefully into the earth.

Behind you, in the field below the village square, another group of farmers is building a set of makeshift pens to hold the livestock when the yard is flooded, and several others are already moving equipment out of the barns. According to Amity's calculations, the dam should be complete in another week, giving the river time to rise before Adren returns.

You don't know why, but you're surprised when you make it through most of the day's work before lunch. You said you were going to do it, of course, but it's not like you really believed it. (Truth be told, you don't believe half the things that come out of your own mouth.)

You and the villagers settle down in the grass while the heat dries the sweat on your backs. You like the easiness of it. The murmured conversations, the sudden bursts of laughter, the way the food is passed among you, hand to hand to hand.

Strangely enough, it reminds you of basic training. Backbreaking marches, water stops in the shade. Jokes made, gourds passed, thirst slaked. All of you dehydrated, exhausted, suffering. All of it shared.

Per usual, Siddie tries to skulk off by herself, but you lose half an hour every afternoon trying to call her back from the western slope, trying to stop her from doing whatever she's been doing up there, and with Ket gone today, that's half an hour you can't afford to lose.

You're not going to be the one caught slacking.

You're not going to be the reason the barricade isn't complete.

You spring to your feet. You chase Siddie down before she reaches the woods, slinging your arm around her shoulders and tightening your grip when she tries to wriggle away. "Where are you off to, Piggy?" You guide her back to the others, lounging in the shade of the lumber pile. "You sneaking off for a tryst in the woods too?"

The villagers laugh.

"No," Siddie mutters.

She tries to shrug you off again, but you pull her closer. "Then why don't you stick around today, eh? I could use someone to keep these farmers in line."

"Keep *us* in line?" Hemmen guffaws into his lunch. "Unlike *some* people, we all showed up for work today."

"Eh, we all showed up." You wink at him. "We just didn't all stick around. Right, Piggy?"

She finally ducks out from under your arm. "My name is *Siddie*."

"Yeah, but you're a piggy, aren't you?"

She gives you a look like she doesn't know what you're talking about, which, come to think of it, maybe she doesn't. Maybe the Amerandines never nicknamed their trainees the way you did, pranked them and harassed them and ultimately welcomed them into the fold the way you did.

"Like pig iron, eh? The stuff used to make steel?" You plop a millet cake into her hand and gesture for her to sit with the others. "That's what you call a kindling before they've been tested on the battlefield."

"Huh?"

Scooping up your bowl, you shovel some of your meal into your mouth before you continue, still chewing. "You're a piggy until you make it through your first combat mission, and after that you get to be called whatever you want, eh? You throw a big party? Everyone chants your name? You're telling me you didn't do that in the north?"

She prods at her lunch. "I guess I wouldn't know."

"It's a whole rite of passage in Vedra."

"Oh."

Hemmen snickers. "That's not what we mean when we call someone piggy." He pushes up his nose with his forefinger, makes a snorting sound in his throat.

Siddie's face reddens.

You flick a wad of millet cake at him, spattering his cheek. "Well, you're not a kindling, Hemmy," you say as he wipes it off, sucks the slop from his thumb. The others laugh, and for the first time that day, Siddie cracks a smile. "You don't get to call her that, eh?"

Ket's back at the barricade the next morning, and you don't say anything to Amity about her absence because you're no snitch, and who are you to stop someone from having a little fun? You're getting the work done, aren't you? Post after post, yard after yard. Maybe Ket slips away for an hour here or there, but you don't mind taking the lead—

Actually, you kind of like it, kind of like being responsible for everyone, for their labor and safety and well-being, though of course you'd never admit it—

(You don't want to ruin your reputation as a slacker or anything.)

Besides, Siddie listens to you better anyway. After the first time Ket ditched out on you, Siddie starts pulling her weight. Digging holes, levering logs into place. You tell her she's got to build up her back muscles if she wants to improve her form.

Can't be a swordmaster if you can't hold your weapon straight, eh?

She redoubles her efforts. Sore shoulders, blistered palms.

After a few days of this, you're even ahead of schedule, the barricade stretching across nearly half of the meadow as the dam below nears completion, and when Amity comes to survey your progress, you can't help but imagine she's impressed, though of course she hardly shows it.

An arch to her eyebrow.

A curve to her lips.

She clears her throat a couple times before she speaks, like the words somehow pain her. "I can't say I'm not surprised. I didn't think you had it in you."

You put your hand to your ear. You've never had the admiration of an Amerandine Deathbringer before, and you don't know if you'll ever get it again, so you're determined to milk it for everything it's worth. "C'mon. Would it kill you to compliment me, Queenie?"

She smiles thinly. (But she *does* smile.) "Nice work, Emara."

You preen.

Siddie averts her gaze, kicking moodily at a tussock of grass, though you don't know why. (She should be as eager for Amity's praise as you are.) But your mother always said no amount of pulling makes the tide come in, so you don't call Siddie back when she slinks away.

Since seeing you hit Hemmen with the millet cake (fast and accurate, as befits a kindling), the farmers teach you a betting game called pitch-cup, which, as the name implies, involves several players pitching stones into a wooden cup. You're pretty good at it, winning a few kidam, a coil of rope, and a horsehair bracelet that way—

(You also lose two han, a pretty piece of quartz, and a carved wooden bowl you stole from some trader down south, but who's counting?)

Siddie doesn't participate, but at least she's not off pouting in the woods anymore. She starts saving you stones from the digging, smooth and round. She starts refilling your water gourd without you asking, setting aside choice bits of meat from the stewpot, saving you the best spots in the shade.

She takes to following you around in the evenings too, like a kid sister, although you never had a kid sister—

Don't remember one from Livia—

Just you and your mother, your aunts and older cousins—

Siddie's what you imagine a kid sister would be like, a little annoying and always underfoot, but you don't mind. You like having someone to boss around. To fetch your dinner, to fold your laundry, to clear the cobwebs from the cabin (although *technically* you're supposed to be doing it), leaving one in place for luck—

She begs you to train her, which you refuse because you're no expert in swordsmanship or anything, but then you catch her swinging her blade in the garden one night after dinner, and even you can see her form is bad enough that she's going to hurt herself if she keeps it up, so you stride over to her, shouting at her to widen her stance, to keep her back straight.

Ben, who normally spends her evenings in the garden with you, watches, but she doesn't join in. As far as you can tell, she's been avoiding anything that reminds her of the attack. She actually seemed relieved when Amity took over weapons training with the villagers. Preferred to dig in the mud with Leum and Kanver.

After that, you spend your days working on the barricade and your evenings with Siddie and Ben. It's odd. You thought this month was going to be a waste. You thought you were going to fritter away all the weeks you could have spent searching for the next wrap, the next Chenyaran wrap, some sign of your family and what happened to them during the obliteration of the Vedran Empire. You thought you were going to squander your days trying to please a bunch of northerners who don't like you, don't trust you, even despise you for what you did in the war.

And maybe you are. (Because Leum certainly still hates you.) But you don't have to see Leum except early in the morning and late at night, and even then you both go out of your way to avoid each other, so it works. (Kind of.) The rest of the time you spend with people who actually seem to like you, and with them, you find you're almost at ease—

The hard work, the shared aches and pains, the jokes no one else understands because they weren't there when Siddie sat on that anthill or Ket strung up Hemmen's clothes in the wild rye because he sealed her toiletries in wax and left them in the dung heap—

For the first time since the war ended, you find you're almost comfortable. You find you almost fit.

One night, Siddie takes up her usual stance in the garden, swinging her sword like she's Callula-on-the-Mountain or something, outnumbered by hundreds of snarling enemies. She's improved a lot since you saw her take Hope's arm off that night, but every so often her arms start flailing, every so often her legs go akimbo.

You nudge Ben in the ribs. "Look at that, Knifey. What does she think she's doing? Dancing?"

Siddie pauses only long enough to stick her tongue out at you.

You don't expect Ben to say anything, because mostly you do the talking while she stands there stoically, so you're surprised when she cocks her head at Siddie, studying her form, and adds, "Keep your shoulders down."

With a quick glance at Ben, Siddie tries to adjust.

"Knifey's right." Taking up a stick, you prod at her upper back. "No hunching."

"I'm not hunching!"

"You are." You swat at her (lightly, of course). "If you weren't, that sword would be easier to swing, eh?"

While she attempts the lunge again, you sidle up to Ben. "You sure you want to help with this, Knifey? What if I'm turning her into a monster, eh?"

Ben's expression creases with guilt. She hasn't said anything more about killing Hope and the others, though you've seen her struggling with it occasionally—

The trembling of her fingers—

The emptiness of her gaze—

She disappears the way Kanver does, the way you do in your dreams, out of the present and into the worst parts of her past.

"I don't know." Ben sighs. "I can't stop her from wanting this, but maybe I can try to keep her alive."

You study the village in the dying light: the golden-thatched houses, the animals milling in the farmyard, Parker crossing the road to Ferra's house with a basket of summer berries. You nudge Ben with your elbow. "That's what it always comes down to, eh? Trying to keep each other alive?"

"I guess." The tips of her fingers start twitching, and she jams them into her armpits to make them go still. "But I wish we didn't have to."

You swing the stick back and forth a few times, listening to its soothing *swish-swish*. "Me too."

With another sigh, Ben moves to adjust Siddie's elbow. "Keep practicing," she says. "You'll get it."

"Yeah." You tap Siddie's leg more times than you probably need to. "And don't forget your stance, eh?"

She scowls at both of you, but she obediently lowers her elbow, she obediently bends her knees.

Inside the cabin, Amity starts coughing. Her cough's gotten worse lately. You wonder if she's caught something, some late summer chill.

Siddie only makes it through a few more drills before she lets her sword fall to her side. "I'm sorry," she says. "I'm not getting it."

Ben pats her on the shoulder. "We'll do it again tomorrow. And the day after that." Tipping one of the stumps near the firepit onto its side, she rolls it toward the west edge of the garden and sets it upright against the slope. Then, after ducking briefly into the cabin, she returns again with her knives.

Thunk! A blade buries itself in the bark.

Drawing another knife, she throws again.

"Whoa. Hey, Piggy, did you see—" You reach out, trying to tap Siddie on the shoulder, but when you turn to find her, she's sitting at the edge of the garden, and she's not looking at Ben at all.

Glumly, she sheathes her weapon, wraps the cloth around the hilt.

"Cheer up, Piggy." You plop down beside her. "Maybe it doesn't seem like it, but you're getting better every day."

(Mostly, anyway.)

"It's not that."

"Then what's wrong with you, eh?"

She glances toward the cabin, as if to make sure no one's watching, but there's no movement in the windows, no sound except for Amity clearing her throat.

All of a sudden, Siddie's eyes well with tears, which is alarming, because ever since you took her under your wing, you've teased her and badgered her and ordered her around, but you haven't made her *cry*. (You're not Leum, for gods' sakes.)

But her tears don't fall, so you're still better than Leum, if only just. While you wait for an answer, Siddie wrings her hands and sneaks another glance at the cabin, shaking her head, and when she looks back at you, her eyes are still wet. "Can I tell you a secret?" she whispers.

AMITY

YOU HAVEN'T SHARED YOUR QUARTERS WITH ANY-
one since your third year at the Academy, so you were dreading
the cramped accommodations the Camassians offered you here. You
thought you'd chafe at such closeness, thought you'd crave quiet and
solitude, but to your surprise you've come to enjoy these evenings
with your kin. Now you find yourself comforted by the sounds of
Emara and Siddie speaking softly in the garden, the regular *thunk!*
thunk! of Ben sinking knives into a log. (You're particularly pleased
to know she's taken up throwing again. Since the attack, you'd been
concerned that she was losing her edge.)

Having finished the dishes, Ket's slipped away (likely to see Tana,
which is an affair you've no interest in, provided it doesn't distract
from their duties), and Kanver is sitting near the fire, polishing the
rust from their glaive. Across the room, you and Leum are gathered
on the floor with a map of the village laid out between you—

All the roads, the gardens, the slope-roofed houses. All the sheds
and stables and animal pens. All the lives you're supposed to defend—

You shiver, despite the heat of the fire. There's a new chill in the
air as the days have grown shorter. Autumn is already upon you—

And Adren is approaching.

You can almost feel her beyond the horizon, creeping over the
landscape like a fire.

Another week, and the battle will be here.

You take up a brush, marking off the progress you've made on the defenses. Nearly three weeks in, and all the livestock have been transferred to their pens in the south meadow, all the stores removed to higher elevations throughout the village. Leum, Kanver, and Ben packed the last of the mud onto the dam this afternoon, so tomorrow when they fill in the diversion ditches, the river will rise. The farmyard will flood. The corral, the sheds, the henhouses, soon all of them will be under a foot or two of water, seeping into the foundations.

When the battle comes, it will have to be swift, for none of your fortifications are meant to be permanent. The dam will have to be broken before the ground freezes and the farmyard rots. The south road will have to be reopened so the harvest can be sold in Windfall. The bridge, though not yet dismantled, will have to be rebuilt.

It's all temporary.

Fleeting.

There and gone.

As you study the map, your vision blurs. Bright light, a faintness in your limbs. Dropping the brush, you shake your head—

It's all that sun from training villagers in the farmyard, or perhaps a lack of sleep. You've had a difficult time lying still lately. Your mind spinning, your skin tingling. Nerves, you think, although you've never suffered from nerves before, never doubted, didn't have to, you were always so self-assured—

Leum gets to her feet to fetch you a water gourd. "Drink."

You take it from her. Sip gingerly, wincing at the burn in your throat. Dust and dry air, or so you tell yourself. "Once the field is flooded, we'll shift your team to building guard posts along the gully," you say, trying not to cough. "After that, we'll start on the br—"

But before you can continue, Emara storms in from the garden. The door slamming open, the wind gusting inside.

On the floor, the map flutters like an injured butterfly.

"You didn't tell us?" Emara lunges at you, not even bothering to remove her sandals. "How could you not tell us?"

You freeze—

Which for you is unheard of. You've never frozen before. Didn't even know you could. Thought you had it drilled out of you when you were young—

You're supposed to act, Amity. You're supposed to take charge. You're a kindling. You're a *Deathbringer*. Where are your instincts? Where is your fight?

But you let her come at you.

She knows.

It's Leum who stops Emara, barreling into her, wrestling her back. "Get away from her. What's the matter with you?"

Emara bats her away, still shouting at you. "Did you tell her? Does she know?"

"Know what?" Leum tries to shove her again, but Kanver catches Leum's elbow.

"Hang on," they murmur. "Just wait."

Emara wipes her eyes angrily, jabs a finger at you. "Why didn't you tell us?"

Behind her, Ben and Siddie appear in the doorway. Ben looks confused, but Siddie won't meet your gaze as she wrings the cuff of her robe in her hands.

Ah, Siddie.

"That's enough," you croak. Slowly, you get to your feet. Your aching head, your weary bones. You try not to let it show.

You lower your hood, and for the first time you allow the others to see the red lines snaking up your throat. They're brushing your jaw now, and the hollows behind your ears. You wouldn't have been able to hide behind your scarf much longer, but you wanted those extra weeks—

You hoped you could make it a few extra weeks—

Through the battle, through victory—

Until you were forced to reveal the truth—

You're dying.

You're burning out. During the war, a third of us died this way. Our veins turning red. Our bodies betraying us to weakness and trembling. Our magic stuttering out when we least expected it. Once it began, the condition was irreversible. We were discharged at the first sign of symptoms, deemed too unreliable for battle.

(To have kept using us would've cost too many lives, you see.)

And we accepted that. It was an honor to die like that, in the sick houses, or wherever we went when they took us off the battlefield.

But we're not supposed to die like that now.

"How long have you known?" Emara demands. "Two months? Three?"

"Five." You try to keep your voice level, but this time you can't stop yourself from coughing. The dry rasp. The ache for breath. "It's why I left the capital," you gasp.

A year and a half after the war ended, and your fate finally caught up to you. A fine web of balar red on your ribs, like lace. You don't know how long it had been killing you before that, the disease gnawing quietly at your insides for months, for years—

Slowly, slowly—

Death by inches—

Death by minutes—

"And you didn't tell us?" Emara knocks over the empty cooking pot, sending it clattering across the floor.

You lift an eyebrow. You try to appear haughty, though you're afraid you only appear weak. "Would it have made a difference?"

"Yes!" Emara upends the kettle, rips the drying clothes from the rafters. "You should've been honest, Queenie! You should've told us everything from the start! Who do you think you are, keeping something like this from us?"

Siddie stops her from throwing a set of bowls against the wall. "She didn't want to worry us!"

"What do you know about it?" Leum snaps.

Siddie swallows, suddenly self-conscious again, fidgeting with her sleeve. "My old master burned out last year. I recognized the symptoms, but not until—"

"So you knew?" Leum advances on her. Hard footsteps, balled fists. "And you didn't tell us?"

Emara intercepts her. "Leave her alone, Grumpy. It's not her fault you didn't see it yourself."

Leum scowls, and for a moment you think she'll push her again, but instead she retreats.

That shocks you more than anything. You didn't think she had the ability to retreat, thought she only knew how to charge. Always forward, like a true vanguardian.

But she crosses her arms and joins Kanver by the fire.

"How long do you have left?" Ben asks from the doorway.

You shrug. An ominous twinge in your neck and shoulder, but you pretend it's nothing. "I'll be gone before winter."

Silence.

Even you're shocked by the sound of it, so final, like a rock sinking into a still lake.

Gone before winter.

And it's already fall.

Emara strikes the side of the cabin with her fist. The walls shuddering. Her knuckles bleeding. With a squeak, Siddie runs for the water and bandages, but Emara waves her away.

Drops of blood spatter the floor—

Balar red.

Leum stares at you, not with the fiery scowl you've all become accustomed to but with a cold disavowal, a deadness in her gaze. "Did you ever think we were going to make it out of this alive?" she asks. "Or was victory the only thing that mattered to you?"

You want to reply, *Of course it was.*

Victory is the only thing that matters, the only thing that has ever mattered. It's the purpose you were trained for. It's the reason you exist.

Three weeks ago, you wouldn't have hesitated to tell her precisely that.

But how can you say that to her now? That her life doesn't matter? That none of their lives matter?

More importantly, how can you believe it? Now, when you know them? When you've come to understand them? Learned their wants and wishes, their hopes and worries and wounds?

(Now, when you love them?)

By the door, Ben stares at you warily. Her mouth is drawn; her eyes, red-rimmed. She doesn't look at all like the sideshow entertainer you met in Windfall. (Stoic and self-possessed.) She looks like a girl, just a girl, scared and weary and thin.

She backs out of the cabin, disappearing into the shadows, and she doesn't come back when you call, "Ben, wait!"

You almost start after her, but you're halted by the sounds of footsteps coming up the flagstone path—

Ferra and Parker. They burst into the cabin, brandishing their spears. (Under other circumstances, you would've been proud of their nimble stances, their ready weapons. You've done a good job training them.)

"What happened?"

"We heard the noise from below!"

"Are we under attack?"

No one answers. Leum and Kanver look to each other. Siddie

stands there with the bandages in her hands. Emara shoulders past the villagers, kicking over a stool on her way out the door.

"Amity." Ferra points at you, at your neck, at your veins of balar red. "What *is* that?"

The rest of your kindred disperse before Onna and the Old Man arrive at the cabin. To be honest, you don't know if you could've kept them there if you tried—

Which, of course, is why you didn't try—

Didn't want to test your leadership, didn't want to know if it would fail—

While you wait like a prisoner for your date with the judge, you see Ket through the windows, returning from her nighttime tryst, but she's intercepted by Leum and Kanver. You hear their lowered voices. You see Ket's startled expression—

Her anguish, plainly written across her face—

Then Onna and the Old Man enter the cabin, and when you look to the window again, Ket's gone.

You sigh. Though you don't want to, you go over it all again. How you're burning out. What burnout is. The fact that you're dying.

"Just you?" the Old Man asks. "What about the rest of them?"

"They're fine."

"Fine as in not dying? What about with you lying to them?" he demands. "Are they even going to stick around after this?"

You stare at your hands, feeling like a child chastised by your elders and betters. A feeling you haven't had since you were nine years old.

(You still don't care for it.)

"I certainly hope so." You try to say it with a little dignity, but the truth is, you don't know. In the war, your commanders never told you everything. They couldn't. It was a strategic necessity, and you accepted that. You accepted that you were going to be used. You were a weapon to be deployed. You were a tool to be discarded. That was your destiny.

Come victory or come death, right?

But given the choice, you don't know if you'd follow a leader who lied to you. You don't know if you'd stay. Which means you don't know if you can still do this—

Without all your kindred on board, you don't know if you can still win.

Onna hasn't said much since you told her about your illness, but she speaks again now. Her voice low, her expression guarded. Unlike the Old Man, who's predictably concerned about the fate of the village, you can't tell what she's thinking. "How are you feeling?" she asks.

"Fine."

"It's a little late to be lying, don't you think?"

You cross your arms. Reluctantly, you relate your symptoms: the burning in your throat, the coughing spells, your occasional dizziness, the sleepless nights, the weakness in your limbs . . .

You know what comes next. Tremors. Fainting. Coughing blood. But you've been spared those, at least for the moment.

"How're you supposed to fight like that?" the Old Man asks.

"Hush now," Onna tells him. "Go fetch me my kit."

He glares at her. "You want me to walk all the way back down there? What about my knees?"

"They'll survive, and so will you. Go."

With a huff, he totters from the cabin, leaving you and Onna alone. You don't know what to say to her, so you allow the silence to fill the room. Silence, you've discovered, makes people uncomfortable, uncertain, prone to error and weakness.

Except this time it's you who's uncomfortable. It's you who's uncertain. You let your gaze drop to your hands, to the red veins appearing at your wrists. You would've had to start wearing gloves soon.

But despite your uneasiness, you remain as stubborn as ever. You still haven't spoken by the time the Old Man returns with a worn carrying case, emblazoned on the side with the sigil of the Queen Commander's army and the calendula flower of the medical corps.

"Your husband was a medic?" you ask.

Nodding, Onna kneels to open the case. As she lifts the lid, you smell the sharp odor of herbal tinctures, the mingled scents of healing salves.

The Old Man glares at you with his milky eyes. "Now what?"

"Now go to bed," Onna tells him. "It's late."

"What are you going to do about her?"

"That remains to be seen."

Dismissed for a second time, the Old Man leaves the cabin, grumbling under his breath. Meanwhile, Onna fetches the kettle. She fills it with water and sets it over the fire. "You should have told us sooner," she says finally.

"Why? So you could kick us out?" You can't keep the bitterness out of your voice. "You didn't want us here in the first place; this would've given you the excuse to renege."

She looks up from the sachets of herbs in her kit, regarding you thoughtfully, almost pityingly. "So we could take care of you," she says.

You don't respond. You don't know how to. You expected her to be angry, disappointed, even pragmatic, like the Old Man.

But you didn't expect kindness. You didn't expect compassion. You can't remember ever having had those. How could anyone treat you with compassion? How could anyone pretend to care for you when they kept sending you onto the battlefield to die?

To die quickly, by blade or balar burn?

Or slowly, from the inside?

How could anyone love you when every time you fought, you were killing yourself for them? Using yourself up for them?

For *their* safety?

For *their* future?

They thanked you, of course. They praised you. You were brave. You were saving them. You were doing the work they couldn't accomplish in their own time.

But they were never going to share that future with you.

Finally, you sit.

Selecting a few items from her kit, Onna steeps you an infusion of herbs and bark and seeds. You sip it gingerly, the liquid soothing on your throat, and give her a nod.

"Thanks," you croak.

"Think nothing of it," she says, returning the tiny pots and paper packets to their proper places. Then, smoothing her hands over her thighs, she looks to you and sighs. "Now, tell me about the others. Are they going to leave?"

"I don't know."

"Why didn't you tell them from the beginning?"

You want to say it was none of their business, but you're so tired now of your own posturing, your own arrogance and pomposity. "I didn't think they'd follow me," you say softly.

Onna sits back on her heels, gripping a glass bottle in her fist. "Do you think they should follow you now?"

You look down at your tea. The last of the steam drifting from the surface, a few stray flower petals floating beneath.

What have you done, Amity?

You gathered your kindred because you needed an army. No, you needed a win. One more victory before the end. You were so obsessed with your own mortality, your own legacy, that you didn't care what happened to them as long as you got to be glorious, important, resplendent once again.

You were using them. You were using them the way you were used. Without kindness, without compassion, without love.

Leum was right. You *did* bring them up here to die.

At last, you meet Onna's unswerving gaze. "I wouldn't," you say.

BEN

YOU HEAR AMITY CALLING YOU, BUT FOR THE SECOND
time in your life, you ignore your orders. You flee from the cabin
and into the woods, following the creek up the west slope. Granite
boulders, tumbled logs. You scramble through the forest until you
reach a clearing among the pines—

Ferns, moss, wet rocks where the spring seeps from the mountainside—

Drawing a knife, you fling it into the nearest tree trunk, the bark
hardly making a sound under the keen edge of your blade.

Three weeks ago, you would've been gratified. The clean entry.
The flawless arc. But it doesn't seem like enough now, does it? One
throw? One perfect throw?

For what?

With a flick of your wrist, you send another knife sailing into a
tree across the clearing.

Thunk!

You leap to the side, twisting in the air, and sink another blade
into a stump. *Thunk!* A rotten log. *Thunk!* A sapling no thicker than
your wrist. *Thunk!*

You don't stop. You can't stop. You have to keep practicing. You
have to be perfect. You jump and spin and dive, throw after throw
after throw, each blade going exactly where you want it to go—

The trees, the clumps of moss, the mushrooms emerging fanlike in the darkness—

Until all your sheaths are empty and you're forced to pause, panting and ankle-deep in the creek. Straightening, you survey your work.

It's perfect—

(But meaningless—)

You calm your breaths. You collect your knives, wipe them off and slide them back into their sheaths.

You thought this was a second chance. You thought that if only you fought well enough, if only you were perfect enough, you wouldn't have to lose any more of your kin. You'd be able to protect them. You'd be able to prove yourself.

But it doesn't matter how skilled you are now, how accomplished, how perfect. No matter what you do, you won't be able to keep Amity alive.

You can fight a lot of things, Ben, but you can't fight burnout.

Pulling your knives from your holster, you throw and throw again.

You're still practicing hours later when Leum comes to fetch you. Your hands trembling, sweat dripping into your eyes. You're so absorbed in it that you almost don't see her approaching, almost hit her, almost fling your knife through her eye socket and into her brain.

It's only your finely honed instincts that allow you to adjust at the last second, sending the blade past her ear instead.

Quickest reflexes in Kindar, not that it matters anymore.

Leum halts at the edge of the trees.

You double over. A stitch in your side. "What are you doing here?"

"The Camassians are gone," she says. "We can go back to the cabin now."

Wiping sweat from your chin, you yank one of your knives from a blackened log. "So you're just going back?"

"What else are we supposed to do? Leave?" When you don't answer, she lowers her head, scowling at you across the clearing. "The mission isn't over, Ben."

"The mission was a lie," you retort.

"So?"

"So why should we follow her when we can't trust her?"

(Not even to tell the truth?)

(Not even to stay alive?)

Leum crosses her arms. "What do you think is going to happen if we quit? Everyone we leave behind will die. The villagers we swore to protect will die. Amity will die."

You flinch, though you don't mean to. "Amity's dying anyway."

"It's the code."

"That was a lie too."

A lie they told us to make us obedient—

A lie they told us to make us into killers—

A lie they told us to make us believe that despite *everything*, we could still be good.

"Huh?"

You sheathe your blade. "I just don't know if I can do it anymore."

"Too bad," Leum snaps. "You're here now. You have to finish this." Then, unlooping something from her neck, she tosses it to you—

Shining, bright—

You snatch it out of the air.

"We still need you," she says.

Looking down, you open your fingers to find a tiny silver medallion winking in your palm. You glance back up at her, surprised. "You still have your Wind Runner medallion?"

We all got them when we arrived at the Academy, when we went from civilians to trainees. Even as we mourned the loss of our families, our friends, our neighbors and communities, those medallions made us feel special. They made us feel important.

We were *kindlings*—

Warriors—

Heroes, pledged to the service of something greater than ourselves—

(The last time you saw your own medallion, you were leaving it on a pillow like an apology.)

"I sold mine last year," Leum tells you. "This one belonged to my brother, Zan. He gave it to me just before he told me to leave him."

You prod the medallion with your forefinger. (It's warm with Leum's body heat.) "Why would he do that?"

"Because he was already lost, and he didn't want me to be lost too." She shrugs. "You seem like you need it more than I do now."

Then she stalks into the forest, leaving you alone in the clearing with your knives, scattered like shrapnel among the trees, the logs, the stumps. You turn the medallion in your fingers, but you don't put it on.

What are you doing out here, Ben? You don't know. You don't remember. Why did you come? You had everything you needed. Your horse, a guide and supplies. You had the chance to make it out of Amerand, to leave all this behind, and you didn't take it.

You should've taken it.

KANVER

NO ONE SPEAKS TO AMITY THE NEXT MORNING, AND
she doesn't try to speak to any of you either. Her flattened lips, her
downcast eyes, her veins vivid in the morning light. Usually, she'd
be checking in with each of you. Usually, she'd be giving you orders
before the work begins.

But today she lets you slip away without a word. (Her gaze out the
window, her hands folded in her lap.)

No one feels particularly industrious, but once you're out of the
cabin, Leum tells you you've still got a job to do. Defend the Camassians. Protect the village. Amity may have lied to get you here, but
the mission is the same.

And it's not like anyone has a better idea, so Emara, Ket, and
Siddie return to the barricade while you and Leum head to the river
to fill in the ditches—

Usually, Ben would be with you, but you haven't seen Ben all
morning, although her belongings are still in the cabin and her horse
is still here, so she's got to be around somewhere—

By now, the Camassians must have heard what's happening to
Amity. They must know, because you should be celebrating. You've
almost flooded the farmyard. You're almost done. But among you
the mood is subdued. The rasp of your shovels, the slop of the mud.
Not even Vander, normally nosier than a gossip in a gambling parlor,

wants to ask what's going on, how bad it really is.

You finish the work in silence, and then everyone drifts away. Maybe you should be doing something else, building guard posts or helping with the barricade, but what does it matter? It's not like anyone can scold you for shirking today.

Sometime in the afternoon, you wind up on the edge of the farmyard while the river overflows its banks. The rise of the water. The grasses undulating beneath the surface. Brook trout, surprised at their newfound space, darting open-mouthed through fences and barn doors.

Up the hill, the village children are racing through the gardens, ducking behind rocks and clambering into trees. Their high-pitched laughter, the patter of feet. Somewhere near the square, a young voice counts haphazardly down from fifty.

You remember this game. You and the little ones played it at the Academy, except you called it Mistwalker. One assassin. The rest of you targets. You were never very good at it, but you still enjoyed playing.

And it's fine . . . for a while. The kids climbing over the terraces, rustling in the berry hedges. The way they shriek when they're routed from their hiding places. The countdown beginning again. *Fifty, forty-nine, forty-seven, forty-eight . . .*

It's fine until you're walking back up the hill, and you're just walking, you don't expect it, you're walking and there's Poppy curled up at the base of a garden wall—

She's got her hands over her mouth to smother her giggles—

But she's not laughing—

And she's not Poppy—

She's not playing—

And you're not in Camas. The scent of black powder wafts over you (stinking, sulfurous). It's all you can smell. Not pine, not wild rye, not the livestock in their makeshift pens—

Just powder.

You smell it everywhere. On the wind. In the meadow. The only way you don't smell it is if you're drinking, and there's no reason not to anymore, it's not like there's anyone who can stop you anymore, so you drink. You break into one of the houses. You drink your fill. You drink more than your fill. You're drifting in it. For a while, you aren't back there anymore, and you aren't here either. You're nowhere. Sleep floods around you, cold and dark, and your eyes are closing, and then you're subsumed. Pleasantly nothing, nothing, nothing until—

"Kanver?"

A thin voice, high and worried. Big eyes like glass floats, bobbing in the water.

Siddie.

You want to cry.

You're not nothing anymore. You're not nowhere anymore. You're you, and you're here (awfully, terribly here), lying among the goats with an empty wine jug—

You're awake, and you remember.

It was a seaside town, and you loved seaside towns. You used to love seaside towns. They reminded you of that slim lens of time before the kindling collectors, the Academy, the war. The lemon sun, the blue blaze of the water. Gulls crying in the air and kelp drying on the beaches, the smell of brine and garbage, fishing nets encrusted with salt.

You remember being small. Your skinned knees, your chubby hands. Your mother, a diver. Not a face now in your memory, just a body, a strong body, brown limbs, the scent of the ocean, long ribbons of hair.

And your sister.

You had a sister, a tiny one. A year old, no more. Pem. That was her name. Pemma. She liked your necklace, you remember that. You had a necklace, given to you by your strong, brown-armed mother. A mussel shell, worn smooth, on a braided red cord. Pem was always sticking it in her mouth, sucking on it happily while you rocked her in your arms.

Then the kindling collectors arrived, as they always did, once every year to test the five-year-olds with their balar lodestone. The darkened room, the crystal blazing in your presence. The first of the stipends paid out to your mother, and then you were gone.

You weren't allowed to take anything when you left. Not even your clothes. You weren't Kanver from—

(Wherever it was you were from—)

(Whatever your town was called—)

You were Kanver, Kindling Trainee of House Kemera. You didn't have a mother. Or a sister. Or a necklace. You left them all behind.

You liked seaside towns. Until this one.

The war was almost over by then, but you had started drinking months ago. Loose and floating, the way you liked it. At the time, you were attached to a regiment that had orders to retake this little seaside town, just a little seaside town, occupied by some Vedran battalion with nowhere else to go, with nowhere left to run.

They had to have known the war was ending. They had to have known they didn't stand a chance.

They should have surrendered. It should've been easy. You were supposed to sit back, let the cannoneers do the fighting. A wall of fire and powder. *Boom boom boom.* No sense risking a kindling in this kind of battle. You were supposed to watch.

But the town.

The little town.

The lemon sun. The blue blaze of the water.

The Vedrans fought back. Buildings burning, civilians screaming, the cannons going *boom boom boom boom boom*—

And in the smoke, kindling magic. Flashes of pink and red and coral. The enemy had three kindlings, then. Three Vedran kindlings and no sign of surrender.

You and another of your kindred were sent in.

You don't remember the fighting so much as you remember the running. The burn in your legs. The smoke in your lungs. The scent of black powder everywhere, coating everything. Your nose, your throat, your tongue—

Maybe it was because of the smoke that you didn't recognize where you were at first, but you turned a corner, and you knew.

The diving harnesses. The fishing nets encrusted with salt.

You knew this town. Had almost forgotten it, but now that you were here, now that you were in it, you knew it well, knew it by heart, by smell, by footstep.

Home.

Home.

You ran, reeled back along the familiar streets like a fish on a line. This boathouse. That shop. These places appearing bright, bright, bright in your memory as their ruined facades emerged from the smoke.

Then the house—

Your house—

Your mother's house—

It was scorched but intact, and no one inside. You searched. Your voice calling, *Mama! Pem!* The old unused words warping in your throat.

You stumbled up the road, the once-familiar roads, searching.

Mama! Mama! Pem!

You found a body—

A small one—

Nine years old and no more. Up the road by a wooden fence, looking like she'd been running. A strong body, brown limbs—

•

She could've been asleep.

You wanted her to be asleep.

But who could sleep in that noise?

The roar, the clash, the cannon fire.

Who could sleep in that smell?

Sulfur and ash.

There was cannon shot in her chest and a mussel-shell necklace at her throat. Red cord. Red blood. Red as your magic. You hadn't seen her in years, but as soon as you saw her, you knew.

Pem.

Pem.

Your sister.

You had a sister.

You'll never have a sister again.

LEUM

YOU'RE ON THE NORTH EDGE OF THE VILLAGE, WHERE
you're trying to figure out where Ben and Amity wanted those guard
posts built along the gully, when Siddie finds you. "Leum!"

"Go away." You're in no mood for distractions. Amity lied to you.
Amity's *dying*. You should've known she was sick. You should've
seen it—

She should've told you—

She should've been honest with you from the beginning, before
you said yes, before you came all the way out here, before you allowed
yourself to believe you could have this again. A purpose, a mission,
all of you together, and who knows how long it could've lasted?

Months?

Years?

Decades?

You deserved to know, didn't you?

Now everyone's uneasy. The villagers are nervous. Ben's still
missing in action, and Kanver's wandered off somewhere (probably
playing Mistwalker with the children or getting lost in the wild rye
again). You've got to focus. You've got to keep things on course.

But Siddie won't be deterred. "Come quick!" she says. "It's
Kanver!"

And she doesn't need to say more than that to get you to follow her. With Burk at your heels, you trail Siddie along the edge of the flooded farmyard to the south meadow. Near the road, you can see Ket and the rest of the barricade team levering logs into the ground, but Siddie doesn't take you toward the barricade. Instead, she motions you through the makeshift livestock pens, past the horses and pigs, and that's when you hear it.

Ohh-oh-ohhh . . .

Someone's singing the lullaby, but it's not Kanver. The voice is too fluid, too smooth, like coins chiming into a very deep well.

Ohhh-oh-ohhh . . .

It's Emara. There, in one of the storage sheds, you find her kneeling over Kanver's unconscious form.

Kanver's been drinking. (You knew they'd been drinking as soon as Siddie said their name.) You can smell it over the heady odors of dung and hay.

"How do you know that song?" you say.

Emara glances over her shoulder, tucks her hair behind her ear. "How do *you* know it?"

"We all do."

A sad smile dimples her expression. "I guess maybe we're not so different after all, eh?"

You glare at her. Of course you're different. You're enemies. But when you don't answer, it makes it seem like you agree, so you round on Siddie. "Who else knows about this?"

"N–no one!" Her broken speech, her backward steps.

You keep advancing. "Not even Amity?"

"To hell with Amity," Emara scoffs.

That halts you in your tracks. You never thought you'd side with Emara on anything, but in this case she's right.

To hell with Amity.

You grunt. You kick at a discarded wine jug, upended nearby. "Where'd they get this?"

Sighing, Emara smooths the hair from Kanver's forehead. "I don't know."

You frown. You're grateful she's taking care of Kanver. It's what you would've done if you'd found them first. But you hate it, and you hate having to be grateful for her too. It makes you feel like you owe her, and you don't want to owe her more than you already do.

"Did someone give it to them?" you ask.

"Doubtful. Everyone knows they're not supposed to be drinking."

"Then they stole it." For a second, you're torn. You want to sit with Kanver. You want to clean them up, but you can't stay here when you know somewhere out there someone's going to find evidence of Kanver's crimes. Broken shutters, shattered crockery, stolen wine—

And everyone already so on edge—

Would Onna kick you out for this? After Amity? After Kanver fell asleep during the attack?

You start for the shed door. "I'm going to find out what happened. I'm going to make sure no one says anything."

"Hold up, Grumpy." Emara stands, scooping up the jug with one hand. "I'll do it."

You scowl at her. "You?"

"Yeah. If Moony did any damage getting this, someone's got to smooth things over, eh?"

"I can do that."

"Er . . . can you?"

You cross your arms. "What does that mean?"

"No offense, but people like me better than you."

"I don't like you."

"Well, you don't like anyone."

You can't argue with her there. The only person you like is lying on the ground at your feet.

"Piggy, get back to the barricade," Emara says. "Make up an excuse, eh?"

Siddie blinks. "You mean lie?"

"Make it a good one. We're going to be gone a while." Emara steps past you. Then, clapping you on the back, says, "Don't worry, Grumpy. I'll take care of it."

You're unconvinced, but you have no choice at this point, so you don't protest when Emara and Siddie run off without you. You check Kanver's sleeping form, wipe a smudge from their cheek. You fetch them some water, a change of clothes.

When you return, Kanver's awake. Confused and small, like a grounded fledgling. They blink up at you blearily. "Leum?"

"Kannie," you say. Their name, a sigh. "What happened?"

They try to ignore you. They try to turn over, and that's when you notice the straw is wet. Their clothes, between their legs, clammy and cold—

A sour smell—

Oh, Kanver.

Their mouth opens. A small cry, wordless and mewling. Fingers plucking feebly at their robes.

You kneel beside them. Gently, you strip off their soiled clothes, clean away the damp straw, mop them up while they cry. Tears forming at the corners of their eyes.

You dress them. You bundle them in a blanket.

"I'm sorry," they say, wet-mouthed and ashamed.

"It's fine."

"I messed up, Leum."

"What happened?"

And they tell you about their dreams, not the ones at night but their waking dreams, the ones where they can't tell where they are anymore, unmoored in time and place, flickering back and forth between the past and the present, between here and the war.

Pem.

Pem.

You remember the name from the Academy, one of those things Kanver used to tell you while you were trying to sleep at night.

Pem.

Kanver's little sister, killed by cannon fire.

"Damn it," you say.

Kanver closes their eyes. They swallow and swallow. "They made up a name for it, you know," they say. "Friendly fire."

You curse. "We've got to get out of here, Kannie."

You've been in Camas nearly a month now. Spent some time with your kin, and that was fine and familiar, but soon the battle will be over. Soon you'll have your spoils. You'll make enough coin for two horses, double the supplies. It might cost more than you expected, but you'll still only need one guide—

"We're going to get out of here." Cradling their head, you make them drink from your water gourd, a few sips at a time. "It'll be you and me, together, wandering the countryside, fighting the fights that need to be fought. We'll be proper kindlings again, living up to the old ways."

They lick their lips. "Except the old ways were bad."

"What?"

"The honor you like to talk about? The kinship? The glory? It was all lies." They look up at you, plaintively, like they're begging you to understand. "We were kids, Leum. We're still kids, or at least we're supposed to be, but they made us into something else."

You make a face. "You sound like Ben."

"Well, maybe Ben's right. We killed people. Do you ever think about how many people we killed?"

"They were enemies—"

"Like Emara? Emara's not our enemy."

You don't mean to, but you look toward the door, like at any second Emara will appear, grinning and waggling her eyebrows and boasting how she covered for Kanver, how it took a little bit of bribery, but a little bit of bribery never hurt anyone, eh?

"And we were killed too," Kanver continues. "Even when we weren't actually dying, they were killing us, little by little, every time they forced us onto that battlefield. I mean, look what happened to Amity . . ."

They're crying again, and you don't know how to stop it. You don't know how to fix them, because the way they're broken, you're broken too, only you don't want to admit it, never wanted to admit it—

"They killed my sister, Leum. They may have killed my mother too. Thousands of sisters and mothers and siblings and kin. All those dead. And for what? The old ways?" Kanver gestures at themself, their pile of soiled clothes. "Look what the old ways did to us."

"No." You get up. You pace the shed, kicking up straw and dust. You peer through the gaps in the walls, like the answers will be out there somewhere, like you'll find them in the light between the slats. "No."

"I'm sorry."

"No!"

You don't even know what you're protesting anymore. You just know you can't accept it, can't accept any of this.

"No. You're coming with me, Kannie. I'm going to get you out of here. We'll leave Amerand behind and the rest of it too." You kneel beside them again, resting your forehead against theirs. "We'll be okay out there. You'll see."

You feel them shake their head. *No, we won't.* You feel their tears fall onto your clasped hands.

Burk curls up between you, nose tucked into the stump of her tail.

Sniffing, Kanver lays a hand on her head.

They sleep again, for a while, while you remain awake, still staring at the breaks in the shed walls.

Outside, the light fails.

Emara returns, some hours later, with a bowl of lukewarm stew and a meaty bone, which Burk takes with a satisfied snarl. Tendon and gristle. The dog munching happily in the straw.

You hunch over your bowl. Potatoes, onions, a slick of beef fat on your lips. "Any problems?"

"Moony got into Hemmen's house, but I took care of it." Emara leans against the doorway, watching you eat. When you don't respond, she adds, "You're welcome."

"I didn't thank you."

"Yeah, I noticed." She rolls her eyes. "Amity probably knows, though."

To hell with Amity, you think, though you don't say it.

"Onna?" you ask.

"Nah."

"Good." You stuff your face with stew.

"How's Moony?"

You shrug. After talking with you, Kanver threw up twice in the afternoon but has been sleeping soundly since. (Not that it's any of Emara's business.) You shovel more of your meal into your mouth and hope she goes away.

She doesn't.

Instead, she picks at the doorframe, pulling out splinter after splinter of wood. "Can I ask you something?" she says finally. "Did you know me before we met in Windfall?"

"What?"

"Did we fight in the war? Me and you?"

"No." You scowl. "I don't know."

"Then what's your problem with me?"

You're tempted to tell her you don't have a problem. You don't get along with anybody, remember? People don't like you, and you don't like them. She's not special.

But you're a terrible liar, Leum.

(And, let's face it, after all she's done for Kanver today, maybe you owe her the truth.)

"You're Vedran," you say.

Emara flicks another splinter from the doorframe. "Not anymore."

"But you were. You were the enemy. We were supposed to hate you, to kill you, if we could."

"Yeah, yeah, and we were supposed to kill you. Whatever. It was war. But the war's over. Vedra's gone—"

"I know," you growl.

"Vedrans don't exist anymore." She throws out her hands, as if to encompass you and Kanver, the dusty shed, the village of Camas, the northlands, the entire Kindar Peninsula in the breadth of her arms. "We're all Amerandines now, eh?"

"I *know.*"

"So . . . this is what? You want to cling to tradition or something? You want things to be like they were? You want to start up the war again? Right here? Me and you?"

"No."

"What is it then?"

"You can't be one of us."

"Why?"

"Because if you're one of us, it doesn't make sense!"

"What doesn't?"

"Any of it!" Your own vehemence surprises you. You didn't mean to shout. Emara's not supposed to be worth your anger, your attention, your anything. For a moment, the two of you are still, listening for footsteps, for voices outside—

But there's nothing—

The sound of the flooded farmyard lapping at the loop road, the pines in the early autumn breeze—

You scowl down at the remnants of your dinner. Mushy carrots and congealed fat. "How can you be one of us?" you mumble. "Because the war's over? Because the Queen Commander said so? We hated each other for *years*. It's what gave us purpose. It's what we lived and died for . . . But if we could've been on the same side this whole time? If we could've been allies? Friends?"

Emara's not our enemy.

You look up at her, and for maybe the first time you allow yourself to see her. Tall, strong, quick to laugh. She reminds you of Kida, actually. An older sister, always joking, always giving you a hard time—

You shake your head. "If we could've been kin this whole time, then we didn't have to be fighting in the first place. We didn't have to do all those things they ordered us to do. We didn't have to be like this . . ." Your gaze drifts to Kanver, passed out in the straw, then back to Emara. "So you see? You *can't* be one of us. You just can't."

Emara says nothing.

(A dent in her expression. Hurt in her gray eyes.)

You don't know why, but all of a sudden you want to shout. You want to leap to your feet. You want to fill the silence. More words. An argument. A fistfight. *Something.* Anything to bridge the space between you—

An arm's length between you, if you would just put out your hand—

But you can't bring yourself to move, and before you can say anything else, Emara turns around and walks into the dark.

EMARA

IT'S EARLY, AND THE VILLAGE IS EERILY QUIET. NO sounds of axes or shovels. No saws. No posts being hammered into place.

The work is done.

After Amity told you she was sick, it took the rest of you a day or two to get back on track. For Ben to return from the woods (or wherever it was she had gone). For Leum to figure out the plans for the guard posts along the gully. For the villagers to take down the bridge.

But you did it. (Even without Amity, without her leadership, her role reduced to obligatory check-ins and training drills with the villagers.) In less than a month, you evacuated the farmyard, dammed the river, dismantled the bridge, erected guard posts along the perimeter, and barricaded the entire southern flank of the village—

(A feat of which you're particularly proud, seeing as it's the first time you've ever really built anything—)

(The first time you've ever really led anyone in anything that wasn't a battle—)

Camas is a fortress now, or as much of a fortress as an unequipped backwater village can be.

With a minimal amount of swagger, you show Onna and Amity

the bulwarks along the south road. The arrow slits, the mud-reinforced logs—

"To protect against fire!" Siddie declares, although the observation is unnecessary. Amity knows the value of a fire-resistant barricade, and Onna lives in wildfire country.

But no one scolds her for stating the obvious.

Ordinarily, you'd look to Amity for approval. This was *her* plan, after all. *Her* mission. But she hasn't said a word since she reached the meadow, toying with the edge of her scarf, which she's still wearing for some reason, as if she can still hide the signs of burnout from you, as if nothing at all has changed.

So you nudge Onna with your elbow instead. "Well? Not bad for a bunch of kids, eh?"

"You're not kids," she says. Then she pats the back of your hand. "But no, it's not bad at all."

And you don't know why, it's not like she's your mother or anything—

(She's nothing like your mother, or at least the way you remember her. Too short, too frowning, too built for the cold—)

But for some reason you're reminded of your mother. (A warm light, a gentle hand.)

"Impressi—" Amity tries to stifle a cough, but it rips through her, doubling her over, making her shake. Between gasps, she slips a flask from her robe, takes a sip of some infusion Onna's been making for her.

It's alarming. The relentlessness of it. The violence of it.

You shift uncomfortably. You try to laugh. "Calm down, Queenie. I didn't *really* think it'd kill you to compliment me, eh?"

"Don't get ahead of yourself, Emara." As she straightens, she looks amused, although to be fair, her amusement's always a hairsbreadth from irritation. "I'm not dead yet."

You laugh. (For real this time.) You've come to expect a lot of things from the Twin Valley Reaper, but you never expected her to crack a joke—

(Even if it is a little morbid—)

"We'd better keep moving," Onna says to Amity. "We still have to check the barricade by the bridge—"

"Now wait just a second!" You plant yourself in front of them, sweeping your arms wide to encompass the barricade, the wet meadow beyond. "We *did* something here, eh? We accomplished something! Can't we revel in that a little longer?"

Amity flicks her fingers. "Revelry is your purview, I'm afraid."

A grin steals across your features. You hadn't thought of it before, hadn't been thinking of much besides your own sense of accomplishment, but now you realize you've stumbled across a rare opportunity—

No, you've earned it—

(A new sensation, but not unwelcome—)

Which makes it even more important to seize upon it now—

You rub your hands together. "Well, if that's the case, I think my *purview* is calling for a party."

"A party!" Siddie's face lights up.

Onna's don't. "A party?"

You waggle your eyebrows at her. "You know. Festivity, merriment, general debauchery?"

"And you want to do this tonight?"

"Well, if I could do it sooner, I would, but it'll take me the rest of the day to arrange for the food, some wine, a little entertainment . . ."

For a moment, she looks thoughtful. Crossed arms, furrowed brow. You even allow yourself to believe she's considering it, but then she looks to Amity, and something unspoken passes between them before Onna turns away and starts back up the road to the village.

"Hey, where's she—"

"You're aware we aren't done here, aren't you?" Amity says. "We still have to contend with Adren."

"All the more reason to party while we still can!"

Amity purses her lips. "There's no time. The Camassians still have work in the fields. You still have lookouts to train. In fact, I suggest you head out there now to relieve Leum and Kanver."

You know she's got a point, so you try not to pout. "So . . . no party?"

"No," she says firmly. "No party, Emara."

"I'm going to throw a party."

Since Amity and Onna moved on to surveying the dismantled bridge with Ben, you and Siddie have been skipping stones through the flooded farmyard, watching them *plink-plink-plink* across the glassy surface.

"Amity told you not to throw a party."

"Amity's not the boss of me." Winding up, you chuck a rock as far as you can throw it. The satisfying splash. "Or you either. Want to help?"

"Me?" Siddie looks around, like you couldn't possibly be talking to her, but there's no one else around. Ket and Tana have slunk off to find some privacy, and, since you haven't relieved them, Leum and Kanver are still up in the hills with the lookouts—

"Yeah," you say. "You ever been to a party before, Piggy?"

"Of course," she scoffs.

She's lying, but if she's never been to a party before, then it's your job—

No, your solemn duty—

No, your *destiny* to instruct her. You beckon her toward you, sling an arm around her neck. "Okay, Piggy. First lesson. It's not a party without a bunch of other people doing all the hard work for you."

"Okay!"

You pat her on the head, and for once she doesn't try to duck out of the way. "Love the enthusiasm. Let's call that lesson two."

"Great!"

As with any covert operation, you know you're going to need someone on the inside, someone who knows the location, the people, someone who will be able to turn potential enemies into allies on your behalf, so the first person you seek out is Tana—

Fortunately, it doesn't take long, because you know she and Ket have been using the market wagon, now parked in the dusty clearing above the cemetery, for their not-so-secret rendezvous. Striding up to one of the large wooden wheels, you knock three times upon the splintered siding.

Muffled whispers—

Creaking floorboards—

A few feet away, Siddie is watching the wagon with wide eyes, her cheeks flushing bright as her balar crystal as she realizes what they've been doing, sneaking away all this time.

You grin at her. "C'mon, Roamie! We know you're in there!"

"Emara?"

"Hurry up and put your trousers on, eh? We need to talk to you two."

Moments later, Ket and Tana crawl from the back of the wagon, flustered and more than a little annoyed with you but (thankfully) fully dressed. You know you're at something of a disadvantage, considering you interrupted what was likely a very enjoyable morning of rest and recreation, so you make your case quickly—

Not that there's much of a case to be made—

Parties are good.

You want to have one.

The end.

"Could be fun," Ket says, grinning. "If you can pull it off."

"Oh, I can pull it off. Right, Piggy?"

Siddie nods, although to be fair, you could say anything at this point and she'd agree. *Want to have a party, Piggy? Aren't I the greatest, Piggy? Why don't you worship at my feet, Piggy?*

Tana frowns at you. "Does my mother know about this?"

You wink at her. "Not if you don't say anything."

Tana nods a few times, like she's getting used to the idea. A party, an act of defiance, a celebration, a rebellion. "Okay," she says finally, and you're kind of surprised, because in all honesty you thought you'd spend another fifteen minutes trying to convince her before giving up and doing it all yourself, although of course you're happy not to.

"Okay," she repeats. "Let's do it."

Ket chuckles. "Really?"

"Yeah. Why not? You don't think I can party?"

"Well . . ."

Tana makes a face at her before turning back to you. "What can we do to help?"

With Tana's assistance, you get Ferra to clear the temporary henhouses from the square. You get Vander to donate a pig for roasting. You get offers of grain and potatoes and whatever's left in the root cellars from last year. No one has much to spare, but everyone wants to contribute something.

"Lessons three and four," you explain to Siddie. "It's not a party without a venue. Or food."

"Okay!"

Racing down the loop road, the two of you find the Old Man beside the flooded meadow, where he's taken to fishing in the mornings, though he rarely catches anything. Just likes to watch the trout jump, you guess.

You tell him you're having a celebration. You ask him to donate the wine.

He squints up at you. "All you've done since you got here is take up our time and our resources, and now you want my wine too? I thought you were supposed to be protecting us."

"We are," Siddie says.

"Yeah," you add. "From being a bunch of tedious old farts."

"Bah."

"It's fine." You wave him off. "You don't have to come. More roast pig for the rest of us, eh?"

"Roast pig?" The Old Man straightens, smacking his lips. "That's my favorite."

You grin at him. "I know it is, Old Man."

In exchange for the jowls (his favorite cut of meat), he offers you several barrels from his store of wine.

"Lesson five," you whisper to Siddie as you skip back to the square. "It's not a party without drink."

"What about Kanver?"

"Yeah." You nod. "We'll watch out for Moony, eh?"

When Leum and Kanver come down from the lookouts, you rope them into helping you too. To be honest, you mostly want Kanver (because Leum hasn't spoken a word to you since that night in the shed), but you don't object when both of them sit down with the village children to start making flags and flower crowns for the festivities.

Lesson six: It's not a party without favors.

With all the commotion, you're certain both Amity and Onna have gotten wind of your plan by now, but you and Siddie don't stay in one place long enough for them to find you. You're sweeping the square of chicken manure. You're turning Vander's spit. You're cajoling musicians into digging out their instruments, which, incidentally, is lesson seven: It's not a party without music.

If there are objections, they're overridden or ignored. Tables are set out. Banners are hung. Clusters of crates and stools appear in the square like mushrooms after a rain.

Near dusk, you and Siddie scamper back to the cabin to scrub your faces and brush the dust from your hair. Rummaging through your clothes, you dig out a set of robes—

Not particularly festive, which is unfortunate, but they're clean and whole, and that's more than you can say for most of your things—

As you change into your party clothes, Siddie sinks to her haunches beside your haphazard pile of belongings, carefully peeling back the paper packaging on one of your wraps. A flash of blue. A diamond of white. "Ooh! This is nice."

You almost snap at her. You almost smack her hands away, almost snarl, *Don't touch that!* You don't want her hands on it, this scrap of your history, your homeland, your culture—

Not her—

Not an Amerandine—

Not the enemy—

She doesn't have the right.

But you swallow a few times. Try to loosen the knot in your throat. Try to remember. Try to let go.

She's not the enemy. She's not Amerandine.

She's Siddie.

So you finish pulling on your clothes. You tie your belt. "Of course it's nice," you say primly. "It's Chenyaran."

"I thought you were Vedran."

You kneel beside her, pulling the wraps from their packages. "I'm not really anything anymore," you say, picking a bit of lint from the fabric. *Here is the story of Vana, Third Queen of Chenyara.* "But my mother was Chenyaran, so I guess I was Chenyaran first."

Siddie hugs her knees. Says in a small voice, "You remember your mother?"

"Yeah." For an instant your eyes burn. Your voice tightens. You pull your mother's wrap toward you. Its ragged edge. Its frayed sentences. "This was hers."

Siddie reaches out, her fingers hovering over the fabric like she can't quite believe it, wants to reassure herself that it's real, this cloth, this connection—

A mother—

A family—

Blood—

"How did you find it?" she whispers.

A month ago, you would've lied to her. Would've made it a good story, something epic or horrific or exciting, something to strain credulity, because it wouldn't have mattered whether she believed you or not. She would've been no one to you. A kid. Some random Amerandine kid. Daughter of your old enemy.

Then again, a month ago, you wouldn't have told her the truth to begin with. Wouldn't have left the wraps on the floor for her to find. Wouldn't have taken her under your wing—

Your minion—

Your little piggy—

So you tell her the real story. You read her what's written, or what you can remember. "When we're done here, I'm going south again," you tell her. "There are more of these out there, and I'm going to find them."

"Because you want to find her?" Siddie asks.

You run your thumb along the stitches. *Here is the story of Emara, daughter of Rava, Weaver of Livia . . .* You want to say yes. Your mother is out there somewhere, and you're going to find her. A long journey. A family reunion. A happy ending.

You want to say no. She's gone. She was taken a long time ago by Yavana, Greater God of Wind, to someplace that you in your earth-bound body cannot follow, no matter how hard you look, no matter how far you run.

Maybe that reunion still awaits you, in the realm of the Dread Empress, through the doors in her Palace of Bones.

But not here.

Not now.

"I don't know," you say truthfully.

Siddie nods. She tucks her arms around her knees again. "Are you going to wear it tonight?"

Sighing, you run your fingers over the fabric. Loose threads. Torn stitches. You've kept it tucked away for over a year, sealed and safe, but Chenyaran wraps were always designed to be worn, to be displayed and shown off, to be admired and envied for their beauty, their artistry, to be read, to tell their stories, to pass on these histories—

No matter how tattered—

No matter how incomplete—

You step out of the cabin, tucking your mother's wrap into place around your neck. It's not the way your mother would have done it—

Chenyaran wraps are supposed to be draped around the shoulders—

A story cascading down your spine—

But there wasn't enough fabric left for that, so you're wearing it like a scarf. The fabric twisted, the tassels tucked under, forming a loop with no ending and no beginning—

Below, the square is starting to fill with people. Musicians tuning their instruments. Tana raising a cup with the Old Man. Ket and Parker bringing out the last few chairs. Onna searching the crowd while Siddie does her best to avoid her, ducking behind houses, the bonfire, the cooks dishing out cuts of roast pork and braised vegetables, juices oozing over steaming bowls of rice. A few kids run by waving tiny paper battle flags, each one painted with the face of a kindling.

You laugh when you see them. Even at this distance, you recognize Leum's scowl, Ben's straw hat, Siddie's enormous eyes. You wonder what yours looks like, but before you can head down to find out, Amity appears on the steps below you.

She looks displeased. (Not that that's unusual or anything.) "You were told, explicitly, not to throw a party."

"Oh, I thought you meant *tomorrow*." You grin at her. "No party *tomorrow*."

"You did not."

"Well, you can't prove it, eh?"

Her lips twitch. "I suppose I can't."

Below, there's an appreciative murmur as the musicians start up a lively Amerandine folk song. The lyrics are different, but you recognize the melody, the rippling beat. You feel it in your chest, your legs, your feet. You know this dance, know the bow, the kick, the twirl. You danced it all the time back in basic training—

And before that, in Livia—

This isn't an Amerandine folk song. It's Vedran. No, Chenyaran. It's all of them and none of them—

It's Kindarian.

Cheering, the Camassians flock to the center of the square. (Lesson eight: It's not a party without dancing.) Hemmen pulls Kanver away from their dinner. Ket and Tana go racing, hand in hand, to join the dancers.

Even Amity, standing beside you, can't stop her fingers from tapping. Her thin fingers, trembling, if only faintly, with burnout.

"I never thanked you," you say abruptly.

Amity raises an eyebrow. "For what?"

"For bailing me out of that card game. I even resented it, eh? Having to be here. Having to fight for you, for this . . ." You gesture to the dancers, whirling through the square like dandelion seeds. "I didn't think this was for me. This wasn't my place. These weren't my people."

"The farmers?"

"Any of you."

"And now?"

"And now I'm partying with the Red Death. So things change, eh?"

She laughs. She laughs so hard she starts coughing again, almost folding in half at the waist.

You want to help her, but you don't know what you can do besides be there with her, so you let her lean on you until she recovers.

"I'm sorry, Queenie," you say.

Sorry you were angry. Sorry you couldn't let it go. Sorry she's sick—

Sorry she's dying.

She swallows a few times, and when she speaks again, it's in little more than a whisper: "I'm sorry too."

You put your arm around her as the two of you survey the party. The night lit up like summer. Sparks fluttering from the bonfire. Your kindred laughing together. Couples twirling across the square. "Admit it," you say. "You're glad I defied orders this time."

She chuckles softly. "Don't tell anyone. I've a reputation to protect."

KET

YOU CAN'T BELIEVE EMARA THREW ALL THIS TOGETHER in less than a day. The colorful flags, the favors, the dancing. You're supposed to look down on the south for their festive, freewheeling ways, but let's be honest, none of the rest of you could've pulled this off—

(None of the rest of you would've dared.)

But you needed this. You all needed this, after you found out you were losing Amity, after all these weeks working at the defenses—

The shared food, the warmth of the fire, the music on the air.

At some point, you see Siddie's turned luminous and tipsy, so you fill her cup with water. You order her to drink. Not long after, you catch Kanver staring longingly at the Old Man's stash: the open bottles and upturned jugs, the puddles of liquid, the abandoned cups.

"Kanver?" You sidle up to them.

They give you a faint smile. "Hi, Ket."

"Want to walk with me?"

"Yeah." They nod a few times. "Let's walk."

You make it to the edge of the square before Ben intercepts you. Twitchy, anxious, like she wants to jump out of her own skin.

(If you had to guess, you'd say she likes a party even less than Leum.)

"Where are you going?" she asks.

Kanver shrugs. "I've just got to get out of here for a while."

"Same." Ben grimaces. "Do you want to stay here, Ket? Kanver and I can check on the lookouts together."

You let them go, their forms disappearing into the darkness while the party spirals on in the square. Music and laughter. You dance with Tana (who's not very good at it, though she declares she'll get better), and throughout the evening you keep finding each other by the fence. Your voices lowered, your heads together, your fingers twining along the rail.

Simple.

Easy.

It's getting late, but no one seems to want to retire yet, and while Tana is by the kegs, refilling your cups, Onna settles against the fence beside you. "So." She sighs. "You and Tana."

You nod, although you're not sure if you're supposed to nod. You've never had a girl's mother sit you down for a talking-to. You've been beaten off with a broom. You've been chased out a window. But in all those other cases, you were already in motion, already leaving. You've never held still long enough for a lecture, so you don't know what to expect.

But Onna doesn't lecture you. "I'm glad," she says.

"You are?"

"She's always been so serious," Onna says. "But you lighten her up."

"Oh." You look to Tana, who's weaving through the dancers with both your cups held over her head. When she sees Onna with you, she makes a face and laughs.

Onna nods. "She needs that, especially after Vian."

"She talks about him a lot." With a smile, you add, "Apparently, we would've gotten along."

"You would've been trouble, that's for sure." Patting you once on the knee, Onna stands. Sighs again. Old laugh wrinkles at the corners of her eyes. "But I would give anything now for trouble like that."

As she walks off toward the bonfire, Tana appears in front of you, handing you your drink with a bow. "What was that about?"

"I think she likes me."

Tana rolls her eyes. "Everyone likes you."

"You didn't, at first."

"I did. I just didn't *get* you."

"And you get me now?"

She taps her cup against yours and takes a swig. "Nope."

You laugh. You drink. You dance. After a little coaxing from Vander, you even sing. An old song, a plaintive melody. You've forgotten how much you like to sing—

Never do it, really—

Not in front of people—

The last time you sang like this was when Vedra surrendered. Fireworks and dancing. It seemed like all of Amerand was celebrating. Flags flying. Kegs emptied. Soldiers kissing in the streets. It was the end of the fighting, after a century, the end of the war, and here you all were, still standing—

You'd made it—

You were fifteen and the rest of your life was ahead of you—

You had so many plans ahead of you—

You're flushed by the time the song ends, dizzy with drink and memory, and you stumble breathless through the cheering crowd (even Leum applauding, albeit begrudgingly) to Tana, who's whistling at you from the edge of the square.

She slaps you on the shoulder as you sit down beside her. "Why didn't you tell me you could sing?"

"You never asked."

"You're going to sing for me every day from now on, you know that?"

"I am?"

"Yeah." She pokes you in the collarbone, accentuating each word. *"Every day."*

Ordinarily, you'd be alarmed by talk like that.

(*Every day* from now on?)

(And you unflinching?)

Instead you laugh, because Tana's drunk. "Sure. Okay."

You stay. You talk. You dance some more. At some point Emara teaches the musicians a Chenyaran love song, which she belts out in a beautiful warbling contralto. Later, Fern crowns Siddie with a circlet of asters, the kid dancing so hard that petals fly from her hair.

With every drink, Tana gets a little louder, a little wilder in the swing of her arms. She stands, pointing at you accusatorily. "You need another refill." She looks annoyed, like your empty cup is an affront of the highest order.

"I'm fine."

"Nooo." Leaning over, she snatches at your cup but can't seem to grasp it. "Oops."

You're on your feet already, steadying her in your arms. "Maybe that's enough for now, huh?"

"I never drink this much, you know." She pokes you again, almost admonishing. "It was Vian who drank, but he's not here anymore, so I guess I have to drink enough for the both of us."

"Well, I think you're succeeding."

"Shh." She digs her fingers into your collar. A thread popping. The crinkling of paper. Before you can stop her, she draws the list from its hidden pocket. "Hey, what's this?"

Your mouth goes dry. No one but you has touched that list since you wrote it, the two of you, on the night of the Vedran surrender—

The ink smearing as you passed the paper back and forth—

All the things you were going to do—

All the promises you were going to keep—

But Tana doesn't open it. Swaying, she presses the paper back into your hands and declares, "I have to pee."

"All right."

You walk her to the outhouse. You sit outside while you wait. You lean back on your hands and watch the Morning Daughter, serene in her shadowed hood.

"You okay?" Leum settles heavily on the step beside you.

"Yeah." And you grin at her, because you mean it. For the first time in ages, you're not thinking of the past or the future or the list in your pocket. You're just here. You're just where you are.

You're okay.

"Tana?" Leum nods toward the outhouse.

"She probably needs to throw up."

Leum's silent for a moment as the two of you listen to the musicians' last song drifting out of the square. The hiss of water in the bonfire and children being hurried off to bed.

"You're happy here, huh?" she says.

You think of the way you've settled in to Camas. You think of the pace, the work, the calm. You think of the pines and the gold of the valley. You think of riding into the hills with Callie.

You think of Tana.

"Yeah." You smile. "I guess I am."

"Does that mean you're going to stay?"

"What?"

"After the battle, I mean."

You should have a ready answer for her. In the past, you would've told her there's a lot of world out there. *There's a lot of world to see.* But you don't know anymore.

Could you stay?

Could you have this? Could you let yourself have this?

The pace, the work, the calm? The green pines and the gold of the valley? The mountains, the freedom, the chill alpine air? You and

Callie? Here? With the villagers?

With Tana?

But you're so used to dodging questions that you don't answer. Instead you ask, "Why? Do *you* want to stay?"

"Me and Kanver are headed over the mountains." She scowls and picks at her fingernails, bitten to the quick. "I guess I just wanted to know one of us was going to be okay."

From the outhouse, there's a *thump*. A muffled curse. Inside, you find Tana fighting with her robes. You help her up. You straighten her clothes.

"I'm tired," she says.

"Oh yeah? I didn't notice."

"Shut up."

"Okay."

Once you're outside, Leum helps you take her weight, and you feel it again, that sense of steadiness, the way you take care of each other. You, Tana, the villagers, your kin. Here, in the mountains, you could be steady—

It could be simple—

Easy—

Every day from now on—

But as the two of you guide Tana up the road, two figures come hurtling toward you—

Kanver and Ben. They're panting and breathless. They're skidding in the dirt. Before either you or Leum can get out a word, Kanver doubles over, gasping. "Scouts," they say. "Three of them to the south. They're on horseback. They're headed this way now."

AMITY

THE VILLAGE PANICS.

Lanterns doused. Doors slammed. Camassians dashing this way and that. Some of the farmers have remembered their weapons, racing over the roads with bows and wooden spears while Onna directs them to the barricade, the guard stations, the broken bridge, but others seem to have forgotten their training at the prospect of a real attack—

Chairs overturned, flags trampled, a child left crying in the center of the square—

Adren is on the way.

The battle is on the way.

You and the other kindlings run through the chaos, calling orders to the villagers, reminding them to report to their posts.

"The *gully*, Parker!"

"Vander, you're supposed to be at the bridge!"

You relish the familiarity of it. The easy mantle of your leadership, your firm and steady hand. No time for resentments now, no room for doubts. You're soldiers again. Taking orders, executing commands. You do what needs to be done, no questions asked.

Still drunk from the party, Hemmen staggers from his front gate, dropping his bow and quiver with a clatter. Shafts scattering, a muffled curse.

"Oof, Hemmy, you don't look so good." Stooping, Emara helps him to gather his arrows again. "You better throw it all up soon and get it out of your system, eh?"

In the square, you sweep the wailing child into your arms and deposit her in the care of a runner, a gangly girl, not much older than Siddie, by the name of Fern. "Get this kid to Onna's—"

You stifle a cough. You don't have time for burnout now, don't have time to be sick. You have too many other things to attend to, too many battles to win. You flag down Onna. "Can you handle things here?"

"You're going after the scouts?" she asks.

You snatch a bow and quiver from one of the passing villagers. You could probably use a sword as well, but if it comes to hand-to-hand combat, you'll simply have to take one—

(That is, if you still can—)

Onna regards you for a moment, and you can feel her studying your sunken eyes, your hollow cheeks.

"I can handle it," she says finally.

You give her a nod. You signal to Siddie. You tell her to fetch Comet and two of the fastest horses the villagers have left. As she sprints away, you start jogging toward the south road while the rest of your kin fall in behind you. "Emara!" you call, wheezing only slightly in the chill air. "With me."

Swatting Hemmen toward the gully, she tips you a salute.

"Kanver," you say. "Can you show us the way?"

They nod.

Emara trots up to you. "You want prisoners?"

You adjust the bow on your shoulder. "One will be enou—"

But the word lodges in your throat. You're coughing again. You can't stop coughing, the breaths hacksawing in and out of your chest. You can't seem to get enough air. You're gasping, wheezing, collapsing—

"Amity!" Leum catches you before you hit the ground.

You shrug her off, or at least you try. (Your feeble flapping, your trembling hands.) At this point, it takes all you have just to breathe.

Then the fit passes, leaving you hollowed out and weak. "I'm fine," you say. "I'm fine." But as you wave her away, you spot a slick of blood on the back of your hand—

At first, you think you've been cut—

(Though there was no one to cut you—)

But there's blood in your mouth, too, on your teeth and tongue—

The others stare, but no one speaks.

(No one wants to say what it means.)

In the back, Ben looks like someone's punched her in the chest.

While the rest of you hesitate, Siddie rides up on Comet, leading two of the Camassians' horses behind her. "What's the matter?" she asks, dismounting. "What are you all waiting for?"

Then she sees it—

The blood on your fist—

The blood on your lips—

"Oh no."

You cringe at the words. The silence broken, the spell undone. There's no pretending anymore, Amity. There's no ignoring it, no denying it, no pushing it away.

You're too weak to be a weapon now, too soft to be the point of the spear. You can't be trusted in battle when one breath can send you to your knees.

And who are you if you can no longer fight? If you can no longer crush your enemies in your fist?

Not the Red Death—

Not the Bolt of Judgment—

Not a Deathbringer—

Not a kindling.

You close your eyes. You try to think. The others are counting on you. They're waiting for your instructions. You have to tell them *something*, Amity. The scouts are still on their way. You can't falter now.

But you can't think beyond the fact that you can no longer do the one thing you were trained for, the one thing you were made for, the only purpose you ever had—

While you hesitate, Leum lays a hand on your shoulder. "What do you want us to do?"

You look up at her. You look up at all of them, at all of their faces, their frightened and beloved faces: Leum, Emara, Kanver, Siddie, Ben, and Ket.

Your soldiers.

Your kindred.

They're still looking to you. They still depend on you, even if you're sick—

(Even if you're dying.)

You don't have time to wallow in self-pity. Your kindred need you. Not your strength or your power but your authority, your leadership, your expertise—

So you pick yourself up. You sway on your feet. You swallow your doubts and lick your lips and hope your voice doesn't crack when you speak.

"Leum," you say. "Will you take my place out there?"

LEUM

THE SCOUTS HAVEN'T BOTHERED WITH HIDING THEIR tracks. The loam cleaved, a path in the trees. They don't know you're here yet, don't know you've been preparing the village for assault, don't know to be wary.

But as soon as they reach the ridge, they'll see the barricade, the flooded meadow, the guards on the perimeter. They'll race back to their camp. They'll warn Adren and the rest of the raiders, and they'll change their plan of attack.

So you have to stop them.

You and Emara.

Kill two. Take a prisoner for interrogation.

Leaving Kanver by the lookout, you ride off after the scouts. You tear through the forest like cannon shot. Twigs snapping, pine needles flying. *Bang.* Nothing left of you but smoke.

Your vision narrows. Branch, limb, a break in the brush. When did Amity start coughing blood? Did she know? Did she hide that from you too?

No, she looked just as surprised as the rest of you—

Just as scared—

The pines close in, branches tearing at your hair, your clothing. Cuts and scratches. Blood running from your brow. You wipe it away, the back of your hand smeared with red.

Then you see something ahead of you. A flashing tail. The shine of a pauldron.

The scouts have heard you.

They're shouting to one another.

Emara draws up beside you. Grim, focused, with her hair flying out behind her like a battle flag. And you don't mean to (you don't even realize you're doing it until it's already done), but you nod at her—

Just once—

Because she's here, and you need someone here, with you, now, when everything else seems to be slipping away—

Your dreams for the future—

Your grasp of the past—

Amity—

Gone before winter.

You draw your sword.

In the hilt, your balar crystal gleams.

You can see the scouts clearly now, charging madly through the shadows. One of them looks back at you, and over the sound of hooves you hear a word of warning.

The second scout turns in their saddle, bow drawn.

Your eyes widen, but you only have time to duck before the arrow is loosed. It flies at you, skimming past your shoulder and into the dust behind you.

The archer nocks another arrow to their bow.

But you're upon them now. You're raising your blade. *Clang!* The first scout brings up his own sword to block you, the impact sending him tumbling from his saddle.

As he rolls to his feet, you leap to the ground, attacking, stabbing, your blades ringing, the mulch flying beneath your feet. Slash, *clack!* You're better than him, but he's wearing armor, your sword shearing off him like water.

He lashes out at you, and as you dodge out of the way, an arrow finds you. (Sharp, quick.) It tears across your calf, causing you to stumble.

The first scout is on top of you in an instant, and you're trying to fight him off, but there's that pain in your leg now. It won't hold for long—

You've got to end this quick.

The scout nicks you across the arm. The shredding of cloth, a hiss of pain. You swipe at him, but he's already dancing out of your reach.

Then Emara tackles him from the back of her horse, plunging her daggers through the gaps in his armor.

The dying gasp.

The blood fountaining around her hands.

He falls to the ground as the other scouts circle you, and out of instinct you find Emara, the two of you fighting back to back. You didn't notice when Hope attacked you a month ago, but Emara is good—

Strong and fast—

She cuts the third scout across the leg as he passes—

She slices an arrow out of the air—

You've got to do something about that archer, so the next time they ride by, you lunge. You curl your fingers into their trousers and wrench them from their horse. Their bow snapping, the arrows rattling from their quiver. They hit the ground, and as the third scout rushes in to help them, Emara flings her dagger—

It sinks deep into his throat.

Below you, the archer pulls a knife from their belt, and for a second you think they're going for your kneecap, your heel, something to incapacitate you, to get you on the ground where they can go for your neck, your ribs, your heart, so you step out of the way—

Except they're not going for you—

They're going for their own throat, digging the blade into it, the blood flowing out of them so fast there's nothing you can do to stanch it.

They die, and then it's just you and Emara and the corpses. She grimaces and scratches thoughtfully at her cheek. "Eh . . . didn't Queenie say something about keeping one of them alive . . . ?"

You shrug. "They wouldn't be taken."

"*Yeah* . . . she's not going to be happy about that."

You pull a pauldron off one of the scouts. Lacquered scales. Pink thread.

Kindling armor.

This is what you wanted. The spoils that'll buy you supplies and a guide. This is what's supposed to get you out of Amerand for good—

You and Kanver—

(If Kanver will come—)

"You either, apparently." Emara elbows you in the side. "Buck up, Grumpy. We survived. There's no reason to pout."

"I'm not pouting."

"Sure, and I'm not Chenyaran."

You almost bristle at that, at the reminder that she's not one of you, was never one of you, because for a few minutes there, for a few precious minutes, you'd allowed yourself to forget. For a few minutes, you weren't Amerandine and Vedran. You were just Leum and Emara. You were just kindlings—

Scattered, shiftless, searching—

Found.

With a sigh, Emara retrieves her dagger, and for the first time you notice her balar crystals are fuchsia in color—

A little pinker than yours, but from a distance they'd look nearly identical—

On a battlefield, they'd look nearly identical.

You said Emara wasn't one of you, but you were lying. Even then, you knew you were lying. You knew she belonged, because when you imagined your future, you imagined her with you—

The seven of you, together—

All of you, together—

For as long as you wanted. For years, if you wanted. For a lifetime, for the rest of your lives—

"You're not Chenyaran," you say.

"Oh, right," she scoffs. "I'm Vedran. I'm the enemy, or nothing means anything and we all spiral into dread and despair."

"*No.*" You scowl at her. Maybe you would've come around to liking her eventually, given enough time, but time is never given, is it? Not for you. Not for Emara. Not for Amity, burning out before your very eyes.

Not for any of us.

So you don't wait any longer, because you don't have any longer to waste.

"You're not *just* Chenyaran anymore," you say.

She frowns, and you're pleased to have caught her off guard, pleased to see the confusion in her dark gray eyes.

You take her arm and grip it tight, so she knows you mean it when you tell her, "You're kin."

BEN

LEUM AND EMARA DON'T RETURN WITH A PRISONER,
but they bring horses and armor and saddlebags, which they dump
out onto the cabin floor. Kneeling, you pick through the scouts' provisions. Weapons, water, foodstuffs. There's only enough for another
day's journey, which means their camp must be close.

Adren must be close.

Soon she'll start wondering about the fate of her scouts. She'll
send more, or she'll come herself, but before that happens, Amity
gives you two options. One, you can fortify the defenses and arm the
villagers. You can prepare for the battle to come.

Or two, you can attack now, while you have the element of surprise. It's a bolder move, a riskier one. You might only be able to take
out a handful of raiders, but after having killed the scouts, you'll have
brought her down by eight, nine, ten fighters. Fifty bandits instead
of sixty. It could be enough to make a difference.

It could be enough to win.

Enough to save the village and your kin.

"So who's going?" Emara asks.

"I can do it," says Kanver.

"Me too," Siddie adds.

Ket shrugs. "Any of us will go."

Leum finishes knotting her bandage, wipes her bloody fingers on a cloth. "Amity stays."

"As do you," Amity replies.

They stare at each other, but neither of them protests. Leum's injured. Amity's sick. They need to rest while they still can.

"Ket and Kanver will stay behind," Amity says. "The villagers will be anxious, now that they know Adren's watching them. They need to remain organized and focused."

Emara elbows you in the ribs. "Guess it's you and me then, Knifey."

You nod. You were always going to be on this mission. A tracker, an assassin, a Mistwalker in training. You were always going to be the one to steal behind enemy lines, to sneak into their camp, to slit their throats in the night.

Siddie climbs to her feet. "What about me?"

"No." Leum yanks her back down by her belt. "Not you."

"Actually," Amity murmurs, "I think she should go."

Leum glowers at her.

"She'll be safer with Ben and Emara than on the front lines here. It'll be good practice for her."

"It's a mission, not practice."

"Yeah, an *easy* mission." Emara laughs. "Killing a few bandits? I could do it in my sleep, eh?"

"Siddie goes," Amity says in a tone firm enough to quell Leum's objections, though you can see her bristle when Siddie lets out a soft cheer. "You can leave her on watch if you think it's too dangerous."

You nod.

Emara licks her lips.

If you leave now, you'll have a day to follow the scouts' trail to Adren's camp. You'll attack in the night, and if you do your job right, you'll be long gone before anyone discovers the corpses, still and cold in their beds.

Your fingers twitch.

Are you ready to kill again, Ben?

You don't know, but you can't back out now. Your kin are counting on you. The village is counting on you.

You have to protect them. You can't let them down.

"Dispatch as many as you can and get out of there," Amity says. "I want all of you back here and ready to fight when Adren comes for Camas."

It's sunset by the time you find Adren's encampment in the hills. Creeping through the graying light, you survey your enemy's defenses: perimeter fences of woven branches, watch stations on every corner. A creek runs diagonally through the camp, separating the livestock and pack animals from the personnel and their horses.

"What do you think?" you ask Emara. "Former military?"

She nods. The camp is organized in the Amerandine style, with tents and paddocks arranged around open quads that checker the muddy field. It means Adren's forces aren't just marauders. They're coordinated, methodical, and likely well trained.

That's something none of you were prepared for. You thought you were fighting bandits, not soldiers.

"See any handcannons?" Emara whispers.

You study her curiously. You wonder if she fought any cannoneers in the war, if she was on the receiving end of their fire and shot. "Not yet," you say.

She rubs her eyes. She nods a few times, as if to reassure herself. "Let's hope not ever, eh?"

You shift uneasily in the mulch. Looking down on Adren's camp, you can't help being reminded of the last mission you took—

The tension on the air—

The sound of the alarm—

The explosion that took the rest of your squad—

You tell yourself this will be different. This time will be different. You're faster now. You're stealthier now. You won't be caught. You won't let any of you be caught.

On the slope where you've tethered your horses, the three of you hunker down in the shadows to wait. Darkness falls. The braziers are lit. As the night crawls onward, Emara and Siddie catch a few minutes of sleep, but you remain awake. You take note of the changing shifts, the rhythms of the raiders moving in and out of their tents.

You're faster now. You're better now. You can protect them.

Soon, the southwest corner of the camp draws your attention. One of the squads seems to be hosting some kind of party, the whole platoon in on it, drinking and carousing, their torchlights bright in the yard.

"Emara," you whisper.

She lets out a snore.

"Emara."

"What?"

"Look." You point toward the host squad's six-person tent, near the low willow fence. It's close to the southwest watch station, so you'll have to be wary, but if you sneak in from the north, no one will see you.

Emara grins.

"One squad," you tell her. "No unnecessary risks."

Siddie crawls up beside you. "We'll have to wait for the party to die down," she says.

"You're not coming," you say.

"Why not?"

"No unnecessary risks." You enunciate each word to make sure she hears you. "Stay out here and keep watch."

"Yeah, Piggy." Emara elbows her a little. "If anything goes sideways, someone needs to make it back to Camas, so Amity knows what we're up against."

You expect Siddie to pout, but she must understand the gravity of the mission, because she bites back her protests. Nods once.

Pulling your jacket about your shoulders, you settle in for the wait.

The moon rises. The hour grows late.

Beside you, Siddie lets out one of her long-suffering sighs.

Emara rolls her eyes.

Eventually, the lanterns dim. The laughter dies. One by one, the raiders stumble to their tents, until there's nothing left of their revels but discarded kegs and empty cups—

An abandoned sword—

A stool tipped sideways in the dust—

You nod at Emara, and the two of you rise. You check your weapons. You shake the stiffness out of your limbs.

"It's happening now?" Siddie whispers, her eyes moonlike in the dark.

Emara grins at her. A flash of teeth in the night. "See you soon, Piggy."

Silently, you and Emara slip down the mountainside, swift as swallows between the trees. At the southwest watch station, a guard paces—

Three steps this way—

Three steps that—

You count their movements, and when their back is turned, you dash for the fence, leaping over the woven branches and into the encampment.

Braziers burn along the fence, lighting the perimeter, so you and Emara duck into the shadow of a tent.

You wait for a moment, holding your breath.

No one sounds the alarm.

Emara draws one of her daggers and grins at you in the darkness.

Digging her blade into the canvas, she slits the side of the tent with a soft *rrrrrip*—

She pauses again—

But no one stirs.

The two of you dart inside, wait a moment for your eyes to adjust. There's laundry piled in the corners and weapons tossed in a heap.

So much for martial discipline, you suppose.

Your nose wrinkles at the smell of liquor and the sweat of dirty soldiers.

Motioning to Emara, you approach the nearest of the raiders, snoring and spread-eagled on their cot. You draw one of your knives.

Six kills, that's all you need—

Quick and painless—

You didn't want this. Didn't want to have to kill again. But now you're here, and this is the way you protect your kin—

With violence—

With bloodshed—

It seems inescapable now, inevitable now. This is what you were trained for, this is what you're good for, so you do it. You do it because it will save lives, because it's the only way you know how to save lives—

By taking them, no matter what that makes you—

Warrior, murderer, hero, monster—

(Perfect—)

(At least for this.)

With a nod, you lift your blade.

SIDDIE

YOU'RE NOT HAPPY TO BE LEFT BEHIND AGAIN, BUT you're determined to prove you're a good soldier, and good soldiers follow orders, so you stay where you are and watch, breathlessly, as Ben and Emara launch themselves over the fence.

Briefly, your gaze darts to the watch station, but the guard is looking the other way. Leaning forward, you watch Ben and Emara dash to the tent, where they split the canvas and slip inside.

Then nothing.

There are no shouts, no cries, no motion at all, and you wonder what it must be like inside that tent now. Ben and Emara sliding between the cots like shadows, their blades sure and bloody in the darkness.

You're so busy imagining it, in fact, that you almost miss the movement in the yard as one of the marauders comes staggering out of a nearby tent. He's dragging his feet and rubbing his eyes and saying something that at this distance you can't quite hear, but you catch the words "cheat" and "you owe me" as he stumbles toward the tent that Ben and Emara are in—

(At least, you think they're in there—)

(You haven't seen them come out—)

You spring to your feet.

They're going to be discovered. They're going to be caught.

No matter how good they are, they can't fight an entire encampment alone.

For a moment, you're frozen there, paralyzed on the hillside. Ben told you to stay. Emara told you to stay. She said that if anything went wrong, you were supposed to ride back to Camas. You're supposed to warn Amity.

And you want to—

You want to be a good soldier—

You want to obey—

But you can't leave Ben and Emara to die.

You race down the hillside, heedless of the sounds you're making in the brush—

The rustling branches, the crackling mulch—

You barely glance at the watch station as you vault over the fence, past the brazier to the front of the tent, where the drunken raider is already reaching for the door flaps, and you draw your sword—

The blade slides through him—

Flesh, muscle, organ, bone—

You thought you'd be ready. After Hope, you thought you'd know what to expect. But you don't know if you ever could've been ready for this—

The way he writhes, the way he tries to scream. You put your hand over his mouth. You hold him while he thrashes in your arms—

Then he dies, and you know it, because all of a sudden he goes limp. You gasp at the weight of him, the impossible weight of him—

(You didn't know he'd be so heavy.)

Gingerly, you lay him down. His sightless eyes, his crooked limbs. For a second, you stare at him, your bloody sword still dangling from your hand.

You did it.

You killed him.

Ben and Emara?

You saved them.

So where's the elation? The sense of vindication?

His open mouth, his bloody tongue—

You want to be sick, but you don't have time to be sick. You need to get out of here. You wipe your blade, then sheathe it. Leaning down, you grasp the dead man by his armpits, try to drag him into the tent. Maybe Emara will be there, spinning her daggers or grinning in the dark. Maybe she'll see you, help you inside, waggle her eyebrows at you and say something like, "Proud of you, Piggy," and maybe she'll mean it—

But you don't make it that far.

There's a shout from the corner of the camp. At the watch station, the guard is lifting a mallet over a hammered brass gong.

And before you can take another breath, the alarm sounds.

EMARA

THE RAIDERS DIE IN THEIR SLEEP, ONE AFTER ANOTHER
after another. Ben looks pale by the time you're done, but her hands
are steady as she sheathes her knives. The two of you slip out of the
tent the way you came. Breathlessly, you pause beside the nearest
paddock, wait for the guard to turn away before you scramble over
the fences—

The willows rattling, the branches flexing under your weight—

You drop to the ground outside. Another pause. Somewhere,
there's a muffled cry, like one from a dream—

Like someone's half-whimpered scream.

No time to linger. Motioning to Ben, you make your way up the
hillside, where you expect to find Siddie practically pissing herself
with excitement.

But she's not there.

The cavernous shadows. The echoing woods.

Ben shoots you a look.

You check the horses (still tethered to their trees). "Piggy?" You
peer into the shadows, panic rising like bile in your throat. *"Piggy."*

That's when you hear it—

The telltale *clang clang clang clang* of the alarm—

Siddie's in the encampment. Siddie's been spotted. At the sound
of the gong, three raiders charge from their tents, surrounding her

before she can clamber over the fence.

Without a second thought, you race down the hillside, followed quickly by Ben.

You curse under your breath. What were you thinking, letting Siddie tag along? The girl couldn't follow an order if it slapped her in the face—

Still, the kid's not giving up, and you've got to give her credit for that. Full-grown raiders, some twice her size, are coming at her from all sides, and somehow she's holding her own, that ridiculous sword of hers carving down to the bone.

An enemy falls. Then another.

But you know she can't keep this up for long. The rest of the camp is waking, raiders hurtling down the paths.

You vault over the fence, landing beside Siddie with both daggers drawn. Ben's less than a second behind you, falling upon the marauders. Spinning, slashing, leaping, stabbing. Bodies piling up at her feet.

(You thank the Shell Collector you never had to fight her during the war. You're not sure you would've made it.)

"Emara! Ben!" Siddie's voice is watery with relief.

"I told you to stay put!" you shout. One of the bandits slices at you, but you're already sidestepping around him, too fast for him to follow. You're behind him now, his back exposed, your blade in his neck. You let him fall, turning quickly back to Siddie. "What are you doing down here?"

"There was someone near the tent! I—"

Before she can continue, an arrow skims your shoulder. At the watch station, the guard's nocking another shaft to their bow.

"Knifey, the archer!" you cry.

Ben barely pauses to look up, and her knife's flying from her hand. It sinks into the guard's stomach, sending them gasping to their knees.

"I was *trying* to save you!" Siddie says.

You snort. "Well, I don't think it worked!" Another two raiders rush you, but you dispatch them easily. Trapping their weapons, cutting their arms and thighs.

Ben draws another knife from her belt. She doesn't look good, you think. Her face is ashen; her expression, drawn. She can't seem to catch her breath, and you'd wonder if she's been wounded, but she doesn't seem to be bleeding—

Sweat beads on her forehead. She squints at you like she's trying to make her eyes focus, trying to see you and Siddie, standing there in front of her, and not whatever nightmare's come over her instead.

You touch her arm. "We've got to get out of here, Knifey."

She blinks up at you. She nods.

Together, the three of you fight your way to the watch station. You're clearing a path while Ben defends the rear, and the raiders are rushing you, another and another and another—

You're a blur of movement. Daggers glinting, fast and fluid—

Blood spattering hot over your fingers—

You're at the edge of the encampment now, boosting Siddie over the fence, but Ben's not with you anymore—

She's behind you—

She's surrounded—

She's still fighting, slicing through her enemies as if they were paper—

Knives flashing and deadly in the firelight—

But she's overwhelmed. In the melee, she's cut across the arm, the side. You see her flinch. You see her falter. No matter how good you are, sometimes the numbers are just against you. Another injury and she's going to fall—

But you can't let that happen.

You're *kin*.

You're not losing her. Years of searching, and you've finally found somewhere you belong, people you belong to and who, despite your heritage, your upbringing, your timeworn allegiances, belong unquestionably to you—

So you go back for her.

You grab her by the wrist. You yank her out of the fray.

"No!" She pulls against you. "Stop! Emara, don't!"

But you don't listen. You're hauling her after you, you're picking her up and throwing her over the fence. "Get Piggy out of here! I'll be right behind you, eh?"

You don't wait to watch her land. Turning back to the camp, you slip between your foes, slick as water. A cut to the neck, the back, the ribs. You're in constant motion, spinning, wheeling, finding your enemy again and again and again. Fingers, forearm, neck, chest. Thigh, stomach, throat. You're a hurricane. You're howling wind and devastating rain, your enemies falling before you like uprooted trees.

From the hillside, you hear Ben screaming, "Emara! *Let's go!*"

Sheathing your weapons, you launch yourself back over the fence. You're tumbling to the ground and rolling back up again, while Siddie plunges into the woods ahead.

You run, and Ben's racing back for you, and you're keenly aware of the uproar behind you—

Shouting, clamoring, the rattle of weapons—

But you've got time. You've got enough time. You're almost at the trees. If you can get to the horses, you can get out of there before any of the raiders can catch you.

You can get back to Amity.

You can warn her.

You can give her one more victory before she burns out.

Then you feel something strike you. You feel it before you even hear the shot—

The sound of thunder, rolling over the hills—

And suddenly you're pitching forward. Something bleeding—

You—

You're bleeding—

Groaning, you roll over. Look back the way you came. By the watch station is a girl, your age—

(She's only your age—)

She has the cloak of an Amerandine captain rippling about her shoulders, and a handcannon smoking in her arms.

Briefly, you close your eyes.

They *did* have a handcannon.

You're trying to stand, but your legs can't seem to hold you up anymore, can't move anymore, aren't working anymore, and Siddie's racing back to help you, she's skidding to a stop beside you, her hands all over you, her tears falling hot and wet on your cheeks.

"Emara! Get up! You've got to get up, Emara!"

You bat at her hands. (Your fingers feeble, your arms limp.) Distantly, you can hear Adren's bandits climbing over the fences. You can feel their footsteps through the earth.

"No, no, no, no." Ben grabs one of your arms, and you try to tell her she's holding you too tightly, but you can't seem to form the words. "Not again. Not this time. Come on, Emara. *Get up.*"

You feel yourself being hauled upright between Ben and Siddie, and now you're being dragged, but there's not enough time. The marauders are charging across the slope below you. They'll reach you in seconds.

You swat weakly at your kin. "Put me down. Get out of here."

Ben grunts. "We're not leaving you."

"Well, thanks." You try to laugh, but it doesn't come out right. You cough, and blood sprays from your lips. "I think I'm leaving you though, eh?"

Siddie stumbles, and you feel the impact go through you like an avalanche. Things breaking. Things are already broken. You cringe.

Ben pulls your arm tighter around her. "Shut up and keep moving."

But you're so heavy now. You're falling now (your limbs all twisted, something wrong inside you), and Ben's pulling you across her shoulders as Siddie turns to face the raiders, her sword long and gleaming with a faint, blush-colored light.

The air ripples around her—

And from her blade comes an arc of fire, so brilliant and blinding it's almost white—

For an instant, it illuminates the frightened face of every charging raider, whose mouths fall open in wonder as the blast sends them sailing backward, splintering the fence and the watch station, all those bodies flying into the paddocks, the tents—

Ben carries you into the forest, and you don't know how she has the strength because she's so much smaller than you, but she's climbing up the hill and toward the horses, and it's hard to see anything now but shadows—

Hard to hear anything now but breath—

Things are going cloudy and dim, and you can't see her anymore but you reach out for Siddie, though you don't know if she's near you, don't know if she cries out or clasps your hand—

But you smile, however faintly—

And you hope she hears you when you murmur, "Proud of you, Siddie."

KANVER

IT'S A GOOD DAY FOR DRINKING. YOU KNOW IT AS
soon as you wake, which is early, before the sun comes up. The dark
is too hard; the air is too sharp. Shivering, you stumble from the
cabin. (Flat skies, frost in the weeds.) You wrap yourself in a blanket,
knowing the liquor could keep you dull, dull, dull, and you want to
be dull now. You want to be drifting and unfeeling now, and you
ache—

The last time you drank, it was Emara who found you. It was
Emara who mopped up your messes and swore the villagers to
silence. It was Emara who saved you.

But Emara's gone—

You feel her absence like a missing tooth, a soft and fleshy place,
a space you keep reaching for, hoping the next time you reach for it,
it'll be filled—

But it isn't—

(Filled.)

And she isn't—

(Here.)

Dawn arrives, and as the clouds blush a beautiful and traitorous
pink, Ben joins you in the garden. She's almost unrecognizable in
the morning light—

A slumped-over Ben—

A crumpled-up Ben—

She's wearing a Wind Runner medallion, Leum's Wind Runner medallion, keeps turning it between her fingers as if she's at prayer—

Across the creek, in the cemetery, you hear the sounds of shovels. Scrape and pebble, sand and heave. Ben puts her head between her knees.

Below, smoke rises from the village chimneys. The smells of simmering broth and searing meat. The farmers are preparing a feast for the dead, which is their way, though you don't understand it, can't seem to grasp it—

If you had a feast for everyone you knew who died, you'd never stop eating.

"Kanver, Ben." Leum stands in the doorway. (Her eyes sleepless, her face made of stone.) "It's time."

None of you know much about Vedran burial rites (or Chenyaran burial rites, for that matter), but you hope, for Emara's sake, that some traditions belong to you all.

You surround her, the six of you like rays of the sun, and you bathe her body. You lift her hands, you wipe down her arms. You swab each of her fingers, from her knuckles to her nails, bitten to the quick—

With a gasp, Ket drops her washcloth, stained pink.

Her shaking hands, her sudden retreat—

You find her standing at the edge of the path, tracing the frayed edge of her collar. Snapped threads, a gaping hem.

"Do you remember the last time you washed a body?" she asks.

"The end of the war." You rub your face, as if that will stop you from seeing it, there, behind your eyes—

The small coffin—

The smaller body—

Pem's body—

With the mussel-shell necklace clasped in her fist—

"I never thought I'd have to do it again," Ket says.

You grimace. Your bones hurt. (The hollows of them.) "Never?" you ask.

"Never."

"In your whole life?"

You don't know why, but you think of a river. You think of life on a river, the flow of it, the way things drift in and out of it, things drifting in and out of your life as you float downstream: minnows beneath the surface, dragonflies skimming the reeds, a twig, a yellow leaf, a weave of algae, a flat-bottomed boat, a gleaming stone, a child in the shallows, up to their knees—

Then they leave, or you do—

They're swept away, or you are. Old age, weak hearts, accidents, disease—

There's movement in the cabin windows. A passing figure, a rustle of clothes. Have the others finished, you wonder? Have they combed the hair and closed the wounds? The long, empty swaths of her, now washed clean?

"Wasn't there always going to be a next time?" you say.

You don't think Ket has blinked once since you got out here. Her gaze fastened on the mountains, her eyes watering in the wind. "I dunno," she says. "I guess I never thought I'd be around long enough to find out."

While Onna and her family prepare an offering for Vastari (some part of a cow, like the Camassians always do for the dead), you and your kin dress Emara in clean white robes. Arrange her hair. Lower her into the plain pine coffin, where you lay her daggers on her chest.

Ket loops a red string around her wrist.

Leum places a dash of salt on her lips.

As you cross your hands over her balar weapons, Siddie lets out a cry (strangled and high) and scurries to the back room for Emara's things. Empty bedroll, cold clothes. Belongings, but they don't belong to anyone anymore, and if they don't belong to anyone, are they still belongings?

Or are they debris?

Soon, Siddie's pulling several items from their packages. Indigo. Ikat. Cotton. The cloth spilling from her arms as she stands.

"They're Chenyaran," she says, kneading the folds between her fingers. "She was collecting them. I thought maybe . . ." She lifts the wraps toward the coffin as if they'll float out of her hands like soap bubbles, or dandelion seeds—

Lifting a finger, Leum traces the edge of the fabric. Printed patterns, embroidered stars. "Would she want them with her?"

"I don't know."

"You're the only one who could've known."

"I don't know!" Siddie's voice rises; her expression contorts. "She didn't tell me! How am I supposed to know?"

None of you answer. Sometimes there is no answer. No conclusions, no solutions. Sometimes there are only hints and guesses, questions and regrets.

As the tears begin to fall from Siddie's cheeks, you put your arm around her.

You forget not to cry.

When you're ready (or as ready as you can be, given the circumstances), Jin and a few others come in to weave flowers in Emara's hair. Faded stalks of yarrow and buckwheat like lightning in a cloud. The air perfumed by sprigs of pennyroyal and sage.

She almost looks beautiful.

She almost looks asleep.

Then the villagers leave, and Amity (always a perfectionist) re-arranges Emara's hair, tucks a strand behind her ear. For a long time, she stands there, gripping the edge of the coffin, and you wonder what she's promising herself now, with the weight of Emara's death on her shoulders and the rest of your lives hanging over her head.

No more of you extinguished?

No more of you dead?

Beckoning for a hammer, she nails down the lid herself.

It's nearly midday when you emerge with the coffin, the six of you carrying her to the cemetery where the rest of the village awaits. Onna, Tana, Poppy, Parker, Hemmen, everyone clad in funereal white.

You lay Emara down with her body facing east. The prayers are said; the offering's ashes, scattered upon the coffin lid.

You bury her.

You bury her.

Far from Chenyara, the cairn is built.

When the villagers leave for their solemn feast, you and your kin remain. Staring at nothing, nothing to say.

Ohh-oh-ohhh . . .

You don't know who starts singing first, but soon the rest of you join in. The lullaby for the little ones, faint and lovely, floating over the graves. The song she sang to you while she sat with you that day, her voice drifting softly through your dreams.

Ohhh-oh-ohhh . . .

Your voices rough. Your throats raw. You hope she hears you, you pray to the gods she hears you, as she makes her way to the Palace of Bones.

You hope she knows she's not alone.

Ben stops singing to throw up in the weeds. Her arms bent, her body curled. You rub her back. You lay your head in the curve of her neck and let her weep.

You move, you move. The path, the broken bridge, the creek. Sometime in the afternoon, you end up at Onna's, where the villagers are gathered, picking over the bones of their feast.

"Handcannons," the Old Man is muttering. "What are we going to do against handcannons?"

Onna glances at him sharply. "Now's not the time, Old Man."

"I'm just saying what everyone is thinking. Didn't the sick one tell us she needed *seven* kindlings? And how many do we have now? *Six.* Against handcannons. And they won't even use their most powerful weapon to defend us."

"You mean magic?" Tana snaps. Her words a lash. "You want them to burn themselves out for us?"

To his credit, the Old Man looks suitably abashed. But that doesn't stop him from muttering, "That's their job."

Stealthily, you steal a jug of wine from the table and slip away again before anyone notices.

He's not wrong. During the war, life for a kindling was fleeting. You were born, you trained, you fought, you died—

Quicker than the blink of an eye—

You understood that. You accepted that.

To be a kindling was to be a corpse.

But that's supposed to be over. The war is supposed to be over. You're supposed to have a future, like Leum wants. Companionship, adventure, freedom from the past—

Only the past won't let you go—

Your nightmares, your waking dreams, your visions of Pem. You can't escape them, just like you can't escape the fighting, the killing, the dying—

You keep losing.

It's in your nature.

(It's in all of our natures.)

Even when we win, we lose.

You move again. The shrine, the woods. You have to move, or you'll sink. You'll be swallowed. You'll drink. You stumble through the trees, dangling the jug from your finger—

You shake it, just a little, to hear the sound of it, like a tiny ocean rolling around inside—

It comforts you, knowing you could drink if you wanted to. (And you want to.)

(You don't want to, and you do.)

You want to be subsumed.

You keep moving. You and the jug and the wine inside. By the time the sun is setting, you're at the cabin again, inside the cabin, where you find Leum and Burk in the front room. Removing your sandals, you stagger up to them, listing a little on your tired feet.

Leum glances at you. You and your ocean. "You're drinking?" she says. (Half question, half accusation.)

You heft the jug, listening to the *slosh, slosh, slosh* of it, and set it down beside her. "I wish."

She takes a swig. She looks surprised, you think, like she didn't really believe you, didn't really think there'd be anything left. Taking a cup from the shelf, she pours out a little wine and sets it beside the meager pile of Emara's things, like a gift—

Like she'll find it waiting for her when she comes back from wherever she is—

Out by the barricade or maybe on patrol—

"I wish a lot of things," you say.

Leum nods. A long, slow nod like she's falling asleep. "Me too."

You sit beside her, but you're heavier than you mean to be. You're a sack of grain. You're a bag of sand. *Whump!* You're collapsing under your own weight, under the weight of your sadness. Any more, and your seams will split.

Leum pulls a length of fabric across her lap—

One of Emara's wraps, woven of so many colors and textures, it reminds you of a landscape seen from a very great height. (Farmlands, roads, rows of flowers.) Siddie didn't know what to do with them, couldn't choose, had never had to choose before and didn't know how, so Leum did it for her, for both of them, you suppose, for Siddie and for Emara—

She kept the wraps. Didn't want them moldering in the ground, all their colors fading, all that brightness fading, there, in the grip of the earth.

"What are you going to do with them?" you ask.

"I don't know."

"Are you going to bring them back?"

"Where? To Chenyara?"

"Maybe."

"Chenyara doesn't exist anymore."

"Yeah."

"A lot of things don't exist anymore, if they ever did." She traces the embroidery with her finger. "That's why I wanted to go north, remember? So we could start again."

At some point, you sleep. You and Leum and Burk together, a bundle of limbs. You sleep, and when you wake again, it's evening, and you're alone. Maybe Leum had watch duty. Maybe she could no longer be still. Above you, Emara's clothes are still dangling from the rafters. Socks and underthings, a pair of trousers, a shirt.

You're lying where Emara's coffin was, you think. You're lying where Emara did.

Then, a *thump* at the window. Two small hands on the sill.

You sit up, bemused, as Poppy tumbles to the floor, nearly impaling herself on her little spear.

"Oops," she says.

You don't mean to, but you chuckle. A low and painful joy in your chest. "What are you doing here?"

She doesn't answer. She kicks off her sandals and begins a circuit of your living quarters. The cook fire, the kettle, the ladles dangling from their hooks.

"It was cleaner when the Old Man lived here." Poppy crosses the room and sits next to you, pulling her spear across her lap.

"Blame Emara," you say, though you don't mean to, didn't intend to invoke her name in this place that's still so full of her—

The drying laundry—

The dimple in her pillow—

The cup Leum left for her, the wine shimmering within—

Seeing it, Poppy frowns. "Tana says you're not supposed to be drinking."

"I'm not," you say. "That's not for me."

She tips her spear this way and that. The weight of it. You can already tell it's unbalanced, not that it matters.

"Does your mama know you're here?" you ask.

She ignores you. "What's going to happen when Adren comes?"

You smooth your hands along your thighs. You try to figure out where to start. "You remember how we saw the scouts before they reached us? The lookouts will see Adren coming long before she gets here," you say. "They'll warn the rest of us, and we'll all go to our positions."

Poppy's brow creases. "What's your position?"

"I'll be on the north road, by the broken bridge. Do you remember where you're supposed to go?"

"I'm supposed to hide."

"Right. You and the other kids will hide in your mama's house."

"What about Emara? Where was she supposed to be?"

You blink a few times. You try to clear your throat. But your voice still cracks when you say, "She was supposed to be on the south road."

She was supposed to be on the barricade, the one she worked so hard for, to guard the village against invasion.

"But she's gone."

You nod.

"So you need someone to take her place on the road," Poppy says. "Like me."

"No!" You bolt upright so suddenly, you knock the spear out of her hands. She jumps as it goes rattling across the floor. *"No,"* you repeat.

You don't want her running around. Don't want her on the streets. You can't find her on the ground like you did Pem—

The smell of powder—

The sound of explosions—

A small body, dead on the ground—

You *can't.*

You take Poppy by the shoulders. Shake her a little bit.

Her eyes widen.

But you don't let go. "Promise me you'll hide," you say. "You stay where you're supposed to, where none of Adren's raiders will find you. You hide, and you don't come out till we've won. Promise me, Poppy."

She regards you solemnly with her obsidian-chip eyes. "Do you promise we'll win? Even without Emara?"

You shouldn't. You can't. Amity would tell you to be honest. Don't get her hopes up. Don't make her believe something that isn't true.

You lost Emara.

You could lose everyone.

But the truth is overrated. The truth is terrible, brutal, banal, cruel. (And you don't want to be cruel.)

So you release your grip. You pick up the spear. You hand it to Poppy and pat her on the head. "I promise." You try to reassure her, but who are you kidding, Kanver? You can't even reassure yourself. "We're going to win."

KET

YOU KNOW YOU SHOULD REST. YOU HAVEN'T SLEPT
since Ben and Siddie returned with Emara's body—

Her big, beautiful body, slung across the back of a horse as if she
were nothing more than baggage—

Loose hair, limp arms, eyelids sunken like she didn't have eyes
anymore, like there was nothing inside her anymore, not her heart
or her tongue, not her soul or her memory or the last breath in her
lungs—

You couldn't look at her. Couldn't stand to see her like that.
Empty and broken. You can't close your eyes without seeing her like
that. You're turning in your blanket. You're finding lumps in your
bedroll. You've got watch duty in a few hours, but you're staring at
the ceiling. You don't want to sleep, don't know what you'll see if
you sleep, don't know what dreams will find you—

You get up. You slip into your clothes and slide your sword
through your belt. You need to move. The open door, the tempestu-
ous dark. You take the steps two at a time. You're quick as the wind,
and nothing can touch you.

You steal across the square.

You're at Tana's window. You're tapping at her shutters.

Above you, a storm is brewing. A moan in the treetops, damp on
the air. Clouds billow across the stars, and you want to be carried

away with them. You want to be lifted, wind-tossed and lightning-struck—

Anything, as long as you don't have to be here, in your own body, with your own thoughts—

The window opens, and Tana appears. Her pursed lips, her furrowed brow. You haven't spoken all day, but you don't need to speak now. You take her chin in your hands. You lower your mouth to hers.

She pulls away. "Not here."

She climbs through the window, and you take her by the hand. You tug her after you. Away, away. Up the hill and through the graveyard. You're not thinking about Emara now. You're not thinking about anything now.

You reach the wagon, the market wagon in the clearing above the cemetery, looking strange now in the shadows. Handles and spokes.

"Ket." There's a tremor in Tana's voice, a ripple of grief.

You pull her toward you. Her wrist, her waist. She's in your arms, familiar in your arms, and you kiss her again. Tongue, throat. You want to plunge inside her. You want to lose yourself in her like a diver in a cave.

Under your hands, you can feel her opening up to you. Her arms, her robe, her legs. You're on your knees in front of her. You're finding the darkness between her thighs.

Then she stops you.

A hand on your jaw. A look in her eyes.

"You don't want to?" you say.

She tucks her clothes back into place. "No, sorry, I just—"

You stand. "Don't worry about it." You're already dusting off your trousers. You're already walking away.

It doesn't take her long to follow. (Her footsteps in the mulch, her hand on your elbow.) "Ket, wait."

You want to believe she's changing her mind. She doesn't want conversation, doesn't want to ask you any questions, doesn't want anything but to push you against a tree and kiss you in the darkness—

But you know her better than that by now.

You pause all the same, even though you don't want to, want to keep moving, want to get lost.

"I thought I could be different," she says. "I tried to be different. I thought if I was more like him . . . like Vian . . . then it would be like he wasn't gone."

You avoid her gaze, searching the woods for an escape. You want things to be easy (a kiss, a touch, a moan), and nothing about this is easy.

"But he's gone," Tana continues. "And I can't pretend anymore."

"You mean with me?"

"I mean, if we live through this, what are you planning to do? Are you going to stay?"

You force yourself not to think about it. The life you could've had up here. The mountains, the pine trees, the freedom, the calm—

The battle is still coming, and when it's over, Camas could be gone—

Trampled gardens, burning houses—

After the battle, you could all be dead.

You—

Tana—

Nothing but corpses in the road.

You shake your head. "I can't."

She's silent.

The wind tears at your clothes, your hair, your hands. You're unraveling. You're coming undone. Your pretenses, your armor. Your heart, exposed, with all its secrets, all the things you held so close.

From your pocket, you remove the pleated page. "I made someone a promise, a long time ago," you say.

"What's this?" She unfolds it. Her gaze darting across its surface. "A list?"

You swallow. You nod.

You remember.

"Her name was Kari," you say.

She was a soldier, like you, but unlike you she enlisted. Volunteers were rare by that time and welcome, so they didn't bat an eye when she told them she was sixteen, though she was scrawny and six months shy. She wanted to fight, she said. She wanted to make a difference, not that she ever got the chance.

You met her after basic training. She was seventeen and at her first posting; you were a kindling, and it was the end of the war. Not much left to do but hold the lands you'd taken, and that was easy enough with legions of cannoneers.

You could've been restless. No one to fight, no battles to win. You could've been bored, like the rest of them, drinking and dueling and gambling, killing time before the official Vedran surrender, when you could all finally leave.

But you had Kari.

And Kari was never boring.

She was always moving, always chasing something. (A feather on the wind, a cloud, a dream.) *There's a lot of world out there, Ket. Don't you want to see it?*

When the news came down that the war was over, that all of you had made it through the fighting, that you were going to live, the two of you danced through the streets—

Fireworks and music—

Parades and applause—

Laughing, she pulled you into a crowded tavern. Cheap drinks and a corner table. Everyone cheering. *Peace! Peace at last!* The two of you ebullient and overflowing. It was her idea to make the list.

You have a future now, Ket.

What do you want to do with it?

Brush, paper, smeared words, spilled wine. You wrote down whatever you could think of, whatever you could dream. You were going to do it together. There was so much world to see.

"What happened to her?" Tana asks, folding the paper up again.

You take it from her. "It was an accident," you say.

Not some life-changing battle but something utterly mundane. Two days after the Vedran surrender, and not everyone was done celebrating.

A drunken wagoner—

A skittish horse—

A cart overturned, and Kari crushed beneath it, broken and empty—

That was the last time you washed a body. That was the last time you stuck around long enough to see somebody die.

After that, you were always in motion. You had promises to keep. You had a world to see.

"I'm sorry," Tana says.

You pocket the list, still incomplete. "That's why I can't stay."

"I'm not asking you to stay." She regards you sadly. All her thoughts swimming behind her eyes and nothing you can do to calm them. "But I can't pretend anymore that it doesn't matter if you leave."

The wind tugs at her hair, whipping it across her eyes, and you almost reach for her. You almost smooth the strands from her face, almost tuck them behind her ear, almost brush her cheek—

You can't stay, but you don't want to go, so you draw out the moment. You don't even breathe. You carve out this second and nestle inside, because as long as you're here, you can still change your mind.

You can still be together.

You can still be okay.

But Tana is already turning away. The storm is already brewing. The raiders are already on the move, and the battle is already coming.

In the distance, the alarm begins to ring.

AMITY

STANDING ON THE BARRICADE, YOU WATCH THE enemy gather. Marauders, horses, torches flaring in the darkness. They're surrounding you. A dozen flames lighting up the field. A hundred. More.

There shouldn't be nearly so many. By your reckoning, you've already taken three of their scouts, a squad of six. Ben says she and Emara slew at least two as they fled and wounded another half dozen at least—

You tell yourself it's easy to light fires. Those aren't reinforcements out there; it's a show, a display meant to frighten and intimidate, distract and confuse. While your attention is on the south road, the raiders will be probing your defenses elsewhere, searching for weaknesses on the western slope, the flooded meadow.

But you planned for this, didn't you?

The lookouts have returned from their outposts. The slope and the meadow have been secured. The villagers are armed; the children are in hiding. Everything and everyone is in its place—

Except Emara.

You imagine her beside you. You imagine her with the wind in her hair. You imagine the shape of her voice on the air.

What's the matter, Queenie?

Don't tell me you're having second thoughts now.

You imagine her loose and relaxed beside you, picking slivers out of the barricade and flicking them onto the road.

But no, that's just you. The splinters pricking your fingers as you peel them from the ramparts and fling them into the night. One after another after another, disappearing—

"Are you okay?" Kanver asks. They're standing beside you, watching you with those sad amber eyes. In their pupils, you swear you can see the light of a hundred fires—

All the enemies that have come to destroy you—

You try to shrug, but it comes out as a shudder. "Fine."

"They're surrounding us." Behind you, Leum returns from her sweep of the perimeter, bounding up the steps two at a time. "They're on our north flank too. Ket and Onna spotted them by the broken bridge."

"How many?" you ask.

She glances at the torches, well out of range and difficult to count. "Hard to tell."

You nod. "Go tighten up our patrols. I don't want any more surprises tonight."

Silently, she obeys.

"Someone's coming," Kanver murmurs.

You squint over the barricade as a horse and rider emerge from the darkness. A flowing cloak. A lashing tail. The pair of them unnaturally beautiful, almost ghostlike, in the gusting shadows.

Halting on the road, the rider glances up at you. To the untrained eye, she might seem casual, might seem careless, but you know she's a predator. (You can sense it from here.) She's neither casual nor careless but controlled, precise, purposeful—

Turn your back on her, and she'll pounce.

"Adren." You try to keep your voice from cracking, but you feel it fracture in the frosty air. You wet your lips and swallow a few times, trying to soothe the ache in your throat.

Leaning over the ramparts, you study Adren's oval face, her delicate features, her hair flying about her in the wind. She's younger than you expected. The way the villagers talk about her (the people she slaughtered, the terror she wrought), you were imagining someone older, worn and calloused by battle, but this girl is your age—

And if she's your age, she's got to be a kindling.

Below you, Adren lets out a whistle. "Is that the Twin Valley Reaper up there?"

You don't answer. Your mind is racing. How does she know you? Were you both trainees at House Vastari? No, Ben or Siddie would've recognized her name. Does that mean you fought together, like you and Leum did at Twin Valley? Or did she see you through the crowd at one of your many parades?

For once, you wish you'd paid more attention to your peers during the war. You need more intelligence on her. You need to know her weaknesses, her preferred modes of attack.

As if she knows you're trying to identify her, Adren grins and leans back in the saddle. Smug and overconfident, although of course she has reason to be.

You swallow again. "Are you the one who killed Emara?"

"Was that her name?" There's a thoughtful pause. "I didn't know she died."

You can't see Adren well in this light, but you think she almost looks sorry.

(But she doesn't get to be sorry.)

(Not yet.)

(Not until you burn her heart from her chest.)

"What do you want, Adren?"

Instead of answering, she tilts her head curiously, her face pale against the black of her cape. "What are you doing here, Deathbringer? You know what we used to say about these old villages. Rations and draftees—"

You and Kanver exchange glances.

But we would've preferred more to eat.

A faintness comes over you, and you grip the ramparts to steady yourself. "They're under my protection now."

"That's what I find odd. What are they offering you, Death-bringer? What could they possibly have that you want?"

You answer her with silence.

She doesn't seem to mind. "I've no interest in slaughtering war heroes," she says, "so I've come to make you an offer of my own. If you and your kindlings leave before dawn, my raiders will allow you to pass unmolested. You'll be free, and you'll be alive, and that's more than most of us can say."

"Or?" you ask.

"Or you choose to remain, and when we invade tomorrow, we'll kill anyone who stands in our way."

You've been threatened before. In fact, you're used to it. All that bluff and bluster, all those delusions of being dangerous.

But Adren isn't bluffing.

(She doesn't have to.)

She already took one of you. She already put one of you in the ground, and she did it without a balar weapon—

Crossed hands, flowered hair, cold daggers in the coffin-dark—

Emara.

Adren may not have used magic, but she doesn't need magic to be a threat. She has handcannons, and you still don't know how many.

You can't help but think of your kin now, dying around you, falling around you like leaves, brilliantly red in the dirt.

"So? What do you say, Deathbringer?" Adren calls. "Are you willing to die for these peasants?"

As she speaks the wind picks up, tearing at your scarf and hair, spiking your lungs with cold. Your throat burns. Your limbs ache.

You try to smile, though you're shivering. It's the chill, or so you tell yourself. It's the illness in your veins.

"To protect these people," you say, "I'm willing to kill every last one of you."

"Suit yourself." Adren sighs. "I suppose I didn't expect anything less."

You see the back of her, but you haven't seen the last of her. Her and that horse. Her and that cape. It's a cloak made for captains, but like the torches, it's theater.

She's not a captain. That's not her rank.

She's one of you.

You shift uneasily. Who was she in the war? Quaternary Class? Tertiary? A specialist, like you? You wish you knew the shape of her balar weapon, so you could anticipate the shape of her attack.

Will she try to infiltrate your defenses in the night, like a Mist-walker?

Or is she a vanguardian who'll attempt a frontal assault?

Quietly, Kanver tells you Onna and the Old Man are waiting. They got an offer on the north road, too, and they want to discuss.

You nod, expressionless. You expected as much. Leaving Kanver on the barricade with the other guards, you descend the steps. To the east, the flooded meadow is jagged with wind. Guard posts lit by orange flames, golden tips upon the waves.

A storm is coming—

Rain—

Snow, too, if it gets cold enough—

As you reach the road, Onna beckons you toward the village, out of earshot of the others.

You follow. (Your shoulders tight, your footsteps heavy.) "They offered to spare you if you gave us up, didn't they?" you ask.

"They said if we let them into the village, they'd leave the rest of us alone," the Old Man says.

Onna frowns at you. "How did you know?"

"It's what I would've done." You pause for a several moments to cough into your sleeve. "If they turn us on each other, the village is theirs."

"Then we don't turn," Onna says simply.

You're surprised by her finality. A month ago, she didn't even want you here, didn't want you or your kin or the violence that haunts you—

Hunts you—

Every breath, every step—

You clear your throat. "Will the rest of your people agree? Now that they've seen the enemy, surrender might be looking like a nice alternative to a swift and bloody end."

Onna turns her husband's infantry knot in her fingers. "You said it yourself. Starvation may not be violent, but it still results in death. And that won't be swift. It'll be slow and painful."

The Old Man scowls. "Why are you acting like there are only two options?"

"What do you suggest?" Onna asks.

He gestures vaguely in your direction. "I'm just saying, we've got a Deathbringer right here."

You stiffen.

"That'd kill her," Onna snaps.

"So? She's dying anyway, isn't she? At least this way, she dies doing what she's supposed to."

You tighten your scarf. You look away.

At this point, you'd lose a couple weeks, at most—

Or maybe only days—

(You're so close to death already, aren't you, Amity?)

(For months, it's been staring you in the face.)

"Just hop up on that barricade and do whatever it is you do." The

Old Man makes a cutting motion with his hands. "If anybody's left alive after that, they'll have no choice but to turn tail and run."

The disquiet you've felt since seeing Adren on the road now creeps into your bones. You're trembling. You can't seem to stop it, which unnerves you more—

You've always been master of your own body—

In fact, you were a prodigy. The fastest, the strongest, the best House Vastari had seen in years. You graduated early, made Death-bringer by twelve, Primary Class by fourteen—

Gods, you even hid the fact that you were dying *for weeks*, even from those closest to you—

Onna rounds on him. "Get that thought out of your head right now, Old Man. These are *children*. They're *our children* now. We're not going to ask any more of them than we've already taken, do you understand me?"

He sulks at her.

"Old Man."

"Bah!" He waves her off. "Yes, I understand."

"Good. Now get out of here, and don't tell anyone about Adren's offer or your disgraceful plan," she says, lifting a finger. "Not a word. Or the consequences will be on your head."

You wrap your arms around your waist as the Old Man stalks toward the village, but you can't stop shaking. You're coming apart.

Noticing your shivering, Onna reaches for you. "Amity?"

You want to shrug her off. You want to snap at her. You want to tell her you're fine. Everything's fine.

But you're not fine—

You're not strong, powerful, glorious—

You're not important—

You're not the weapon the Old Man wants you to be, the weapon you were trained to be, the reason you were celebrated for all those many years—

You're not the Reaper—

You're not the Red Death—

You're just a kid.

You're just a dying kid.

And still they want to use you. They want to burn you up and snuff you out so *their* lives can be lit a while longer, so *they* can survive.

But you?

Never you.

You're crying. You don't even realize it until Onna pulls you to her. Strong arms, broad chest. "Shh," she says, cradling you, gently, like a child—

Like someone's child—

"It's okay," she says into your scarf, your hair. "You're okay."

But you're not.

"I'm sorry." You can't catch your breath. "I'm sorry."

"Shh. It's okay. You don't have to be sorry."

But you are. You're sorry you're not stronger. You're sorry you're not the weapon they need.

You're sorry you don't want to die for them.

(You don't want to die at all.)

You're not ready. You never were. You lied to yourself, again and again. You told yourself you accepted your fate. You just needed a mission. You just needed a victory. You needed to go out fighting. That's what you told yourself. You needed to go out blazing like a star.

But fighting this battle was just an excuse to fight *something*—

To feel like you could win against *something*—

But you should have known, Amity—

(We know better than anyone—)

No one wins against death.

You're going to lose people tomorrow. It could be Leum. It could be Ket or Kanver. It could be Ben or Siddie or Parker or Tana or Poppy or Onna herself—

It could be you—

Crossed hands, flowered hair, your body crowned and withered in the coffin-dark—

You don't stop crying. You bury your head in Onna's chest.

BEN

YOU REMEMBER THE FRONT ROOM OF THE CABIN feeling cramped. Kitchen, cook fire, bedrolls, blankets. Foodstuffs on the shelves, weapons on the floor. You had to sleep outside because you couldn't breathe with so many bodies nearby, couldn't roll over without running into one of your kin.

But there's too much space now with only the six of you. Cold and cavernous. On the earthen floor, Leum prods at the fire, sending up sparks. In the corner, Siddie's huddled in her blanket, petting Burk between the ears. There's even enough room for Ket to pace, corner to corner, stepping over Kanver, who's spread-eagled on the floor.

Everyone avoids touching Emara's hanging laundry, the cup of wine someone's left by her things.

It's almost like they're waiting.

It's almost like they think she'll return.

You tried, Ben. When she didn't die out there by Adren's encampment, you tried to bring her back. You'd left your old squad in the rubble, but you tried to bring Emara back. Her wound packed with rags, her breath coming fast and shallow. You remember talking to her, though you don't remember what you said.

You wanted to keep her awake.

You wanted to keep her alive long enough to make it home.

In the doorway to the back room, Amity clears her throat. She looks tired, with the signs of burnout feathering her cheeks and forehead, jaw and chin. She says Adren made all of you an offer, made one to the villagers too. "We're being asked to betray them," she says. "They're being asked to betray us."

"Will they?" you ask. "How many of them know about this?"

"Whoever was on the north road to hear it." Amity ticks off the names on her fingers. "Tana, Parker, the Old Man. Onna's sworn them all to secrecy. She doesn't want word getting out."

"Does it matter?" Ket shrugs. "No one in their right mind would take that offer."

Amity shakes her head. "Don't underestimate the power of self-preservation."

In the ensuing silence, the others look to one another, and you watch their resolve settle over them like night over an ocean—

Black, penetrating, inexorable—

They're not leaving. They couldn't now if they wanted to.

They're *kindlings*.

"We're with you, Amity," Siddie says in her small, bright voice. "To the end."

"Come victory or come death," Kanver murmurs. They still haven't moved from their place on the floor.

Leum and Ket nod.

You don't say anything. You're staring at the cup. Emara's cup. The wine untouched, the surface slicked with dust.

What's the point, if no one's going to drink it?

You imagine dumping it out in the morning. The sound of it splattering against the flagstones or mixing with the rain. You imagine your fingers numbed by cold, your damp hair, your drenched clothes. Your insides feel hollow. You're so empty, you ache.

"Ben?" Amity's watching you from the doorway.

Crossing your arms, you give her a sad smile.

Then you sleep, or you try to, because whatever happens, you're going to need rest. Throughout the night, your kin wander in and out of the cabin. Shifts on the perimeter. Restlessness rearing its head once again.

Dawn's still a couple hours away when you wake for your watch. Wind rattling the shutters. Scattered raindrops outside. With a shiver, you strap on your gauntlets and buckle on your knives.

Amity and Ket are already on patrol, but in the front room you find Leum, Kanver, and Siddie curled up together. A bundle of limbs. Under Leum's arm, Burk perks up as you slide past. (Her tail thumping, her soft *haroomph*.)

You lay another log on the fire. You put a finger to your lips.

She places her head on her paws again, watching as you don your hat, throw your coat over your shoulders.

You step outside.

You should head toward the barricade, where you're supposed to relieve Ket, but you hurry toward the stables. You open the doors. You saddle your horse.

You knew as soon as you heard the offer that you were going to take it.

A sudden wind rattles the temporary stables, searingly cold through the cracks in the walls. You're going to be wanting for warm clothes in this weather, but you couldn't risk packing. You didn't want the others to wake—

To watch you—

To try to stop you—

You're returning to Windfall, where you'll replenish your supplies. From there, you'll return to Gateway. You'll rehire your guide. You're running away, but you're good at that, aren't you?

(This isn't your first time.)

As you lead Penumbra out of the stables, someone steps in front of you. A sword on her back. A dog at her side. She glares at you, defiant, fierce.

You climb into the saddle. "Get out of my way, Leum."

She doesn't move. "Where are you going?"

"You know where I'm going."

Leum hunches her shoulders and sticks out her chin; though you can't see her expression, you know her well enough now to know she's glowering at you in the darkness. "You can't leave."

"I can't stay."

"We can't do this without you."

"You're wrong."

You almost tell her that it's not you she needs. She needs the Sparrowhawk. She needs the assassin. She needs the Quickest Blade in Kindar. She needs the girl she thinks you are—

A kindling—

Devoted, honorable, fearless, resolute—

But you haven't been any of those things in years.

"I'm sorry," you whisper.

Leum still doesn't move, forcing you to ride around her, forcing you to acknowledge her (her presence, her opposition, her judgment) even as you try to avoid her.

"Coward," she calls you. A word like a knife. She doesn't let you go without wounding you, without reminding you that she's here—

You're leaving her here when you could've stayed and fought—

You're leaving all of them—

Leum, Siddie, Amity, Kanver, Ket—

You're leaving them to die.

You were still recovering from your last mission when Vedra surrendered. Your bones mending, your wounds healing. Another few weeks, and you would've been assigned a new squad, given new targets, dispatched into danger again and again and again, so when you heard kindling warfare had been outlawed, you were actually relieved.

You didn't have to be a kindling anymore, didn't have to be an assassin, didn't have to return to battle, didn't have to take any more lives.

You thought you were out.

You thought you were free.

Five days later, the messenger arrived. The Queen Commander (Long May She Reign) had need of your talents. To the public, kindlings were history, barbaric relics of a barbaric past, but the Great and Harmonious Reunification was new and tenuous. Its success required vigilance. It required agents who would protect the queen and her interests, to ensure, quietly, that no one dared disturb the new and uneasy peace.

In short, it was an offer, one made only to assassins, spies, and Shieldbearers, who once guarded the queen. You'd be promoted, afforded a handsome salary, although, of course, you'd no longer be a specialist. Amerand, newly unified, had no use for the old ranks and titles, so you'd never make Primary Class or even Tertiary.

But you'd still be a Mistwalker, in practice if not in name.

You knew that if you agreed, you'd one day become Amerand's greatest assassin, its deadliest weapon, deployed not in flash and powder but as a knife in the dark.

It was what you were trained for.

Some would've said it was what you were born for.

But the truth is, you were afraid—

Afraid of death, of what it had done to those closest to you, of what it would do to you now if you took its hand—

That was when you became a deserter. Took your knives and your balar weapons, left your Wind Runner medallion upon your pillow, and limped into the dark. It was the end of the war, so no one came looking. You sold off your armor. You begged for a while. You had few marketable skills, so you performed on the streets.

You became the Sparrowhawk.

You were the Quickest in Kindar.

It wasn't what you imagined for yourself, but you didn't have to kill anyone for it, and you didn't have to watch anyone die.

Beyond the barricade, the enemies' torches have all burnt out, leaving only the somber glow of their campfires, the silhouettes of their tents against the sky. As you ride up to their perimeter, a pair of guards emerge from the shadows, and you feel a sudden twinge in your gut—

They're fully armored and bristling with weaponry—

Bows, arrows, knives, swords—

All this against the Camassians' wooden spears, the handful of weapons Leum and Emara took from the scouts—

As if sensing your disquiet, Penumbra shifts beneath you, her hooves sounding hollow on the hard-packed earth.

"I'm taking Adren's offer," you say.

One of the guards sneers at you, and you're glad of the darkness because she can't see you flush with shame.

The other beckons to you, and you follow him through their field camp. You pass paddocks, racks of polearms, the rustle of tent flaps being pulled back. From the shadows, you feel the eyes of your enemy upon you, contemptuous and hot—

Someone mutters under their breath.

Someone spits in your path.

As you near the center of camp, Adren appears before you. You recognize her from the attack—

Her cloak—

Her delicate features—

You remember her watching you hoist Emara onto your shoulders. You remember the handcannon smoking in her arms.

"So you're getting out," she says. "Smart."

You don't reply.

"What's the matter? You've got the rest of your life ahead of you now. Don't waste it being ashamed."

You rub your eyes. Your hand comes away wet. "Are you going to allow me to pass or not?"

"By all means."

You click your tongue. You kick your heels. You ride out of there, and the last you hear of her is her cruel and unwavering laughter, chasing you down the field.

But she's wrong, isn't she, Ben? You're not smart. If you were smart, you never would've come here—

You never would've thought you could make it through this without letting someone die, without letting someone slip through your fingers because you weren't good enough or strong enough or fast enough to keep them alive—

And the worst part of it is, after all these years, you're still not brave enough to stick around and face it.

No, it was Leum who was right.

You're a coward.

You always have been.

Part III

THE BRAVE

LEUM

YOU WAKE TO SILENCE AND STILL THICKETS. NO birds singing, no insects stirring. Even the wind has died, leaving the clouds churning on the mountaintops, black and unspent. It's as if the entire world is holding its breath, waiting for the storm to break—

For the blood to be spilled—

Around you, the air is electric. Almost vibrating, almost alive. The sensation sings along your nerves, making your skin prickle and the hairs on your arms stand up. You remember this feeling from the old days. Tension, anticipation. But you never felt such hollowness, such dread.

Emara is gone.

Ben is gone.

Amity always said you needed seven kindlings for this mission, but now you number only five.

Careful not to disturb Kanver and Siddie, you slip out of your blankets. By the fire, Amity and Ket are already up and moving about. The scents of brewing tea and mineral oil, the sounds of embers and whetstone.

Without a word, you wash your face in the basin. You comb the snarls from your hair. Unraveling your strop, you sharpen your razor and, stroke by stroke, shave the sides of your head.

A cold blade—

A nicked scalp—

As you bend over the basin again, you feel a hand on yours. Scarred, strong. "Let me," Ket says. Gently, she takes the razor from you and with smooth, steady motions, she removes the hair from your neck to the crown of your head.

You towel yourself dry. Mesmerized, you run your fingers over your scalp, feeling the curves of your skull beneath the skin. You know before Ket passes you the mirror that you look good—

Clean, neat—

Like a kindling, you think, although you don't know what that means anymore—

If it ever meant anything at all—

By now, Kanver and Siddie are awake, and the cabin fills with dozens of utterly ordinary sounds: a kettle boiling, a groan and a yawn, feet shuffling across the floor, the rasp of a drawer opening, then closing again. The sounds of your kin.

Beside you, Ket cleans the razor, spools up the strop. "It doesn't feel like a month, does it? Since we got here?"

"It feels longer."

Like a lifetime, you think. Like so much more than four weeks.

"Not long enough, though, huh?"

You close your eyes. Inside, a part of you is unwinding, dissolving. All those futures you dared to imagine. Long days, quiet nights, the ebb and flow of your voices, the rhythm of your lives, all of it dissipating. All that time you could've had.

"Forever wouldn't have been long enough," you say.

Ket nods, but you don't think she's thinking about the rest of you. She's not looking at you or Amity or Kanver or Siddie. She's staring out the window, toward the village square. "I know what you mean."

You've never seen all your weapons at once, didn't realize how beautiful they'd be, with the mingled glow of your balar crystals bathing the cabin in shades of rose, red, and peach.

You slide your sword into your belt, feeling yourself shift at the familiar weight of it, the perfect balance of it, both comforting and deadly.

Amity's the only one without a weapon. A queen without her crown. She looks naked without it, vulnerable, with the signs of burnout creeping across her face.

She draws your attention with a wave of her hand, and you all go still. Waiting. That tension again. (Trapped thunder, heavy air.)

You expect her to say something inspiring. A word of wisdom, a rousing speech. She's your general, after all, and that's what generals do. They give you courage. They give you hope. They give you something, anything, platitudes, even, to take with you into battle as you confront your death.

But you don't need courage.

(You already have it.)

And you don't need hope.

(You're not all going to make it.)

You've thinned the enemy ranks a little, but not enough now, not enough to win. Not without Emara, not without Ben—

"I was wrong," Amity says finally. "I was wrong to deceive you. I was wrong to lie. I thought I needed one more battle to give my life meaning, to go out with a victory, the way I always thought I should. But I was wrong there too. This battle won't give my life meaning—"

She stops to cough into a handkerchief. Flecks of blood on the cloth. Then she looks at you. Just looks at you. Her eyes kind, her mouth soft. It's the tenderest you've ever seen her; you almost find it disquieting. The Twin Valley Reaper isn't kind, isn't soft, isn't tender. She's sharp as steel, she's hard as stone, she's resplendent and untouchable and fathomless as the sea.

But you don't know the Reaper. You never did.

This is Amity we're talking about. Prideful, fallible, compassionate, magnificent and devastatingly mortal. Her attention lingers on each of you like she's capturing a piece of you, somehow, something she can take with her, whatever comes next.

You look back at her. (You don't scowl.) You promise to remember.

Amity.

Kanver.

Siddie.

Ket.

The five of you in the balar light, just before the storm.

Then Amity smiles, and the tension eases like a long exhalation or a lingering embrace. "I love you," she says. (Her voice clear and plain.) "Take care of each other."

The sky darkens as you descend from the cabin. Wind racing through the village, clouds amassing overhead. From up here, Camas almost looks deserted (the square empty, the houses secured), but here and there is a flurry of activity: a door slamming, a sudden cry, runners in straw coats darting from post to post.

At the base of the path, you glance southward. A makeshift infirmary below the cabin. Fallback positions along the road. You pray to Callula you won't have to use them, that the air won't be filled with the screams of the injured, that the defenses will hold, that the raiders don't get in.

As if sensing your mood, Burk nudges you with her snout. Cold nose, soft fur. You scratch her behind the ears.

Beyond the livestock pens, you notice waves on the flooded meadow, white-capped and sharp as smiles.

"Hey, Leum." Kanver's standing behind you. Tousled hair, lopsided expression. They've got their polearm slung across their shoulders, so

casually your old sergeant would've had them digging ditches for dis-
respecting their weapon. "Thanks for getting me out of that alley,"
they say.

"In Windfall?" You snort. "You loved that alley."

"I love you more."

You pull them to you, bury your face in their neck. The clean
smell of them, almost like a child, almost like you're children again.

"I'm sorry," they mumble. "I wish I could've been what you
wanted."

You squeeze them tighter. "I never wanted you to be anything
more than who you are."

"A nonbeliever?"

"Enough." You shake them a little, as if that will make them
believe you. "You're enough, Kannie, just as you are."

They touch their forehead to yours. Feathery hair. An ember in
their voice. "Maybe I don't believe in the code anymore, but I never
stopped believing in you." Then, with a smile, they slouch off toward
Onna's, where the children are already in hiding.

Kneeling, you rub Burk's ears. "Go with Kanver. I'll see you
later."

She's just a dog, so she probably doesn't understand concepts like
"later," but she's a good dog, so she trots after Kanver when they
call her.

As they approach, Poppy flings open the door, racing across the
garden with her little wooden spear. "Kanver!"

"What are you doing?" Kanver squats down in front of her. "You
promised me, Poppy. What did you promise me?"

The girl scowls at the ground. "Stay hidden," she mumbles.

"That's right." Reaching out, Kanver ruffles her hair. "You stay
hidden. You have to watch out for Burk, okay?"

Still clutching her stick, Poppy throws her arms around the dog's neck. Even from a distance, you can tell Burk hates it (ears back, eyes showing white), but she lets the kid cling to her, like she understands, even though she's a dog, that sometimes we need to be held, and sometimes we need to do the holding.

Tana appears to usher Poppy and Burk inside, and you think for a second that Ket, who's crossing the square, will go to her. Say something to her. Kiss her goodbye. Because if she doesn't do it now, she might never get the chance—

But they hardly look at each other, like looking at each other is somehow too painful, and Ket doesn't say a word to Tana as she and Kanver head north from the square.

You wonder if it's the last time you'll see them, disappearing around the bend in the road. Is that it? Your last look at them? Not even their faces, just the backs of their heads?

You want them to turn. You want to call out to them. Another look, that's all you want. Another word, another moment, another minute together, a second, a breath, you'd take any amount of time together as long as you could postpone your parting, the uncertainty of ever seeing them again.

But if there's anything you've learned from being a kindling, all those years of separations, departures, deaths and farewells, it's that you don't get to say when things end.

On the south side of the village, Emara's barricade stretches from the rocky western slope all the way to the flooded meadow, where archers have been stationed to deter an attack from the water. Here, the land is so open, you can see the bulk of Adren's forces gathering out of range: the armed marauders, the trampled grass, the horses stamping in the stormy light.

You join Amity by the road. She seems tired already. Ragged, frail. In lieu of her balar weapon, she's carrying one of the swords you took off the scouts, but it looks too heavy for her, dangling from her hand. Beckoning you aside, she mutters, "The villagers have been prepped for a cavalry charge, but what concerns me are those handcannons."

You squint at the bandits in the distance. "Wish we knew how many they had."

"I was counting on Ben to find out for us."

You tighten your grip on the hilt of your sword. Ben would've been perfect for this, for locating the flash and the thunder, for finding the cannoneers in the crowd. She would've been perfect for dispatching them too. Her throwing knives, her deadly aim.

"Will you help me?" Amity asks. There's an uncharacteristic shiver in her voice, not from her illness, but because she means more than she's saying.

(She means she might not be strong enough. She might falter. She might collapse—)

(A dizzy spell—)

(A coughing fit—)

(She might not be able to lead you through this, and if she can't do that, someone else will have to.)

You nod.

Amity swallows, grimacing at the pain, and pats you on the shoulder. "It's going to be a long day."

As she departs, Siddie trots up to you, looking sweaty and pale. She was supposed to be a runner, racing back and forth between positions with the other kids her age, but now she's needed on the barricade.

There were supposed to be four of you: Amity, Emara, you, and Ben. You might've managed without Emara. It would've been hard, but with luck you could've done it.

But you still needed Ben. Without her, the defense of the barricade will be stretched too thin.

Hence, Siddie. She'll be supporting Amity on the upper end of the field, where your forces are concentrated, while you command the rest of the defenses alone.

"You okay?" you ask.

She nods, wiping at her mouth with the back of her hand.

"You throw up?"

She winces. "Is it that obvious?"

"Don't worry." You shrug. "We've all done it."

For some reason, this seems to reassure her. She runs her fingers over her clothes, her belt, her scabbard, and finally goes still. "I don't know if I'm ready," she whispers.

You frown. "For the battle?"

"For being a kindling."

You don't look at her. You can't look at her. Her worry, her hope, her determination. She's not the kid who barged into the Grand Hotel a month ago, tripping over her own sword.

She's stronger now.

She's taken lives.

(She's seen them taken.)

And you're proud of her, proud of how she's grown, what she's learned, who she's become, but you also know it means you failed her.

"Too bad, kid," you tell her. "You're already a kindling."

She barrels into you, hugging you swift and hard. Her skinny arms, her shoulder guard shoved painfully up against your cheek. It's uncomfortable, but you don't struggle.

(Sometimes even you need to be held.)

Then she runs off toward Amity, and there's something in your eyes, so you blink rapidly to clear your vision. You need to be focused. It's almost time. On the other side of the barricade, Adren's forces assemble. Archers. Infantry. Cavalry. They're so close now, you can count the tips of their polearms as they gather.

You feel moisture on your cheeks, brush it away with your finger. Raindrops, at last, spattering the villagers, the barricade, the field—

You ready your sword. You call to your forces.

The clouds burst open as the battle begins.

SIDDIE

YOU DIVE FOR COVER AS ANOTHER VOLLEY OF arrows showers the field, dozens of shafts striking wood, earth, grass. You hit the mud. You hold your breath. Was anyone wounded? You listen for screams—

But there's only the wind, the rain, the roar of the enemy—

All those evenings, Ben and Emara tried to prepare you. They tried to tell you it would be chaos, fury, confusion. They said it would be hard not to lose your head, but you had to focus.

The Camassians are counting on you.

Your kin are counting on you.

You blink rain out of your eyes. Along the barricade, the archers (*your* archers) are already reaching for their quivers.

"Ready?" you call.

Targets sighted, bowstrings taut.

"Loose!"

A hail of arrows, pointed and sharp. In the meadow, the raiders duck behind their shields and launch a volley of their own.

"Take cover!" you cry.

Their arrows fly at you. *Ssnk! Ssnk!* Shafts quivering in the barricade, points embedded in the wood.

It's been hours of this. They fire on you; you fire on them. You patch up the injured. You do it again. At this pace, Adren might wear

down your defenses eventually, but it could take days. After everything you'd heard about her, all of you were expecting full-throated
aggression, a relentless assault, but you can't say you're disappointed
with what you've got.

(You haven't lost anybody this way.)

Peering through the barricade, you spy Adren astride her black
horse, sitting back, almost lazily, while her archers prepare another
volley.

Amity staggers up to you. Her breathing shallow, her face flecked
with mud. Anxiously, you study her for signs of collapse—

(Leum tasked you with watching her, told you to get help if she
fell—)

But there's nothing. If anything, Amity seems more alive than she
has since you got here. Ferocious and bright—

"Something's wrong," she says.

"What?" You duck as the air fills with arrows, sinking into the
ground, thudding into the barricade. Down the slope, someone cries
out, and you see one of the villagers clutching their scalp as they
scramble for cover. "I thought we were doing okay?"

"So is Adren," Amity replies.

Behind you, runners race through the field, collecting fallen
arrows to refill your quivers.

Amity jerks her head toward the rocky western slope. "Go check
the perimeter."

You don't move.

You can't leave her, can you? Leum told you to watch her. Leum
told you to protect her. She's your commander. You can't just leave
her here while she's sick.

"Siddie!" She yanks you toward her as another flight of arrows
strikes the barricade. *Sssnk! Sssnk!* A shaft buried where you were
kneeling seconds before.

Your eyes go wide.

"*Think*, Siddie," Amity says. "What about Adren's cavalry? What about her handcannons? We know she has them, but she hasn't used them. She's waiting for something, and we need to find out what."

You glance at Adren. Her haughty figure, her cloak in the wind. You remember the way she looked the night she shot Emara. You remember the flash. Her indifference.

The thunder.

The blood.

You gulp. "Okay."

"Good." Amity points up the hillside. "Start with the west."

You're still a little clumsy, but at least now you're fast. You dash up the slope, scrambling over the rocks, steep and slick with rain. You're above the infirmary. You're behind the cabin. You check with the guards, but they haven't seen anything. No movement on the hillside, no sign of raiders in the trees.

You don't know if you should be concerned or relieved.

Maybe Amity was wrong. Maybe this was all Adren had planned.

But you have to be sure. As you come down through the square, you almost collide with another runner.

"Fern!"

"Siddie!" Her wet hair clinging to her forehead, her cheeks red with cold. "What are you doing here? I thought you were supposed to be on the barricade!"

"Amity sent me to check the defenses. Any news?"

"I just got back from the gully." She motions behind her, where the loop road skirts the creek. "Parker and Hemmen seem a little tired, but they say no one's tried to cross yet."

You glance between the houses on the north edge of the square. Empty terraces, quiet gardens. No one's there.

As you try to sort out whether that's good news or bad, there's an uproar at the broken bridge—

Someone shouting—

A clash of weaponry—

Squealing, Fern ducks behind you, and it's not like you're happy to be under attack or anything, but you can't say you're not almost pleased.

She thinks you can protect her.

She thinks you're strong.

"It's coming from the north road!" You draw your sword. "I've got to go!"

Fern clasps your hand briefly. "I'll tell Amity! Be safe, okay?"

You're already sprinting away, calling over your shoulder, "You too!" You race out of the square, past the apple trees on the side of the road, and as you round the bend toward the broken bridge, you see raiders swarming the barricade. Weapons jabbing at the defenses, armor shining black in the rain. Some of the Camassians have been wounded, but Ket and Kanver are still standing, still fighting with the defenders that remain.

Gripping your weapon, you launch yourself into the melee. You're hacking at the enemy, you're forcing them back.

"Siddie? What are you doing here?" Beside you, Ket slashes at one of the raiders, sending him flying backward into the creek.

"Amity sent me to check the perimeter!"

And she was right, wasn't she? Adren's half-hearted assault in the meadow was nothing but a distraction. The real battle is here.

"Keep moving, Siddie!" Ket calls to you. "We've got this under control!"

And you should go. You know you should. You have orders. The whole perimeter. You're supposed to report back to Amity. You're supposed to be at her side.

But you can't leave Ket and Kanver like this. You can't run off while they stay behind to fight.

That's what happened to Emara that night.

You left her.

You left her with the enemy.

You left her to die.

Snarling, you slice one of the marauders across the chest. A shallow wound, blood blooming across his clothes as he barrels toward you. With a yelp, you spin out of his way, but you're too hasty, Siddie. You're off-balance.

But you're not the same kid who stumbled into Windfall.

You remember your stances.

You keep your feet.

Using your momentum, you throw yourself at him, knocking him into the path of Kanver's glaive.

They swipe at him.

His blood hits your face.

You almost drop your weapon. You almost double over and retch. All around you, fighting and bloodshed. Confusion and fury. You wish Ben and Emara were here. As much as they tried to prepare you, you still wish they were with you to guide you through this.

Kanver takes your hand, helps you to your feet. With the corner of their sleeve, they wipe at your cheeks. "Siddie. Siddie, are you still with me? You're okay. You're okay."

As you stand there, dazed, your gaze drifts over their shoulder. There's movement down the loop road. Two strangers, armed and dangerous. They're creeping out of the gully. They're skulking across the road toward the terrace gardens.

A brittle cold settles over you.

No.

No, that can't be right. Fern was just there, wasn't she? Said nothing was wrong? There are guard posts down there, archers in stone fortifications dotted along the creek. Someone should've noticed the marauders. Someone should've stopped them.

What was it Fern said?

Parker and Hemmen seem a little tired . . .

Oh, Siddie.

You tried to do your job. You tried to follow orders. You tried to be a kindling. You tried to protect your kin. But how could you know? When to follow orders? When to fight? When to run? The battle's everywhere. It's all around you, happening on all fronts.

"Siddie, what's wrong?" Ket grabs your shoulder. She follows your gaze. Through the downpour, you see another raider slink from the gully—

Spiked with armor, gleaming in the rain—

"Breach!" Ket cries. "Raiders in the village! Breach!"

Around you, the others are pointing and shouting. Kanver's shaking you. They're calling your name.

You blink, but you can't seem to focus. "Parker . . . ," you whisper. "Hemmen . . ."

What happened to them while you were up here fighting?

How many raiders have you let in?

KET

ONCE YOU SOUND THE ALARM, THE RAIDERS REDOUBLE their assault on the broken bridge. They clatter over one another. They're clambering over the fences. You're trying to repel them, but your defenses are failing. Onna's favoring her leg; Tana's been cut across the shoulder. Here on the north road, you're being overwhelmed by invaders, while down the slope, their brethren slip into Camas unopposed.

"I'm sorry." Siddie stares down the hillside, her weapon limp in her hand. "It's all my fault."

You don't know what she's talking about, but if you don't do something she's going to go into shock. You take her by the shoulders. You speak in low, hurried tones. "Siddie, listen to me. Whatever you did or think you did, it doesn't matter anymore, okay? It happened. What matters now is what we do about it."

She blinks a few times. "Huh?"

"I need you to run to Amity. You're the fastest here. You need to get back there and tell her what's going on."

"Okay." She nods faintly, but her eyes are still unfocused.

"Siddie." You shake her a little, until she looks up at you. "We're counting on you."

The poor kid swallows. Pale-faced, blood-spattered, drenched with rain. But she nods all the same. "Okay."

You can't afford to watch her as she races away. From inside the village, the raiders will have the drop on your defenses. The guard posts at the flooded meadow, Leum and Amity at the barricade. If you don't stop the incursion now, they'll slit all your throats from behind.

You have to go.

"Kanver!" For a second, you want to fight your way to them. Want to stand with them again. Want to hear their low voice amid the trickle of dishwater, the clatter of bowls being placed on their shelves—

The calm of it—

The peace—

(They were never meant for battle, you think. They should've been an artist, a painter, maybe, who made a study of beauty, or a shepherd roaming the hills with their herd—)

Across the defenses, they catch your eye. "Go!" They smile at you, kind and wide. "I'm okay, Ket. Really, I'm okay."

You can't spare another second for goodbye. Pointing, you pick two Camassians who've proven themselves adept in the open. "Vander, Ferra—"

You know Tana should be your next choice. She's fast, strong, determined. In practice, she could hold her own against two or three villagers at a time—

But this isn't practice. She has a better chance of survival here behind the fence than exposed on the loop road—

And you want her to survive.

So you don't look for her in the melee. (Don't know if you could leave her if you did.) Motioning to Vander and Ferra, you take off down the road. The three of you racing by the apple trees, feet skidding in the gravel, and barreling past the terrace gardens as two more marauders scramble out of the gully.

You draw your sword. You meet them head-on.

One of them swings at you with a spear, but you parry, sidestepping around him as you slice him across the shoulder. He stumbles, but another two raiders are coming at you now, their blades arcing toward you, and you barely have time to dodge out of their reach before they're on top of you again.

You block. You duck and feint. You find an opening. An exposed wrist, the inside of an elbow. Your blade slashing, your enemies falling back.

Out of the corner of your eye, you see the Camassians flanking a fourth marauder, stabbing at him with their wooden spears.

Ferra gets him through the gut. A spurt of blood on the pale wood.

You don't know how many more have already infiltrated the village, but for now the loop road is clear. Ordering the others to defend the creek, you sprint for the guard post, where you find Parker and Hemmen on the ground—

Bows snapped—

Throats cut—

"No!" Someone rushes up behind you. The smell of lilacs in the rain—

Tana—

She followed you here. Dropping her spear, she flings herself at Parker and Hemmen, but you catch her. Her wiry strength, her flood of grief. You wrestle her away.

"What are you doing here?" you ask.

She ignores the question, still struggling in your grip. "How did this happen? They were two of our best archers."

You push her back. You place her spear in her hands. "You've got to get out of here, okay? Get back to the bridge. Report this to Kanver. We need archers to fill this guard post, as soon as they can be spared."

She glares at you. Tears on her lashes. "Send Ferra. She's faster."

"But you're right here."

A furrow appears between her brows. "I'm not leaving you, Ket."

You don't know how to argue with her. (You've never known how to argue with her, in part because she's usually right.) So you call for Ferra. You send her up the hill. As she races away, you hear a whimper behind the guard station.

(Now that's a surprise. You didn't think the raiders would've left anyone alive.)

"Old Man?" Tana says.

He's slumped against the stones. Head bent. Arms around his knees.

"What're you doing out here?" she asks, kneeling in front of him. "You're supposed to be hiding with—"

"Tana." You touch her shoulder. "Go help Vander by the creek."

She looks at you, confused, but both of you know Vander can't hold the gully alone, so she shoulders her spear and runs off.

You stand over the Old Man, staring down at his thin, trembling shoulders, at the liver spots on his balding head.

"I thought they'd honor their word." He looks up at you, eyes clouded and wide. "They told us that if we let them into the village, we'd be spared."

You grab him by the collar. You pull him to his feet. "What did you do?"

But you know already. You knew as soon as you saw him sitting there. That's why you sent Tana away, after all. You didn't want her to hear it, not now. Not in the middle of battle. She didn't need to hear it, and neither do you.

He took Adren up on her offer.

He let the raiders into Camas in hopes that the villagers would be left unscathed.

He moans. He looks to Parker and Hemmen, their bodies drenched in the rain. "I gave them a sleeping draught! I thought they'd be safe!

Our people were supposed to be safe! It was you who was supposed to die, not us!"

You drop him. You let him fall to the ground, where he prostrates himself before you, groveling in the mud. You shake your head. You back away.

"*Ket!*"

You look up. Tana's at the edge of the gully, driving foe after foe back into the creek. Jabbing, thrusting. She dances away as one of the raiders slashes at her ankles, but her strength is flagging. The wound in her shoulder's bleeding heavily through her robes.

You search for Vander, but he's on the ground behind her. You don't know if he's breathing. You can't tell from here.

Tana's alone.

Tana needs you.

You don't think. You move. You sprint toward her, but in the gully one of the raiders is getting to his feet. He's hefting his spear—

The gleaming point—

The blackened shaft—

A trained soldier would see him. Kanver or Leum or even Siddie would see him. But Tana's not a soldier. She doesn't know to look. She's battling back the other raiders. She's leaving herself exposed.

You're too far, Ket. You're too far from her. You thought that was better, thought it was easier not to get too attached when there was so much else out there, so many places to see, but the truth is you never wanted to keep leaving. You never wanted to keep moving. You were just too afraid of losing anyone else the way you lost Kari, and you thought if you never loved anyone else, never let yourself be at home with anyone else, you'd be safe.

But you're too late.

You already loved Tana. You were already attached. After Emara died, you tried to break things off to protect yourself, but instead you gave up what little time you had—

Hours—

Only hours—

A wind-tossed night, a grim sunrise—

But those are hours you could've spent together. Hours you could've kissed her, held her, loved her. Hours you could've passed together in peace—

You lunge as the weapon flies through the air. You fling yourself in front of her.

The spear goes through your thigh. (Torn muscle, scratched bone.) You try to land on your feet, but your leg collapses beneath you. You're on your knees in the mud.

"Ket!" Tana rushes to your side. She's under your arm. She's helping you up. "That was stupid!"

You try to grin, but it comes out as a grimace. "Don't you mean brave?" Testing your leg, you hiss at the pain, but you can't think about that now. You've got to fight now, because running's out of the question. In fact, you can hardly stand—

Which is fine, because for the first time since Kari died, you don't want to run. You stagger forward as the raiders charge from the gully. You raise your saber. You find the weak points in their armor. Behind the knee, under the arm. Their pained cries fly from their throats as you cut them—

The neck—

The meat between the ribs—

Again and again, you and Tana drive them down the slope, but as soon as they fall back, they're replaced. You glance up the road. Ferra should've gotten to the bridge by now. Kanver should've sent down the archers you asked for.

But there's no sign of reinforcements.

You and Tana are alone.

Across the creek, more of Adren's bandits are wading into the water, swarming up the shores of the creek like black-armored beetles.

There are too many of them. You're going to be overwhelmed.

Tana must realize it at the same time you do, because she reaches for your hand. Her palm calloused, her grip firm. "Don't leave me, okay?"

As the next wave of raiders storms out of the creek, you squeeze her fingers. You give her a smile. "I'm not going anywhere."

KANVER

YOU SHOULD'VE HEARD FROM KET BY NOW. SHE should've come back. She would've sent someone back, if she couldn't come herself, which means something must've gone wrong, but you try not to think about that as you drive the raiders away from the broken bridge.

You slash at one of them, and as your glaive shears along the side of her helmet, you think you hear the sound of a scream—

Distant, yelping—

The scream of an animal or maybe a child, like the screaming you hear when you close your eyes and you forget you're not back there anymore, not in the war anymore, the war that ended two years ago, although you still don't know if you believe it—

You want to turn. You want to know if that was the screech of metal or the voice of a child or only your imagination, but you can't look back. The defenders are counting on you. Ket's counting on you. You can't falter now. Spinning your glaive, you rake one of the raiders across the chest. He cries out and tumbles into the creek.

Then Onna shrieks. *"Poppy!"*

That's when you turn. That's when you see the girl standing on her back doorstep, staring at something on the loop road—

Raiders—

They've surrounded Ket and Tana by the guard station—

They're creeping out of the gully nearby—

She's outside. Your mind churns like a waterwheel stuck on a log. *Poppy's outside. She's outside—*

On the air, you think you smell sulfur.

She's in danger.

With a cry, Onna rushes from the ramparts, but you catch her by the arm. "No!" You shove her back into line. "Stay here. I'll get her."

"But—"

"The enemy's already in the village. You can't protect her now, but I can."

(At least, you think you can.)

You have to.

You can't fail again.

Onna grips your hands, her fingers slick and cold with rain. "Thank you."

"Send archers down the loop road," you tell her. "Ket and Tana need help."

Without another word, you dash away. You race down the road, under the apple trees, where you nearly stumble over a body—

Ferra's body—

Dragged here, by the looks of it. The disturbed leaves, the broken twigs. In the mulch, you spot two sets of footsteps heading toward the square.

Somewhere above you, Poppy screams again.

Leaving the body, you vault over the rock wall and into the gardens. (Gourds ripening on the vine, carrots thickening in the ground.) "Poppy!" You can see her over the second wall. That braided hair. That tiny spear. She's close. You can get to her. You can keep her safe. "Get inside!"

But you're too focused on the child. You're not paying enough attention to your surroundings. You're not watching your flank. The first arrow comes at you, sinking into the ground at your feet.

You glance to the south. Along the side of the house, a couple of marauders are doubling back toward you. They must have been heading toward the village square when they heard you shouting.

You dive for cover, but Poppy hasn't moved. She's still standing there, in the open on the edge of the terrace. In a few seconds, the raiders will come around the corner of the house. They'll see her.

She's outside.

She's in danger.

"Poppy!" You leap to your feet. "Inside! Now!"

She turns to you, wide-eyed, like she didn't even know you were there. You watch the recognition dawning over her face, agonizingly slow. You're keenly aware of how exposed you are in the lower garden. An easy target. Nowhere to hide.

Then, with a squeak, Poppy runs for her back door. Her feet moving fast. Her braids flying behind her. You know you should get under cover, but you have to see that she makes it. You have to know that she's out of harm's way.

At last, she scrambles up the stone step and back into the house, where she slams the door behind her.

You let out a breath.

She's okay.

She's safe.

But you're not. No, Kanver, you've lingered too long. *Sssnk!* An arrow gets you in the shoulder. Something inside you tearing. You duck below the wall again, feeling the arrowhead dig into your muscle as you throw yourself against the stone. It's going to hinder your movement, it's going to slow you down, but you can't pull it out if you can't bandage it yet. With a grimace, you snap the shaft off at its base.

Above you, the raiders must have reached the corner of the house by now. You imagine them stalking toward you, step by step through the garden.

Gritting your teeth, you launch yourself onto the upper terrace, where you duck an arrow, the sound of it whispering past your ear. You find your feet in the grass, advancing on the archer as she nocks another arrow to her bow, but before you can reach her, the second raider charges you with a sword.

You jab him with the blunt end of your weapon, forcing him back, and slice at the archer, the tip of your glaive carving circles in the air. It pains your shoulder, the embedded arrowhead rending your flesh, but down on the road three more invaders slip past Ket and Tana and head toward the terraces. No time to worry about your injury now.

You're flanked, caught between the swordsman and the archer, but even injured, you're more than a match for them both. You dispatch the swordsman quickly, you cut the archer across the leg. But the other three raiders are in the garden already. In another few seconds, they'll reach the upper terrace—

Onna's house—

The children—

You race along the stone wall to the top of the steps, where you face off against the new marauders. Two spears and a greatsword. Leaping and slashing, you force them back down the stairs while the archer picks up her partner's fallen sword and assaults you from the left.

They surround you as you back toward the house, trying to keep them at bay. Your weapons clashing. Their blades finding your foot, your arm, your thigh.

You kill both of the spearmen, but someone slashes you from behind. You almost twist out of the way, but your injuries are slowing you down, and you feel the wind on your back. You feel your skin open up. You hiss through your teeth—

It stings, but you can keep fighting—

You have to keep fighting.

For Poppy.

(For Pem.)

The archer comes at you again with her borrowed blade, but you knock her weapon out of her grasp. Crying out, she stumbles backward as the raider with the greatsword charges. You try to parry, but the wound in your shoulder is worsening. You can't turn your weapon in time. You slice your enemy across the stomach, but not fast enough to stop their momentum.

As they fall, their blade bites into your calf—

Through the muscle and down to the bone—

You stagger. Almost trip over your fallen foe. You can't put your weight on your leg anymore, and while you try to regain your balance, the archer slips under your polearm. You try to spin out of her way, but your wounded leg won't cooperate. You barely escape the reach of her blade.

Rearing up again, you ram the butt of your glaive into her skull. She drops.

Your vision blurs. You're soaked with blood. You can feel it running out of you, fast fast fast, but you can't think about that, because as you're turning for the house, trying to make sure Poppy and the others are okay, there's a blossom of fire at the east end of the garden—

It takes a second for you to understand it—

Fire?

Just a flash of it?

In this torrent of rain?

You're diving for the ground when the bullet reaches you, something hard and round searing through your center—

Then pain—

Then thunder—

The dissonant scents of salt and sulfur—

Pem.

Pem.

She's in danger, you think, but you're wrong. You're the one in danger, Kanver. You're the one exposed. You can see your enemy now, another five in the garden and one of them with a handcannon.

Below, Onna's archers have arrived on the loop road. They're taking up posts in the guard station while Ket and Tana force the enemy back into the gully.

You let out a little gasp of relief.

No more raiders are getting into Camas that way.

You're hurt, and you're dizzy, but you pull yourself to your feet. You need cover. There's a boulder behind you, only waist-high and about as wide, but it'll have to do.

You have to protect the children.

You scramble behind the rock as another bullet clips the stone. Your breath is coming fast now, fast as the blood running from your leg, your back, your stomach, but you can't seem to get enough air, can't seem to focus, can't seem to get the smell of gunpowder out of your senses, and you want to tell yourself it's not real, you're not back there, the war is over, and you try to believe it—

Pem.

No. You shake your head. Not Pem. Pem is dead. Pem died years ago in that seaside village. But *Poppy* is here. *Poppy's* alive. You can still save her.

Wincing, you peer over the top of the rock. The raiders are advancing. They're almost at the house.

One of them shouts.

For a second, you see the mouth of the handcannon. Black and unknowable.

Then you duck as a chunk of rock shatters above you, dust raining into your hair. Ignoring the pain in your leg, you pull yourself into a crouch.

Deep inside you, your magic kindles—

Red as cannon fire—

Warmth and a spark—

Then it's racing through you, through your blood and your veins. In your glaive, the light of your balar crystal flares red.

With a cry, you leap from behind the rock, magic blazing along the edge of your weapon—

For an instant, the eyes of your enemy go white with fear—

Then you're sweeping your polearm through the air, magic bursting from your glaive in a perfect crimson arc. It strikes your enemy with the force of an explosion, sending them flying onto their backs.

Three of them are nearly sliced in half. Scorch marks. Sizzling flesh. The gun falls from the cannoneer's hands, cloven neatly in two.

You collapse. Your injured leg can't hold you up anymore, and you fall to one knee on the flagstone pathway as the remaining two raiders get to their feet.

Groaning, you crawl toward the house. You need your back against something, can't allow yourself to be flanked.

They charge. Swords, daggers, and you with your glaive. From the ground, you fight them off, your polearm keeping them at a distance, but you're too weak, the weapon trembling in your hands, and you cut the legs out from under one of the raiders, but the other gets you, a sword sinking into your chest—

You gasp—

A wet sound in your throat—

Something wrong with your lungs, then. Something bleeding deep inside you.

But you need to keep fighting. You summon your magic (one last time) and with a sweep of your arm, you let it fly.

A burst of red light.

Your enemy (your last enemy) staggering backward with a burn in their chest. (Charred bone, smoking fats.) They collapse in the garden, dead in the rain.

Wincing, you pull yourself onto the stone step at the back door. Probably unnecessary, with Ket and Tana holding the line at the gully, but you want to be here, just in case.

Your glaive slips from your hand, clattering onto the flagstone, but that's okay. You don't need it anymore.

The kids are safe.

"Kanver!" The door is wrenched open, and Poppy's face swims into focus above you. Dark, serious eyes. That family frown.

You make a face. "You promised." You try to push her back into the house, but you're too weak, and she doesn't move. "Get back inside."

"Kanver," she says. Her voice is watery, her tears falling onto your bloody clothes. Her hands hover over you, but there's nothing she can do.

You motion her away from you. "Stay inside," you murmur. "I'll be right here. Your mama will come get you when it's safe."

Sniffling, she nods and lays that little wooden spear across your chest.

You grip it tight as you watch her enter the house again, go into hiding again, the door sliding closed behind her. With a sigh, you lay back. Rain spatters your face, but you don't see the clouds, you don't smell the storm. You don't smell the granite or pine—

You smell salt on the air again, but this time it isn't marred by gun smoke—

Just salt and the mineral scent of the sea. You're drifting again, peacefully, peacefully—

In the distance, you think you hear a handcannon, but this time it doesn't trouble you. How could it trouble you? It can't reach you now—

You or the children—

Safe inside.

SIDDIE

YOU'RE PASSING THE INFIRMARY BELOW THE CABIN
when you hear thunder behind you. The sound of a handcannon.
You skid to a stop.

Did it come from the broken bridge or the breach in the gully?
The flooded meadow or somewhere inside Camas?

Because you failed?

Because you didn't check the perimeter like you were supposed to?

You search the roads, but you can't see anything from here.
Pounding rain, closed shutters, damp thickets. For a second, you
consider running back. Ket and Kanver might need you. Someone
might've been shot.

But you still have to warn Amity about the breach—

You hesitate too long. Time's slipping away, but you don't know
what to do. You need someone to tell you. North or south? Bridge,
barricade, or gully? No matter what you do, you're leaving someone
to die. How are you supposed to choose?

With a pit in your stomach, you race back to the barricade, where
the fighting has gotten worse since you left. Arrows whizzing into
your ranks while Adren's horsemen harry your defenses. Scattered
bodies. Blood-soaked earth.

As you pick your way through the chaos, you swear you hear

another shot in the distance, but you can't be sure. The fighting is so loud. The clash of weapons, the thunder of hooves. Villagers crying and shouting over the sound of the rain.

"Amity?" You scan the battlefield, but there's no sign of her. She's not calling orders. She's not racing through the ranks. You were supposed to watch her. You were supposed to be there if she had another fit.

Did she collapse while you were gone?

Was she hit?

Your voice cracks with panic. "Has anyone seen Amity?"

"She went to help Leum!" In front of you, one of the villagers lifts a hand, pointing down the meadow—

Then there's a bang. Unmistakable, this time, now that it's near.

The villager dies, and for the second time today, someone else's blood spatters your face—

"Handcannon!" The cry goes up along the barricade. "Hand-cannon!"

"Siddie, take cover!" Someone pulls you to the ground as another bullet strikes the barricade near your head. Splinters flying. A cut on your cheek.

Dazed, you touch your face. Blood on your fingertips and not all of it yours.

"Did you see it?" Leum's crouching over you. "The handcannon. Did you see where it was?"

Maybe you answer. Maybe not. You try to get up again, unsteady on your feet. You were supposed to be doing something, weren't you? Before the villager—

Before his face—

There's another shot, then another, but you don't know where they come from, don't even know where they hit.

"Siddie!" Leum snaps at you. She's crouched beside Jin, tying a bandage around their forearm. "Pick up a bow and give everyone some cover!"

You rub your eyes.

You have to get up. Taking Jin's bow from their hands, you nock an arrow, sight, loose. Across the field, one of Adren's archers staggers back.

Behind him, you catch a glimpse of the enemy forming ranks. Marauders lining up shoulder to shoulder. A wall of them, all heavily armored. They're rattling their shields. They're stomping their feet.

In front of them, Adren has dismounted from her stallion. She's prowling up and down the line.

"An infantry charge?" You look to Leum, confused. "Isn't it too soon for that? They haven't broken our defenses."

"I know." She scowls as she knots Jin's bandage. "There's something we're not seeing yet."

You loose another arrow.

This time you miss.

There's another gunshot. An explosion rippling the air. But it doesn't look like anyone was hit.

Someone scrambles up beside you, ducking as cannon fire bursts from the enemy line.

"Amity!" you cry.

She looks exhausted, pale and shaking, but her voice is sharp as ever when she demands news of the perimeter.

Breathlessly, you tell her about the breach, the gunshots on the other side of the village.

She coughs. "That's one handcannon. What about the rest?"

"I don't know. I didn't see them."

"Have you found any of them yet, Leum?"

On her belly, Leum peers through the barricade. "Don't even know how many there are," she mutters. "Three, maybe four?"

"It's three." With great effort, Amity pushes herself to her feet. "I'm going up the road. Maybe I'll spot one from—"

That's when the bullet finds her.

"Amity!" Leum shouts.

You blink, and Amity's falling. She's gripping her leg. Another bullet strikes the ground beside her as Leum yanks her out of the line of fire. Blades of grass and bits of mud flying.

She's hurt.

Amity's hurt, blood seeping through her fingers as she presses her hands to her thigh.

One of the villagers shoves a bandage into your hands, though you don't remember calling for it, don't remember saying anything, but maybe you did. At the Academy, they taught you that a wound to the thigh could kill you. Five minutes, they said. That's all it takes.

"It went through," Leum mutters.

Irritably, Amity snatches the bandage from you, loops it under her leg. "I can tell."

"Don't think you'll bleed out, though."

"Good." Her trembling fingers fumble at the cloth, struggling to wrap it. "I can't be bothered with bleeding out today."

With a grunt, Leum swats Amity's hands away and finishes dressing the wounds herself, knotting the bandage so tight that Amity winces. "You need to get to the infirmary."

Amity's already trying to stand, leaning heavily on her sword. "Not a chance."

But her strength fails. Her leg buckles under her, and it's only Leum who keeps her upright.

For a moment, Leum glares at her. Eyes bloodshot, jaw set. "If they get through the barricade, we're going to need someone to lead us," she says firmly. "It better be you."

Amity looks like she wants to object, but before she can speak, she doubles over, coughing. You try to help her. You try to go to her, but she waves you away—

Now even the back of her hand is vined with red, crawling over her knuckles toward her fingertips.

You remember when this happened to the Swordmaster.

After this, she had little over a week.

"Okay," Amity wheezes. Jagged and brittle.

"Siddie," Leum snaps at you. "Take her."

Your mouth opens in protest. You're being dismissed?

But you don't get out a word of complaint before Leum grips your shoulder. "You're the only one I trust her with."

"No." You jerk out of her grasp. "Not me."

You didn't obey orders.

You didn't check the perimeter like you were supposed to.

You let the raiders into the village.

"I messed up," you tell her. "I already messed up."

She shakes her head, and you think for a second that she's going to yell at you. She's going to tell you to shut up, this is a battle, it's no time for whining, do what she says and get moving—

Instead, she grabs you by the back of the neck and presses her forehead to yours, the way she does with Kanver—

The way she does with her kin—

You never realized before how much gold she has in her eyes. Warm as sunlight, soft as sap.

"Then you really are one of us," she murmurs. "When we have no good choices, we still have to choose."

You feel something break inside of you. Your pride, your ambitions, your illusions of glory. Is this what it means to be a kindling?

Your losses?

Your mistakes?

"Okay." You pass her the bow and arrows. You get Amity to her feet.

Without a backward glance, you help Amity through the meadow, through the chaos, through the dead on the field, toward the make-shift infirmary below the cabin. She's leaning heavily on you, dragging her injured leg, but she's so thin now, she's so light or maybe you're stronger than you were, because she weighs almost nothing, like she's made of nothing more than fire and nerve—

Behind you, the sound of the fighting fades to a dull roar, like the sound of the ocean through a sand-scoured shell.

You're almost there. You've reached the road.

Then, in the distance, the barricade explodes.

BOOM.

You're almost knocked to the ground. You almost take Amity down with you. Over your shoulder, you see flames in the air, bits of wood and smoke, defenders flying backward and landing crumpled in the grass—

And a haze of light, the color of lavender, quickly dissipating but instantly recognizable—

Kindling magic.

At the front of her forces, Adren hefts an iron shield. From the crystal at its center, there's another blaze of light, but this time it doesn't strike the barricade. Instead, it unspools before the raiders, settling in front of them in a pale, undulating ribbon of fire.

No.

You can't believe it.

Adren's not just a kindling, she's a *Shieldbearer.* A specialist. Rare. You've heard stories about Shieldbearers, the elite guard of the Queen Commander (Long May She Reign). Their magic is impenetrable. Their reflexes are quick. At one time, they were known as the Walls of Amerand—

And now you can see why—

As the raiders begin their infantry charge, Adren's barrier spans the front of their ranks in a river of pure balar magic—

Blazing and impregnable—

Adren already broke your defenses with one blast from her shield. If no one figures out how to stop her, she's going to break Camas and everyone who stands in her way.

LEUM

WHEN YOU WAKE, YOU'RE ON THE GROUND. COLD earth. The smell of singed grass and charred stone. You try to move, and you groan. Your head is throbbing; your back aches. You must have been blown off your feet when the barricade broke. You remember wood splintering. You remember bodies flying through the air like debris—

You remember fire the color of lavender. Those purple hues were rare for a kindling, but no rarer than a Shieldbearer—

Or a Deathbringer—

You try to breathe. All around you, the Camassians are still fighting, running, shouting, firing arrows at the advancing invaders—

But as soon as the shafts strike Adren's barrier, they're incinerated. They burn up like sticks of incense and fall harmlessly into the grass.

"Aim up and over!" You stumble among the villagers, pointing toward the sky, and the next volley soars over the top of the barrier, raining down on the raiders from above.

You're rewarded by a few shrill cries, but behind the front line, Adren's infantry simply raises their shields, arrows pinging off steel—

And the forward march continues.

"Hold!" you shout. "Save your arrows!"

But you don't know for what.

As Adren advances, her balar barrier burns anything it touches.

Grass, lumber, cloth, bone. If she gets into the village, she could raze everything in minutes—

The gardens, the sheds, the livestock, the homes—

You have to stop her, but you don't know what else to do. You don't know how to fight a Shieldbearer. No one ever told you how to fight a Shieldbearer. They were supposed to be guardians. They were supposed to be on your side.

Your gaze darts across the lavender shield, trying to find an opening, an opportunity, some way to break the barrier before Adren reaches you.

You could break her balar weapon. (That'd be easiest.)

You could break *her*. (That'd be best.)

But you can't do either of those things from here. No, from here, your only option is to break the barrier itself—

And the only way to break magic like that is with more magic—

It'll cost you months of your life—

But you'll die anyway if you don't try—

You run into the road, into the ruins of Emara's barricade, where among the smoldering logs and scorched scraps of timber, you turn to face your enemy—

The archers, the cavalry, the armored infantry—

Adren and her glowing shield, her captain's cloak damp and heavy—

You draw your greatsword.

You can already feel your magic pulsing inside you like an ember awaiting timber. Planting your feet, you summon your power from deep in your core, drawing it through your veins, down your arms and into the palms of your hands, where it's channeled into your balar weapon—

The crystal flashing—

Fire dancing along the edge of the blade—

You bring your sword down, sending a swath of pink fire curving from your sword. It crashes into Adren's barrier in an explosion of light—

Blinding and cacophonous—

You close your eyes. You look away.

When you look back again, the barrier remains.

Through the pale purple of her magic, Adren smiles. (Distorted but serene.)

You try again. And again. Arcs of light, spears of flame. You send them crashing into the barrier, one after another like waves—

Roar and radiance—

Brilliance and blaze—

But nothing happens. All that, each blast taking more months off your life than the last, and the barrier's still unscathed.

You wipe your eyes. (Sweat, tears, rain.) You can't do it. You're not strong enough. Maybe if there'd been more of you—

If Ben hadn't left—

If Emara was alive—

Maybe you could've done it together, all your magic combined.

But alone? You could burn up all the years of your life and never break through.

Wearily, you watch the edge of the barrier ripple toward you, hissing and crackling on the gravel, in the puddles of rain. Adren's almost upon you. She's going to go through you. She's going to set her raiders loose on the village, and there's nothing you can do to stop her.

But everything ends, doesn't it?

First the war—

Then this—

Our time of valor dead and gone—

No heroes in the new age, Leum. No purpose, no mission, no reason for being.

Were you wrong to come here? Were you wrong to believe?

Then, a disturbance among the infantry. Confusion, screams. There's fighting in their left flank, you think, on the western edge of the line. Weapons clashing, marauders falling. A gunshot, another. Frowning, Adren glances over her shoulder, and as she does, her attention wavers. Her barrier shudders. Sudden fissures appear in the light—

Behind the line, there's the *crack!* of a handcannon—

In that instant, Adren's barrier dissipates. Her focus broken, her magic dissolved. Before she can gather herself again, a lone figure in a straw hat comes hurtling out of the ranks behind her—

Ben.

She's racing away from them. She's clutching something under her arm—

A handcannon. She got one of their handcannons. She even fires it at Adren as she passes, but the bullet goes wide.

Adren doesn't bat an eye. She's summoning her magic again. She's reactivating the barrier. It unravels from her balar crystal, streaming for the front of the line—

For a second, you think Ben's going to collide with the blaze. She's going to burn up. She's going to fry. But she doesn't balk. She bolts toward you, leaping through the last gap in the light before it closes behind her.

She drops the handcannon at the base of the barrier, all its wooden pieces igniting before Adren or anyone else can save them, and races up to you. Scratched, bleeding, panting, drenched—

"You came back," you say obviously, like saying it will mean you're not dreaming, will mean she's really here.

She tips back her hat. Mud on her cheeks, a glint in her eye. "I'm no coward," she says, "and I'm going to prove it to you."

BEN

YOU WERE ALREADY HOURS AWAY WHEN THE STORM broke. The black clouds, the driving rain. You were shivering in your robes, should've stopped to make a fire, to find shelter on the road.

But you had to keep moving. You thought if you kept moving, you could outrun the battle—

The idea of the battle—

The knowledge that it was starting—

Or was going to start soon—

You had to keep moving, faster, farther, as if you were being pursued. You charged down the mountain (flooded trails, slick stones) and by the time you felt Penumbra sliding beneath you, it was too late—

You were thrown from the saddle, landing hard in the mud, and as you got to your knees, the medallion fell out of your collar—

Leum's Wind Runner medallion, winking in the silver light—

You'd forgotten you had it.

You'd forgotten a lot of things, actually. Why you were here. What you wanted to prove. But you hadn't proven anything, had you? You were still a deserter, still a runaway, still so scared of the past that you doomed yourself to repeat it.

On the side of the trail, by the buckwheat flattened by rain, you spun the medallion, watching the dayfly flicker between your fingers. A flash in the darkness, but only fleeting.

And you knew then that you had to return.

You couldn't be a kindling if you were a coward.

You couldn't be the best if you ran.

You couldn't say you loved them if you left them.

You couldn't be perfect if you didn't change.

Taking a slip of paper and a nub of charcoal, you scribbled a note, wrapped it around the medallion. You stuffed it into Penumbra's saddlebags and mounted up again in the rain.

Your destiny was never over the mountains. It wasn't in Ifrine, or Riven, or Kun-kala, or Yansen beyond the sea.

It was here in Amerand, the land that created you, the land that made you what you are—

You rode back to the village, and as you reached the valley, you saw that the battle was well underway. Cavalry charging the barricade. Gunshots on the line. Just out of range, Adren's infantry was readying for an advance, but you didn't know why until you saw the first burst of balar light.

Adren.

You ducked at the explosion, but you didn't stop riding. You had to rejoin your kin, but the south road was blocked by Adren's forces, the flooded meadow impossible to cross. Urging Penumbra westward, you climbed up the ridge, parallel with the offensive, until the land grew too steep for her to pass.

Dismounting, you kissed her quickly on the nose. "Find me when it's over." And with a final pat, you set her loose.

Through the trees, you could see the curve of the balar barrier ahead of the front line, and despite your fear, you smiled.

You'd always wondered how you'd measure up to a Shieldbearer—

Now was your chance to try.

The barrier would be impenetrable, but even Shieldbearers have limits, and Adren had left her flank unfortified. You took off again, leaping and stumbling down the slope, toward the village, until you reached an outcropping where the barricade met the hillside—

Just in time—

As the edge of the barrier rippled past you, searing the moss and lichen from the rocks, you leapt from your perch—

Over their heads—

Into their ranks—

You landed among them, moving swiftly through their defenses. Armor, sword, arrow, pike. You were a shadow. You were quick with your blades.

Then came the gunshots—

Three of them—

Bang. Bang. Bang.

You ducked, but not before noting the cannoneers in the melee.

Selecting a knife from its sheath at your waist, you fought your way to Adren. (The curve of her back, the black of her cape.) But the blade had scarcely left your hand when she ducked out of its path, the knife slipping past her, and you wondered if it was true, if Shieldbearers were clairvoyant—

How could she have known you'd attack in that way?

(She wasn't even looking at you.)

But there was no time for shock. You'd had your chance, and you'd missed it. You were surrounded, and the only way out was through the flickering barrier, weakened when Adren's attention wavered. Snatching a weapon from one of the cannoneers, you pointed it at Adren—

You'd never held a handcannon before—

(It was heavier than you expected—)

(The way Emara was heavier when her spirit had left her—)

You pulled the trigger.

Bang.

Now you stand before Leum, who's shaved since you saw her last, her topknot high and tight. Despite her customary scowl, it's hard to believe she's the same girl who approached you in Gateway. No longer a vagabond but a warrior. No longer a stranger but your kin.

"You look good," you tell her.

"You don't."

You laugh. You can't help it. The familiar abrasiveness. The begrudging conversation. You wish you had time to provoke her. To tease her and prank her. You should've been more like Emara, you think. You should've been in the thick of things instead of alone.

But you're here now, and Adren is approaching, the last remnants of the barricade are burning, and you don't know where Amity is—

(You pray to the gods she's alive—)

But the villagers will be killed if you don't act quickly. You pull Leum aside. "We need to fall back."

She looks startled. "What?"

"We need to retreat."

It should've been obvious. You could try to break the barrier, but even if you managed it, Adren would simply summon it again. The surest way of eliminating the threat would've been to kill Adren, and you already tried that and failed.

Besides, the raiders are nearly upon you. Even if they didn't have the barrier, they're too close to be stopped now. You can't let them loose upon the Camassians—

They're better armed—

They're better trained—

Without fortified positions, the villagers will be slaughtered in seconds.

Leum should've already had them withdrawing to the secondary defenses by the infirmary, although, to be fair, you don't know if it even occurred to her.

She's a vanguardian, after all. Vanguardians don't give up, don't run, don't retreat.

"But they'll get into the village," she says, still uncomprehending.

You place a hand on her shoulder. "They're already going to get into the village."

She looks up at you, and for the first time since you met her, you think she looks frightened. Both of you know the secondary defenses are little more than a few low walls along the road, a few extra quivers stashed behind fences. Enough to keep fighting. Enough for a last stand, nothing more.

You hope you make it to the end.

You hope to be there. You hope to bear witness. You hope you're still fighting when they strike you down beside your kin.

Sheathing her sword, Leum calls for the retreat.

AMITY

YOU'VE ALWAYS FOUND SOMETHING SO BEAUTIFUL about destruction. The tongues of fire, the shrouds of smoke, the rubble of the battlefield—

Char and corpses—

Blood and steel—

From the road, you and Siddie watch, spellbound, as Adren advances through the ruined barricade, past burning logs and the bodies of your dead, while behind her the marauders send arrows arcing over the rim of her balar barrier and into your fleeing defenses. Feathered shafts stippling the field. Villagers falling forward, pierced through their backs.

Leum stops to help someone to their feet. Together, they stumble onward, past a slender figure, who pauses briefly to draw a knife from her belt.

Through your mind flits the memory of a child, mantis-thin and just as quick, flinging blades at impossible angles, impossible speeds—

"Is that Ben?" Siddie gasps.

No, it can't be.

(Can it?)

A second later, you glimpse the flash of a blade, poised for a moment at the peak of its flight before lancing downward on the other side of the barrier, piercing Adren's armored shoulder.

It *is* Ben.

It has to be.

She came back.

She chose you. Chose to stand with you, chose to fight with you, to die with you, if fate decrees.

You want to call to her. You want to let her know you see her, you forgive her, you love her, would've loved her even if she'd stayed gone.

Adren staggers. In front of her, the barrier quivers. But she doesn't stop. The march continues.

At this rate, they'll reach the village in a matter of minutes. All those marauders loose among the children, the elderly, the unsuspecting defenders to the north.

Minutes.

That's all you have, Amity.

That's all you have left to stop this.

"Amity!" Siddie's voice reaches you as if from a distance. She's pulling you toward the infirmary, but you resist. You can barely stand on your own two feet, but you resist.

The villagers need you.

Your kindred need you.

You know what you have to do.

Mustering your strength, you shove Siddie away from you. "Help Leum and Ben," you tell her. "Get the Camassians to safety."

She seizes your arm again. "I'm supposed to take care of you. Leum trusted me to—"

"No."

Below you, the fleeing defenders have reached the outskirts of the village. They're scattering between the houses, hopping fences, hobbling through the gardens toward the infirmary.

You lay your hand over Siddie's, your voice breaking, though you don't mean for it to. "They need you more than I do now," you murmur.

For an instant, her eyes spill over with tears, mingling quickly with the last drizzle of rain.

"It's okay, it's okay." You cup her face between your palms, brush her cheeks clear with your thumbs. "It's okay to be sad, but we've got to keep going. It's okay."

She lets out a sob. Then, with a nod, she races down the hillside to join the others.

You watch her go. Still scrawny, you think. Still growing into that sword of hers. But more graceful now than ungainly. More kindling now than trainee.

Gritting your teeth, you limp up the road, past the infirmary. Slowly, much too slowly. Blood running down your leg, pain radiating through you with every step.

You drag yourself up the path to the cabin. Over the wet grass and into the interior, still warm from the cook fire. Tottering through the front room, you're overwhelmed by the smell of your kin. Soap and mineral oil, leather and steel.

You're bleeding all over the floor now, but you suppose that can't be helped. Falling to your knees in front of your belongings, you draw out a silk package. Each tie loosened, each fold of cloth peeled back, until the light of your balar crystal escapes at last—

Bright as a bloody sunrise on your cheeks, your chest, your palms—

Your crown—

Your other half—

It's a simple circlet, austere in its curves. The smiths of House Vastari weren't jewelers, after all, weren't trained to craft trinkets and finery. One look at this, and anyone can tell it's a weapon.

You lay a hand over the red cabochon. All that power at your fingertips again, at your beck and call again, deadly and comforting.

You were trained for this. You were made for this.

Not peace but war.

You lurch from the cabin again, across the garden and toward the lip of the terrace. You need a good view of your enemy. Someplace high.

You don't make it past the firepit before you're seized by a coughing fit, worse than any you've experienced before. Each breath an agony. Each step a struggle. Your legs go out from under you. Your hands splay in the mud.

But you can't stop now, Amity. (The others still need you.) You're stumbling forward. You're spitting blood.

Gasping, you stagger to the edge of the garden. Below you, the defenders have taken cover behind low walls and fortified fences, exchanging volleys of arrows with the marauders behind the barrier, but Adren won't stop coming.

The light ripples, lavender and mauve. The faint blush of a bruise. The delicate purple of dawn.

Another barrage of arrows comes raining down upon the villagers, crouched behind the secondary defenses. Swiftly, Ben draws Siddie into the shelter of an overturned cart, but they're too exposed down there on the road. They only have seconds before Adren's barrier reaches them.

But Adren has made a miscalculation, shielding her horde from a frontal assault. Now that the war's over, she must've thought she was the only one who'd burn herself out for a fight, but she should've known better when she met you last night.

You're the Twin Valley Reaper.

Lifting your chin, you place your crown upon your head. Deep inside you, your magic kindles—

It's been so long since you used it that you can actually feel it draining the life from you now, feeding on you like a flame on tinder—

Searing through your veins, your lungs, your heart—

Then it stutters out, leaving you cold.

"No," you mutter. *"No."*

This is why kindlings were removed from the field when they started burning out. With their ailing bodies, they couldn't be trusted not to choke and sputter when everyone needed them most.

But you can't choke now. You can't fail.

Taking a breath, you summon your magic again. (Blistering and raw.) You realize you're shaking, though not with fear or even pain now but anticipation—

You look toward the battlefield, take stock of your enemies. Archers, swordsmen, cavalry—

All of them insects, writhing and wet in the rain—

Overhead, the sky flashes, and you allow yourself a final forbidding smile.

You remember this.

You were forced into this, once, but now at the end you choose it. You choose to be a weapon. You choose to be the Reaper, the Red Death, the Bolt of Judgment spearing down from the firmament.

You choose what you fight for.

You choose what you die for, and it isn't glory or self-importance but to protect the people you love.

You lift your hands.

You wish you had more time, but if your time is ending, you couldn't ask for a better end than this.

You and a battle—

You and a mission—

You and your kin.

LEUM

THE ENEMY IS IN THE VILLAGE. WHILE ADREN'S BALAR barrier burns across the road, behind her loose bands of raiders disperse among the houses, kicking down doors, trampling gardens, killing any defenders they find in hiding.

Ferra's home is lost.

The makeshift infirmary is overwhelmed.

You peer over a low wooden fence, where you've taken cover below the cabin. You need to find Ben. You need to find Siddie. Together, you might be able to break Adren's barrier. Together, you might stand a chance.

But Ben and Siddie are pinned behind an overturned cart. Adren is almost upon them, her magic radiating toward them, sizzling over the gravel, the weeds. It's only ten paces away. Eight. Seven.

They're trapped.

They're going to be burned alive.

But as the barrier reaches the cart, its sides igniting, sending spirals of smoke into the air, the sky erupts with thunder—

Krrra-aak!

On the road, there's a strangled cry—

The smell of singed hair—

You look upward, searching for lightning, but the clouds are dark and eerily still. The rain has dried up. Even the wind has died.

Overhead, the storm is poised like an avalanche, swollen and ready to fall.

You sneak a glance over the fence, but the raiders look as mystified as you are. There's some sort of commotion behind the front line. A few shouts. A trail of smoke. Adren's so close now, you can see her confusion through the shimmering light. Her lips parted in some unspoken question—

But then her eyes widen, and her gaze goes skyward—

She's lifting her arms—

She's changing the angle of her shield—

Krrra-aak!

The bolt comes down before Adren can shift her barrier. Garnet in color and crackling with heat. It spears one of the marauders from above, raging through him like lightning, and for an instant he's illuminated—

You see the entirety of him alight from within—

Veins, muscles, organs, bones—

Uncanny and beautiful—

Then the magic bursts. It rips him to pieces. And he's gone.

Almost as quickly, another bolt streaks out of the sky.

Krrra-aak!

You know this.

You've seen this before.

Years ago, on a mountaintop, with the night sky roiling and bunching overhead and thousands of Vedran soldiers swarming up the slopes.

You look back, over your shoulder, and there's Amity on the edge of the garden. She looks so calm up there, in her crown (composed, regal, her balar crystal glowing bloody and red at her brow), and you're struck, all of a sudden, by how much like herself she looks now.

Maybe she's missing her armor. Maybe she's unsteady on her feet.

But there she is.

Amity, Kindling Primary Class, Deathbringer of Her Queen Commander's Army. The Bolt of Judgment. Kemera's Knife.

The Twin Valley Reaper.

But something's wrong. For an instant, red lightning flickers across the sky, forking and dissipating without ever striking the ground—

A stutter in her magic, but only briefly. Seconds later, three more bolts of balar fire spear from the clouds, scattering Adren's forces—

Thunder and screams on the air—

Distantly, you hear Ben calling the others to battle. You know you should join them. The enemy is fracturing. Adren's barrier can't cover all of them. Now is the time to strike.

But you can't take your eyes off Amity.

There are red lines crawling along her cheeks now, threatening to swallow her. You've never seen it happen before, never watched it with your own two eyes, but you know she's burning out. She's drawing on the last weeks of her life, using them as fuel, using herself as fuel, as kindling, to give the rest of you a fighting chance.

But you have to stop her.

A few more weeks, or less than that now, days, hours, minutes, but that's still something, isn't it? You can give that to her. A little more time. A little more time with the people who love her.

You just have to stop her.

"Amity!" Your voice fractures in your grief.

She looks down at you. For the briefest of seconds, she holds your gaze with her own, and she doesn't have to say anything for you to know she's saying goodbye.

Then she gives you an order.

"Go."

And you obey.

You're a soldier, and she's your commander, your general, your kindred, your queen, and you obey her without hesitation.

You draw your sword and launch yourself into the melee.

Adren's magic flows upward like a ceiling of lavender glass, sheltering her forces as they fall back behind sheds, houses, trees, anything to get out of the open, out of Amity's line of sight.

Krrra-aak!

Ruby light explodes over the road.

Another raider falls.

Jin runs up beside you. "Is this Amity?" they ask. Breathless, awe-struck. "She's burning herself out for us?"

You nod. For a second, you think it's raining again, but no, those are just tears on your cheeks. Turning, you wipe your hand across your eyes and hope Jin doesn't notice. "Come on."

The remaining marauders have concentrated around Adren at the intersection of the south and loop roads, where they cluster beneath her barricade, but Amity's magic keeps faltering. Her bolts aren't striking anymore, evaporating into the clouds before they ever find their targets—

Then nothing—

The absence of thunder, the sky clear and dark—

You want to look for her.

You're afraid to look for her.

(What if you look and she's gone?)

But you don't have *time* to look for her, Leum. You still have to fight. You join the villagers as they advance on Adren's forces with wooden spears and scavenged weapons, battling your way through the enemy, but before you can get to Adren, a single blaze of light sears out of the sky—

Krrra-aak!

Amity's magic explodes against the barrier. Beneath her shield, Adren's arms shudder at the impact.

Krrra-aak!

Adren falls to one knee.

Krrra-aak!

In her shield, the crystal shatters, shards quickly losing color as they're flung away from her.

Overhead, the barrier flickers once and evaporates.

Her balar weapon is broken.

Her forces are exposed.

Amity did it.

Amity saved you, or at least she gave you a fighting chance.

There among the villagers, you, Ben, and Siddie race toward Adren, but you don't make it two steps before you're halted by cannon shot spraying gravel at your feet—

Then another, bursting through one of the farmers, who charges past you—

Stumbles—

Collapses—

"Cannoneers!" Siddie shouts.

You duck, pulling her down with you. "I know!" You yank her behind a tree at the fork in the road. Glancing around, you spot a flash at the corner of Ferra's house, a second behind the infirmary fence.

Two handcannons. They have two handcannons left.

Another villager, too slow to find cover, falls.

Ben skids to a halt beside you, on her knees in the mulch. "I'll get the one by the infirmary." Her voice is low and fast. "Can you two handle the other?"

She doesn't wait for you to respond. She knows you can. She knows you have to. Drawing her knives, she dashes off again as cannon fire explodes around you.

Siddie covers her ears. "We have to get out of here!"

Twisting in the dirt, you peer around the tree to see seven raiders creeping toward you from Ferra's house. Besides the cannoneer, there's four infantry and two archers, an arrow narrowly missing you as you pull out of sight again. *Sssnk!* The shaft quivering in the earth.

You glance at Siddie: her smudged cheeks, her bloodshot eyes, her greatsword trembling in her hands.

"Ready?" you ask.

She nods.

She's lying, but that's okay. She doesn't have to be ready.

She's got you.

You wait for a pause in the shooting, then you dash out from behind the tree with Siddie on your heels. You have to be quick now, racing through Ferra's garden. You dodge another arrow, slipping past the tip of a spear and under the shaft, your enemy within slashing distance now, your blade sinking into the meat of his thigh.

Another arrow whizzes past you, but you've already moved on. You're leaping at the next marauder, your blade cleaving through the air as they stagger backward under the onslaught. Siddie's behind you, disarming the injured spearman with a deft flick of her weapon while the others close in around you.

You feel a grim sense of satisfaction come over you. You're used to this. You were used for this, in the war, battling among the infantry, breaking through the enemy lines like a battering ram. You're used to being surrounded. You're used to leading the charge.

It may not be like it was. It will never be like it was. (It shouldn't ever be like it was.) But in the end it's still you and your squad—

A little smaller now, a little changed—

After everything, you're still here, still fighting for each other.

Ahead of you, one of the marauders trips, their heel catching on something (a rock, a trowel, the edge of a garden bed), and you're upon them in a flash, your sword sinking clean through their chest.

Blood on your hands, your neck, your face—

You're vaulting off them, past them, and straight to the cannoneer. They get off one shot, powder burning the side of your neck, but you're too fast. You knock the weapon out of their hands, send it flying into a patch of half-trampled vines, and slice them across the throat.

Behind you, the second handcannon goes off near the infirmary.

You duck out of instinct. Ben was supposed to take care of the other cannoneer—

What happened to her?

Whirling, you turn to check on Siddie, but Siddie isn't behind you anymore. She's on the loop road, dashing across it and into the brambles on the other side, where she flings herself through the thorns and against the low rock wall of a garden terrace.

A bullet chips the stone by her head.

You see the second cannoneer now, behind the upturned cart on the south road, firing across the garden at Siddie, who's jumping at every explosion, squeezing her eyes shut like if she can't see anything, nothing can see her.

At the corner of Ferra's house, the raiders are regrouping. They're collecting the first handcannon from the vines. Stupid, Leum. You should have picked up the weapon when you had the chance—

Too late. You're already racing toward Siddie, knowing it'll put you in danger too, but you can't leave her. You can't let her die. As your feet fly over the gravel, a bullet clips you in the leg. You stumble, but you keep running.

A face full of brambles. Scratched cheeks and hands. The wall at your back.

Siddie gapes at you. "You came back for me!"

"Don't be stupid," you grumble. Your leg hurts. Your trousers are torn, blood running down your ankle.

It's lucky they didn't hit bone.

Across the road, three of the raiders split off toward Parker's house with the first handcannon, but the others move in your direction, weapons drawn.

You start up, but before you can get to your feet, another bullet drives you back under cover. You curse. You can't make a break for it without being shot, but you can't stay where you are or the marauders will be on you in a matter of seconds.

You're pinned.

Siddie must know it too, because she glances at you, panicked, as the next bullet strikes the ground at her feet. "What do we do now?"

KET

"SIT BACK," YOU SAY.

Behind the shelter of the guard station, Tana obeys. Once Kanver sent down the archers from the bridge, you were able to close the breach. Tana insisted on wrapping your thigh, but her shoulder's still bleeding. You tear off a bandage with your teeth.

Thunder rumbles off the mountains. A growl, a roar. To the south, a red beam of light lances out of the sky.

Krrra-aak!

"What was that?" Tana looks up, frowning. Her brow bleeding, her lip split.

You don't look up, don't want to see it again, that balar lightning bursting from the clouds, can't see it again without thinking of Amity, of what's happening to her, what she's doing to herself, and if you allow yourself to think about that, you won't be able to keep going, to keep fighting—

And you need to keep fighting, Ket.

"That's the Twin Valley Reaper." Hurriedly, you finish binding Tana's shoulder and struggle to your feet.

"Amity?"

You nod grimly, casting about for a walking stick. "There's only one reason she'd burn herself out like this."

Your kin are in danger.

You need to get to them. Quick. Scooping up an abandoned spear, you draw Tana to you. Your lips in her hair, your hand at her waist. "I'll come back to you," you whisper.

You start for the square, but even with your makeshift walking stick, your leg's already failing you. You don't make it two steps before you pitch forward into the road—

Before you hit the gravel, Tana catches you. "I said I wasn't leaving you, and I meant it."

"You can't come with me." You try to pull away, but she tightens her grip.

"Can't I?"

"It's too dangerous." You think of Kari under the wheels. You think of Emara in her coffin. You think of Tana impaled on a spear.

Krrra-aak!

Another bolt strikes on the other side of the village.

Krrra-aak!

You don't have time for this. Amity needs you. Your kindred need you.

But you're injured. Your leg is throbbing, bleeding heavily through your bandages, threatening to buckle with every step.

Tana pulls your arm over her shoulder, taking your weight. "You need me," she says. "You can't do this alone."

You bite your lip. You never wanted to need anybody again, never wanted to depend on them, went out of your way to avoid it, actually, so you never got too attached—

But you need Tana now. You can't do this without her.

(Even if it puts her at risk.)

So you grit your teeth and give her a nod and let her lead you up the slope.

As you reach the village square, the lightning stops. In the sudden silence, you hear cannon fire in the distance. From the square, you can see all the way down to the south road, where one of the raiders is crouched behind an overturned cart with a handcannon in their arms.

Bang.

"Who are they shooting at?" Tana asks breathlessly.

Down the loop road, you see someone peer over the low rock wall.

A sour expression. A freshly tidied topknot.

Leum.

And Siddie beside her.

Tana sees them at the same time you do. Turning, she helps you toward the cannoneer, but you don't even make it across the square before a second shot rings out from your left.

Something hot and fast grazes your shoulder.

Tana cries out as you drag her toward cover, but you don't think she's been hit. "I need you to check on Amity," you tell her, pushing her toward the western slope. "She'll be someplace high."

"But you—"

You duck as another bullet strikes the mud of the square. A cannoneer at the corner of Parker's newly reconstructed house. "I need you to do this for me," you say. "Please."

Tana grips your hand a second longer before she turns and runs, quick as she can toward the cabin, but you're still out in the open. You have to move. Dragging your leg, you veer toward the direction of the shot, into Parker's garden at the edge of the square, and there among the scorched apple trees, you find your enemy—

The cannoneer behind one of the unburned walls—

An archer behind a weatherworn juniper—

A swordsman with two curved blades charging at you through the mulch—

You draw your sword, your saber ringing against his. *Clang! Clang!* You block and parry, but you're slower than you should be.

Hesitant. You're testing your weight every time you take a step, not knowing when your wounded leg will fail you.

Bang! Mud and leaves spray up at your feet.

The smell of loam, damp with rain.

Too close. You throw yourself behind one of the trees, out of sight of the cannoneer, and duck as the swordsman comes after you again.

Parry, feint, another bullet flying past, another slash. You're evading their attacks, but only barely, each one whispering closer to your ribs, your arm, your neck. The swordsman is practically on top of you, driving you backward as his blades shear across yours.

You shove him off you, and you're on him again in a flash, slicing up, down, forcing him off-balance, and then all it takes is a touch—

A kiss of your blade on the inside of his wrist—

And he drops his sword.

You're ready for it. You snatch it out of the air, and in one smooth movement you send it flying end over end toward the corner of the house, where the blade embeds itself deep in the cannoneer's chest.

Her weapon falls from her hands, landing by the doorstep with a clatter.

You're too far to reach it before the swordsman finds you, but without his second weapon he's off his guard. You finish him off in three quick strikes and turn on the archer, but she's dropping her bow. She's fleeing through the garden and down to the loop road, where you spy two raiders with knives in their backs.

For some reason, you think of Ben.

But it can't have been Ben. Ben's gone. Ben left you.

Didn't she?

You stagger toward the abandoned handcannon, but your attention is drawn by gunfire on the south road. *Leum*, you think. *Siddie*.

Limping, you head for the overturned cart, where you set upon the second cannoneer. Their astonishment, their fear. You slash them across the throat before they can even get to their feet.

You pick up the handcannon and shove it into the hands of the nearest runner, Fern. Glazed eyes. A cut across her cheek. "There's another one of these by Parker's house," you tell her. "Get them both to Onna."

Nodding, she clasps the gun to her chest and dashes off.

"Ket!" Down on the loop road, Siddie hops one of the rock walls and barrels toward you, followed at a much slower pace by Leum. She's limping, a bloody bandage knotted around her shin, but other than that, they both seem okay.

"I saw the lightning," you say as they reach you. "Where's Amity?"

"At the cabin . . ." Leum's gaze drifts over your shoulder, where, at the edge of the Old Man's garden, you see Tana, kneeling over someone—

Heavy on the ground—

"Oh no," Siddie whispers.

"What about Kanver?" Leum asks.

You glance over her shoulder, like you expect to see Kanver behind her, slouching toward the rest of you with their glaive on their shoulder. "They're not with you?"

Both Leum and Siddie shake their heads, and in your stomach you feel a cold pit of dread. You thought you saw Kanver leave the barricade while you were defending the gully. They were moving southward. You thought they were heading for the square. If they didn't make it here, then . . .

No.

No.

You can't think about that yet.

All around you, the raiders are scattering, their formations breaking as the Camassians drive them out of the village and into the meadow.

"They're retreating," Siddie murmurs.

"Not all of them," you say, scanning the nearby houses, the gardens, the broken fences, where skirmishes are still taking place. "Where's Adren?"

BEN

IT TAKES YOU LESS THAN A MINUTE TO DISPATCH THE cannoneer by the infirmary. A leap over the fence, a well-thrown knife, a kill. You retrieve your blade, and you're just reaching for his weapon when out of the corner of your eye you spot Adren slinking away from the battle.

For the briefest of seconds, you think she's retreating. After Amity's onslaught, her raiders are scattering, her forces are crumbling. Maybe you and your kin were simply too much for her, even with her shield, her broken shield, now in pieces in the middle of the crossing.

But she doesn't flee to the south like you expect. Instead, she steals a sword from a corpse in the road and sneaks into the garden behind Ferra's house.

You take up the handcannon, but when you try to fire it, nothing happens. Its chambers empty, its mechanism useless and cold—

No ammunition on the raider's corpse either, and you don't have time to search for more—

Adren's getting away.

The weapon's no good to you now, so you toss it to the nearest villager and sprint after Adren. Making your way toward Ferra's, you see Leum fighting on the other side of the house, carving through a squad of raiders like an axe through a rotten log. Hurriedly, you steal through the backyard, pausing only once to pick up a fallen sword

It's not your weapon of choice, but you've only got a dozen knives left on you, and you're going to need a bigger blade before the day is done.

You poke your head around the corner.

Bang.

A bullet strikes the garden wall across the road.

Someone's shooting at Leum and Siddie, huddled in the berry brambles. He must have gotten the handcannon you left with the villager, must have killed her for it, must have had more bullets on him. Now he has Leum and Siddie pinned near the intersection while a pair of raiders advance on them from the loop road.

Across the way, Adren has reached the gate that leads to Parker's garden. Her back is to you. Your line of sight is clear.

You reach for your knives—

You could kill her now. You could finish this.

But you'd be leaving Leum and Siddie to die—

As you rise, not one but two blades leave your fingers. They separate in midair, sinking into the backs of the marauders, who collapse in the gravel before they can reach the other side of the road—

You vault after Adren, toward the garden gate, where she turns, swiftly, her sword coming up to block your attack—

Clang!

She's fast. That's the first thing you notice. Finding her feet quickly on the splintery wooden stairs, she lashes out at you, almost experimentally, forcing you back.

"You should've stayed gone," she says.

"I couldn't leave them," you murmur, "even though I tried."

"Then you're a fool."

"Am I? Your shield is broken. Your forces are scattered. You can't hope to win now."

For an instant, her gaze drops to your gauntlets, your balar crystals glowing blossom-pink on the backs of your hands. Her lips twitch. A funny little smile. "What do you think winning is?" she asks. When you don't reply, she shakes her head slowly, like a snake. "It's destruction. All I have to do is kill enough of you, and you'll never recover."

You think of the stores she already pillaged, the lives she already took. You think of the fields left unattended while the defenses were being built.

You think of the cold.

The temperature dropping already. Your breath fogging in the air.

You think of starvation and the coming winter.

"After a point, the only real victory is desolation," she continues softly. "The war taught me that."

You think of your squad in the rubble. You think of Emara dying in your arms. You wonder if you can ever come back from that, if there can ever be victory after that, if you can ever win after that or if the only thing left for you will be loss—

But you don't believe that, Ben. You never have. You believe in second chances. You believe in fresh starts. That's why you came here in the first place. That's why you couldn't run when you tried.

After everything you've lived through, after all the death, destruction, and loss, you still believe that things can be better—

(That *you* can be better—)

You press the attack. You're lunging, feinting, but your sword is a distraction, a way to keep her attention on your advance and not your left hand, not on your holster, not on the knife you slide from its sheath.

A flick of your wrist, and it strikes the step, its point embedded deep in the wood.

You try not to stare—

Can't afford to process—

Can't afford the hesitation—

You missed.

While your attention's still on the knife, Adren swings. She's got the higher ground, the longer reach, and you jump backward, dodging, parrying, the strength of her blows sending shivers along your blade.

She fights like Leum, like a vanguardian, like a person so surrounded by death she's become one with it. *Clang! Clang! Clang!* It's almost enough to put you off-balance, but you're not so besieged you don't see her wrench your knife from the stair and fling it back at you, the point going end-over-end through the air—

You duck, the weapon whistling past your ear, and pull another blade from your belt, hurling it at her as you charge her again with your sword.

She sidesteps easily, but you're expecting that, another knife already leaving your hand, but this one misses her too, sailing into the rock wall at the top of the terrace.

You throw again and again—

Two, three, six of your blades lost to your surroundings—

But you can't seem to hit her. You've never missed this much in your life.

You know it's backward, but you can't help feeling pleased.

At last, a challenge.

At last, a chance to test your speed.

Adren's at the top of the terrace now, the cold nipping at her delicate features, turning her cheeks pink. A few steps below her, you tear one of your knives from where it's lodged in the rock wall.

You know she's watching it, waiting for the moment the blade leaves your hand, but you don't throw it. (Not yet.) You leap up the stairs, slashing at her ankles with the tip of your sword, and you're on the top step now too, forcing her onto the flagstone path to Parker's back door.

Then, overhead, the flash of her blade—

But you're ready for this. You catch her sword with your own, deflecting it as you step inside her reach—

Your knife comes up—

You hear her gasp (a quick sound by your ear), and then she's staggering backward, touching her side, her eyes widening at the sight of her own blood on her fingertips.

It's nothing but a scratch, more fabric than flesh. Anyone else and you would've gotten their ribs.

But she's not just anyone—

And now she knows you aren't either.

Turning, she flees, and you chase her across the garden, but it's like she understands you now, understands who you are and how you fight, and every move she makes forces you to throw away another of your knives. You're down to five, then four, and maybe she even allows a couple of them to graze her—

Her arm, her cheek, blood spattering the grass—

But soon all your sheaths are empty, and it's just you and her and your swords, and you hate to admit it, but you know you couldn't have left Amerand without facing her—

Couldn't have called yourself the Quickest Blade in Kindar without fighting her—

All of a sudden, Adren stumbles. Maybe she's tiring. Maybe she didn't *allow* you to hit her after all. Maybe her steps are slower, her sword work sloppier.

You hack at her, driving her toward the back of Parker's house, and yes, you're right, she's retreating now, more desperate now. She's trying to put some distance between you, but you keep charging after her, relentless in your attack.

A jump, a slash, your swords clashing, and then you're springing apart again, coming together again, dodging, parrying—

Out of the corner of your eye, you see Ket dispatch the cannoneer by the cart. You watch Siddie breaking from cover, followed closely by Leum, her gait a little off, something wrong with her leg, but they're safe. They made it—

Some of them made it, at least. You're still missing Amity. You're still missing Kanver.

It's not perfect. (You'll never be perfect.) But this time you know you did your best.

In that instant, you feel your sword catch on Adren's. You feel it shiver (a ripple of wind across the flooded meadow), and there's something about Adren's strength or the angle of her attack, but the steel can't take it.

The blade shatters as Adren flings open the back door and disappears into Parker's house.

You launch yourself after her—

The abrupt change in light—

The interior cool and dim—

She almost slices your head off as your eyes adjust, but you duck, lashing out with your broken sword.

You hear the tearing of fabric before Adren dances out of your reach again. She escapes across the kitchen, kicking kettles and cauldrons into your path as you advance on her.

She's breathing harder now, her hair falling from its perfect pins and into her face, but she's still got her sword, so you grab for Parker's cutlery, arranged neatly on the counter. A cleaver, a carving blade, a paring knife—

Not much, you think, but they'll have to do—

You throw the paring knife first, the slim blade lodging itself in Adren's shoulder as she tries to spin away.

She snarls, wrenching it out of her flesh and flinging it back at you.

You duck, but it clips your scalp. A dizzying flash of pain. You must be tiring too, your limbs growing weak, your blood flowing freely down your neck.

Adren runs from the kitchen, but you're not done with her yet. You fling your broken sword, catching her in the calf as she crashes through the screen into the next room—

Smoke-stained beams, the smell of fresh thatch—

She trips, rolls, coming up on her feet again but limping now as you charge after her. Snatching a blanket from the floor, you toss it at her, the cloth opening up like a sail—

You fling the carving blade through it, the steel shearing the fabric as you dive for Adren's feet, coming up underneath her as she lunges sideways to avoid the knife.

Her eyes widen, but she sees you too late. You're already hooking her sword with your cleaver, forcing her to drop her blade.

The sword falls as she twists out of your grasp, but you don't stop to grab it. You chase her out the front door, into the garden, where she stumbles through the fruit trees, the corpses littering the mulch—

Her exposed back among the branches—

An easy target—

The cleaver strikes her between the shoulder blades as she reaches the road, clambering across the gravel. With a grunt, she tears the cleaver from her back, lets it drop with a clatter. She's tripping, falling, scrambling toward the slope below the cabin—

But there's nowhere for her to go.

Leum, Ket, and Siddie have seen her. They're closing in from your left. In the middle of the road, you retrieve your cleaver. Blood dripping from the edge of the blade.

Adren's reached the side of the road now, and among the weeds you see her fumbling with a villager's corpse—

A runner, you think, with an arrow through her back—

Fern—

As you recognize her, Ket shouts, *"Ben, wait!"*

But she's too late.

In front of you, Adren flips onto her back, and she's holding one of the handcannons. Bellowing, fire-breathing, threatening to swallow you whole—

Your knife comes up—

Your muscles tense for the throw—

But the bullet strikes you before the cleaver can leave your hand.

In the distance, someone is screaming.

You sink to your knees.

You were too slow, Ben. You were too slow, too out of step with time. A decade ago, you would've been unmatched, unstoppable, the Quickest in Kindar and no mistake, but you were simply born too late.

The time of the kindlings is over. Our weapons outdated, our skills obsolete. The invention of the handcannon changed everything for us, for the world, for you. The Vedrans knew it. Adren knew it.

Maybe you knew it too. Maybe that's why you wanted to leave, to try to outrun the spread of powder and shot, these weapons of war, before they caught up to you.

Because who could win against a bullet?

Not even you.

SIDDIE

AND YOU UNDERSTAND, FINALLY, WHAT LEUM WAS trying to protect you from.

Ben, collapsing in the gravel—

Kanver and Amity, missing, absent—

Emara, already underground—

To the south, smoke rises from the meadow. Corpses litter the gardens. Allies, enemies. For some reason, they all look the same when they're dead.

On the side of the road, Adren's checking her handcannon, something wrong with it, with its fatal mechanism. It won't fire anymore. It's dead in her arms.

Ket and Leum rush to Ben's side. They're checking her pulse. They're putting their hands over her wound.

Was this what you wanted?

Was this what you asked for, when you asked to be one of them?

To lose them? To watch them fall?

You didn't know.

You didn't listen.

Clutching your sword, you stalk toward Adren as if in a trance. You can't seem to stop yourself. Your agonizing steps, your weapon dragging in the mud. For the first time since you lifted it from the Swordmaster's corpse, you notice how heavy it is. You don't understand it. You're stronger than you've ever been, but you can barely lift your blade—

With a disgusted sound, Adren tosses the handcannon aside. She stares up at you as you tower over her. She's unarmed and defiant—

No, not defiant—

Furious and incandescent.

She understood. *She* knew what you didn't, what it meant, what it really meant to be a kindling—

The way you loved them. The spaces they left.

She knew, and you hate her for it.

She lifts her chin. "Well, kid?" The words are a challenge. The words are a plea. She lost the battle. She lost her horde. But maybe these are only the latest in a long string of losses that have shaped her, turned her, twisted her, made her, the same way they've shaped Leum or Ket or any of your kin. If you end it now, if you end *her* now, she doesn't have to lose anything ever again.

Grimly, you lift your greatsword.

Beneath you, Adren swallows. Maybe she smiles.

Maybe she's ready.

Maybe she wanted it to end this way.

(Maybe she just wants it to end.)

But your arms are trembling. Your breath is coming short. You can't do it. To take another life? To strip someone else out of the world, this world, which has experienced so much loss already?

A century of it—

Generations of Chenyarans, Vedrans, Amerandines—

Kindlings, soldiers, civilians, infants and children, the young and the old, loss after loss after loss and none of you untouched—

You can't do it.

As you hesitate, Leum steps in front of you, and before you can stop her, her sword comes down, spearing Adren through the heart.

There's a shudder, a spray of blood, and then Adren goes still.

In that moment, the whole world seems empty and cavernous, like there is too much space and too few souls to fill it, and you want to fill it again, you want to have them back, you want to have them all back, you want and you want and you want, but it doesn't matter what you want, because the living are living and the dead are dead.

"Why?" You're sobbing. You're screaming. "Why? *Why?*"

The words only echo (cruelly).

Why? Why? Why?

You try to lash out, but there's nothing to hit. Everything is so blurry and so far away, and nothing can touch you and you can touch nothing, so you scream and you rail and it doesn't do anything, it doesn't do any good.

"Why?"

The ache inside of you, the ache of the world—

That such things can happen—

That such things *do* happen—

Then Leum is beside you. Dropping her sword, she pulls you into her arms, and in that instant you're not alone, she's with you, she's holding you, too tight and just tight enough, she's speaking gruffly into your hair.

"I'm sorry," she's saying. "I'm sorry. I'm sorry. I had to do it."

And you don't know if she did or if there was another way, if there could have been a future in which Adren lived, after the destruction she wrought, after the people she killed, but you know that this was a choice someone had to make, and you couldn't, so Leum did.

You understand finally why she fought so hard to protect you. She didn't want you to have to experience this. The violence, the carnage, the lives you took and the lives that were taken from you, the anger, the sadness, the absence, the grief—

But you did, and you're one of them now. You're a kindling now. Maybe you didn't know what you were choosing, a month ago, when you stormed into that hotel, when you trailed them up the mountain, in all your stubbornness of spirit, but you chose it. You chose them. Chose to follow them. Chose to love them, and losing them was the hardest thing you ever had to live through, but loving them was the best thing you ever did. You chose it. Again and again and again.

Now you just have to live with it.

LEUM

THE THREE OF YOU STAND IN THE VILLAGE, SUR-
rounded by broken fences and flattened gardens, survivors hobbling
between corpses, trying to identify their loved ones. As the wind
stirs your hair, you hear a keening on the air, a whimpering, more
felt in the bones than heard.

It starts to snow—

Feathery flakes alighting on the faces of your kin and melting
away just as quickly. There and gone. A star, a sliver, a drop of water—

Then nothing. A memory of beauty. A lingering sensation of cold.

Snow falls upon Camas in hushed curtains, dazzling and white.
For a moment, you think the whole world will be carpeted. Lovely.
Serene. All that carnage swept under a rug. But the ground is too
wet. The earth is too warm. Rain, blood, ash, bodies—

Nothing sticks.

You lay Ben inside the cabin, her body at rest beneath a sheet.

Then Onna finds you with the news about Kanver, the words
hardly leaving her mouth before you shove past her.

No, no, no, no—

Your denial. Your panic.

Heedless of your wounds, you flee across the square, vaulting
over the fence and into Onna's garden, where your injured leg falters.
You stumble. You scrabble at the mud.

You can't seem to stand up. Can't seem to find your balance. You're running, or you're crawling. Around the side of the house and into the backyard, where you see their body on the step—

Kanver—

You're not a kindling anymore. You're just a kid, a kid like any other, who's lost her friend, her family, her sibling—

No, no, no, no—

You fall to your knees. You pull them into your lap. Awkwardly, clumsily. They're heavier than they should be. You keep losing your grip as you cradle their body, rocking them back and forth—

Oh-oh-ohhh . . .

You try to sing to them, like you sang to them when you were little, like Emara sang to them a week ago, like all of you sang to Emara, like the song will reach them wherever they are, across the realms of life and death, like that will be enough to let them know they're not alone, even as they ascend the steps of the Palace of Bones.

Ohhh-oh-ohhh . . .

You want the song to find them, but you choke on the melody. Your shoulders trembling, your sobs soft and quick.

It isn't working.

It doesn't comfort you.

They can't hear you.

They're gone.

Standing, you try to lift them on your own, but their body is too loose, too pliable. They're slipping out of your grasp—

"Let me help you." From behind you, Onna steps forward. She's injured, you notice. Dried blood matted in her hair. With a solemn expression, she reaches for Kanver, takes their body in her arms.

You growl at her.

Kanver isn't hers to carry. Kanver isn't hers at all.

But she doesn't let go. "They saved my daughter," she says. "They saved all the children. When the raiders breached the gully, it was

Kanver who stopped them. Every single one."

You try to imagine it.

Kanver in the garden.

Kanver and their glaive.

You don't want to imagine it. You don't want to imagine them dying, you want to imagine them alive. You want to imagine them sitting with you, spine to spine. You want to imagine them giggling in the grass or sleeping upright against a tree. You want to imagine their voice drifting from the bunk beside you, crackling and warm in the dark.

You squeeze them tighter. You bury your face in their hair.

Onna takes most of the weight when you carry Kanver to the cabin and lay them beside Ben.

Then the garden, where Ket, Tana, and Siddie are gathered on the terrace. They look so clear after the storm, with the air gleaming around them, soft and bright.

As you cross the grass, Ket looks up. "Kanver?" she says.

You shake your head. You draw up beside her.

At first, Amity looks like she could be sleeping. Her closed eyes, her slender shoulders, the graceful curve of her neck—

But she isn't sleeping.

She's too still. Her skin is entirely vined with red now, vulgar and bright, rivers of it twisting along her throat, her cheeks, out of her hair and down her forehead, beneath her balar crown.

Burnout.

You want to take comfort in the idea that this is how she would've wanted to go. Not quietly, not peacefully, but *raging*, fighting, smiting her enemies from on high like the God of War herself. Wrathful, merciless. Callula incarnate—

Except gods don't die.

If this were the war, she would have been celebrated, valorized.

Her coffin adorned in silk and carried on a litter through the capital. Her name remembered, recorded, repeated.

Amity, Kindling Primary Class, Deathbringer of Her Queen Commander's Army.

Here, there will be no parades, no accolades. A quiet burial, some flowers on her grave. Her name remembered by but a few.

But they knew her, and that's something, isn't it? That they knew her the way no one in the capital would have? She would've been an icon, yes, but not a person. A weapon, a symbol, but nothing more.

Here, she was real. Here, she lived.

Beside you, Siddie is crying. Her expression twisted, her tears glittering on her cheeks. She's the only one of you who's seen this up close, watched her old master burn out in her arms.

She kneels beside the body. She removes the balar crown (the crystal glowing only faintly in her proximity, not the vibrant bloody red it should be but the faintest blush of peach).

"Will you help me with her?" Siddie's voice is small.

You swallow. You nod.

Together, you carry Amity inside to join the rest of your kin. That makes four of you. More than half of you gone.

You cross her hands, lay her crown upon her chest. You cover her with a blanket. Not crimson silk but a quilt, lovingly stitched together out of scraps, the pieces a little faded, a little frayed: a gift from the villagers, when they found out she was ill.

It doesn't seem worthy of her, but for some reason it feels right.

A day of funerals, burials, farewells. All that ceremony only to leave you feeling hollow. All those words and none of them seem to matter—

Whispers on the wind—

Tossed stones in the sea—

You stare at the graves, and you think of drifting.

You think of horizons shifting.

Rain, cloud, a twinkling star. You think of washing up on another shore, clean and cold. Everything numb but new again, in a land where nothing hurts.

Onna remains with you in the cemetery long after the villagers have left for their paltry feast. You don't understand it. A table of dishes seasoned with tears? A few lean cuts of meat? You don't know how any of them can eat at a time like this, after a loss like this, but truth be told, you don't know if any of them are.

Maybe they're staring, silent, still—

The food untouched—

The wine unswilled—

Maybe they don't know what to do with themselves any more than you do.

Maybe the motion is what matters. The traditions, the preparations, the things you do not because you want to do them but because you need something to do. Some flowers, a feast, a vigil, a song—

But none of you feel like singing today.

You sit on your haunches. Dull-eyed and haunted.

The mounds of earth, the stone cairns.

At the head of Kanver's grave, someone has left a small wooden spear, endearingly tilted in the mud.

Thoughtfully, you lift your old medallion to your lips. Skin-warmed, thin. A parting gift from Ben. You found it on Penumbra two days ago when she wandered into Camas, into the ruins of Camas, ragged-black and rain-soaked, after the battle was done.

The medallion had been tucked into her saddlebags, wrapped hastily in a note—

Behind you, Siddie lets out a whimper. Turning, you see Ket with an arm around her, you see Ket hugging her to her side, and you wonder if they've been waiting for you, if they didn't want to leave without you, didn't want to separate, now, with only three of you left.

You stand, stuffing the medallion back into your collar.

"Okay," you tell them. "I'm ready."

But before you can leave, Onna steps forward and takes your hands, all of your hands, clasped gently between hers.

Her steady fingers, her roughened palms.

Your own hand feels small in comparison. Like a child's hand, though you're not really a child. Enveloped and secure.

"You don't have to go," she tells you, looking at each one of you in turn. "You're ours now. You belong to us. You can all stay here, with us, if you want to. You can make this your home."

Siddie starts crying again, and Ket looks thoughtful, but you pull out of Onna's grasp.

Home?

Home.

Home—

You don't know the meaning of the word. You never had one, never had one you can remember, at least. After the kindling collectors took you, every place you lived was always supposed to be temporary—

House Kemera—

The bivouacs and field encampments—

The towns you came to after the war, searching for your squad—

You were a traveler. You were just passing through.

Stumbling away, you withdraw the note from your pocket. You read it again.

Ben left you everything she had. A guide in Gateway. Enough funds for supplies. Her horse. It's all arranged. You could cross the Candiveras tomorrow if you wanted. You could get out of Amerand, like you planned from the beginning.

You could finally leave—

You could finally be free—

Free of the past, free of your ghosts, free of everything this country did to you, made you do, took from you. Your identity, your purpose, your kin.

But you don't know if you want to be free anymore.

This is where Amity died. This is where Ben and Emara died. This is where Kanver died. Their bodies are here on this hillside. Their memories are here in this valley.

If you stay, you can be with them. You can visit them. You can imagine them all around you: the things they did, the things they could've done. Amity and Onna could've supervised the repairs and restorations: the breaking of the dam, the dismantling of the barricade. Ben could've ridden into the hills for the cattle drive, learned to throw a rope with as much finesse as a knife. By the time the harvest was over and the barns had been refilled, Emara could've gambled away her balar weapons in some foolish bet with Hemmen, although he never would've held her to it. And in the winter, when the nights were cold, Kanver could've sat by the fire telling stories to the children. Made-up stories. True stories. Quiet stories, where no one dies and nothing bad ever happens, to lull them into sleep.

You wonder if that's what home is supposed to look like.

You wonder if home is here.

KET

FOR THE FIRST TIME IN A LONG TIME, YOU'RE NOT going anywhere. With the hole in your leg, you couldn't go anywhere even if you wanted to. Couldn't make it down the mountain. Couldn't climb onto Callie's back. Thanks to that spear, you've finally been forced to be still.

A strange sensation. You thought you'd feel restless. Jittery and caged. But the thought of being settled? The thought of being home?

Here? In the Candiveras?

(With Tana?)

It quiets something in you that hasn't been quiet in a long time. Those massive peaks. That wild vastness. Your own insignificance, except to those who love you—

If she loves you—

If she could maybe love you, given enough time, if she wants to give it to you—

You just have to ask her for it.

(Although, ironically, you haven't had time.)

The day after the funerals, Tana rode off with a dozen other villagers to bring the cattle down from the high country. Couldn't wait. Couldn't leave them up there with the snows already coming in. A week, she's been gone, while you've had time to think, and thinking's never been your strong suit.

You wish Emara were here. When it came to other people, she was the best of you. Good-natured, gregarious, perceptive. She would've had some sound advice for you, would've suggested a gesture, something romantic, something grand—

Or maybe not—

Maybe she would've told you Tana doesn't *need* gestures, doesn't *do* grand. Maybe she would've waggled her eyebrows and said, *C'mon, Ket. What's the matter with you? Just talk to her, eh?*

You don't know. You'll never know.

Meanwhile, you're stuck with Leum, who has no interest in romantic overtures, and Siddie, who's still recovering from the battle. Sometimes you hear her crying at night. Sometimes you hear her turning in her dreams. Restless now like the rest of you.

You wonder if they're going to take Onna up on her offer. They've been helping the Camassians with the restoration, so they don't seem like they're in a hurry to leave, but now that the bridge is rebuilt and the farmyard's been drained, you're finally picking over the spoils you were promised in the beginning.

Much of it's worthless, as far as relics go. Brittle swords. Cheap pikes. Shields that would've been doled out to draftees. But as you sort through the dreck, you find bits of kindling armor: a cuirass, a damaged helmet, a pair of greaves.

You place these in a growing pile. A pauldron, a gauntlet, a lamellar skirt missing a third of its plates.

"There's so much," Siddie murmurs, turning the gauntlet in her hands. "But it doesn't seem like enough, does it?"

Leum grunts. She tosses a spear into a pile for the villagers, to be melted down or kept for the future, in the event that Camas is attacked again.

"What are you going to do with your share?" Siddie asks you.

"I dunno." You pick up a dagger. You place it with the scrap. "What are we going to do with any of it?"

The spoils.

Ben's travel fund.

Amity's cabin, the land it's on. She left it to all of you, to be split equally among you. That's what she was doing the day you met Ben in Gateway. She was meeting with a property agent. She was drawing up a will. Knew, already, that she might not make it, and if she wasn't going to make it, she still had to take care of you.

"Emara would've gone south to find her family," Siddie says. "She wouldn't have needed to steal anymore."

Leum snorts. "Yeah, but she would've done it anyway."

"What about Kanver?" Siddie asks. "Would they have gone with you to Ifrine?"

Leum glowers down at her hands. "Don't know if I'm going to Ifrine."

"Oh yeah?" You cock your head at her. Try not to look too eager. "Does that mean you're thinking of staying?"

She shrugs, which is all the answer you're going to get from her, at least for the time being, so you turn to Siddie. "What about you?"

She fidgets with the gauntlet, plucking at its lacquered scales. "I don't . . . I mean, I haven't—"

"She's sticking with me," Leum interrupts. Then she scowls, more at herself than either of you. A wrinkled nose, some pink in her cheeks. If she were anyone else, you'd think she was embarrassed. "I guess," she adds gruffly. "If you want to."

Siddie screws up her face, like she can't bring herself to believe it. "Really? You mean it?"

"I said it, didn't I?"

You laugh.

"Shut up." Leum prods at your leg with the toe of her sandal. "We know *you're* staying, at least until that's healed. How's it feel?"

With a grimace, you shift out of her reach. "The wound? Or the idea of sticking around?"

"More than a month in some northlands backwater," she says with a smirk. It's what you said to her when she told you about Camas on the roof of the Grand Hotel. "With nothing better to do than clean up after the cows."

"I can think of something better." Siddie waggles her eyebrows. An imitation of Emara. "I bet Tana can too."

You chuck one of the helmets at her. It strikes her in the shoulder, but she laughs and tosses it onto the pile.

"But after," Leum says seriously. "You're staying in Camas?"

You lean back with a grin. "I guess we'll see."

She comes riding down the north road on Adren's black stallion, on her brother's black stallion, and when she crosses the bridge, she slips from her saddle and flings herself into your arms—

You stagger, a little, on your crutches, but you don't let go. You're clutching her waist, her mud-spattered clothes—

She smells like pine and lilacs, windswept and free—

You want to keep holding her. You could hold her forever. But she leans back with a grin. "So?" she says. "Have you made up your mind yet?"

You almost laugh. She must already know, right? She must be teasing you.

"I knew what I was going to do as soon as I took that spear for you."

"Only because you couldn't go anywhere until it healed."

You chuckle. "Do you want me to say it or not?"

"Yeah." She pokes you in the collarbone. Once, twice, as if in challenge. "Say it."

"I want to stay."

Before the words have even left your mouth, she grips the back of your neck and pulls you in for a kiss. A soft moan. Chapped lips.

You grin at her. "But only if you want me to."

In response, she kisses you again. "What do you think?"

When she finally releases you, you lead her to the side of the bridge, where you lean against the railing. Setting your crutches aside, you remove the list from your pocket. The worn creases, the faded ink. An unfinished record of Kari's dreams.

You wanted to think you were doing this for her, but let's be honest, you were doing it because you didn't know what else to do. Had to do something after she died, and this was all you had.

But you have a home now.

You have a future now.

"To show you I mean it." You start to tear the list in half, but Tana stops you.

"Don't." She slides it from your grasp, unfolds it thoughtfully between her hands. "There's a lot left here to do."

The giant cedars on the eastern coast—

The flower fields of what used to be Chenyara—

The Morning Daughter—

You saw her this morning, snow-capped and clear, but now the clouds have come in, gray-veiling her features, her folded hands. You shrug. "I don't need to do it anymore, though."

Tana frowns. There's that look again, her thoughts diving and resurfacing in the well of her mind. "I wonder if I do."

"What?"

"My life has been so small," she says. "For a long time, I didn't mind. I didn't even notice. It was Vian who always talked about leaving . . . although when I think about it now, I don't know if he really would've done it, if he'd had the chance. I think he loved the valley too much to ever be away from it for long." She wipes her eyes, takes a slow breath. "But I'm not like him. After all this, I think I want my world to be bigger than this valley. I think I want to travel. I want to experience things."

You smile faintly. A little painfully. "There's a whole lot of world out there to see?"

Nodding, she traces the smudged ink with her fingertip. "For a while, anyway. Camas will still be here when I want to come home." Then she folds up the paper again, passes it back to you. "What do you think? Would you come with me, once the village is stable again? We could even cross some things off this list, if you don't think Kari would mind."

"She wouldn't." You smile, remembering Kari's ink-stained hands, her trill of a laugh. "I actually think she'd like that."

"But?"

Your hand falls to your injured leg. No one knows yet how it'll heal. If you'll need a cane after. If you'll be able to climb or ride or run after.

"But I might be a little slow."

"I don't mind." Tana takes hold of your hand. "We have plenty of time."

You kiss her again, and again after that, and each kiss is the first and the last. The start of your future, the culmination of your past. Moment after moment after moment, you come to rest—

Spectacularly, ordinarily still.

LEUM

YOU AND PENUMBRA WATCH THE SUNRISE FROM THE outskirts of the village, where you told the others to meet. Frost in the thickets, Burk biting at the weeds. Behind you, the thatch-roofed houses, the gardens wilting in the cold. You're going to miss it, you think—

The harshness of it—

The beauty of it—

You don't know exactly when Ket arrives, but at some point you look over and she's standing on her crutches beside you, breaths fogging in the air.

You scowl. (You still don't like being snuck up on.) "How long have you been there?"

"I dunno." She grins at you. "A few minutes, I guess."

Silently, the two of you survey the valley: the gray fields, the slate-blue river, the mist rising from the cattle as the sun warms their backs.

"You can still change your mind," Ket says quietly.

"Yeah." You sniff. You pretend to adjust your balar weapon, wrapped in cloth and strapped to the saddle. "But I won't."

You're leaving, you and Siddie. (Whenever she gets here, anyway.) You're going to Gateway to collect a refund from Ben's hired guide, and after that you're going south—

For Emara—

For Emara's family—

She was looking for her mother, Siddie said. *Emara, daughter of Rava, weaver of Livia.* It's not much to go on, but you have a name, a place, the wraps, stowed safely in your pack—

You've found family with much less than that.

You're going to track down her mother. A brother, maybe. Grandfather. Cousins. You're going to give them the artifacts she collected. You're going to tell them who she was, what she did, the joy she was capable of. She should be part of their history, lovingly embroidered in white cotton thread.

This is the story of Emara, daughter of Emara, kindling and kin.

You look toward the cemetery. (The cairns, the graves.) Emara, Kanver, Amity, Ben—

Seeing the direction of your gaze, Ket nods. "Don't worry. I'll watch over them."

Which is funny, because she's got it backward. *We're* the ones watching over her—

Over you—

Over all the brave, the haunted, the restless—

We always have been.

We always will.

You blink a few times. Must be the cold, stinging your eyes. "And Amity's cabin?" you ask.

None of you knew what to do with it. Couldn't stay there. Couldn't sell it. So you're keeping it, at least for now. Who knows? Maybe someday, one of you will need it. Maybe one of you will settle there, after all your adventures, after traveling far and wide, and find the peace she always said she wanted—

(Although, of course, she was a liar.)

The garden, the foothills, the sunsets, the quiet—

Maybe someday that'll be for you.

Ket nods again. "Tana's going to help me until I can get down there myself."

Below on the loop road, Siddie appears on Amity's old warhorse, Comet, who seems less than pleased with his new rider, tossing his head in irritation as she urges him up the slope.

"About time," you say as she draws up to you. "Are you ready to go?"

"Oh!" She glances at Ket, wide-eyed and breathless. "Already? I, uh, I thought I'd get to say goodbye—"

"Should've thought of that before you decided to be late."

Ket smirks. "Don't let her rush you." She limps up beside Comet. "I'm counting on you to write me, okay? I know Leum won't."

You grumble under your breath, but you don't try to deny it.

"Okay." Siddie gives her a smile. (Sad and bright.) "I will."

With a grin, Ket slaps her on the knee and steps back.

Morning's unfurling across the valley now: pink on the mountaintops, mist rising from the river. As if at some hidden signal, the three of you turn south, toward the rest of the peninsula—

Toward Amerand—

You don't know how long you'll be gone. Months? Years? Maybe one day you'll meet back here, in the dead of winter or the riot of spring. Willows leafing out in the streambeds, calves tottering after their mothers, lupine carpeting the cemetery, quiet and still.

Or maybe, once Ket's leg is healed, you'll meet on the road. The three of you (and Tana) and whoever else you find: siblings from the Academy, brothers from the battlefield, strangers from Vedra, soon to be kin—

That's what home is.

The people you love. The people you fight for.

You and your squad, wandering the countryside, choosing your own causes, keeping your own code—

All of you together and none of you alone.

ACKNOWLEDGMENTS

THOSE CLOSEST TO ME KNOW THAT *KINDLING* WAS written during a particularly difficult time, and I will be eternally grateful for all the love and support that sustained me through this period in my life. To my family, I would not be here without you. Thank you for everything. To Cole, I love you. To Tara and Emily, your friendship never fails to buoy me. Thank you for allowing me to share my fears, my doubts, my setbacks, my victories, and everything in between (and, of course, for every Whine & Cheese). To Parker, the conspiracy continues! Thank you for the pure joy of Mystery Club, always but especially during the times when I really needed it. To all the friends and neighbors who reached out to us, who prepared meals, who sent gifts and well-wishes, it meant the world to know that you were thinking of us, that you were holding us in your hearts, that we were so very loved and cared for.

My deepest thanks, as always, to my literary agent, Barbara Poelle, for being a tireless advocate and the fiercest of champions, and for understanding, sometimes even before I do, exactly what my creative spirit needs. I'm honored to be one of your authors, and I'm eagerly settling in to bear witness to your goddess years! Additional and overflowing gratitude to Sydnie Thornton, Ellie Lynch, and the teams at IGLA and Word One Literary.

To my editor, Emilia Rhodes, thank you for your patience, your understanding, and your unflagging belief in this story. Thank you for answering every call and talking me through every thorny question and navigating us so smoothly through the transitions of these past few years. I am pleased to report that I am back in fighting shape, and I am so excited for what we do together next.

Thank you always to the team at Clarion and HarperCollins, including but never limited to Mary Wilcox, Erica Sussman, Briana Wood, Erika West, Mary Magrisso, James Neel, Kristen Eckhardt, Michael D'Angelo, John Sellers, Patty Rosati, Mimi Rankin, and Christina Carpino. Special gratitude to Valerie Shea and Samantha Hoback for the keenest of eyes and the sharpest of figurative red pens.

I have been blessed with the most beautiful books, and *Kindling* is no exception. Thank you to designers Kathy Lam and Celeste Knudsen for outfitting this story in such style, inside and out; to Kiuyan Ran for the cover illustration, rendering my brave, haunted battle-children in all their glory; and to Shing Yin Khor for the maps, which have brought the northlands to life in such perfect detail.

I am hugely indebted to my readers: Emily Skrutskie, Tara Sim, Randy Ribay, Karolina Fedyk, and Sophia Babai. This book is better, richer, and more nuanced because of your advice and expertise. My thanks as well to Loree Joses for so kindly providing me with a wealth of details about ranching in the highlands. All errors or oversights are my own.

Enormous thanks to Tommy Harron, Grace Rolek, and the HarperCollins audio team for breathing life into Miuko, Geiki, and the world of *A Thousand Steps into Night*.

I am profoundly grateful for my film agent, Sean Berard, who never makes me feel like I'm asking too many questions. Thank you for always knowing how to put things in perspective. Further thanks go to Semi Oloko and everyone at Grandview LA for their support.

I would never have written this book if not for my colleagues at the Angels Theatre, particularly Jeff Olson and Brandon Townsend, whose informal crash course in cinema history introduced me to *Seven Samurai* and its American remake, *The Magnificent Seven*. I never expected that discussing films while sweeping floors and cleaning the popcorn machine would lead, decades later, to me putting my own spin on this classic tale, but I guess it goes to show that passion is infectious and inspiration can come from anywhere and everywhere. Thank you.

Finally, thank you to my readers. Thank you to everyone who has followed me from the magical high seas of The Reader trilogy. Thank you to everyone who found me through *We Are Not Free* and the Japanese American incarceration camps of World War II. Thank you to everyone who became fans of the goofy, spooky spirit world of *A Thousand Steps into Night*. And thank you to everyone who is just joining me now for a retelling (and a return to my heartbreaking roots). I'm grateful for all the time and care you put into reading and loving these stories, as eclectic as they are. No matter where we go next, I promise you new, unexpected adventures to come.